Revelations

on the

Battery

a novel by

Andi Thomas Peters

Revelations on the Battery

ISBN Kindle: 978-1-955032-06-3
ISBN Paperback: 978-1-955032-07-0
ISBN Hardcover: 978-1-955032-08-7

This is a work of fiction. Names, characters, businesses, places, events, locales, and incidents are either the products of the author's imagination or used in a fictitious manner. Any resemblance to actual persons, living or dead, or actual events is purely coincidental.

Also by Andi Thomas Peters

The Purple Fence on the Boardwalk

Hired Hit on Jessamin Island

Dedication

The novel is dedicated to the one and only Susan Sparks.

I would have never survived my third year in law school without you. That year was tough, but life has been tougher. You have continued to provide unconditional support, sage advice, and many belly laughs along the way.

In addition to your numerous hats—minister, standup comedian, best-selling author, speaker, and lawyer—you wear your cowboy boots marvelously. This one is for you, girlfriend!

Prologue

Somebody opened the floodgates...

Wrapped in a wool blanket and sitting under the heater in the marina dock house, Sammie shivered from head to toe. The room pulsed in cadence with the red and blue lights reflecting on the walls. The sirens from the emergency response vehicles and the incessant ringing of the marina phone echoed in her ears. Dizzy and numb, she could only stare uncomprehendingly at the blood splattered all over her.

Sammie closed her eyes to block out the chaotic scene outside. Before today, the marina had been her refuge—the peaceful place where the sun, water, and briny breeze provided perfect accompaniment to the nautical flags rhythmically blowing from the sterns of the luxury yachts. The smells of the Charleston Ashley Dockage had permeated through Sammie's skin injecting a natural anesthetic. But, today, the scent was rancid. Black smoke engulfed the sky from the burning yacht.

Sammie thought pursuing her legal career in her grandfather's firm was her destiny. Her husband seemed perfect too. But, her choices had only brought disappointment and misery. Her life spiraled downward. She found it surreal that she, Samantha Parker Spencer, would topple the Spencer reputation and unleash the family secrets.

She may never know who pulled the plug on her life raft. But, one thing was for certain, she was sinking fast. The blood on her hands was proof of that.

PART ONE

A southern belle breaks rules when Momma isn't watching...

Chapter One

Lucy & Sammie

It was the third consecutive night that Lucy and Sammie worked past midnight. Long hours were typical and expected of associates at their prestigious law firm. In addition to the ridiculously long hours, the roles of associate attorneys included subservience and sacrifice. Any chance of a social life was typically squelched by a text or call from one of the partners at any hour. But, associates were willing to pay the price because, after seven grueling years, the brass ring awaiting was an invitation to join the coveted partnership.

Spencer, Pettigrew & Hamilton was located in Charleston, South Carolina, the state's oldest city. Its Colonial style office building dated back to 1765 and had a highly desired Water Street address. The large windows in the partners' offices provided expansive water views of the Charleston Harbor and Sullivan's Island. A select few could see Fort Sumter, where the first shots were fired starting the Civil War.

In addition to posh offices with amazing water vistas and associate attorneys at their beck and call, partner status at Spencer, Pettigrew & Hamilton afforded other perks. The title of partner entitled one to leave the office at a reasonable hour, free booze in the Cooper Conference Room, and free lunches at the popular restaurant, C. Christopher's on the Cooper, located directly across the street. But, most importantly, partner status guaranteed a six-figure paycheck.

The firm's historic location, the coveted Fortune 500 client list, and the rich salaries made Spencer, Pettigrew & Hamilton one of the most desired destinations for lawyers in the South. Lucy attributed her six-year survival in the firm to her best friend and colleague, Sammie Morgan.

Sammie never mentioned her family connection. Of course, everyone knew of it. After all, she was a Spencer.

Sammie had a calming and practical influence over the rebellious interloper from rural South Carolina. Her friendship gave Lucy confidence about her future at the firm. Sammie made Lucy feel like she was smart and worthy, despite the fact that she wasn't a Charleston blueblood.

Sammie worked as hard or harder than anyone, and her intellect was never questioned. But her grounded, compassionate, and unpretentious personality traits were the reasons that Lucy often forgot that Sammie Morgan was a Spencer.

Lucy couldn't recall exactly why she instigated the fourth floor, midnight ritual with Sammie. It had been provoked by giddiness due to sleep deprivation at the end of an 18-hour workday. The fourth floor was bestowed upon the most powerful partners. When Lucy and Sammie entered the fourth floor sanctuary, the intimidating extensive hallway was always eerily quiet—so quiet that you could hear an antique clock ticking from within one of the partner's offices.

During their late-night visits, Lucy enjoyed perusing family pictures and other personal items that provided a hint into the partners' private lives. With each passing year, Lucy's awe of the men who inhabited the fourth floor was replaced with a light-hearted irreverence. As she walked past the gold-framed partners' portraits lining the hallway, Lucy would cross her eyes, stick out her tongue, make wiggling bunny ears on top of her head, or turn her hands backward pushing up her nostrils with her thumbs. In addition to the facial expressions in her repertoire, Lucy began mimicking an eccentric characteristic or acting out a scandalous event that had circulated through the rumor mill.

The law firm grapevine provided an abundance of tales about the partners. The leader of repugnant conduct was Holmes Stockton, IV. Holmes was a tremendous flirt who tested the firm's sexual harassment policies. The reprimands he had received didn't stop his habit of gawking at women's breasts. The most recent report on Holmes was linked to Cavelle Gibson, one of the most tenured secretaries and assigned to the managing partner, no less.

Secretaries were among the bottom rung of the law firm's hierarchical ladder, unless you were the managing partner's secretary. Then, your status propelled you above all the associates and even some partners. Cavelle understood her power so she wasn't scared to speak her mind.

"Holmes, didn't your parents teach you to look people in the eyes when you speak to them?" Cavelle chastised him on the elevator one morning. "My eyes are on my head, not on my chest."

"Your chest is much better looking," Holmes reportedly said, laughing.

One night, Lucy waltzed into the office of Holmes Stockton, IV, plopped down in his oversized leather chair, and grabbed one of the many vintage pipes neatly arranged on his desk.

"Come on in here, Samantha Morgan," Lucy grunted, in her best Charleston accent. "You are such a pretty thang and have a delightful pair of breasts. Come and sit on my lap, darlin', so I can get a closer look at those gems."

Sammie laughed so hard at Lucy that she uncharacteristically and embarrassingly let out a most ungenteel snort. Sammie loved Lucy's free spirit and found her irreverent sense of humor refreshing.

The playful visits to the fourth floor aided Lucy's perspective. She became less intimidated and fearful of the Spencer partners, with one exception—Franklin Hamilton, the reigning managing partner. Lucy never dared to venture into his massive fourth floor office. His office was a shrine, a holy place. Even when he wasn't there, it commanded a respect that even Lucy honored.

Lucy wondered how she was going to survive the next several months without her best friend. Sammie's first child was due in late May. Working outrageous hours, Sammie's feet had swollen, and her blood pressure had spiked. The results from Sammie's stress test at her last obstetrics visit caused her doctor to order bed rest for the remainder of her pregnancy. So, in addition to the four months maternity leave offered by the firm, an additional two months had been tacked on for bed rest. Tonight would be Lucy and Sammie's last fourth floor jaunt for a while, so Lucy wanted it to be memorable. She was going to attempt to crack the code allowing entry into the Cooper Conference Room.

The conference room, located by Frank Hamilton's office, was only available to firm partners. The mahogany doors to the conference room were formidable—15-feet high with paneled insets and large brass knobs and foot plates.

The doors were always locked, and entry required a confidential code on a panel box located outside of the doors. Lucy always surmised that this firm tradition of restricted access must have originated from a partner attempting to relive his fraternity days. The associates and support staff, or pledges in fraternity ranks, were simply unworthy.

Earlier, Lucy had been summoned by a partner to drop off a document revision to the Cooper Conference Room where the parties were in the midst of final negotiations. With the document in hand, Lucy patiently waited outside the conference room doors when Cavelle, the only non-partner who knew the code, entered. Cavelle hovered over the code box to block Lucy's view of the combination. Lucy discreetly watched.

During their final fourth floor outing before Sammie's extended leave, Lucy pulled Sammie down the hallway outside of the conference room and told her what she saw.

"I'm sure I can figure it out," Lucy said.

Sammie was not the least bit interested.

"Lucy, forget about what you saw," she cautioned. "Do not try to enter any code."

Despite Sammie's pleas otherwise, Lucy was determined. As she examined the placement of numbers on the code box, she noticed that it was loose and slightly dismantled. Then, she noticed that the conference room doors weren't securely closed. Lucy was so excited that she could barely get the words out. Sammie saw it too, and her instructions were calm, clear, and resolute.

"Lucy do not go in there. You know it's against the rules. We could get into trouble."

Sammie turned and quickly walked away. Sammie's reaction highlighted that despite their friendship, they were indeed wired differently.

Lucy had endured six long years and was on track to becoming one of the first female partners. Now, she was standing at the Cooper Conference Room door yearning for a glimpse of one of the privileges of partnership. Her conscience warned her not to enter the room. Curiosity and disregard for shallow rituals quickly over-ruled the warning. She opened the door.

The layout before her was more impressive than she could have imagined. Mahogany paneling encased a long hallway. As she proceeded slowly down the hall, she noticed two small rooms, one to the right and one to the left. These were the break-out rooms where respective parties would retreat to discuss points of compromise during deal negotiations. There was no expense spared on these small rooms. Oriental rugs covered the wide wood-plank floors; expensive artwork hung on the grass-cloth walls, and houndstooth chairs surrounded marble tables. At the end of the narrow corridor, another set of large wooden doors stood before her.

Approaching these doors, Lucy felt like an intruder engaging in some type of criminal act. But, her defiance won again. She pushed the last set of doors. They didn't budge. She pulled the large brass handles and still nothing. There was no key lock on the door nor code box in sight. Thinking they must be stuck, Lucy attempted to shake them. When the right door moved a little, she realized that the doors were on gliders. As she slid the large wooden door, a magical setting appeared before her.

The room was grand. Intricate crown molding encircled the twenty-foot ceiling. Everyone had heard of the room's views of the Cooper River. Given the abundance of ebony wood, Lucy was surprised that the room was so bright. Ornate chandeliers hung overhead, but they weren't the source of the light flooding into the room. The light shone from the shipping vessels docked in the Charleston Harbor.

The room's focal point, its centerpiece, was a substantial table reflecting a pink hue. Lucy surmised that the wood was some exotic species, like the fifteen chairs on each side. The back wall was flanked by a full-length bar with wooden shelves housing decanters of liquor, an assortment of wines, and crystal glasses etched with SPH. She examined one of the crystal glasses and thought it was interesting how something as simple as a glass could be so revealing. The weight of it in her hand spoke volumes. The glass was saying, *I am important. I am successful. I am only owned by the finest and richest.*

She wanted to celebrate her first visit to the Cooper Conference Room with a shot from the rare bottle of Pappy Van Winkle 23 Reserve but reconsidered. With its $3,500 price tag, the contents were probably measured as meticulously as the firm's collections. She placed the bourbon bottle and glass back on the shelf. She surveyed the room one last time, absorbing its tradition, power, and arrogance.

She slid the door shut and headed back down the hallway to exit the cherished space. A memorandum addressed to the partners of Spencer, Pettigrew & Hamilton was taped to the main door: *Effective immediately, the security code will be changed from 1023 to 6690.*

The note explained why the panel box was disengaged. Whoever was working on changing the code hadn't finished the job. Lucy decided to keep the memorandum identifying the new code to herself. Sammie wouldn't be interested in this news right now. This would be a secret that she would reveal after Sammie had settled into being a new mom—the perfect welcome-back-to-work surprise.

A southerner knows their raising...

Chapter Two

The Spencers

Samantha Parker Spencer Morgan, Esquire, came from a long line of barristers. Her great grandfather was one of the founders of the law firm. And, her grandfather had been a formidable presence at the firm for many decades. Sammie's father, Samuel Parker Spencer, IV, was destined and groomed to follow the Spencer tradition of lawyers. All was on course.

Sam IV, pegged "Sam Quart" in college, and later shortened to Cort, graduated in the top of his class at Yale Law School. With his gift for numbers, he obtained a specialty in tax law. Upon graduation, he was recruited by the top investment banking firms in New York City and also received numerous offers from law firms, including his father's firm. To the chagrin of his father, he chose Wall Street over Water Street.

Cort's passion for his beloved Charleston soon triumphed over his large Wall Street paycheck. He returned to the Holy City, but not to the family firm. Samuel Parker Spencer, III, came to accept his only son's rejection of the Spencer tradition because Cort was a rising superstar with the rapidly growing local bank, Palmetto Bank & Trust. Better yet, the bank was a longstanding client of the Spencer firm.

Sammie's mother, Eleanor Glenn Spencer, known as "Glenny," had youthful aspirations to become a fashion designer. This vocation was a perfect fit for her alluringly simple, yet elegant, classy style. Glenny's beauty was natural—high cheekbones, almond-shaped eyes, and full lips glossed with pale pink lipstick, her only makeup. Despite her age, Glenny Spencer still turned the heads of young men.

After graduating from The Savannah College of Art and Design, Glenny landed a job as a designer in a fashion house in New York. When she and Cort moved to Charleston, she became a buyer for one of the exclusive boutiques on King Street in downtown Charleston. She terribly missed the city that never slept. She had relished her frequent trips to New York. But, selecting designer clothes for sale in the Charleston boutique wasn't the same as designing them. She privately began memorializing her own design ideas, partly as consolation for what she had given up.

Sammie was completely in the dark about her mother's creative talent until she found some sketches many years later. Sammie had never viewed her mother as anything other than a great nurturer. After learning that the designs were her mother's originals, Sammie was curious why she had never pursued her talent.

"Mom, these are really good. When did you do these?"

"Oh, honey, before you were born," Glenny answered, embarrassed that her daughter had found some of her original scribbles.

"Did any of these ever get made?"

"Lordy, no. I never showed them to anyone," Glenny said.

"Why not?"

"Because I had you."

"You abandoned this gift because of me? I don't believe I ever objected to you working."

"Of course, you didn't. I guess I've never told you of my difficulties with pregnancies. I had lots of miscarriages. After the third one, I quit my job. I assumed my work travel might have had some type of impact. Then after still other miscarriages, my doctor advocated adoption. He didn't believe I could carry a child full term. We felt so blessed when you were born that I didn't want to miss a single minute with you."

Listening to her mother's explanation of her sacrifice to raise her only child, Sammie felt guilty and selfish. She didn't need to work at all—the trust fund established for her at birth had climbed as rapidly as her father's position with the bank. But, Sammie was determined to return to full-time hours at her grandfather's law firm after her maternity leave.

For as long as Sammie could remember, she wanted to be an attorney at the family firm. She felt a sense of duty to carry on the Spencer tradition. After all, Samuel Parker Spencer, V, had not been in the cards. Though Sammie's father had remained silent on her desired vocation, her mother's view was conveyed clearly and often.

"You don't need the stress of the long hours, the tedious work, the partners' egos, or the unappreciative clients," she said, repeatedly. "Your father fell on the sword to break tradition. You have the freedom to pursue your own dreams," Glenny counseled her daughter.

Glenny Spencer's dream for her daughter was marriage and grandchildren, lots of them. Sammie saw things dissimilarly. She had goals and wasn't going to let a child sidetrack her. She could be a great mother and a great lawyer.

After Mack Spencer Morgan was born, Sammie became conflicted. She could imagine her grief when she learned about her baby's momentous milestones from her sitter. Conversely, she didn't want to throw away all of her hard work to fulfill her dream of partnership in her grandfather's firm. She had invested too much time and energy not to try to juggle a child and a career.

Sammie's first week back in the office picked up exactly where she left off six months earlier. There had been no easing back into the frenzied pace. By Thursday, she justified taking the morning off for some extended time with her son since she had clocked nineteen hours the previous day. It was a beautiful fall day, and she needed some fresh, salty air to clear her head. She loaded Mack into the jogging stroller and headed south in the direction of her childhood home.

Dougie and Sammie lived north of Broad Street near the College of Charleston. It was a very nice area for young families, but nothing like south of Broad where Sammie had grown up. Her childhood home, in the heart of the historic district, was surrounded by the Cooper and Ashley Rivers. As she headed down East Bay Street and turned onto the idyllic, picture-perfect street of her parent's home, Lucy's candid assessment of her upbringing began ringing in her ears.

"Sammie, you grew up in the Battery, attended the best private girls' school, and had a summer job sailing on the Ashley River. To top it off, you had a guaranteed job at the most prestigious law firm in the southeast. If you don't call that spoiled, I don't know what is."

Sammie realized that Lucy was right. To this point, she had lived a glamorous, stress-free life with everything falling perfectly into place. But all the easy and glamorous roads were becoming bumpy and treacherous. Nothing was easy. She began to question everything. She attributed her doubts to her hormonal volatility. Her erratic mood swings were the only explanation for her reservations about her grandfather's firm, her career, and even her marriage.

Sundays are for confessions; the other six days are for transgressions...

Chapter Three

Lucy

Lucy grew up in Edenville, South Carolina—population 10,000. Though only fifty miles from Charleston, the cities were poles apart. At least, that was Lucy's impression when she first moved to Charleston. The only feature shared by the two towns were the church steeples throughout the downtown skylines. The church goers, however, were a rarer breed from the ones in her father's small Baptist church.

The majority of Lucy's father's congregation were employees of the town's primary employer, Mooney Mill. Folks in Edenville didn't see college as an option, much less law school. Lucy Tate was different. She was determined to escape. Her brains were her passageway out of Edenville. She certainly wasn't going to make it to the promised land on her beauty.

When Lucy looked in the mirror, she didn't appreciate her long, naturally-curled eyelashes or her thick, shiny black hair. She couldn't see past her sharp nose and the mole above her right jawline. These Tate trademarks had only been impediments to her summer job in the mill's spinning room. She had even named her mole, Gertrude, because it had seemed to take on a life of its own.

"Gertrude and I are off to make some towels and wash cloths," Lucy would announce to her mother when she dropped Lucy off at the mill gates.

Lucy became a proficient doffer in the spinning room. There, the spinning machines transformed cotton fibers into threads and captured them on a bobbin. A doffer's job was to quickly remove the bobbins filled with thread and replace them with empty ones. The spinning process required that the machines move at high velocity, spraying cotton particles into the air.

Although Lucy wore a hairnet during her shift, it didn't prevent the cotton from blanketing her thick braid. By the time her shift was over, her long eyelashes even looked like they were dusted in white snow. Lucy attributed her now overactive sweat glands to the extreme heat she endured those summers working in the mill. Worse than the cotton adhering to her drenched skin, the remnants stuck to Gertrude like glue.

Lucy embraced her *Linthead* status, the title bestowed on the Edenville populace by the rival high school in the next county. Her summers in the mill taught her more than how to spin yarn. They instilled in her a healthy drive and perspective. Mooney Mill also illustrated the benefits of a *diverse workforce* long before it became the new buzz word in the professional world.

A *diverse workforce* was becoming a mandatory criterion by large corporations when retaining law firms. The resumes of the attorneys at Spencer, Pettigrew & Hamilton were virtually homogeneous. They told the same story—southern white men from well-to-do families who had ventured north for Ivy League degrees before returning South. To play the "diversity" game, the prominent Spencer firm established the Thomas Pettigrew Scholarship. The recipient was guaranteed a job with the firm for one year upon graduation. If the work was exemplary (the standard for associates at the firm), employment could be extended. The scholarship also paid the final year's law school tuition.

Applications for the prize weren't accepted. Only one student was eligible—the student with the highest-class rank entering the third and final year at the Charleston School of Law, like Thomas Pettigrew. Of course, Thomas Pettigrew had been a white male. Since he was from the "wrong" side of Broad and not Ivy League educated, the firm viewed him as an appropriate namesake for the scholarship promoting diversity.

Lucy's cynical view of the Pettigrew diversity scholarship was radically altered after her grades arrived in the mail the summer after her second year. She examined the transcript closely to ensure there was no mix-up. But there it was—her name in black and white: Lucy Marie Tate, Class Rank: 1.

If her class rank was correct, Lucy would be the recipient of the Thomas Pettigrew scholarship. But, she was skeptical. Lucy's class rank had never cracked into single digits. She had perched at number ten the past two semesters. She was convinced there was a computer glitch.

The registrar's office confirmed that Lucy was indeed first in her class, and a zero had not been omitted from her rank. The scholarship meant that she would be associated with the most prestigious firm in the South and would reduce her tuition debt. Filled with relief, freedom, and exhilaration, Lucy entered the spinning room that day appreciating the place and the people that shaped her work ethic.

But, as graduation grew near, Lucy began questioning herself. *Would she measure up intellectually? Would she fit in with the other lawyers whose pedigrees and backgrounds were quite sophisticated? Had the firm ever foreseen that a Linthead could receive the scholarship?*

If you don't stop crying, I'll give you something to cry about...

Chapter Four

Sammie

Sammie had overestimated the therapeutic effect of the Battery's waterfront. The salty breeze blowing off the Cooper and Ashley Rivers, the sound of the waves crashing on the sea wall, the shade offered by the canopies of oak trees, and the rich architectural history of the large antebellum homes had always soothed her soul. Today, however, the view of Sullivan's Island from the promenade wrecked any curative power. Memories of her high school visits to the island's beach were as intrusive to her thoughts as the loud horns of the cruise ships arriving into the harbor. She tried to stop her tears by focusing on her son who was cooing in the jogging stroller. She tried to convince herself that he was worth her mounting insecurities. But, with each step she jogged, she couldn't help revisiting the decisions of her past.

Isabelle Lynch—Sammie once had considered her former soccer teammate as her best friend. Isabelle's confident spirit was raw and hypnotizing. Her persona wasn't fed by a designer's name on her clothes, the manufacturer of her car, or the zip code of her home. There had been no one like her at Pinckney Hall, Sammie's private, girls' school. But, after high school, they lost touch.

Sammie wondered if she could do things all over again, would she make the same choices? Now, she believed that Isabelle's comments about her "phoney-baloney" school friends had unfairly influenced her. She had tried too hard to fit in with Isabelle's groupies.

Had she been too quick to judge Kurt Girard at the back-to-school dance her senior year? Had his comments impacted her actions on Sullivan's Island? Sammie's recollection of both was crystal clear. She ran faster to clear her brain. But, no matter how fast she ran, her tears kept pace. She relived her past all over again.

Chapter Five

Sammie

Sammie abhorred the back-to-school high school dances hosted by her all-girls' school, Pinckney Hall, for the nearby all-boys school, Tradd Preparatory. She found them demeaning—a means to introduce the girls to potential future husbands. But year after year, it was the same old story. The boys and girls mostly remained huddled in their respective corners.

The only mingling that ever occurred was at the party at Chet McDaniel's house after the dry dance. The McDaniel's were of the opinion that teenagers were going to congregate somewhere, so they preferred to host the high school gatherings where they could chaperone the activities. Sammie learned from previous parties that the stainless-steel Subzero refrigerator in their carriage house was always stocked with an assortment of imported beer for the attendees.

Their home was classic Georgian architecture and Sammie's favorite in the Battery. The modern updates had kept intact the intricate mantels and ceiling medallions and refortified their expansive piazza. Sammie wasn't the partying type so at these gatherings, you wouldn't find her in the carriage house but on the McDaniel's third floor piazza. It stretched the length of the house and provided a spectacular view of the Charleston Harbor.

Since Chet was a senior, it was rumored that the post-party at the McDaniels after the back-to-school dance was going to be epic. The only remarkable thing for Sammie about these back-to-school dances was that they were mandatory for the Pinkney Hall girls but not the male invitees from Tradd Prep. The so-called popular boys never attended but headed straight for the McDaniel's house. Now that she was a senior, it would be the last compulsory dance she ever had to attend. Like all the others, she would stand against the wall and watch the few brave souls who ventured onto the dance floor. But, as they say, there's a first for everything. And, she would have never imagined that the first time she set foot on the dance floor would be with a newbie.

"Newbie" was the name penned on those who didn't have a Charleston County birth certificate; a newbie was considered second-class Charleston material. At small, private schools like Pinckney Hall, a newbie stuck out more than the white loafers and bow tie on Alfred Holloman, V, nicknamed "A-Hole" by the popular Tradd Prep boys. Word had quickly circulated in the cluster of Pinckney Hall girls that the newbie's name was Kurt Girard. His family had recently moved to Charleston from Atlanta.

Sammie had inherited her father's rejection of the "inside the historic district" society rules. So, when Kurt Girard approached her at the beginning of the last song, "We've Got Tonight" by Bob Seger and the Silver Bullet Band, she accepted his invitation to slow dance.

"Thanks," he said, looking down and blushing at the awkward moment at the end. "I noticed that you hadn't danced all night. Guess it took the last song for me to finally get up the nerve."

At the time, Sammie found his vulnerability refreshing. She couldn't think of one Tradd Prepp guy with such transparency.

"I'm glad you asked me," she said, surprising herself.

Sammie thought that Kurt was cute. His style wouldn't be found on the racks at Penn Ltd., the preppy shop on King Street where all the Tradd Prep guys bought their identical clothes. Like the Tradd Prep guys, Kurt was clean-cut, but he had a distinctive look—a sort of Indiana Jones ruggedness.

"Are you going to the after-party?" he asked, during their slow dance.

"I don't know yet."

"I haven't decided if I'm going either. I just moved here from Atlanta. I haven't met Chet. The guys I've met went dove hunting. I don't really feel comfortable just showing up at his house."

"You should go. You could meet some people. And, who knows, maybe I'll see you there."

"OOOOh! I can't believe that you slow danced with a newbie stranger!" Katie Rose Clinton exclaimed, when Sammie returned to the cluster of Pinckney Hall girls.

At that moment, Sammie decided that she definitely was going to the post-dance party and with the newbie.

"Well then, I guess you won't believe that I am going with him to Chet's party either," Sammie said, walking back to Kurt Girard.

"I just had an idea," Sammie said to Kurt. "I live a couple of blocks from the McDaniel's. Parking is terrible around the Battery. If you want to park at my house, we can walk to the McDaniel's from there. That way, you don't have to walk in alone. I can introduce you to my friends."

When Kurt arrived at Sammie's, he introduced himself to her parents and thanked them for the parking spot. He and her father talked about his move to Charleston and how he was adjusting. He communicated that it was harder for his sister than him. It was for him, after all, only until December. He had enough credits to graduate early and was going to backpack through Europe for a while. He seemed comfortable in the presence of her parents as if he would rather talk to them than head to the party.

When they finally left, Sammie learned more about his family walking to the McDaniel's. His mother had grown up in Charleston, and his grandmother's health was failing. His father had sold a software business, so they decided to move back so that his mother could help take care of his grandmother. His sister was a sophomore at Pinckney Hall and hated it. She missed her friends in Atlanta. Sammie felt sorry for her.

"I'm sure it's hard, but she'll love Charleston. She should join the sailing club. I'm the President. I can teach her."

"Doubtful. She's more of an artist than athlete. But, thanks for the offer. I'm sure she'll be fine. Everyone loves Camilla."

Apparently, everyone loved Kurt Girard too. Sammie didn't understand his hesitancy about attending the party. The minute he walked in the door, the popular guys were pulling him into the carriage house. Like the other parties, Sammie grew tired of listening to her friends scheme about potential hook-ups. She always gravitated to the kitchen to help Mrs. McDaniel. Though she had heard it all before, she loved hearing Mrs. McDaniel's stories about the renovation approval process with the Historic Society. Tonight, however, the rumored "throw down" was true. A catering company, not Mrs. McDaniel, was scurrying around the kitchen. They were passing out pimento cheese and bacon crostini and miniature crab cakes on a silver platter. Sammie ventured outside to listen to the band.

Before long, Kurt reappeared.

"This band sucks. I hear the piazza has the best view for watching the boats in the harbor. Come with me," Kurt said, grabbing her hand.

Kurt's demeanor seemed to have taken a 180-degree turn. He wasn't the reserved person on the dance floor or standing in her family's den. She smelled beer on his breath. She noticed Katie Rose staring in their direction, so she instructed herself to take a chill pill, as she was commonly chastised by Isabelle.

"Okay, their piazza is one of the best in the Battery."

They climbed the three stories to the expansive piazza and headed to the porch swing. Kurt surprised Sammie with his knowledge of historical landmarks within view—Fort Sumter, Fort Moultrie, and Castle Pinckney. He even educated her about the unique triangular shape of the Sullivan Island Lighthouse.

She was enjoying her time with him. He put his arm around her shoulder and leaned into her. Before she knew what was happening, he kissed her.

"You are so beautiful," he said.

He pulled her closer and kissed her again. This time, he injected his tongue into her mouth. She had never been French kissed before. She didn't like it one bit. She tasted beer.

"What do you think you're doing?"

"Making out? I like you," he said, leaning back in for another kiss with his hand sliding up her leg under her dress.

She grabbed his hand and slapped him.

"Geez. Where did that come from?" Kurt asked. "I thought you seemed cool. I never would have pegged you as a SOBB, but, boy was I wrong," he said getting up from the swing and walking away.

Sammie wanted to yell, *I thought you were too*!

Though new to town, Kurt had learned that "SOBB" stood for "South of Broad Bitches"—the stiff, aloof girls who lived south of Broad Street in the Battery. She ran home but found herself staring at his car parked in their driveway. She had enjoyed talking to him and feared she had overreacted. When she awoke the next morning, she ran to the window and looked for his car. It was gone. She never heard from him again.

Sammie knew that she wasn't a SOBB, but she questioned who she really was. She didn't seem to fit in anywhere.

Chapter Six

Sammie & Isabelle

The following week, Sammie was reminded of Kurt Girard's South of Broad Bitch label. Her club soccer team had finished their match on Rutledge's soccer field. Rutledge was a large public school across the bridge in Mount Pleasant. The entire Rutledge football team was on the adjacent field in the middle of spring football drills. Isabelle, Sammie's best friend and soccer teammate, attended Rutledge and had a severe crush on Joe Parrish, a Rutledge football player.

After their soccer match, Isabelle asked Sammie to stay and watch the rest of the football practice. Sammie had never watched a football practice. In fact, she had never attended a football game. She had ridden to the soccer game with her parents and didn't have any other plans.

"I can take you home," Isabelle said. "I am permitted to cross the bridge, you know."

Isabelle's backhanded comments always struck a nerve. Sammie thought the "crossing the bridge" comment went much deeper than the fact that her house was on the tip of the Charleston peninsula, the most expensive and desired real estate in Charleston County. The area, bordered by the Ashley and Cooper Rivers, contained the residences built by wealthy plantation and store owners in the 1700s. The Georgian-Palladian architecture, wrought-iron gate work, lush gardens, and carriage houses were meticulously described in the guided carriage tours throughout the city.

Isabelle and her friends viewed any resident on the Charleston peninsula as uppity. Sammie was determined to shatter their stereotype. Though she felt like a fish out of water, she agreed to hang out at the publics' football practice.

"Who is #24?" Sammie asked Isabelle.

It didn't take football acumen to scout out #24 as a star.

"Oh, that's Dougie Morgan," she said. "He's hot, and he knows it."

"What do you mean, he knows it?" Sammie asked.

"He's broken more hearts in Charleston County than anyone I can remember," Isabelle said. "Dougie's been the starting QB of the football team since his freshman year. He works summers at the Shem Creek Marina. I'm surprised you haven't met him or at least heard of him with all your sailing regattas."

Sammie ignored the jab. She watched the entire football practice and refrained from asking any more questions. As it concluded, Isabelle flirtatiously waved at Joe.

"Looking good, Joe!"

Despite her intermittent digs, Sammie found Isabelle's bluntness and lack of discretion authentic and refreshing. There was always a hidden agenda at her private school. Isabelle, on the other hand, went after things full throttle whether it was scoring soccer goals or chasing boys. It wasn't just her vivacious personality that made her stand out. Her auburn hair, green eyes, and perfectly proportioned figure enhanced her charm.

At the end of football practice, Joe sauntered over to Isabelle and Sammie. He was covered from head to toe in dirt, sweat, and grass stains.

"What's up?" Joe mumbled, throwing back his wet hair.

"We finished our club futbol match and decided to watch some reeeealll football before heading to the beach," Isabelle said, turning one syllable into four.

"This is Sammie. She's on my soccer team," Isabelle continued. "Wanna go to Sullivan's Island with us to cool off?" Isabelle chimed, twirling her hair.

"Sure," Joe said. "I'll get some of the guys. We've got to shower and then have a short team meeting. But after, we'll pick up some beer and meet ya at Station 23."

"Sounds like a plan," Isabelle said, winking at me.

"Isabelle, I thought we were only staying to watch the practice," Sammie said after Joe jogged away. "You didn't mention anything about the beach."

"You said you didn't have any plans. We'll only stay for a little bit."

"I don't know any of these guys. Can you take me home first?"

"Well, you can call your mommy to pick you up, but I'm not missing one minute with Joe," Isabelle said, rolling her big green eyes like she was talking to a 3rd grader. "And I bet #24 will come," she added, curtly. "Dougie is one of Joe's best buddies. Come to think of it, y'all would be a perfect pair. He's as beautiful and athletic as you are and loves the water too. The only problem is that he doesn't have a number at the end of his name."

Sammie had never been attracted to the likes of George Baker, II, Thomas Hodges, III, Julius Kensington, V, or the others that hadn't made it to the numbers and were simply juniors. In fact, Sammie always had found it curious that the passing of a family name seemed so important, but the boys were penned with stupid nicknames like Little Georgie, Trey, or JuJu, quite the opposite of regal. But, Isabelle's comment struck another nerve, so she caved.

En route to Sullivan's Island to meet the boys from Rutledge, Sammie coaxed herself that she wasn't a SOBB. She would relax and follow Isabelle's lead. And, maybe today, she would feel like she belonged.

Southern girls can be meek and mild, sassy and brassy, trashy and classy all at the same time...

Chapter Seven

Sammie & Isabelle

If there was one thing you could say about Isabelle Lynch, she was full of life. She was always on her A-game whether it was on the soccer field, in the classroom, or just singing to a song blasting in her used Volkswagen Beetle. Her infectious personality and energy sucked people in and could suck the life out of you too.

Isabelle secured a great spot at Station 23, as instructed by Joe, and had her Bluetooth speaker cranking Van Morrison's *Wild Night* when the boys arrived. Sammie always wondered how Isabelle's eclectic range of music had developed. She had introduced Sammie to many new artists and songs. Isabelle apparently had great taste in boys too.

Sammie had not been impressed with Joe earlier, perhaps because he was sweaty and covered in dirt from football practice. His husky build must have been due to all the football pads. Now, his tight shirt highlighted six-pack abs. Two other cute boys accompanied him, one carrying a cooler and the other a brown bag. The one with the brown bag was mouth-droppingly handsome. All were wearing flip flops and baseball caps, but the hunk was wearing his hat backwards. He had a confident swagger unlike any boy she knew from Tradd Prep. His baggy athletic shorts and loose fitting t-shirt didn't mask his tan, toned legs.

"Isabelle, and I'm sorry, I forgot your name," Joe said.

"I'm Sammie."

"Oh yeah, I knew it was a guy's name," Joe continued.

Sammie flinched. She loved her name because she was named after her father, but at times like this, she desired a feminine name like Isabelle.

"This is Dougie," Joe said, pointing to the really cute one with the backward baseball cap and brown bag. "This is Matt," pointing to one carrying the cooler.

"Natty Lites anyone?" Matt asked.

"Sammie hates beer," Isabelle said, "but I'll take one."

Sammie could have killed her. She felt like a prude on her own even without her friend highlighting the fact.

"No problem, Dougie has Firefly," Joe said.

"Sammie would love some," Isabelle said, popping the top of her beer. "She is a southern girl to the core and loves her sweet tea, right?" Isabelle returned Sammie's bewildered glare with a big, toothy, mischievous grin and wink.

"A girl after my heart," Dougie smiled. "I'll fix you one. You want it with lemonade or straight up?"

Sammie took a deep breath. She had no idea how she wanted it because she didn't even know what *it* was. But, she thought whatever *it* was, *it* was probably illegal to drink. She reminded herself that she wanted to fit in and relented to the peer pressure.

"I'd love it with lemonade, if you are sure you have enough," Sammie said.

The concoction did taste like sweet tea, so Sammie rationalized that it couldn't be all that bad. Still, she sipped it slowly listening to Isabelle's playlist and trying to keep a low profile. When Jerry Butler's "Cooling Out" boomed, Dougie grabbed Sammie's hand.

"I love beach music. Dance with me," Dougie said.

Instantly, Sammie was twirled around on the sand with Dougie's gang watching. She could tell he was the leader of the pack.

The sweet tea and lemonade (and whatever else was in her cup) was going to her head and heart. She was falling for this Dougie. She understood how Dougie had broken every heart in Charleston County, and at that moment, she didn't care if she was the next victim.

As she spun under Dougie's arm, his free hand slipped behind her back and pulled her close. She could feel his breath on her neck. Given his ruggedness, she was surprised by his smooth dance moves. His swagger and magnetism were reeling her in.

After Matt left and Isabelle and Joe went for a walk down the beach, Dougie spread out a beach towel in the sand. He asked her to join him.

The sun was setting, and nothing could rival a Charleston sunset. Dougie laid down and started looking up at the sky. At this particular moment, Sammie longed to be more like Isabelle. She felt awkward and stiff sitting up straight, but she didn't know what to do.

"You have a much better view of the stars if you lay down," Dougie said, tugging on the back of her shirt. "Look at all of them out tonight."

Sammie was speechless, and her heart was pounding out of her chest. She wanted to ignore her rule-following, "Miss Goodie Two Shoes" voice and just roll with it.

Dougie was easy to talk to. She was feeling at ease. She forgot that she was lying next to one of the most popular guys at Rutledge. He asked her about her soccer team and her other interests. He talked about his summer jobs at Shem Creek. She talked about hers at the Charleston Ashley Dockage.

"You're so cool. I've never met anyone like you," Dougie said.

Before Sammie could say another word, Dougie slid his arm under her back, pulling her closer. He leaned into her and kissed her gently on the lips. She thought she was going to faint. She couldn't catch her breath. His soft tongue entered her mouth. Sammie felt him pull back and was mortified that she might have gasped. Dougie's kiss was far better than Sammie's first kiss from Kurt Girard just a week ago. She didn't want him to stop. Her mind was racing with pleas not to stop. Perhaps he heard them, because he came back into her mouth and kissed her longer. His kiss moved to her neck and then her chest.

Sammie couldn't process all that her body was feeling—it was limp yet burning with excitement at the same time. Before she knew what was happening, she felt Dougie's hand under her soccer shorts. She was suddenly aware of the involuntary effects that his touches were causing. The lack of control over her own body scared her. When

Dougie placed Sammie's hand down his shorts, she was embarrassed that she was so inexperienced. She was going to let this moment take her wherever Dougie Morgan wanted it to go. That is, until she heard Isabelle's laughter coming up the beach. She yanked her hand from inside Dougie's shorts.

"Leave it to Isabelle to kill the moment," he said, sitting up.

Dougie was cool and collected as Isabelle and Joe approached hand-in-hand, but Sammie's head was spinning. Her insides were on fire. She worried that Isabelle would sense something had happened.

Sammie stood up quickly.

"I've got to go, Isabelle."

"Can't you stay just a little longer?" Isabelle said with a pouty face, resting her head on Joe's shoulder.

"I can give you a ride if you don't mind riding in a pick-up truck with sweaty football gear," Dougie said.

"Dougie Morgan, what would your girlfriend say about that?" Isabelle asked. "And, Sammie lives across the bridge—South of Broad."

At that moment, Sammie's heart sank. She felt like a fool. Obviously, she was just a beach hook-up. The comment about where she lived wounded her. Sammie tried to hold back the tears that began welling up in her eyes.

"OK, I was just trying to be polite. You know, us guys across the bridge aren't so bad," Dougie said, coolly. "Catch you girls, later."

He grabbed his beach towel and brown bag and left.

Isabelle leaned into Joe.

"I guess we better be going too. You're going to call me, right Joe Parrish?"

"I'll think about it," Joe said, laughing.

Then, Joe pulled Isabelle into him, and they began kissing. Sammie felt even more like an idiot. It was like she wasn't even there.

"So, Missy, what happened with you and Dougie?" Isabelle asked about five seconds after getting in the car. "When Joe and I walked up, you looked like you had been caught with your hand in the cookie jar," she said, laughing.

"Isabelle, he has a girlfriend," Sammie said, flatly.

"Well, he seemed really into you."

"Who is his girlfriend?" Sammie asked, nonchalantly.

"Donna Boykin, she's the chief cheerleader."

"What's she like?"

"She has huge boobs, a teeny waist, short blonde hair, and a killer tan. Plus, although I'm not a good judge of asses, the boys are goo-goo-eyed over hers. And basically, she's a slut. The joke about her at Rutledge is 'Who is Donna Boykin boinking?' I guess Dougie likes the sluts with tits and ass, like everyone else. Boys are sooooo shallow like that."

Sammie wished she hadn't asked. Her stomach started hurting. She had just let a stranger go farther with her than anyone ever had, and he was probably going to be boinking Donna later. Sammie turned up the volume to "Rolling in the Deep" on the radio to cut off the conversation. It worked. Isabelle started bellowing to Adele's new song.

The drive over the bridge seemed to take forever. Sammie wanted to get home and crawl under her covers. When Isabelle finally made the turn onto Sammie's street, Sammie thanked Isabelle for the ride home.

"The beach was great too. I'm too uptight sometimes. I'm glad you made me go."

"Oh, girl, you are fine. Correcto in the uptight column, but we can work on that and work on Dougie too" she said, winking. "He'll dump 'Who is Donna Boykin Boinking?' before too long. None of them last. See ya at practice tomorrow."

By now, Sammie's head pounded. She didn't know if it was from the four headers during the soccer game, the sweet tea and lemonade drink, the kiss, what had followed, or a combination of all of them. It was only 8:00 on a Saturday night, but she retreated to her bedroom. She tried to get Dougie Morgan out of her splitting head, but she knew she'd never forget the quivering sensations and burning desire that still raged throughout her body.

Chapter Eight

Sammie

Sammie's senior year was flying by. Between *among* the sailing team, club soccer, and college applications, she had little time for anything else. She did find time, however, to periodically scan Isabelle's *Facebook* page for any photos of Rutledge beach parties. Unfortunately, Dougie wasn't on *Facebook* and Donna Boykin's page was private. Her only means to learn anything about Dougie's activities was reading the Sports page of the *Post & Courier* every Saturday to check out the articles about the Friday night football games.

As the season progressed, the articles heralding Dougie Morgan's football prowess seemed unending. *Rutledge 17-Reynolds 10. The winning touchdown drive was set up by a 52-yard pass from Dougie Morgan to Brandon Nichols. Rutledge 38-West Ashley 35. Dougie Morgan scored in the last minute on a one-yard quarterback keeper.*

Sammie pictured Donna Boykin shaking her pom poms as she cheered for her boyfriend. She was envious that Donna and Dougie were celebrating the victories that Sammie only read about in the newspaper.

After football season was over, Sammie discovered from the sports section that Dougie was a great basketball player too. While reading the blurbs, she would rewind time to Sullivan's Island and relive the romantic memory. Sadly, it was apparently just another day at the beach for him.

Throughout the spring soccer season, she longed for Isabelle to provide some tidbit of information about Dougie. She assumed Isabelle never mentioned him for a number of reasons, the primary one being that he had no interest in her. Sammie certainly wasn't going to bring him up or admit to searching for him on Isabelle's *Facebook* page or stalking him in the *Post & Courier*. She was embarrassed that she had schemed for a happenstance meeting. But, she hadn't run into Dougie during her frequent visits to the Shem Creek Marina Grill.

As the skipper in the Sailing A-Division, Sammie's top finishes in local regattas provided periodic distractions from Dougie Morgan. The *Post & Courier* assisted her attempts to forget about her interminable crush, since whatever he was doing didn't appear in the paper. She had given up on any *Facebook* intel. But as they say, things happen when you least expect them.

After celebrating Sammie's first-place finish in the James Island Regatta, Glenny apologized that she would have to leave early from the soccer match due to a bank dinner party. Sammie was glad that her parents were going to enjoy a night out. Her mother's world evolved around Sammie's activities. She frankly wished her mother had some other outlet—a garden club, a bridge group, or even a part-time job in the clothing boutiques on King Street. Sammie worried about what her mother would do next year when she left for college.

Sammie texted Isabelle to ask for a ride home after the soccer match. Sammie kept her new BMW a secret since her car was much nicer than those of her teammates, if they had a car at all. Isabelle didn't need any more fodder.

"Kelly and I are hitting a party on Sullivan's after the game, but you can come with us, and I'll take you home after that," Isabelle responded. "It's going to be a blast!"

Kelly was a new member of their club soccer team and also attended Rutledge.

"Are you sure guests are welcome?" Sammie asked.

"Guests? You kill me. There aren't engraved invitations! LOL. At Rutledge beach parties, the more the merrier."

Though the publics were more inclusive than Sammie's schoolmates, she found them intimidating. They exuded an independence and an *eat shit* confidence. She wondered how many of them would be there. She worried about her reaction if Dougie was there with his girlfriend. Would he even remember her? She decided to suck it up. She was headed to Yale University in the fall where she didn't know a single soul there or in the entire state of Connecticut. It was time that she stepped outside her comfort zone, if only for one night.

Sammie's head was not in the soccer game. She was completely distracted by the beach party and whether Dougie would be there. Since the last outing on Sullivan's Island, she hadn't been with anyone else nor did she have any desire. Dougie Morgan consumed her thoughts. She was content to listen to Adele's *21* album on her iPod and reminisce about that evening.

The referee finally blew his whistle, and Isabelle, Kelly, and Sammie scurried to the restroom to change. Though the party was on the beach, Sammie would have preferred a shower but settled for Isabelle's baby powder and dry shampoo. Walking on the boardwalk path through the trees at Station 23, her heart was in her throat. When she saw the mob on the beach, she wanted to sprint away. Isabelle sensed Sammie's apprehension and clutched her arm.

"You are one hot chick," Isabelle said. "These Rutledge boys are going to think they have died and gone to heaven."

Isabelle quickly surveyed the crowd and made a beeline towards Joe and his gang. They, all gripping solo cups, were huddled in a semi-circle near the sand dunes away from the swarms of publics on the beach. Sammie spotted Dougie immediately. He looked even better than she remembered. Her eyes locked on his.

"What's up boys?" Isabelle chirped, boldly sashaying right up to the group with Kelly and Sammie in tow. "You can start having fun now. We're here! Our soccer game lasted forevvvvvvver. Anyway, guys, this is Sammie. You remember Joe? He's mine," she said teasingly, as she curled her arm under his while laying her head on his shoulder. Then, she pointed at the other boys standing in the semi-circle. "Matt and Dougie, you met them before. This is Barnyard."

Sammie thought she had heard a lot of stupid nicknames, but "Barnyard" won the prized blue ribbon. She wanted to ask how his nickname originated. Barnyard was a huge dude with a red bandana covering his head like a pirate. He had a gut that would rival the belly of a middle-aged, sedentary man.

"Isabelle, where have you been hiding Sammie?" grunted Barnyard, "I've never met a girl named Sammie. But it turns me on. Saaammeee!" he said in a high-pitched tone. Sammie thought that he sounded like a squealing pig, which might account for his nickname.

His comments didn't appear to bother the others in the least. Sammie thought that they probably just blocked out this obnoxious creature. She wondered how Barnyard was in the cool guys' inner circle. She wanted to garner the nerve to ask Barnyard if he got his name because he wasn't the sharpest pitchfork in the barn. She refrained for fear that she would likely just offend all of Isabelle's friends and completely ratify her SOBB status.

"Let's go grab some sweet tea," Dougie said, grabbing Sammie's arm. "I have some in my truck."

Before Sammie had time to get excited that Dougie had remembered her, he asked Kelly to join them.

Kelly and Sammie followed Dougie away from the party down the beach. They took a path intersecting two sand dunes. His Ford F-150 truck was parked behind a large oceanfront home.

"This is the Kapp's house. I work for them. They move to Florida in May and don't return until October. Pretty sweet, huh?"

He unlatched the tailgate and opened a cooler, not just any plastic cooler but a sizable marine offshore cooler.

"This is Mr. Kapp's cooler. I'm pretty sure it's never been used," Dougie said. "Mr. Kapp is the type that has the boat with all the toys but doesn't know how to use any of them. So, tonight, it's our bar."

Sammie bit her tongue to keep her from asking what he meant by "bar." She watched him carefully this time. The glass bottle appeared to contain tea. He poured it over ice and then added lemonade. Dougie noted Sammie's scrutiny.

"Firefly is vodka but infused with tea from the Charleston Tea Plantation. It's sweet tea with a kick."

"I remember that I liked it," Sammie said, attempting to hide the quiver in her voice after watching him mix it.

"The only thing better is if you add lemons," added Kelly.

"Sorry, fresh out of fruit, but I'll give yours an extra splash," Dougie said.

Kelly giggled. Sammie could tell that Kelly, like every other living female, was smitten by this charming, athletic star. She felt a twinge of jealously watching Kelly's amorous gaze as Dougie mixed the drinks. They gathered up the red solo cups and headed back between the dunes and to the beach.

"What took y'all so long?" Isabelle boomed. "I'm so thirsty. I want the one that has more tea than lemonade, right Joe?" as she grabbed his hand and interlocked her fingers in his.

Sammie didn't know what to make of that comment. Did Isabelle mean that the vodka made her less inhibited or acquiescent? Sammie was already spellbound by Dougie, so she cautiously sipped her "sweet tea" for fear of losing all control.

Sammie quickly forgot that she was a guest at the publics' party and felt at ease with Isabelle's friends. There was no mention of Sarah Katherine's new loaded Range Rover, Ann Spencer's new Louis Vuitton bag, or Maddie's recent invitation to a debutante party. They were just a group of teenagers having fun.

Sammie was having a lot of fun until Dougie announced that he was leaving. He had the early shift the next day at Shem Creek.

Sammie was disappointed. Her curfew wasn't until 11:00 p.m. She wanted to spend more time with him. She felt like she was holding a winning lottery ticket when Dougie asked her if she needed a ride home.

"I have to drop off something at the Lockwood Marina. Don't you live near there?"

"Yes, I live pretty close. I don't think Isabelle is ready to leave any time soon, so a ride would be great."

"Would you like to see the Kapp's roof deck?" Dougie asked, walking back down the beach towards his truck. "It's pretty incredible."

"That seems awfully close to trespassing on private property," Sammie said, instantly mortified with herself.

Dougie laughed.

"The stairs to the deck are in the garage where the lawn mower and all the other yard maintenance stuff that I use is stored. I have a key, so technically, I'm not trespassing."

"Well, if you have a key," Sammie said, trying to make a quick recovery, "I'd love to see the view."

Dougie fixed another drink before unlocking the storage area. It had been about two hours since Sammie's first drink. She never drank anything, so she was still a little tipsy.

"This place has an old school sound system," Dougie said, climbing the stairs, "and even older music selection."

He punched on the CD player and grabbed a cushion from a wooden bin. Sammie wondered how many girls he had brought here. He seemed to have a well-rehearsed routine. But, at that moment, she didn't care.

They climbed the enclosed staircase which led to a deck with panoramic views of the ocean, the intracoastal waterway, and the Charleston Harbor. The shrimp boats were chugging up the Cooper River, and Sammie's favorite low country music was playing in the background—waves crashing, gulls squawking, and cicadas chirping.

Boz Scaggs' song, "Georgia," interrupted the ocean noises. Dougie put his drink down, grabbed Sammie's hand and started shagging with her like he did last fall. This time, Sammie was determined to remember every touch, every move, and every expression. She knew that she may never see him again.

"I've thought about you a lot," he said. "I started to call you a couple of times to see if you wanted to hang out."

"Well, why didn't you?"

"I figured you had your own friends and parties to go to," he said.

Sammie thought this may be the last time that she saw Dougie Morgan. She coached herself to be bold for once.

"I wish you would have. I've thought about you too."

They sat down on a chaise lounge and talked about their plans for the upcoming year—what it was going to be like in college on their own. The conversation was easy and relaxed as their first time on the beach. Sammie didn't want the night to end, but it was getting close to her curfew.

"I probably need to get home," she said, regrettably. "Don't you have to drop something off at the marina?"

"I do but can do that any time. I just wanted to have a reason to take you home."

Sammie thought she was going to melt. It wasn't just out of convenience that he offered her a ride.

"So, I'll take you home but not yet," Dougie said, moving closer to her.

Though she really wanted to know how many girls he had taken up to the Kapp's deck, Sammie felt inspired by Isabelle's confidence and "live for the moment" attitude. She leaned into Dougie's chest. Unlike their first touching, Sammie eagerly welcomed Dougie's advances. His tongue touching hers sent shock waves throughout her body. Their connection felt so natural that she didn't even flinch when his hands smoothly untied the straps on her sundress. She didn't resist him when his kisses moved to her exposed chest while he pulled her sundress and underwear down her hips. Her heart rate skyrocketed. She realized that she didn't even know her own body parts. It was apparent that Sammie Spencer had been one tightly wound girl who had no idea what she had been missing. An inconceivable sensation was taking over her. She moaned and gasped for air. Dougie moved up to Sammie's face and removed something from his pocket while kissing her.

The ecstasy she had been feeling deflated as she realized he had been prepared for someone else since he didn't know she was going to be at the beach party. But her guarded instincts disappeared when he unbuckled his belt and unzipped his pants. She lost all concept of time and responsibility.

Since their first kiss on the beach, Sammie had fantasized about him and this moment. It was far better than she had imagined. Nothing had given her greater pleasure—not first place regatta finishes, perfect test scores, or soccer goals.

"Can I call you tomorrow?" Dougie asked.

And from that night throughout the summer, Sammie and Dougie were connected. They were a team, best friends, soul mates, spiritual partners, sexual partners— whatever other words there are for the love of your life. Dougie and Sammie were perfect for each other and madly in love physically, emotionally, and mentally ... forever and ever...'til death do they part...or so Sammie thought.

Take the bitter with the sweet...

Chapter Nine

Sammie

Sammie had worked hard to follow in her father's footsteps and gain acceptance into Yale. She had also landed a spot on the sailing team. Likewise, Dougie was headed to Clemson to play football. Due to the demands of both of their schedules, they only saw each other during holiday breaks.

After college, Dougie returned to Mount Pleasant while Sammie stayed in New Haven, Connecticut to enter Yale Law School. Dougie landed a job at RePro, Inc., where business was booming. The company focused on managing product returns for grocery store items and over-the-counter drugs, including reimbursement coupons. Consumers' use of coupons was at an all-time high. Despite the room for advancement in this growing company, Dougie disliked being chained to a desk entering data. He found it excruciatingly monotonous. He missed interacting with people and being outdoors.

Initially, he had been a good sport about weekend travel and attending first-year law school social functions, but it was short-lived. He became very vocal. He hated being around her law school friends.

"I have nothing in common with those brainiacs," he said. "I can't stand to hear those nerds talk about their trial team competitions and case law studies. I'd rather be in my cube at RePro entering coupon data."

Sammie kept her disappointment to herself when, during her second year, Dougie added a weekend job at the Bohicket Marina on John's Island. She understood that he missed the water, so the work was a good outlet for him. But, the job would interfere with the already limited weekends that they had together.

Their visits became limited to breaks and holidays, like the previous four years. Their intermittent phone conversations became strained. Sammie understood that the distance would either solidify their relationship, or they would drift apart. During their reunions, they immediately reconnected and couldn't get enough of each other. Their love life would always pick up where they left off.

Upon her return to Charleston after graduation, Sammie moved back home while she studied for the bar exam. She couldn't begin her dream job until she had passed the mandatory test for obtaining a law license. Spencer, Pettigrew & Hamilton required its prospective attorneys to succeed on the first attempt—there were no exceptions, even for a Spencer. The fact that no Spencer had ever flunked the bar exam was added pressure. Dougie understood Sammie's stress and the time needed for studying. He added double shifts at the Bohicket Marina to keep himself occupied. After all, he was saving for their future.

"I'm always going to be here for you. I understand how important this is to you. It's only for a couple of months. We're going to have forever together."

Dougie's proposal reflected his amorous spirit and was perfect. Sammie was completely unaware that Dougie was going to propose that night especially given how the night had started. Dougie's plan for the evening was a quick dinner in Mount Pleasant before heading to a Sullivan Island beach party with his old Rutledge buddies. Sammie wasn't too keen on the beach party. It seemed like they had been there, done that. They should have moved beyond old high school gatherings.

"I need to go by the Kapps for a minute, if you don't mind," Dougie said, crossing over the Cooper River bridge. "And while we're there, I want to show you what they've added to the deck."

Sammie didn't mind at all. She loved the Kapps' rooftop deck. What was there not to love? It was the place where she had lost her virginity to the high school hunk who had grown even more handsome over the years. She started thinking about that first time. Now, the difference was there was no uneasiness or apprehension. Her insecurities in that department were in the distant past. She smiled thinking about the intense passion they still had for each other. She wished they could stay on the Kapps' rooftop and skip the beach party.

"You head on up," Dougie said, pulling into the driveway. "You're going to love the addition."

Sammie took the stairs two at a time. It was the best time of day for gazing across the Atlantic, watching the flocks of pelicans flying in their "V" formation, the pod of

41

dolphins swimming by, and the seagulls scavenging for crumbs left by beach visitors. There was nothing more peaceful than the sights and sounds of life near the ocean.

The deck spanned the entire length of the house and ran parallel to the ocean. But then it took a 90-degree turn to capture the views from the marsh. It was on the marsh side that she noticed the new addition—a hot tub. The temperatures were mild even in the low country winters, so hot tubs were not commonplace. Selfishly, the hot tub was much more inviting than the beach party. She removed the cover, turned on the jets, dropped her sundress, and climbed in. The sexy voice of William Royce Scaggs, still the artist of choice on the Kapp sound system, crooned across the deck from the built-in speakers.

"I should have known better than to turn you loose up here unsupervised. Who would have ever thought that Sammie Spencer would turn into a delinquent?"

"Well, you know that the ocean sounds make me crazy. I can't understand why the Kapps don't use this deck, their hot tub, their bikes, their kayaks—well any of their things. You would have to peel me off this deck to send me to work."

"Now, hop out," he said. "The hot tub was going to be for later."

"Later? Aren't we going to dinner and to the beach party?" Sammie asked, attempting to feign disappointment.

"Nope, change of plans. I brought some dinner."

While Sammie prematurely dipped into the hot tub, Dougie had dispersed several votive candles around the table. He had set out the feast that he had stashed in the cooler—fresh oysters, shrimp, salad, and succotash—all of Sammie's favorite things.

Dougie popped the cork on a bottle of champagne, filled two flutes, and got down on his knees. He grabbed both of Sammie's hands.

"Sammie Spencer, you're the love of my life. I knew it the moment I first laid eyes on you. Will you marry me?" he asked, handing her an oyster shell with a ring inside.

After dinner and more champagne, they eventually collapsed on the chaise lounge in each other's arms until awakened by the sunrise. She and Dougie had survived the difficulties of a seven-year, long-distance relationship. The worse days were behind them. As, Mr. and Mrs. Douglas Wayne Morgan, the world was their oyster.

Chapter Ten

Sammie

Sammie couldn't wait to tell her mother about the engagement. Her father was another story. Though Cort admired Dougie's work ethic and appreciated his middle class background, Sammie sensed an uneasiness between them. Her father had a guarded mistrust of Dougie. She assumed it was simply a father's protective instinct for his daughter, and in her case, his namesake and only child.

As expected, Glenny Spencer was ecstatic with the news. Unbeknownst to Sammie, her mother had been maintaining a wedding file for years. The large manilla folder was filled with pages from magazines ranging from flower arrangements and the reception menu to parting gifts for the guests. Sammie was overcome with pride when she realized that the wedding folder also contained several Eleanor Glenn Spencer sketches for her dress. After all, Glenny's goal for Sammie was marriage and babies, lots of them. The added bonus was Sammie's fiancé was delightfully handsome. Like all women, she was drawn to Dougie Morgan's charm and jaw-dropping good looks.

Soon after the proposal night, Cort alerted Dougie that a sales position was available at Worth Pharmaceutical Company. He had maintained contacts at the company from his stint in New York, and they had reached out about possible candidates since the position was for the Charleston area. Though Cort Spencer wasn't the meddling type, he was aware of Dougie's aversion to the traditional office job. He believed that Dougie could excel in sales due to his engaging personality. He viewed the inquiry as serendipitous. As a result of Cort's recommendation, Worth requested an interview between Dougie and Worth's regional sales manager. Sammie hoped Dougie would not reject this opportunity due to her father's involvement.

Dougie was never impressed with those in Charleston who worked for family businesses or landed jobs through family connections. He also shunned the social opportunities that were afforded him due to his wife's maiden name. Nothing could be less desirable than associating with the next generation of Charleston aristocrats in Dougie's mind.

In reality, he was emboldened by Sammie's stable upbringing and trust fund. But, he wanted to make it on his own. He had landed jobs at RePro and Shem Creek on his own merits and initiative. He was perfectly capable of paving his own career path.

Dougie was so miserable at RePro, he couldn't let his pride get in the way of a possible escape. He readily agreed to the interview. Dougie reasoned that since Sammie's father didn't know the interviewer, it was ultimately up to him to perform well. He even called Sammie's father to thank him.

Sammie was glad that her father had meddled. She agreed that Dougie would be successful in sales. His various jobs at the Shem Creek Marina had exposed him to a range of social classes—from the boat owners to the boat mechanics. Dougie could communicate with anyone on any level.

Dougie researched all about Worth Pharmaceutical and learned that the company was known for its research and development in pain management medicines. The more he read about the company, the more excited he became. Sammie observed his competitive nature kick into gear as he described the exotic trips awarded to its tops sales representatives. She was flabbergasted that Dougie asked her father to provide interview tips. Cort was pleased to help and met with Dougie numerous times before his interview.

Cort questioned Dougie extensively not only about Worth but also about RePro and his previous employment at Shem Creek. He identified and highlighted strengths and skills garnered from those jobs that would be easily transferable into sales.

"Dougie has inside information about the drug industry and can speak the language," Cort surmised. "His knowledge of pharmaceutical reconciliations at RePro gives him an advantage over other candidates."

Sammie was pleased with her father's interest in Dougie and shared his enthusiasm. She also was ashamed and embarrassed that her father had learned more about Dougie's jobs than she ever had known. She would talk incessantly about the mergers and acquisitions that she worked on at the firm, but Dougie never offered any detail (nor did she inquire) about what he did every day. He seemed disinterested in talking about it, and she sensed that he felt that his job was inferior to the prestige of working at a law firm.

On the day of Dougie's interview, Cort called to wish him luck.

"Just relax and be yourself," Cort said. "If this job doesn't work out, there will be others, and this may be a practice run for the next opportunity. Let me know how it goes today if you have time."

Dougie seemed grateful for the call. It seemed to calm his nerves.

"I never noticed it before, but you are a lot like your dad," Dougie said. "You are both so easygoing. I'm going to go kick some ass in this interview. I'll call you and let you know how it goes. I love you, Sammie."

Sammie agreed that her father was cool under pressure but disagreed that his calm nature had been passed to her. Her stomach was a ball of nerves. She couldn't concentrate on the shareholder agreement she was revising. At this moment, exceptions to restrictions for stock transfers or the procedures for exercising rights of first refusal seemed so trivial. She could only think about Worth Pharmaceutical and Dougie.

Cort called Sammie's office to communicate Dougie's job offer from Worth. He said that he had not properly celebrated their engagement, so they needed to plan a double celebration. Sammie assumed that Dougie hadn't shared the news with her because he didn't want to bother her at the office. When Sammie hung up with her father, she immediately called Dougie to congratulate him. Oddly, Dougie had yet to hear from Worth.

Dougie repeatedly asked if his future father-in-law had pulled some strings. But, he seemed to let it go. He was excited about the opportunity. He was going to knock it out of the park.

One thing Dougie couldn't ignore, however, was Cort's location for the celebration. Cort and Glenny did not appreciate Dougie's contempt for Charleston's high society scene. Sammie had not yet broken the news that a big wedding with a reception at the country club was not in the cards.

Sammie agreed that Herons, Dougie's choice, sounded like the perfect location. Dougie had discovered the bistro on Johns Island while working at the Bohicket Marina. Getting there was part of the adventure—grand oak trees draped with

Spanish moss provided a continuous canopy over the winding road. His praise was effusive.

"The food is even better than the drive. I love the fried flounder, but the menu is varied. There is even an escargot appetizer to satisfy Glenny's love of French cuisine. And, you know how Cort loves she-crab soup. Well, theirs has jumbo lump crab meat. And, it has an extensive wine list," Dougie said, gushing.

The restaurant was outside the security gates of private Seabrook and Kiawah Islands, so if the atmosphere was elegant enough for its wealthy neighbors, Dougie was confident his future in-laws would approve.

Dougie was right. Glenny hired Herons to cater the reception for the small April wedding on the beach at Sullivan's Island. Sammie looked like royalty in her Eleanor Glenn Spencer original. The weather was equally grand—blue bird skies and seventy degrees. The coastal breeze even held the pesky no-see-ums at bay.

Everything was falling perfectly into place for the newlyweds. They settled into a routine. Sammie found that she could work the required long hours at the law firm without feeling like a neglectful wife. Dougie's sales territory continued to expand requiring him to travel most of the week. He was rewarded by invitations to the Worth retreats at five-star resorts.

Dougie's time away provided Sammie with guilt-free nights with her best friend. Lucy served as Sammie's culinary guinea pig—tasting the new recipes before their introduction to Dougie. Sammie loved her husband. Sammie loved her best friend. Sammie loved her job. Life was better than good; it was idyllic.

Be ready for the shoe to drop ...

Chapter Eleven

Sammie

Dougie was a rising star at Worth. Along with his territory, the scope of his sales targets expanded as well. In addition to hospitals and doctors, he now had responsibility for pharmacies, clinics, and long-term care facilities. Sammie couldn't pinpoint the exact time when she noticed a change in her husband.

"I'm worried about you," Sammie recalled saying one weekend when Dougie was too tired to run or bike with her. "Are you taking on too much?" she asked.

"Interesting question from someone who works 12-hour days," Dougie said, brusquely.

"But, it's not the same. I get to fall asleep in my bed every night and don't bounce from one town to the next," Sammie said, attempting to highlight aspects of his job that could be draining.

"You should know that the travel is the main reason I love my job," he said.

Sammie knew that Dougie wouldn't survive in an office environment. He loved visiting new cities and meeting people. Everyone was drawn to Dougie. He was beating sales goals and was consistently invited to the lavish Worth trips honoring the top performers.

"I know. I'm not expressing myself clearly," she said, thinking that the conversation was heading in the wrong direction. "You love to exercise too. It just seems that you don't have the energy for anything but work."

She decided not to add that their sex life was waning. The weekends were never long enough to analyze Dougie's mood swings. Monday mornings arrived too quickly. Their lives resembled a hamster wheel with no exit.

One Saturday when Dougie bailed on a run, Sammie actually didn't mind. She needed to bounce some things off Lucy on a new matter involving an executive compensation assignment for a public company. Lucy was always available for Sammie's last-minute invitations for either runs or dinners.

"I don't know why I got this assignment," Sammie said. "You have more experience in dealing with public companies."

"Maybe, but you can do anything," Lucy said. "And I can help you."

If Lucy's work plate wasn't full, she would have silently questioned Sammie's new assignment too. But, she had more work than she could do, and she knew that the Spencer name afforded Sammie certain internal perks. Though they would be considered for partnership at the same time, their friendship was solid. They didn't compete with one another like the other associates. They were more like a team. Lucy gave Sammie drafting pointers during the entire six-mile run.

each other

Dougie was napping when they finished. Sammie quietly retreated to the spare bedroom that had been turned into their home office. She fired up the computer and worked on her assignment while Lucy's tips were fresh in her mind. She was making good progress when the low battery notification alerted her to connect to a power source. The charger wasn't on the desk. She couldn't afford to lose her work and began to panic. Dougie's briefcase was on the floor. He often researched potential customers on their laptop, so Sammie unconsciously assumed the charger was inside. It was locked.

She tiptoed into the bedroom and found Dougie's keys. The small key fit. As the latch clicked, a weird sensation sizzled through her body like she was violating her husband's privacy. She brushed it aside because they kept no secrets. As she opened the briefcase, she quickly learned that she was wrong.

Along with the expected numerous drug samples, she found some unexpected items. There was a stack of handwritten notes with the Worth logo:

I enjoyed meeting you at the regional sales meeting. You have gotten off to a great start! You have star potential. Congratulations!
Best,
Cathleen McKinney

It was great spending time with you at the retreat. You are building quite a network. Keep up the good work! Worth values relationships. Relationships are the key to success.
Best,
Cathleen McKinney

There were several others praising Dougie's sales success and his growing client base. Why would he keep these?

Well, I must say that I am not surprised that your sales exceeded all expectations. How do you keep busting the projections, Dougie? What is your secret? If you share your secrets at the Christmas party, I'll share mine.
XOXO,
CM

The hugs and kisses abbreviation certainly intimated something more than a professional relationship between her husband and this co-worker. It made her feel queasy.

Then one from December...

I can't wait to see you at the Christmas party. I hope you're still going solo so I can give you an advance tutorial of some new products. I'll be wearing your favorite red dress—at least at the party. Can't wait for our private after-party!
XOXO,
CM

Sammie sat down in the chair and threw up all over the floor. As she was heaving, Dougie walked into the room. He turned white when he saw the notes in her hands and the vomit.

"Sammie, what have you been you doing?" he asked, accusingly.

She continued to retch.

"What am I doing?" she asked, tears streaming down her face. "The question is what have you been doing? Who is Cathleen?"

Sammie couldn't look at him and buried her face in her hands.

He left the room, returning with towels and ammonia. Sammie felt like every internal organ had erupted out of her. She was weak. She felt dizzy.

"Sammie, I know this doesn't look good, but you've got to believe me. It's not what it looks like," Dougie said. "Cathleen is my boss. Shit, she is everybody's boss. She's the manager of the entire Southeast division. It's her job to meet all the sales reps and keep up with our performance."

"Really? Performance?" Sammie asked, regaining some composure. "What kind of performance? A boss shouldn't be saying these things! No one should be saying these things."

Her tears were replaced with anger.

"Please calm down. I can explain," he said, as he paced the room, running his hands through his hair.

"I'm waiting," Sammie said, tersely.

Dougie knelt down at Sammie's feet. He took her hands in his.

"I'm going to be completely honest with you."

His eyes filled with tears. Sammie had never seen Dougie Morgan on edge, much less close to crying. But he was completely falling apart. Her anger quickly turned to heartbreak and despair. She didn't know if she could handle what he was getting ready to tell her.

"I am used to women hitting on me, Sammie," he said, as tears rolled down his cheeks. "It has happened for as long as I can remember. But when I met you, I felt like someone loved me for who I really was, not what I looked like. I want to succeed in this job. I want to make you proud. I want to prove to your father that I am worthy to be your husband. Hell, if it weren't for him, I would still be entering coupon data at RePro."

Sammie's emotions were conflicting. It was heartbreaking to see Dougie cry, but she couldn't connect where this was going. Was he getting ready to tell her that he was having an affair?

"My boss flirts with me. At first, I thought it was her way of giving positive reinforcement to the sales force. But, she singled me out and has been very aggressive. The woman literally harasses me. Who has ever heard of a man being sexually harassed by a woman?"

The resentment in his voice vanished and was replaced with panic.

"I want to keep my job. I am really good at this job. I haven't slept with her, Sammie. I swear to God."

"If nothing is going on, then why would she write you notes?" Sammie asked. "Not only is it unprofessional but also rather stupid for a boss to document actionable behavior—especially if you have made it clear that you are off limits."

"It's not that simple, Sammie," Dougie said. "I have just been caught up in a terrible situation. For the first time in my life, I feel like I am controlled by someone who is too powerful for me."

"That's sick. All of it is sick," Sammie said, becoming angry again. Her emotions were running the gamut.

"We'll sue her Dougie," Sammie said. "She is poison. The firm has the best employment lawyers in the state. We can stop this."

Sammie's anger at Dougie switched to anger at his boss. She wasn't naïve to disgusting workplace practices. She certainly had heard of distasteful and repulsive activities at the firm—affairs that everyone knew about but ignored. But, a woman taking advantage of a man was new territory.

"Sammie, don't think I haven't thought about reporting her," Dougie said. "But, I can't. It's a no-win situation for me. If I took on a powerful Worth executive, I would be forever scarred in the corporate world. Who would hire a man who sued a woman for sexual harassment? Think about it, Sammie. I would be a laughingstock. I could never get another job."

He was right. The only thing he could do was quit, but that was so unfair. As his head lay in Sammie's lap, she stroked his hair.

"Dougie, you've got to stand up to that woman. What's she going to do, fire you? If she does, then you can consider whether to report her. I mean these notes are enough to establish a claim. You must keep everything that she sends to you—voicemails, emails—everything."

"That's just it, Sammie. She is very careful. Her emails are professional. That's why I have kept the notes. I have them all. I'm actually glad that you found them. I haven't slept in months."

Sammie was zapped. Her long run with Lucy just earlier that morning seemed like weeks ago. She went to the bedroom and collapsed on the bed. Dougie followed her. They laid on the bed speechless for some time. Sammie's instincts had been right.

Dougie had not been himself. He had seemed so distant, sad, and withdrawn. Cathleen McKinney had messed with the wrong woman's husband.

Dougie and Sammie came up with a plan. Dougie would tell Cathleen that her last note was commingled with some client orders and that Sammie found it when working from their home office. Dougie would remind Cathleen that Sammie is a lawyer and wants to sue her. She shouldn't contact him again. If Cathleen reacted poorly, he would offer to resign. The plan should resonate with his boss. After all, Cathleen would have a hard time spinning the last note to her underling.

According to Dougie, Cathleen was very professional, but a bit cool about his news. The following months resurrected old times. Dougie was ever present on the weekends despite his travel schedule. Dougie and Sammie sailed, ran, cycled, and their sex life returned with an increased passion.

Sammie took a Friday off of work to accompany Dougie on a weekend sales retreat at a luxury resort. Their marriage was better than ever, so Sammie didn't want to bring up Cathleen McKinney, though she was anxious about whether she would attend. Sammie was relieved when Dougie showed her the attendance list. Cathleen McKinney's name was absent.

The weekend was perfect. The spouses of the Worth Pharmaceutical stars were catered to with unlimited spa accounts. While Dougie was attending meetings, Sammie relaxed with a manicure, pedicure, facial, and a massage. They had wonderful meals with great wine. Mack was conceived on that magical weekend.

Given her mother's difficulties with pregnancies, Sammie was very apprehensive but tried to maintain positive thoughts. When her doctors assured her that all was well, Dougie and Sammie surprised the Spencers with the news. Glenny Spencer was over the moon, as Sammie knew she would be. She cautioned Sammie to take it easy.

"Sammie, I don't want to upset you, but you know the problems that I had. You work so hard and have a lot of stress in your job. We both worry about you. You know your father doesn't care whether you continue at the firm."

Sammie anticipated her mother's cautious advice. She knew at some level her mother was right. Sammie would reassess her career goals after the baby was born. She loved to work. She loved the challenge of the projects. She even loved dealing with difficult clients and quirky egotistical partners. Her job was part of her identity. She didn't want to be known as Dougie Morgan's wife or Cort Spencer's daughter. She wanted to be Sammie Morgan—that attorney at the Spencer firm who knew her stuff. As long as there were no issues with her pregnancy, work helped keep her mind off all the changes happening to her body.

Sammie continued to work at her usual frenzied pace until her April visit with her obstetrician. Her high blood pressure and the results of the stress test concerned her doctor. She advised that Sammie take medical leave until the baby was born. Had it not been for her mother's troubles, Sammie probably would have ignored these orders, because she felt fine. But, nothing was more important than this new life growing inside of her. April 8th would be her last day in the office.

Lucy was beside herself.

"How will I survive until October?" Lucy asked.

Lucy had become obsessed with her billable hours, her collection percentage—all those things that become more important the closer you get to first consideration for partnership. Sammie, on the other hand, had something growing inside of her that had completely changed her priorities. Sammie was looking forward to her break from office politics.

Sammie spent the weeks before Mack was born interviewing potential nannies. She planned to go back to work full-time. She felt even more obligated to return given the fact that she had been provided two months of medical leave in addition to the generous four-month maternity leave. She had plenty of time to find the perfect caregiver. What she didn't anticipate was the limited pool of potential candidates. After each interview, she became increasingly depressed at the options. Her calls to day care facilities revealed even more obstacles—all had extensive waiting lists. She was beginning to panic. Dougie inquired daily how the search was going. One night, Sammie was exasperated and sobbed as she discussed her frustration to him.

"I guess I could call Norma and see if she has any ideas," Dougie said, referring to his mother. "She knows lots of girls from teaching at the high school. There may be someone that she can recommend," Dougie added.

"That's a great idea," Sammie said, feeling hopeful.

Dougie didn't communicate with his mother often. In fact, he seemed estranged from both his parents. The fact that he never called Norma bothered Sammie. It also bothered her that he called his mother "Norma." It seemed cold and detached. But, Dougie had made it clear that he didn't appreciate Sammie's efforts to involve Norma and Dougie's father, Olin, in their family life.

"Sammie, don't interfere," he said. "My relationship with my parents isn't like yours. It's not your problem to fix."

When Dougie offered to call Norma about nanny recommendations, Sammie felt cautiously optimistic that the baby would bring them closer. When they first shared the news, Norma seemed excited about becoming a grandmother and genuinely disappointed of the timing of Sammie's due date.

"I'm really sorry that Olin and I aren't going be there when the baby is born," Norma said. "We planned a cross country trip to celebrate my retirement."

Dougie had not mentioned his mother's upcoming retirement to Sammie.

"I am taking off the last two weeks of school. It's unused vacation time, and I have to use it or lose it," Norma said. "We've always wanted to do this, and with the paper mill on down time, the timing is right for Olin."

"We'll visit as soon as we get back."

Sammie appreciated that her parents were more involved in her life than Dougie's were in his. She couldn't understand it, but, clearly, it was not a subject that he liked to discuss.

"I'm happy to meet with your mother to discuss her ideas," Sammie offered.

"No, I'll do it," Dougie added, quickly and firmly. "It will make her happy that I need her help."

Sammie stayed out of it for the time being but was not going to let Norma leave for her trip before finding out if she had any ideas. The following week, Dougie said his mother had called with a promising lead.

"Her name is Heather Yardley. Here's her number. She graduated from Rutledge several years ago and is taking classes and trying to get a certificate in early childhood development at the community college. Sounds good, don't you think?"

"Oh, Dougie. I hope this works!" Sammie said, excitedly.

"Norma thinks she would be perfect, but of course, your standards are probably higher than hers."

Sammie cringed at the comments about her higher standards. Several months into serious dating, Dougie had slipped and told Sammie his mother's first impression of her. "She's so spoiled, salt wouldn't save her," he quoted his mother's words. When he saw the hurt on Sammie's face, he attempted to laugh it off.

"You can't blame her. She has the same chip on her shoulder that everyone else does at Rutledge for those who grew up on the peninsula. Of course, she loves you now, just like me."

Sammie believed that Norma still didn't like her. The limited times she had been around her over the years, she was always distant. Glenny had picked up on similar vibes.

"It's not just you. It's the Spencers, period. Give her time," Glenny advised.

Sammie hoped that the time was now. Getting Norma's input for someone to fill such an important job should give Sammie some brownie points with her mother-in-law. For once, she had a feeling that it was all going to work out.

If it was any better, it'd be a set up...

Chapter Twelve

Sammie

Sammie called Heather and thought that she sounded excited about the opportunity. They agreed to meet for lunch the next day. Heather suggested the Shem Creek Bar and Grill. It was near the community college, and she had class later that afternoon. Sammie instantly thought Dougie would have a bias towards anyone who knew about Shem Creek Bar and Grill, the adjoining restaurant to the Shem Creek Marina.

Sammie spotted Heather immediately. She was a cute blonde with a golden tan and to-die-for figure. She stood up and extended her hand.

"Hello, Ms. Morgan, I'm Heather Yardley. I assume you are Ms. Morgan because…," she blushed realizing that she may have offended Sammie, "well you're clearly about to have a baby! How exciting! I luuuuvvv babies."

"Yes, it's quite obvious, right? My first, and I didn't realize how uncomfortable these last months were going to be. I just keep getting bigger and bigger."

"Well, you're definitely having a boy," Heather said.

"Why do you say that?"

"You're all out front! With a girl, you show more in your hips, according to old wives' tales anyway. You better have picked out some good boys' names."

"Dougie, my husband, will love that. Speaking of Dougie, you come highly recommended from his mother. I don't know what she told you about our situation."

"Well, I know that you are a big-time attorney that works long hours and that your husband is in sales and travels a lot. I need a three-month internship to receive my certificate. I checked today and working as a nanny would satisfy my requirement, so you would be helping me out. I love children. I have four siblings. I'm number two. Both of my parents worked, so I took care of the others for as long as I can remember. When are you going back to work?"

"It depends on when this baby decides to arrive. I have a four-month maternity leave. It … he," Sammie smiled, patting her belly, "is due May 31st. If all goes well, I will go back in October. I'll be working full-time and that can mean some late hours. But, my goal is to work a normal schedule—from around 8 to 6. What do you think of those hours?"

"I go to school full time and work two jobs, so having one job that would count for school hours sounds cushy," she said. "I would love to keep him. I take care of babies now, part-time."

"Really, where?" Sammie asked, thinking Heather was a gift from heaven. She was going to be great.

"I work the late shift at a day care in Mount Pleasant. You can call the director. I can provide you as many other references as you want."

Sammie was glad that Heather had offered references—another plus in her opinion. She certainly didn't want to get off on the wrong foot by making her feel that she didn't trust her.

"My husband will want to meet you too," Sammie said. "Here's my email address. Please send me the number for the day care director and numbers for some other references. I'm sure they will all have glowing reviews, but it's the lawyer in me. Due diligence is drilled into me."

"Don't take this wrong," Heather said, twisting her hair, "but I would wonder about you if you didn't check me out. I mean, you are trusting me with your baby. You have my number. Let me know of anything else I can provide. I know it's a scary decision, but I know what I'm doing. Well, when it comes to children," she giggled.

They ordered lunch and proceeded to talk about Heather's classes, her long-term goals, and her brothers and sisters. At times like this, Sammie was sad that she didn't have any sibling stories to share, but Heather started feeling like a sister to her—a younger, prettier, and thinner version of herself.

Heather seemed to have an untainted view of the world, although Sammie was confident that Heather's life had been much harder than hers ever was. Heather had that Rutledge I-can-take-whatever-you-throw-at-me attitude.

Sammie called Dougie on the way home and couldn't stop talking. Heather was a great discovery and all due to Dougie's mother. Sammie hoped that Norma would be proud to have played such an important role in her grandbaby's life especially since she couldn't be there for the birth.

"Slow down, baby," Dougie said. "Are you sure you have gone cold turkey on the caffeine? Sounds like you've had three double cappuccinos."

"She is perfect, Dougie. I do need to check out her references, but I know they are going to be great. I can't wait for you to meet her. You have to call your mother and thank her, thank her, and then thank her again!"

"Guess ol' Norma is good for something. I'll call her tomorrow. I'll check in with you later tonight. I am taking this new doc group out for dinner."

"Well, don't schedule any doc meeting next Friday. I want you to meet Heather. Oh Dougie, this is going to work out. I just know it. I am so happy right now."

"I'm always happy when you're happy. Get some rest. You do know what that means, right? I love you and will call you later."

Sammie's gut was right. Heather's references were sterling—"a natural with children," "responsible, mature, and wise beyond her years," "grounded and goal-oriented," "a loving, patient soul." Sammie's favorite was: "If I were looking for a nanny, Heather would be my first choice, by far, no question." Dougie loved her too.

"She reminds me of you," he said.

"Ha ha! Maybe twenty-five pounds and eight years ago."

Heather was right about the old wives' tale. On May 30, Sammie gave birth to a nine-pound, 22-inch long boy. Mack Spencer Morgan was princely. He was blessed with Dougie's piercing blue eyes and blonde curls and Glenny Spencer's olive skin.

Sammie's favorite nurse, Terpetha, repeatedly said, "Uh huh, girl, you got youself a looker. That poor baby is goin' to break some hearts. Mack, baby, don't you go messin' around with the girls. You better be a good boy or Terpetha will find you. Uh huh, I sure will. Miss Sammie, you let me know if you need anything because, girl, when you leave this hospital, you gonna have your hands full with that one. Yes siree, you will," shaking her head as she walked away.

Sammie didn't know that she could love anything more than Dougie Morgan, until Mack came into her life. The first two weeks were a blur. Her years as a lowly associate had provided her plenty of practice in the sleep deprivation department, but there was no practice for delivery of a nine-pound baby.

"That boy stretched your belly honey," Terpetha warned, "but he will fix it in due time when he starts suckling. Those boys suckle harder than girls. I'm sure of that. Your belly will be back in shape in no time at all, yep, no time at all."

When Sammie nursed Mack, she could literally feel her stomach muscles contracting. Though it was quite painful at times, worse than any menstrual cramp she could recall, she felt so connected with Mack during feeding times. Sammie was determined to establish a schedule with her hungry newborn. To ensure consistent feedings, she started the timer on her running watch.

"Only Sammie Morgan would nurse in 'chrono mode,'" Dougie said, laughing.

The summer went by too quickly. Despite his expanding territory, Dougie was committed to limiting his travel to day trips. Sammie had completely forgotten about Cathleen McKinney. She seemed like a thing of the past. She was a test of their marriage that had only made it stronger.

When the severe heat of the summer months began to cool, Sammie would spend mornings and evenings taking Mack on long walks and runs in the jogging stroller, a gift from Sammie's parents. Mack loved the constant movement. Sammie was finally getting her running legs and stamina back, though it was a weird sensation running with breasts engorged with milk production.

Lucy would accompany her on some nights. After one long run where Sammie had cut it too close to Mack's feeding time. Lucy, dripping with sweat as usual, pointed at Sammie's chest.

"I've seen everything now. You still don't sweat, but your boobs do!"

Sammie looked down at her running top. Two, huge wet rings surrounded her breasts.

"Oh no! That is my milk letdown. When it comes close to feeding Mack, my body produces this stuff like clockwork. We've got to turn around."

Lucy was stupefied.

"What are you going to do when you come back to work with all of that?" Lucy asked, pointing her index finger at Sammie and making a circling motion. "You are coming back, aren't you Sammie? I need your momma, Mackie," Lucy said, bending down to

Mack's face. "Our firm needs your momma. You're gonna share her with us, aren't you?"

Mack gurgled and smiled from ear-to-ear at Lucy.

"See, Sammie. Mack approves. And the Seamark deal is devouring us all. We need you back. I've been marking off the days on my calendar like a kid counting down for Christmas."

"Yes, I'm coming back silly," Sammie said. "And I told you about Heather. I know it's going to be hard at first, but I know I'll be leaving him in good hands. Hopefully, that will ease the separation anxiety. I know my hormones are still adjusting to all of this," as her eyes welled up with tears, "but I cry in a skinny minute thinking about leaving him."

"Mack is the prettiest baby that I have ever seen and soooo sweet. I know it will be hard, Sammie. But you are too talented and too smart to throw away your career."

Sammie's view seemed to change with the tides. But, Lucy's remark hit home. Sammie thought about her own mother. She had thrown away her career. Sammie didn't want to look back in thirty years and wonder what could have been.

Busier than a church fan in the dog days of summer...

Chapter Thirteen

Lucy & Sammie

Sammie thought it seemed like only yesterday when she was leaving for the hospital with her stopwatch indicating that her contractions were two minutes apart. Her four-month maternity leave had passed too quickly. As the fateful time of her return to work approached, Heather visited to play with Mack so he would be comfortable with her. She meticulously took notes of his schedule.

"It's important that his routine isn't altered," Heather instructed Sammie like she was the mother.

Sammie was confident in Heather's abilities, but the pit in her stomach wouldn't go away. She was conflicted about leaving her baby in the arms of someone else while she returned to the grind of billable hours. And, from Lucy's account, there was more work to do than hours in the day.

Charleston was investing millions of dollars to make its harbor the deepest on the East Coast. This meant its port would become a major attraction for mega-container ships. The firm's client, Seamark Shipping Empire, was getting ready for the increased activity at the port with its logistics and supply chain offerings. The corporate group was knee-deep in a major acquisition by Seamark.

Sammie was tasked with preparation of all the disclosure schedules, a tedious process at best. She would be diving right back into an unpredictable schedule. She agonized over asking Heather to work extended hours on her very first day.

Dougie came to the rescue by altering his travel schedule. He could focus on his new doctor customer who spent this time of the year in his multi-million dollar home in the exclusive, luxury resort of Kiawah Island. With Kiawah's growing retirement population, the doctor was joining the banks, law firms, and other professional service providers by opening a pain clinic in the shopping village outside of its private gates. Dougie assured Sammie he could keep busy in that area for several weeks. Sammie suspected that Dougie's enthusiasm for staying local may have been influenced by the fishing hobby he shared with the new doctor. Kiawah offered access to channels and marshes full of saltwater fish.

Whatever the reason, Sammie was comforted that his new customer was less than an hour drive from Charleston and afforded Dougie a flexible schedule. He pushed all his appointments to the afternoon so that Heather could arrive at noon. He would relieve her no later than 8:00 p.m.

"Thanks for rearranging your schedule," Sammie said, tearfully. "I have no idea when I'll be home."

Dougie tried to console her.

"Sammie, I need to know that I can do this," Dougie said. "And, it will be good male bonding time for us boys."

Sammie knew he was right. Dougie had demonstrated that he was more than eager to participate in the parenting role. She had picked up on Dougie's comments about her "supervision" whether he was changing a diaper or helping Mack become accustomed to a bottle. She needed to relinquish control.

"Try not to worry," Dougie interrupted. "You have everything taken care of, as usual. All the bottles are marked with feeding times in the fridge. Are you sure you want to keep nursing? It seems like an awful lot of work, and I can't imagine how you are going to pump at work."

"Well, I want to at least try. I know this sounds weird, but it gives me a connection to Mack when I can't be with him. I just need to hang in there a little bit longer."

"You're a wonderful mother," Dougie said. "I knew you would be. And, you're a fabulous lawyer. Go have fun today. I know it's going to be hard, but it will get easier each day as you get back into a routine. We will be fine, won't we buddy?"

As Sammie headed out the door, she took a mental picture of Mack with his father instead of his nanny. She would cling to this image to get her through her first day back in the office.

Dougie checked in with Sammie numerous times. He reported that Mack didn't seem to skip a beat going to Heather. Sammie thought that his report should have been comforting. But, this news made Sammie jealous. On the other hand, if Dougie had said Mack cried hysterically, Sammie knew she would have lost it.

Sammie called Dougie at 8:30 p.m.

"It's going to be midnight before I get home," she reported, weeping.

"Oh babe, I'm sorry," Dougie said. "Everything is good here. I got home a little early. Heather said that Mack had a great day. We are keeping the same schedule tomorrow. I'll wait up for you. I love you."

Sammie's second day was better than the first. Given all of her assigned tasks for the Seamark deal, she didn't have time to think about anything else. She had even forgotten about her apprehensiveness of breast pumping and storing her milk in the break room refrigerator.

When Sammie arrived late that evening, Dougie had the table set and candles lit. A spinach salad with large, pink shrimp was waiting in a serving bowl.

"I picked up these beauties on the way home—straight from the shrimp boat."

Sammie's conflicting emotions evaporated. In addition to Lucy, she had missed the work environment—the hustle and bustle of activity, the stress of deadlines, the challenging analysis—even the egomaniacs and politics. She and Dougie were respecting each other's schedule and job demands. She fell asleep with a clear sense of purpose and direction.

In the South, girlfriends are as tried and true as grits for breakfast...

Chapter Fourteen

Lucy And Sammie

Though Lucy knew Sammie was dealing with a lot of mixed emotions about returning to work, Lucy was elated that her extended maternity leave was over. The minutiae of drafting the dull indemnification provisions in the Seamark purchase agreement didn't bother Lucy now that Sammie was working with her through the wee hours of the morning.

Lucy expected their friendship to pick up exactly where it left off prior to Sammie's maternity leave. One thing she didn't consider was Sammie's commitment to breast feed for several more months. Initially, Lucy was grossed out by the process and the milk bottles in the break room refrigerator. But, having her cohort and confidante back in the office quickly trumped her discomfort.

Even better was that Sammie's return coincided with the firm's upcoming lavish dinner party honoring Franklin Collins Hamilton, III, for his twenty years of service as the managing partner. Due to deadlines in the Seamark deal, Lucy was going to have to miss the throw down. Now, Sammie would be working with Lucy while everyone else in the firm would be dining on seafood delicacies and toasting Frank Hamilton. The Cooper Conference Room was being renamed the Hamilton Boardroom and a new, bronze door plaque was being unveiled at the dinner.

The renaming of the conference room may sound rudimentary, but any change in the firm's deep longstanding traditions was extremely rare. This move was momentous and cause for a big celebration. In Lucy's mind, it presented an opportune time to reveal the secret that had been looming over her during Sammie's leave—her knowledge of the code to the Cooper Conference Room. Since she and

Sammie would be spending the evening working, it seemed only fitting that they should be the first to visit the new Hamilton Boardroom.

Frank Hamilton reflected and represented the impeccable reputation of the firm. Without uttering a word, all six feet and four inches of Mr. Hamilton's fit frame commanded respect. His dark hair was slicked back, with a hint of gray around his temples. He had Southern manners—always picking up the check, opening doors, and standing when a woman entered a room. Lucy knew that there was definitely no one like him in Edenville. Frank Hamilton seemed more gentlemanly than any of the Charlestonian aristocrats.

Lucy naively thought that Charleston men, like Frank Hamilton, married the most beautiful women and bred perfect children. Margaret Calhoun Hamilton, his wife, was no exception. She was a former Miss South Carolina who still maintained her size 4 figure. Despite the rumors of injections and fillers, Margaret (or "Daisy" as she was known in their country club circles) was a natural beauty—olive skin with no apparent sun damage or age spots, piercing green eyes and healthy, brown hair naturally highlighted from hours spent at the club playing tennis and golf.

Simply being in Daisy Hamilton's presence at firm social events exacerbated Lucy's insecurities. Raised in a mill town, she had never been schooled in the do's and don'ts of Charleston etiquette. Cocktail chit-chat had never been one of Lucy's strengths. She struggled to contribute to the topics of conversation with Daisy or any of the other partners' wives for that matter. Further, Daisy's harem, as Lucy called the collection of women that flocked around the managing partner's wife, made her feel dowdy in the style department.

Lucy was relieved that she couldn't attend the event. Thanks to the Seamark deal, she could avoid the head-to-toe examination by Daisy and her harem and their disapproving glares. Sammie was also more than happy to miss the shindig. If she was going to be away from her family, she preferred to be billing hours not spending nonbillable time with colleagues, especially on a Friday night. She had been looking forward to her own celebration—a weekend with her family after her first week back to work. But, when her Friday evening plans were ruined by new deadlines, she called Dougie to deliver the news.

"Sweetie, don't worry about it. My customers don't like Friday afternoon appointments, so I'll be home earlier tonight. Mack and I will enjoy a guy's night."

Sammie was stunned at the time when Lucy stopped by with a lunch invitation.

"I can't believe it's already 12:30. I'm not even halfway through these disclosure schedules. I can't take a lunch break."

"Ah, come on. We're the only ones missing the big party tonight. We deserve some fresh air. I'm craving some pimento cheese from Magnolia's. I'll call in a to-go. Walk with me to get it. We'll walk fast."

Sammie loved the fried green tomatoes from Magnolia's, and she hadn't had anything fried since learning she was pregnant. Lucy's normal walking pace was breakneck speed, so Sammie justified the break from her diet with the exercise and fresh air.

"I have the code," Lucy blurted the minute they stepped out of the building. "Sammie, I have the code!"

"What are you talking about, Lucy?"

"Remember before you left for maternity leave, I found the Cooper Conference room door unlocked. It was unlocked because the firm was changing the code. I saw the conference room, Sammie."

"No, you didn't!"

Based on Sammie's reaction during their last fourth floor visit, Lucy awaited a lecture. Sometimes talking to Sammie was like talking to your mother. Sammie towed the line and reeled Lucy in.

"Oh, yes, I did. It is more amazing than you can imagine. And, I know the new code. It's been killing me the whole time that you've been gone. I almost told you on one of our runs but knew you had more important things on your mind. I've been dying to tell you all week. You have got to see this room, Sammie. It's spectacular."

Lucy talked animatedly about the room the whole way to Magnolia's and back. Sammie couldn't care less about the room. But, Lucy's description piqued her curiosity.

"Lucy, I can't believe you went into the Hom-mill-tan Bored Room," Sammie said, mocking an affluent Charlestonian accent. "But, it sounds interesting. Check with me later after everyone is at the party."

Less than thirty minutes had passed since everyone had left for CCCs when Sammie's phone rang. She suspected it was one of the partners who was adding one more item to her do-list while sipping scotch.

"Sammie, this is Norma. Olin and I are back from our trip. I wanted to see if there was a convenient time that we could come see the baby."

"Oh, Norma. Welcome back. We would love for you to meet Mack. Just say when. And Heather is working out great. She's been a life-saver."

Her compliments were met with absolute silence.

"I'm sorry, but who is Heather?" Norma asked.

"Heather Yardley, the nanny you recommended."

"Heather Yardley, did you say?"

"Yes. We hired her, and she is great with Mack."

"Oh, I see. I know her, but I wouldn't recommend her or anyone for that matter. I thought I had made myself clear on that subject."

Sammie couldn't remember the rest of the conversation. She felt faint. Why would Dougie lie about his mother recommending Heather? Didn't Heather mention Dougie's mother during their interview? Her muddled thoughts were racing chaotically. She felt the rapid letdown of her milk immediately prior to it gushing out of her like a garden hose. She laid her head down on her computer keyboard and let her tears flow.

She finally pulled herself together. She had a strong urge to check on her son. Plus, she needed to change. As she was getting ready to make a quick exit, Lucy appeared at her door.

"Now that everyone is gone, wanna go check out the conference room?"

"Look at me, Lucy. My blouse is drenched."

Lucy knew instantly from her friend's shaky voice, body language, and panicked eyes that something other than her blouse was bothering her. She seemed on edge, and it looked like she had been crying.

"Are you okay?"

"No, I'm not," Sammie snapped. "Look at me! I was interrupted with a call, and my milk started coming in before I could pump. I am going to run home and change."

"You're coming back, right? Don't forget about the conference room—or I should say the new Hom-mill-tan Bored Room."

Although Sammie had earlier used the same drawl, she apparently didn't appreciate it from a Charleston outsider like Lucy.

"Don't you think we have more important issues to deal with tonight?" Sammie scolded.

Sammie regretted her remark noticing the hurt in Lucy's eyes. But, in addition to all the work, she now had to change her clothes, check on her son, and tell Dougie about the call with his mother. She thought that he said he would be home early today, but her recall was hazy. The days were running together. Why couldn't she remember ordinary details anymore?

When she pulled into the driveway, Sammie wondered why Dougie's car was behind Heather's, blocking her in. Sammie's heart started racing. She took deep breaths to calm her nerves and quietly entered the house.

She immediately spotted Dougie on the sunroom sofa drinking a beer. Heather was walking in Dougie's direction with a glass of wine in her hand. Upon seeing Sammie, Dougie jumped up from the sofa. Heather turned around quickly. Dougie announced that he had just gotten home and talked Heather into a glass of wine. An awkward silence hung over the room. Heather placed her wine on the table and started rambling about the day with Mack. Her voice reverberated panic. Sammie couldn't listen to the babbling noise. Cutting off Heather mid-sentence, she excused herself.

Mack was whimpering as Sammie approached his room. She picked him up, collapsed in the rocker, and held him tightly. He began rooting around at her chest. He was awake and obviously had not been fed. Dougie appeared at Mack's doorway.

"Babe, is everything alright?" Dougie asked. "You're home early and seem upset."

"My blouse got soaked by my milk letdown, so I came home to change. And, I do find it peculiar that Heather is still here, drinking wine, and Mack hasn't been fed. So, yeah, I guess I'm a little upset," Sammie mumbled, trying to control her emotions while attempting to feed Mack.

"He must have just woken up. He was sleeping when I got home. I had a long, hard day and got here later than usual. Heather was working on a school project and seemed really embarrassed that she had lost track of the time. I told her that I would feed Mack when he woke up. I offered her a glass of wine to cut the tension. But, I am sure that wasn't what you expected to see. I'm sorry, sweetie. Let me take Mack while you change."

His explanation made Sammie feel like an insecure, dramatic spouse. If the tables had been turned, Dougie probably wouldn't question the situation. But, then there was this one little complication of how he knew Heather. She decided to tackle that issue another day. She had too much work to get done and didn't need to start an argument or hear further rationalizations. She just needed to get back to work.

When Sammie returned to the office, Lucy thought she looked rotten. Her blue, sparkly eyes were now puffy and red. In the past, nothing seemed to shake Samantha Spencer Morgan. But something was off. Lucy decided not to push the conference room.

"Hey, I'm going to make some coffee, want me to bring you some?" Lucy asked Sammie.

"No thanks. While I'm nursing, I'm trying to avoid the caffeine."

"Okay, I'll check on you later."

It was midnight when Lucy stopped by Sammie's office again.

"Ready for a break?" Lucy asked Sammie. "Since we couldn't attend the renaming ceremony, I think it's only fair that we should get the first view of the Hamilton Boardroom."

Sammie rolled her eyes.

"Lucy, if seeing that room is so important to you, I'll go," she said. "But, you need to start acting like a partner, not a rebellious associate," she said.

Though the blow hurt Lucy's feelings, deep-down she knew if she was to become a partner, she needed to act like one. Lucy pushed rules to the limit. She, however, no longer viewed the firm's traditions and rules with trepidation. It was like she was in church in Edenville all over again. There, some would say, Lucy's actions were irreverent or even bordered on sacrilege.

Now, she just hoped she could pull it off. She wondered if her shaking hands would correctly enter the right new numbers. What if she punched them too quickly? Would the system automatically lock up? Would security be notified? Would an alarm be triggered? She took a deep breath and hit 6-6-9-0. There was a clicking sound. She turned the big brass doorknob, and the door opened.

As Sammie and Lucy walked down the hallway, past the impeccably furnished break-out rooms towards the newly named Hamilton Boardroom, the conference room doors were slightly ajar. They heard noises. They tiptoed closer and then heard a high pitch shrill.

"Giddy up, Hoss."

They peered in and froze, as if they were stuck in quicksand. Their mouths gaped open. There on the conference room table where many multi-million deals had been consummated was Barbie Benfield, the mail room manager, donned in a red cowboy hat and boots on top of the room's namesake—the firm's managing partner. Frank Hamilton's hands were holding on tight to Barbie's 34D breasts. He was enjoying this bonanza. Sammie gasped and grabbed Lucy's arm. They ran down the corridor, through the large doors, and down the fourth floor hallway.

Lucy was scared and prayed that their beloved managing partner was so enthralled with his rodeo that he didn't hear or see them. But she felt more than fear—something deeper, something stronger, the kind of disappointment that leaves you feeling empty. The aura of the room along with the flawless image she had held of their leader had been decimated by his celebratory christening of his conference room. Franklin Hamilton was far from perfect. The sophisticated firm was not perfect. In fact, Lucy thought sadly, Charleston really wasn't any different from Edenville after all.

Pretty is as pretty does...

Chapter Fifteen

Lucy

During the last six years, Lucy and Sammie were usually the first associates to arrive at the office. In fact, neither ever had arrived after 8:00 a.m. Lucy thought Sammie was justified in arriving later than normal given the hours she logged her first week back to the office. Still, Lucy was worried about her. It was 10:00 a.m., and Sammie was AWOL.

Lucy returned from the break room with her third cup of coffee. Lucy was having an unproductive morning pacing the hallway. Like all the associates' offices, her office was on the opposite end from the break room and had no views of the Cooper River. The only scene from Lucy's window was the parking lot. For once, she didn't mind her barren view because she could survey the lot for Sammie's car. On Lucy's trek back to her office after more coffee, she poked her head into Sammie's assistant's cubical.

"Shirley, have you heard from Sammie? She hasn't shown up yet. This isn't like her. I'm getting a little worried."

Shirley was a young, capable assistant who juggled assignments by their actual priority in terms of deadlines, as opposed to the status or gender of the attorney requesting the work. With many of the others, their allegiance was to the partners first, who were all men, and then to the male associate attorneys.

"I agree," Shirley said. "Sammie has incredible energy, but even she may have hit a wall with a newborn and the hours she billed last week. And, Cavelle called and said Mr. Hamilton wants to meet with her at 11:00. I've tried her cell and her home number, but she doesn't answer. So, if you hear from her, she needs to get in ASAP."

Lucy felt like Shirley had just stabbed her in the gut with a knife. Why would Frank Hamilton want to meet with Sammie? Had he seen her in the boardroom? A wave of guilt washed over Lucy. Her sweet, innocent friend only went into the boardroom to appease her and had objected all the way. Lucy thought it would be so unfair if Frank Hamilton had seen Sammie but not her. Lucy's head was pounding. When Lucy turned the corner heading back to her office, her assistant Roberta was smirking. Roberta was the opposite of Shirley.

"Mr. Hamilton wants to see you at 11:00," Roberta said. "Do you know what that's about?"

Lucy could place a bet on the subject of the meeting, but there was no way she was disclosing anything to Roberta who was the biggest gossip in the firm. Sammie and Lucy secretly called Roberta, "Gladys" for Gladys Kravitz—the nosey, abrasive neighbor on the old TV show "Bewitched."

"No, I don't," Lucy said, trying to maintain her composure since Roberta, a/k/a Gladys, was carefully watching Lucy's reaction. "I hope it means that we have a new transaction since the Seamark deal will close soon. You know me, I thrive on M&A's," Lucy said, attempting to sound upbeat.

"M&A's'?" Roberta asked, confused.

Though Roberta had been assigned to Lucy for the past three years, her question demonstrated her complete lack of knowledge about Lucy's area of practice and expertise. She was more attentive to everyone else's business.

"Yes, mergers and acquisitions—what I do," Lucy responded, patronizingly.

Lucy could feel Roberta's eyes rolling as Lucy turned and shut the door to her office. At that moment, Lucy wished she knew breathing exercises. This has to be what an anxiety attack must feel like. She instructed herself to take a deep breath. Inhale. Exhale. Her heart was racing, and her mind was following suit. Was Frank Hamilton going to fire them? Lucy couldn't lose her job. Unlike Sammie, Lucy didn't have a trust fund safety net. Her mind jumped to news of a termination percolating through town. She could already hear the rumor mill. *Did you hear that Lucy Tate was fired? Bless her heart. The first Pettigrew scholarship winner, and the first to get axed.*

Lucy perspired to the same degree as if she were on a long run with Sammie. She couldn't understand why Sammie hadn't come in nor returned her calls over the weekend. She was ghosting Shirley as well. Sammie never ignored a call from Shirley, and before the weekend, she had always returned Lucy's calls.

At 10:30, Lucy's hands were shaking as she called Sammie's cell. Sammie's phone went straight into voicemail. *You've reached Samantha Morgan. I'm unavailable to take your call but leave a message.* Trying to disguise her angst, Lucy said, "Sammie, call me, please. We have a meeting at 11:00—with Frank Hamilton."

Lucy then tried Sammie's office phone. Same result—voicemail.

At 10:45, Lucy went to the bathroom to splash water on her face and collect her thoughts. She grew angry. *There is no way she could be fired for catching the managing partner fucking the bimbo mail room manager named after a fashion doll.* She couldn't recall a time that she had been more nervous; the two-day exam required to obtain a law license was a piece of cake compared to what she was feeling. She had not eaten all morning, and, after the four cups of coffee she had chugged, she thought that she needed to get something on her stomach to ease the queasiness. But she decided against that—barfing on Franklin Collins Hamilton, III, would be her death sentence for sure.

While at the elevator bank, Lucy took a deep breath. When the doors opened to the fourth floor, she took another deep breath and headed to her meeting with Frank Hamilton.

"Mr. Hamilton is stuck on a call but should be done shortly," Cavelle said. "Can I get you some coffee?"

"No thanks, Cavelle," Lucy said, her voice cracking.

The last thing Lucy needed was more caffeine. While waiting, she was startled by a tap on her shoulder.

"Good morning," Sammie said, calmly.

Sammie was super composed but didn't look so hot.

"Morning? It's 11:00. Where have you been?" Lucy asked. "You haven't answered your cell."

"Dougie unexpectedly had to go out of town. I gave Heather the morning off because who knows when I will get home tonight. I intentionally turned off my cell so I could spend some uninterrupted time with Mack."

Lucy refrained from asking her why she hadn't returned her calls over the weekend.

"You've never done that before. I have been freaking out about this meeting."

"Interesting. We both have a meeting with Frank. Don't overreact, Lucy. Really, what can he do to us? We are the ones with the goods on him."

Sammie had incredible common sense, solid judgment, and maintained a level head under pressure. Sammie would roll her eyes when Lucy attributed her calm demeanor to her upbringing. Lucy would argue, "If you know someone is there to catch you when you fall, you aren't afraid to fall. If I fall, I will bust my ass."

But this time, Sammie had underestimated their managing partner.

Cavelle walked from her office. In addition to the only secretary with access to the boardroom code, Cavelle was the only secretary whose workstation wasn't a modular cubicle but a real office with windows, and it adjoined Frank Hamilton's.

"Oh, hello, Sammie. I didn't see you. Sorry to make you wait. Mr. Hamilton is off the phone now."

Cavelle knocked a couple of times before opening the door.

"Sammie and Lucy are here for their appointment."

He waved them in.

Frank Hamilton's office looked like it belonged in a magazine. There was a long black leather couch, anchored by two wing chairs, upholstered in some expensive fabric, with exaggerated high backs and scrolled arms. Oriental rugs of varying sizes covered the Brazilian cherry, hardwood floors. A mirror with ornamental scrollwork was mounted above a chest, which was rumored to house very expensive Scotch whiskey. Various legal and business magazines were carefully placed on the coffee table. Even the casual observer would notice Frank Hamilton's image on the covers.

Lucy and Sammie were directed to the tufted, cream, leather chairs facing his large pedestal desk. Typically, Frank Hamilton's office looked warm and inviting, but on this day, it was stifling. She could feel her sweat glands kicking in. She tried to focus on the soothing views of the Cooper River from the floor-to-ceiling windows instead of the managing partner's stern glare.

"Well, I'll cut to the chase. I've requested this meeting for a couple of reasons. The first reason involves your respective positions with the firm. As you are aware, we are in the midst of challenging economic times, and law firms are not immune to the repercussions. Setting aside the hours generated by the Seamark team, the billable hours for the corporate practice group last month were the lowest in fifteen years. And after Seamark closes, there aren't any other deals in the pipeline."

Lucy's head started pounding. Work is down. No new deals are in the works. A message needed to be delivered; if you break the rules of the Spencer firm, someone will pay. Frank Hamilton was too smart to mess with a Spencer. *Please Lord, help me stay calm*, Lucy silently prayed.

"We do not have the workload to sustain the hours to which you both have been accustomed," Frank Hamilton continued. "As you know, your billable hours and collections are two very important factors considered for partnership. Sammie, I am confident that you don't want to be viewed as receiving special treatment when the partnership vote occurs."

Lucy and Sammie sat silently wondering where this was going.

"Though the corporate deals are down, Randy Baker's domestic practice is booming. He just landed the James Putnam divorce, and he needs immediate help. The assets to be distributed will make it the largest equitable distribution case in South Carolina's history."

Sammie and Lucy looked at each other incredulously. They had spent six grueling years in the corporate group honing their skills. They were both good and enjoyed the corporate area. Neither of them had any interest in being a divorce lawyer.

"The management committee decided to move you both to Randy's practice group," Frank continued. "Lucy, I told Randy that you would be available immediately. We have already received a hefty retainer, so there is an unlimited opportunity for billable hours. Sammie, you will remain in the corporate group until the Seamark deal closes and then make the move to Randy's practice."

Lucy couldn't believe what she was hearing. She would be starting all over. Clearly the underlying message was that partnership was not happening in the near future. She dug deep for the control to stay calm and fight off tears.

"You are two very bright young women, so I don't have to tell you billable hours are not the sole criterion for partnership decisions. One of this firm's strongest traits is our culture. We are a family. Loyalty, confidentiality, and trustworthiness are equally important factors in partnership decisions."

Lucy saw where this was going. She was being sent to purgatory to bill lots of hours. If her penance didn't kill her, the other factors were going to be the pretext for her partnership rejection.

"As someone who has some history with this firm, I appreciate that some of the firm's policies and traditions may appear obsolete or a bit strange. But until the partners, who are the owners of this firm, vote to change any rule or policy, they must be followed. It has come to my attention that both of you violated one these rules. We don't need to discuss it again."

He then paused and sort of chuckled. He clearly was punishing Lucy and Sammie in a roundabout way for violating the firm boardroom rule. Lucy didn't believe that he was looking out for their workloads. Instead, he was writing their death sentence. Everyone knew Randy Baker was eccentric and worked crazy hours. Sammie and Lucy were deal lawyers—their clients were corporations not C-suite executives who had been caught cheating on their wives.

"You two actually remind me of the shenanigans I had with Sammie's father," Frank said, his eyes fixed on Sammie. "Back then, there were paper ballots for job offers. Your father and I were both confident, young men and made a wager about who received the most votes."

Frank kept staring directly at Sammie. It was like Lucy wasn't in the room anymore.

"The ballots were on your grandfather's desk. It was late. No one was in the office. Sam cracked his father's office door until the image before us stopped us dead in our tracks. Your grandfather was on his sofa, and let's just say he wasn't there alone. So, we never found out who won the wager."

He turned and began staring out his window like no one was in his office. Lucy and Sammie sat frozen in silence trying to digest his message. He then turned back to face them.

"Get to work, girls."

Lucy viewed Frank Hamilton's disclosure about Sammie's grandfather as blackmail. Since he had kept silent about Sammie's grandfather, he expected Sammie to return the favor. But one thing was clear. If word got out about Frank Hamilton and Barbie Benfield, neither Lucy nor Sammie would ever make partner.

Leaving Frank Hamilton's office, Lucy wished she had listened to Sammie. Entering the conference room was worse than a career limiting gesture. It was career suicide.

Ain't no education in the second kick of a mule...

Chapter Sixteen

Sammie

Waiting on the elevator back down to their offices, Lucy put her arm around Sammie.

"That was interesting. Are you alright?" Lucy asked.

Sammie was numb from this last kick in the teeth. She needed a sanity check, and Lucy was the only one she trusted.

"Do you have time to go to lunch?" Sammie asked. "I'll treat you to Magnolias. It's such a pretty day."

Though Magnolias and a whole host of alternatives were within a short walk from the Spencer office, Lucy never took the time for sit-down dining.

"Sure, that would be great," Lucy said. "But you don't have to buy my lunch. Let's go right now."

It was a cool crisp fall day. When they started down East Bay, Sammie took a deep breath. Where would she begin?

"I need to get some things off my chest, and I want you to promise to be one-hundred percent honest with me," Sammie said.

Lucy looked at Sammie strangely.

"Girl, do I ever filter my opinion?" she asked, pointedly.

"Good point. But this is about Dougie. I need you to be objective and not sugarcoat anything," Sammie said, with tears building in her eyes.

"Oh, honey. What is it?" Lucy asked.

"I really don't know where to start. I have so much guilt for working and leaving Mack every day. And, my raging hormones are making me sensitive and possibly delirious. I need a sounding board."

"You know I am always here for you, Sammie," Lucy said, "but you also know that I don't have the slightest idea about the havoc wreaked on your body after birthing a child and pumping milk—which totally wigs me out, by the way. But, go ahead. I knew something was bothering you."

"When I went home to change on Friday, I had just hung up on a call with Dougie's mother. I know I've told you that they have a weird relationship. Anyway, remember how Dougie's mother was the one who referred Heather?"

"Yeah," Lucy said, "she knew her from the high school, right?"

"Yes. But when talking to Norma, I thanked her for recommending Heather, and she was clueless."

"What do you mean?" Lucy asked, sympathetically.

Sammie could tell from Lucy's tone that she sensed where this was going.

"Norma said that she didn't."

"That doesn't make any sense. Why would Dougie tell you that she did?"

"Exactly. Anyway, after she said that, my chest tightened. Then, the milk started oozing. You saw my blouse. So, I went home to change. Dougie wasn't expecting me. Heather was still there though Dougie was home, and..." Sammie paused.

"Were they fucking?" Lucy asked, bluntly.

"No. God, no," Sammie said.

"Well, then what?" Lucy asked.

"It was just this weird feeling I had. Maybe it was my imagination. I was still reeling from my conversation with Norma, but I felt like a stranger in my own home."

"What were they doing?" Lucy asked.

"Dougie was on the sofa in the sunroom drinking a beer, and Heather was walking towards him with a glass of wine. It's hard to describe," Sammie continued, "but she was obviously embarrassed. There was this awkwardness in the air. Dougie said that he had just gotten home, that Mack was sleeping, and Heather was getting ready to update him on the day. She quickly put down her wine and started rambling about Mack. Her voice was jumpy. I stopped by Mack's room on my way to change, and he was wide awake. When I picked him up, he was clearly hungry. So, while Dougie and Heather were enjoying a drink, Mack was awake and had not been fed. And, then there's the lie about his mother recommending Heather. There was something too familiar between them."

"What did Dougie say about it?"

"He said that he got home late, and Mack was asleep. He said he felt bad about being so late, and Heather was frantically working on some school assignment. He told her that he would feed Mack when he woke up, popped a beer, and asked her if she wanted a glass of wine while she gave him a rundown of the day."

"You didn't ask him why he lied about it?" Lucy asked.

"No," she said. "I had to get back to the office and didn't want to get into it with Heather there. I was hoping to talk to him over the weekend. But then one of his new customers invited him to go on a fishing trip. He had been such a trooper all week rearranging his schedule to accommodate mine, I encouraged him to go. He left early Saturday morning. Over the weekend, I started thinking that I overreacted. My first week back to work had taken its toll."

Lucy listened patiently but was uncharacteristically subdued. Lucy put her arm around Sammie and squeezed her tightly but remained silent.

"Well, what do you think?" Sammie asked. "Be honest."

Lucy paused.

"I do think it's weird that your nanny would be having a glass of wine with your husband. Maybe they did know each other somehow, and Dougie didn't think you would consider Heather if he had recommended her. So, he used his mother as a pretense. Or, perhaps, it was his way to act like Norma is engaged. You know he has to feel badly that your parents are so involved and supportive, and his are basically nonexistent."

Lucy's plausible rationales made Sammie feel even more foolish.

"We both overanalyze things—it's our training. It does sound like Heather is a great caregiver. For once, I don't know what to say. I don't have experience in either the relationship or parenting department. But, I am here for you. You can tell me anything, and it will go no further. Sometimes it just helps to talk things out instead of keeping everything all bottled up. That's when mole hills turn into mountains."

"I already feel better," Sammie said. "Thanks for listening. Heather is good with Mack. She seemed her usual peppy self this morning and apologized profusely for Mack not having been fed on Friday. She basically mirrored what Dougie said. Now, let's order so we can get back to the grindstone."

When they returned to the office, Sammie couldn't concentrate on work. She felt fat and ugly. Heather was cute and perky. Sammie was jealous of her figure, her time with her son, and now her friendship with her husband. Despite Lucy's legitimate rationalizations, Sammie wondered if Lucy's opinion would have been the same if Sammie had told her everything.

Don't judge a book by its cover...

Chapter Seventeen

Barbie & Lucy

Sammie and Lucy were clueless, Barbie Benfield thought. She needed three jobs to pay her bills and save for her dream—something high paid associates at the best law firm in South Carolina would never understand.

Barbie liked Sammie Morgan and Lucy Tate. They weren't arrogant like all the other Spencer attorneys. They treated her like a human being instead of some lowly mail room employee. Most of the attorneys never spoke to her and when they did, they talked in a condescending tone like she was a ditz. The only two attorneys who had shown her respect now probably thought she was some sleazy bimbo looking for a sugar daddy—a bail out. That was far from the truth. And, she wasn't going to pretend nothing happened. She was going to clear the air—but just with Lucy. Everyone knew Lucy wasn't born or even raised in Charleston. She was a preacher's kid from a dinky town. If anyone shouldn't judge, it should be a PK from Edenville.

Barbie attempted to gather her thoughts and courage. She took a deep breath and dialed Lucy's extension.

"Lucy, this is Barbie in the mailroom. There is package for you. I wanted to make sure you were in your office before dropping it off."

Lucy wasn't expecting any sort of package. And the last person Lucy wanted to see was Barbie. When Lucy heard a timid knock at her door, the usual beads of sweat materialized on her forehead.

"Come in," Lucy said, pretending to be engrossed in a document to avoid eye contact.

Barbie stepped in and shut the door behind her.

"Lucy, I don't have anything for you. I used that as an excuse to talk to you. I know what you saw. I know what you think, but you don't know me, Lucy. You know nothing about me. I don't know why I feel like I have to explain myself but, for some reason, I do. I am a good person. I don't have a law degree, but I have dreams of my own. Being manager of a mail room is not my goal in life. I want to be a massage therapist. I go to community college and work two other jobs. I'm saving to open my own business."

"Barbie, that is great. I had no idea," Lucy said, wiping her forehead, wondering how her dreams landed her on the conference room table. "But, you don't have to explain anything to me."

"I want to. This isn't easy for me, so I need for you to just listen."

Lucy was impressed by Barbie's poise and self-assurance. Lucy seemed more uncomfortable in her office than Barbie appeared to be.

"I get to the office every day at 5:00 a.m.," Barbie said. "I have to collect any outgoing mail that has been generated from the attorneys who work late—like you. I drop the mail directly at the main post office on my way to my 7:00 a.m. class. One morning, Frank came in early. I scared him because he thought he was the only one in the building. He looked at me funny and questioned what I was doing. From the tone in his voice and his eyes, you'd think I had broken into the firm. I could tell he thought I was up to no good."

Here comes the testimony and plea for repentance, like those she had heard repeatedly in her father's church, Lucy thought.

"I told him about my classes and my jobs. I was afraid I would be fired," Barbie said. "He congratulated me, though he still seemed suspicious. The following week, he was in the office early again. I knew then that he was checking up on me, which to tell you the truth, really pissed me off. I mean I am busting my ass here. I didn't need some stuffy lawyer looking down on me like I was up to no good."

Though Lucy found this background interesting, it still didn't explain how Barbie ended up on the conference room table.

"His early morning schedule became a routine, and he became more talkative. He asked me about my classes and what I was studying that particular week. I certainly never imagined that anyone like Frank Hamilton would have any interest in me. It made me feel good, you know, that he was interested in what I was doing."

Lucy recalled similar feelings when Frank Hamilton first talked to her. She couldn't believe that someone as powerful and busy would take the time to converse with a lowly associate. Associates and mail room employees obviously held the mighty Frank Hamiltons of the world in the same light.

"One morning, he said his neck was especially tight. He had fallen asleep sitting up reading documents," Barbie continued. "He was tilting his head from side to side. He said he was working out a muscle spasm."

Lucy thought Frank Hamilton probably was already plotting how to get in Barbie's pants.

"I told him I would work out the crick in his neck if he wanted me to," Barbie said. "Lucy, at that point, I just viewed him as sort of a friend—nothing more, nothing less. He had several knots in his neck, and I worked them out."

Even if Lucy didn't know the ending, at this point, she would have predicted the outcome.

"He was impressed. He said I was going to be a big success. One morning, he asked me if I would mind working on his shoulders and back—they were stiff after a weekend of golf. I was so excited that he asked. I mean I was thinking that I may really be good at this. After I worked out the knots, his head flopped backward and right into my boobs. I about died. I knew he could hear my heart about to explode. I didn't know what to do. He clinched his fingers around mine. He asked me to touch him some more. Lucy, I was scared. I didn't want to lose my job. But, I ran out of his office."

Lucy's impression of Barbie was flipping. She needed her job. Frank Hamilton was the most powerful person in the firm. He was taking advantage of his status and hers. Lucy cringed.

"He got in early the next morning and asked me to meet him in the Cooper Conference Room after I got out of class that evening," Barbie continued. "He said he just wanted to talk to me. He gave me the code—6690. June 6, 1990 is my birthday."

Lucy couldn't decide which was more amazing—that Frank had provided Barbie with the cherished partner code to the conference room or that he changed the code to Barbie's birthday. No doubt, he had ulterior motives.

"I did go that night, mostly out of curiosity. But, he didn't try anything. He told me that he hadn't been touched in a long time, and he loved how I touched him. He was very apologetic and said that he was out of line. It would never happen again. He exposed another side of himself. He was a needy man. Frank Hamilton was vulnerable."

Or manipulative, Lucy thought.

"Frank only wants and needs what we all do—to feel loved. Now, he turns to things in an attempt at fulfillment—like being managing partner, his board positions, social hierarchy, a house with more square footage, a car with more horsepower, a yacht instead of a motorboat. Material things have been substituted for what is lacking in his marriage. I'm not stupid, Lucy. He would never leave his wife for someone like me. And, I don't want him to. It's really quite simple. He's benefitting me as much as I am benefitting him."

Then, Barbie Benfield abruptly turned and left Lucy's office. Throughout the rest of that day, Lucy found herself admiring Barbie's moxie. She was treated like a second-class citizen at the firm. Lucy had been friendly to Barbie but admittedly, had thought she was a bimbo. Lucy would never have considered that Barbie juggled two other jobs and classes, all in pursuit of a dream. Things aren't cut and dry.

God bless Barbie Benfield and may one day her large cup runneth over.

Homemade sin is ugly...

Chapter Eighteen

Lucy

Lucy didn't know what shook Sammie up more—seeing Frank and Barbie on the conference room table or hearing about her grandfather's escapades. Though Frank Hamilton didn't exactly say he and Sammie's father witnessed a sexual encounter, that was certainly the inference. Sammie was already dealing with suspicions about her husband's scruples. Now, the sacred image of her family's legacy had been scarred. Sammie was astute and attentive, but she seemed to have gone through life with blinders on. Then again, Lucy was learning that there was an amazing talent among Charlestonians for concealing their true colors.

The Edenville, South Carolina, populace wasn't as cunning or deceitful. Edenville folks understood that sin was to be expected, and many liked to talk about it. Lucy heard a lot about sin from all the time she had spent at the "Born Again Baptist Church." Admittedly, she was jaded, but truth be told, Lucy never trusted Dougie Morgan. She didn't think he measured up to Sammie. Something about him reminded her of the Sunday faithful in her father's church congregation.

Though dramatically less polished than Charleston, Lucy's hometown had more similarities to the Holy City. Gossipmongers resided in both cities—the only difference was the subject matter of the chatter. The women at the Charleston Country Club gossiped about their friends' latest enhancement procedures or their interior decorators' upgrades to their vacation homes. The women at the Born Again Baptist Church obsessed about who was spotted in the liquor store across the county line or rejoiced in the discovery that the coconut cake made by Ella Jenkins from an old family recipe and a hit at the covered dish lunches actually came from the Piggly Wiggly. The pattern was consistent whether you are in Charleston or Edenville—people were focused on their outward appearances instead of nourishing their inner soul. That was bizarre to Lucy. The Christian way should be the latter.

Lucy considered herself a spiritual person though she had resented her mandatory, weekly church rituals: Sunday school, Sunday morning worship service, choir practice, and then Sunday evening worship service. Instead of feeding her spirit during the long hours spent in church, the church nourished her imprudence.

Her pastimes during worship services included distorting her father's headshot displayed on the Welcome cards, playing tic-tac-toe with her best church friend, Tracy Luck, or crawling under the church pews. Sunday nights offered rowdier behavior. After Lucy and Tracy grew bored with Ding Dong Scramble—ringing the doorbells of nearby homes before running—they focused on Juanita and Bud Hathaway's house. Juanita was their Sunday school teacher, and her husband, Bud, was the head of the deacons, the group of men selected to oversee the business aspects of the church. The Hathaways seemed to enjoy being at the church as much as Lucy's parents.

After Tracy and Lucy discovered that the path through the woods behind the church led to the Hathaway's house, the "yard game" was created. The Hathaway's yard was filled with numerous ornaments ranging from crosses and cherubs to gnomes to sheep. Juanita would have never guessed that Lucy was the brainchild behind the rearrangement of her yard art. After all, Lucy was the preacher's daughter and Juanita's star pupil.

The only part of Juanita's class that Lucy found tolerable was the Sword Drill competition. The game involved standing in a circle with closed Bible in hand while Juanita selected a book and chapter. When Juanita's announced, "Draw Swords!", the class would feverishly flip through their Bible to find the reference. Lucy was always first to find the passage. She didn't care about the points she racked up. She enjoyed the other reward—reading the scripture and then explaining the lesson. She liked to think of it as the Lucy Tate version of the Bible. Lucy couldn't believe the Sunday that Juanita selected 2nd Samuel Chapter 11.

"Lucy, please read verses 2-5."

The class loved Lucy's lay person interpretations, and she was going to have fun with this one.

"David saw Bathsheba taking a bath. He thought she was beautiful and immediately desired her, despite the fact that she was married. They hooked up," Lucy said to the muffled giggles of her classmates, "and Bathsheba became pregnant."

Juanita glared at Lucy over her cat-like glasses as Lucy finished the story.

"Bathsheba's husband was in the army at the time. David tried to cover up his romance with Bathsheba by ordering her husband home from war in hopes that he would, well, you know, have relations with his wife."

The class suppressed laughter again. Juanita shook her head.

"David wanted Bathsheba's husband to think the baby that she was carrying was his. But Bathsheba's husband chose to remain at war. So, David ordered that he be placed on the front lines of the battle, so he would die."

"And God punished David for his sin and took the life of his and Bathsheba's baby," Juanita added, attempting to cut-off Lucy's rendition.

"What is the lesson of David and Bathsheba, Lucy?"

"Well, Ms. Hathaway," Lucy said, "the moral is that you don't put yourself into tempting situations because it is easier to avoid temptation than to resist temptation. So, you must do as Forrest Gump did and "Run, Forrest, Run! Run, Forrest, Run!"

The class broke out in laughter and started chanting along with Lucy, "Run, Forrest, Run! Run, Forrest, Run!"

Ms. Hathaway was not amused.

"Lucy Tate, I don't think your father would find this funny. We are done with this game. It's time for the revival."

Lucy loved when her Sunday night schedule was altered by a revival. She found the services entertaining. The traveling evangelists had a unique way of tapping into the repenting nature of the community. It seemed like the entire town of Edenville, as well as every Baptist from nearby towns, were drawn by these traveling road shows.

The sanctuary of the Born Again Baptist Church couldn't hold these masses so a huge tent behind the church was erected with a platform along with hundreds of folding chairs. That night's performer was Reverend Carlton Bumgarner, an evangelist from Alabama, whose team had placed fans in each chair that when unfolded revealed a picture of the fine reverend.

Despite his props, Reverend Bumgarner had the same effect as all the others who had toured through Edenville. When his booming spiel about sin, confession, and forgiveness reverberated from the large speakers, the men fell to their knees.

"As God said in Isaiah 64:6, *we are all **IN-fected** and **IM-pure** with **SIN**. When we display our righteous deeds, they are nothing but filthy **rags**.* Yes, brothers and sisters, we need to toss our filthy rags and our sinful ways and confess our sin to the Lord Almighty. He will forgive us if we repent. The Proverbs instruct us: *People who **CONCEAL** their sins will **NOT** prosper, but if they **confess** and turn from them, they will receive mercy.* God **WILL** show us mercy."

Reverend Bumgarner was a mirror image of the previous revival evangelists. When they had the sinners in the palm of their hands, they smelled money.

"Let us show God our praise for his many wonderful blessings and for his continual forgiveness by our tithes and offerings."

Reverend Bumgarner motioned the ushers to pass the empty Kentucky Fried Chicken buckets down the rows of sinners. This was the time the sinners filled the makeshift offering plates with cash to finance the next leg of the reverend's evangelical circus. He then called on those who would like to share their stories of salvation.

Juanita Hathaway was not one to dodge the spotlight or refrain from an opportunity to re-tell her story of salvation. The members of the Born Again Baptist Church had heard it numerous times, but the tent revivals attracted members from other nearby churches and non-believers. Like Reverend Bumgarner, Juanita truly believed her story would save the heathens and draw the church-goers closer to the Lord. While Lucy found the revivals amusing due to the sheer drama they elicited, she could probably recite Juanita's testimony word for word. She was not in the mood to hear it again.

As Juanita made her way down the aisle to share the platform with Reverend Bumgarner and witness to the masses, Lucy turned to Tracy.

"Let's sneak out," Lucy whispered. "Juanita will be at it for a while and then with all the others following her, we probably have at least two hours for the yard game."

Lucy and Tracy ducked out the back as Juanita began.

"Preacher Bumgarner, the Lord works in miraculous ways. The good book says, 'Ask and it shall be given of you. Seek and ye shall find.'"

They could hear her over the big speakers that had been placed in every corner of the tent as they ran through the woods.

"Reverend Bumgarner, I decided to try that 'asking out' on one of my Piggly Wiggly days. I do hate to go to the Pig. I got in my car and headed down Cannon Boulevard and got stopped at that dadblamed light on Main. Y'all know that light, that loooong one. Well, I just looked up to the heavens and said, 'green light, green light, Lord,' and don't you know, it changed, just like that, no waiting. I said, 'Hallelujah,' this asking really works and decided to ask for a parking space at the Pig. So, I called on the name of the Lord, and said 'Lord, I'm about to give out of gas, please find me a space,' and do you know, a truck backed up about that time from a space on the front row, and I slid right in. I let out another 'Hallelujah'. The Lord is a miracle worker. Well, that day, I decided the sky's the limit. I'm going to ask the Lord to work a miracle on my register receipt. Bud and me were right down to our last pennies. The mill had been on short time, and we didn't have much to eat on. I asked the Lord, 'give me a sign'. The Pig had a hunk of tenderloin a week-old on sale for $1 a pound on the very day that I asked the good Lord to help me with my grocery bill. I picked up a few other staples, and do you know that when I checked out, the bill came to $10 not a penny more. Now if that ain't a sign from heaven, I don't know what is. Hallelujah."

Lucy and Tracy were nearing the Hathaway's house, and the tent revival was but a hum in the distance. They had never been caught making their creations because the Hathaway's schedule was as predictable as deviled eggs at a church potluck. When church was in session, they were there. Since tent revivals lasted hours, the girls had big plans for all the objects in the yard—arranging them into sexual positions.

Tracy and Lucy positioned the sheep with the gnome and then noticed a flickering light from the den. They were worried that others may have picked up on the Hathaway's consistent Sunday night routine and, that perhaps, they were being robbed. They crept up to the back of the house to peer into the den windows. Their mouths dropped at their discovery. The flickering light was from the Hathaway's TV. Bud had skipped the revival to watch a movie—a pornographic one. They noticed that Bud was not alone. Judy Canup, the soprano from the church choir, came dancing in the room donning some sort of kitten outfit. While Bud's wife was pouring out her soul to the hundreds of sinners under the canvas tent erected by Reverend Bumgarner, the Born Again Baptist Church's head deacon was enjoying his own private performance.

As Lucy listened to Sammie discussing her revelations about Dougie and the nanny, Bud Hathaway resurrected in her memory. Her gut told her that there was more going on than Sammie knew or wanted to know. Lucy learned at an early age that in her simple town, sin was enthusiastically confessed to receive pardon. In the sophisticated town of Charleston, sin was relentlessly concealed to escape humiliation. Filthy rags of sin existed everywhere. Sammie Morgan and Juanita

Hathaway had more in common than one would have ever imagined. Edenville and Charleston weren't so different after all.

Idle minds are the devil's workshop...

Chapter Nineteen

Sammie

Work has a way of prohibiting your mind from wandering, Sammie thought. She didn't have time to dwell on Frank Hamilton's revelations. She had to crank out the compromised positions on the Seamark Asset Purchase Agreement. After retrieving the new revision of the 100 plus pages-agreement from the copy room, she noticed the message light on her office phone blinking. Then, she noticed the time.

Sammie had been so focused all afternoon that she hadn't realized it was already 5:30. She had a missed call from Dougie on her cell too. Her stomach knotted up. Dougie was supposed to return from his fishing trip in time to relieve Heather. She couldn't help but worry that two calls close to his arrival time meant that he would be late. She couldn't possibly leave the office. Even before the listening to the predictable message, she could feel her milk starting to let down. She was beginning to be amazed at the connection between stress and her milk production.

Hey, babe. I also left you a message on your work line. I hope you get one of them. I am almost home and picking up some dinner. I can stop by your office and bring you something. Let me know how you're doing and if I can do anything. Hang in there. I love you.

Sammie returned Dougie's call, her stress subsiding.

"You are so sweet. Thanks for the offer, but we are having a working dinner to go over these last changes. Cross your fingers that this last draft will be acceptable. Did you have another good day of fishing?"

Sammie had never found Dougie's fishing stories interesting, but now she wanted to hear all about it. During their brief calls over the weekend, the liveliness in his voice was demonstrable.

"It was great," Dougie said. "I can't wait to tell you all about it. I'll try to stay up, but if I crash, wake me up when you get home. Love you."

"I love you too," Sammie said. "Hopefully I won't be too late, but don't worry about waiting up."

Dougie sounded happy. She, on the other hand, was feeling suffocated by the lack of control over her life. She walked down the hall to deliver her revisions to Walker, the partner in charge of the deal, or "Walk-All-Over-You," as Lucy called him.

Walker was on the phone when Sammie arrived at his door. His acknowledgement, as usual, was pointing his index finger to the associate chair, which meant she had to sit and wait for him to finish his call. He had no respect or appreciation for anyone's time but his own. Funny, before, she had always defended his arrogant behavior.

"He was an associate once too," she rationalized to Lucy. "He has earned partnership and is probably only mirroring how he was treated along the way—his version of retribution."

"Fuck a bunch of retribution, he can retribute my ass," Lucy responded.

Sammie smirked thinking about Lucy's way with words. But, it was more than her Lucy-isms that she found captivating. It was the lessons from her humble background that Sammie took to heart. She no longer wanted to sit in Walker's office like an indentured servant listening to his belligerent remarks to the opposing counsel. But you had to give it to Walk-All-Over-You, that is, unless you were on the receiving end of his tirades. He didn't back down to pompous, New York lawyers who attempted to intimidate their southern counterparts. Every other Spencer lawyer cowered at their perceived superiority—but not Ivy League educated Walker. He seemed to thrive on trading punches with New Yorkers. He finally slammed the phone down.

"God damn it," he screamed. "That prick is reprehensible. At the last hour, he is changing the deal terms. This is bullshit. Why are you here?" he asked Sammie, wiping the beads of sweat forming on his fat, shiny, bald head with his starched white handkerchief.

"I incorporated the changes you requested," Sammie said, handing him the document.

"Didn't you just hear anything I said?" he yelled. "There will be more changes, so I don't have time to look at this dribble. I've got to call the client and find out what they want to do. Sit down and take notes," he said, tossing her a legal pad.

"Janet, Janet!" he yelled. "Get in here and dial up Zach DuBose."

Janet was Walker's skittish secretary. Lucy was confident that she popped Xanax all day, so Lucy referred to her as "Manic Janet." Janet punched the speaker option on Walker's phone and dialed the client. She obviously was used to this kind of treatment.

"Walker Winston, III, is calling for Mr. DuBose," Janet announced.

"He is on another call. Would you like me to take a message or put you through to his voicemail?"

Walker's demeanor took a 180-degree turn when addressing their client's assistant.

"Walker, here. Thank you so much. I'm quite sure you don't know the length of that call but excuse me for inquiring anyway. We are busy here and trying to make the best use of our time tonight."

"I understand," the assistant responded. "All I can tell you is that three hours is blocked on his calendar for the call."

"Please have Zach call me as soon as it's concluded. It doesn't matter how late," Walker responded, politely.

Clearly agitated at the client's unavailability, he slammed the phone down.

"When is dinner going to be ready?" Walker snapped at Janet. "Might as well eat while we're waiting."

Manic Janet scurried out to check on the order. Walker fumed at the news that CCCs was a delivery person short. An ETA couldn't be given.

"God damn it," Walker yelled again. "Did you tell them that you would pick it up?"

"Yes sir, I did, but they are backed up," Manic Janet said.

"Well then, I'm going up to the boardroom. Call me when dinner arrives or if Zach calls back," Walker Winston, III, ordered.

Sammie knew Walker was going to fetch a drink in the Hamilton Boardroom while he waited. She thought that any civilized person would have excused her at this point. But, he left her sitting in the associate chair when he stomped out of his office.

"Looks like it's going to be a long night," Sammie told Manic Janet. "Since there is nothing for me to do until the client returns the call, I am going to run home quickly and help get my son to bed. I should only be an hour, but if anything happens before I get back, you can call my cell."

"Sure," Janet said, irritated.

Sammie had wasted enough time in Walk-All-Over-You's office. She had fifteen minutes before Mack's bedtime. She didn't wait on the slow elevator but sprinted down the stairs to her office, grabbed her purse, and ran to her car.

While uncharacteristically speeding down East Bay, while rummaging in her purse for her phone. She realized that she had left her phone in her office so she couldn't let Dougie know she had broken away and to keep Mack up until she got home. She ran a couple of caution lights in pursuit of her mission. She smiled, thinking that Lucy would have been proud of her driving tonight. Lucy always made fun of Sammie's strict obedience to speed limits and other rules of the road. She accused Sammie of driving like a Grandma. Lucy would say that '"Bill Blauers doesn't like when Granny Sammie drives."

When Lucy first heard the expression "billable hours," she thought someone was talking about a guy named "Bill Blauers." But, it didn't take her long to learn not only what billable hours entailed but also the importance of them.

The almighty billable hour was the method attorneys used to charge their clients. Any time spent working or thinking about a file was recorded into the firm's accounting database. Numerous billable hours equated to higher bills and thus more money in the partners' pockets. An associate lawyer's sole value was measured by the number of billable hours generated. Everyone knew that billable hours was also the key to partnership.

Lucy liked to joke about the time she spent with "Bill." "Bill wouldn't leave me alone this weekend. He's so annoying and demanding." "Bill and I had an all-nighter. He has incredible stamina."

Sammie's recollection of Lucy's comments lightened the intensity of her frantic mission, that is, until she saw Heather's car in the driveway. She thought Dougie had said that he was almost home an hour ago or did he say he just leaving Kiawah? She couldn't remember their conversation details. She also couldn't remember if she had communicated to him that Heather couldn't stay late. It was all she could do to keep up with all the deadlines in the Seamark deal and Walker Winston's demands.

Sammie hoped that Dougie hadn't been delayed because now that she was home, she would have to relieve Heather. She couldn't very well receive a call from Manic Janet with her cell phone sitting in her office. And, Walker Winston would bust a gut if Sammie wasn't at his disposal.

Sammie raced up the front steps. She could use Heather's phone to call Dougie hoping that he was simply delayed in picking up dinner. All was quiet when she opened the door. She tiptoed down the hallway to Mack's room. She hoped that Heather was still rocking him, and she could take over. But, Mack was sound asleep in his crib.

Sammie walked back down the hallway and turned into the kitchen. Heather wasn't there but an open champagne bottle was—on the counter and almost empty. The galley-type kitchen emptied into a sunroom with large, french doors leading to the backyard. Sammie had instantly fallen in love with the house with the views from the expansive, brick patio. Amongst the large oak trees, the former owner, an active member of the Garden Club, had masterly created a private oasis rhododendrons, azaleas, hydrangeas, camellias, and other plants.

From the sunroom, Sammie heard the bubbling noise from her first anniversary gift. Her wobbly legs foreshadowed what she knew she was going to find—her nanny and her husband in the hot tub drinking champagne.

Sammie snapped. She left a note.

Dougie and Heather:

Whatever it is you have going on…you are free to pursue. I'm out.

Sammie

She opened the refrigerator, grabbed Mack's milk bottles, ran to her room, and quickly packed as much as she could. She went into Mack's room and stuffed some things into his diaper bag. Then, she lifted her sleeping baby and held him tightly as she ran out of the house.

What was she going to do? What would she tell her parents? What would they think of her? A sense of failure and stupidity washed over Sammie. She shockingly kept her composure as she pulled into her parents' driveway.

"Mom, I have a huge favor." Sammie said. "Can you keep Mack tonight? I have to go back to the office. Dougie won't be back until late, and our nanny can't stay any later. I'm sorry I didn't call but realized I left my cell at work. Before you start lecturing me, the deal closes soon."

Sammie was talking a mile a minute, and her voice was cracking.

"Darling, of course it is okay. And, I'm not going to lecture you, but you have got to slow down. Listen to yourself. Do you need some dinner?"

"No thanks," she said. "I've got to get back to the office—dinner is being brought in. I'll probably be in trouble for leaving. It may be a long night, so if it's alright, I'll just crash here, that is, if I get to leave."

"Of course, it is, but Sammie, these hours."

"I know, Mom. But, it will settle down soon."

Glenny reached out to Mack who was now awake but happy as a clam.

"Come to me, my beautiful grandbaby. Come to your GG."

Grandmother Glenny, or her preferred name, GG, had converted a guest room into a nursery soon after Sammie's announcement of her pending pregnancy. She adored Mack. She adored children.

"I hate to say this sweetie, but you look tired. Look at this angelic boy. Is your job worth it? That's all I am going to say. Go back to work. I'll have your bed made up, if you get to leave tonight. I love you Sammie."

Sammie hugged her mother tightly and then like a robot, headed back to Spencer, Pettigrew & Hamilton.

I may as well be talkin' to a fence post...

Chapter Twenty

Sammie

The next morning, Sammie asked her mother if she and Mack could extend their stay until the Seamark deal closed. The negotiations had stalled due to last minute changes. There would be many late nights, and Dougie had a hectic travel schedule. Sammie assured Glenny that it was only for a couple of weeks. Sammie wasn't surprised by her mother's reaction.

"Of course, you can stay. I wish you'd reconsider my offer to keep Mack. You don't need a nanny when you have me. And, I'm not going to meddle, but think about your priorities," she said.

At least she had been consistent. Glenny thought a mother's place was at home with children. Her view was starting to win Sammie over. She was sacrificing her marriage and time with her son for what? Partnership in a firm where it was becoming quite clear that it wasn't the place that Sammie had revered all these years. She started blaming herself for whatever was going on between Dougie and Heather. A week passed. She was devastated that Dougie had not contacted her.

She broke down and came clean, to an extent, with her mother. She didn't know why she defended Dougie. Sammie explained that her schedule had created tension between them. Dougie felt like his job was not as important, that he was required to change his schedule at a moment's notice.

"You do work a lot, Sammie."

Her mother's comment reinforced her feelings of guilt. She knew her mother's opinion on that point wouldn't change if she confessed that Dougie hadn't actually expressed the things she had communicated. Sammie had done lots of thinking over the past seven days. She not only felt responsible but also that she may have overreacted about the situation with Heather.

Glenny waited to deliver the letter left in the mailbox until after Sammie returned from a run with Mack. "Mrs. Douglas Morgan" was in generic type on the front of the envelope, but the Worth logo engraved on the seal made it apparent that it involved Dougie.

"There is a big glass of ice water by the swing and one of my new specialty cocktails," Glenny said to her daughter, taking her grandson from Sammie's arms. "I'll get Mack dinner and bathed. Let me know if you need anything else."

Sammie knew her mother understood that things were worse than she had divulged. A letter from her husband in her parent's mailbox was the proverbial nail in the coffin. The specialty cocktail she had left by the porch swing was her way of saying, *I know something is not good. I'm here if you want to talk*. But, her mother didn't pry.

Growing up, whenever Sammie got upset, she and Glenny would head to the porch swing. They called it "porch time." Often, they simply rocked in silence while listening to the horses clip-clop down the cobblestone street. Other times, they'd talk things out. In retrospect, Glenny had allowed Sammie to navigate the direction of those times together.

Sammie sat in her spot on the swing, gulped some water, wiped her wet palms on her shorts, and took a deep breath before ripping open the envelope. Her hands were instantly wet again and shaking uncontrollably. She gripped the letter tightly.

Dear Sammie:

I have almost called like a thousand times but decided to write a letter. That is weird because you were always the easiest person for me to talk to about anything. You know me best. You always loved me for who I am. I miss you, Sammie. I miss Mack. I miss everything about our family.

I wasn't completely honest about Heather, but I didn't lie either. I have known her a long time. Her brother was a friend of mine from high school. Remember Barnyard? Heather was like a little sister to me. When Norma recommended her, I knew she would be great with Mack especially after I learned that she worked at a day care. I should have told you that I knew her but thought if you knew she was Barnyard's sister, you wouldn't give her a chance. I swear there is nothing going on between us. We are old friends. That's all.

The night you saw us in the hot tub, Heather had learned that she aced her project. It's going to be in some kind of publication that is a big deal. I won't go into details about her hard life. You don't understand the struggles of some people. I am not trying to criticize the way you were raised, but most people haven't had it as easy as you. I'm really proud of her and wanted to celebrate her news. I realize now that it was really stupid to not let you know about my history with Heather. You wouldn't have jumped to the conclusions you did. I'm hoping now that you know the background, you can see that it was nothing.

You have to know deep down how much I love and idolize you. I would never do ANYTHING to jeopardize what we have. Before you, I was never confident in who Dougie Morgan was. I was good at playing the part of who people thought I was or should be. Then you came along, and I couldn't understand how someone as beautiful as you, with your brains, your education, and your family background could love me. I've never felt like I was good enough for you or your family. But, I have learned that I am. I'm doing great in my job. I wanted you to notice. I wanted your eyes to light up like they used to when I walked into a room. I want to make you proud. I believe that I will do that soon—really soon.

All I can say is that I was wrong. I was wrong not to tell you about Heather. But as God as my witness, there is nothing going on with her. There never has been and never will be. I need you Sammie. I love you so much. I don't know how I can live life without you in it. I will do anything to get you to come home. We have a son. We are meant to be a family. All of this has been killing me.

Please, let's talk. I am off to Charlotte for meetings about my new extended territory and then Georgetown on my way back. I will be home next Friday. After that, I can rearrange my schedule to whatever suits you best. I just need to see you. And, you can call me at ANY time.

All my love, now and forever,

Dougie

Sammie placed the letter beside her on the swing as tears were streaming down her face. Was she going crazy? Why was she so paranoid? As she thought about it, Dougie and Heather weren't sitting close to each other in the hot tub, so why did she assume something was going on? Why had she jumped to an irrational conclusion? And would she have dismissed Heather because she was Barnyard's sister? Sadly, part of her believed that he was right. Lucy had even considered the possibility. She thought that deep down she was a SOBB after all.

The timing of Dougie's note seemed serendipitous or prophetic. Sammie would be leaving Monday morning with Walker to meet with the New York lawyers. They were trying to salvage the Seamark deal. The client believed if everyone sat down in the same room, it would be more civilized and productive. If all went well, the deal would close, and she would head to Randy Baker's practice to join Lucy. She had no desire to work on divorce cases. There was no better time to resign from the firm. She could be the wife to Dougie that he deserved. Most importantly, she needed to do what was best for Mack. In her wildest dreams, she never envisioned raising a child in a broken home. She had to save her marriage for Mack and for her. And, this time, things would be different.

Sammie was ready to begin a new chapter. She picked up her phone, and with shaking hands, she texted Dougie.

Got your letter. We do need to talk. Let's plan on Friday. I'm out of town until then too—in New York for Seamark.

Dougie responded immediately.

Can't wait to see you! Any time works. The sooner the better. Good luck in New York. I know you'll do great. I love you so much.

Sammie's heart quivered but in a good way. It was a sign that she was doing the right thing. She and Mack would surprise Dougie with the good news of their homecoming on Friday.

PART TWO

Molds are for clay, not people...

Chapter Twenty-One

Lucy

Randy Baker and his brother, Eugene, were misfits at Spencer, Pettigrew & Hamilton. Their background, dress, and habits didn't fit the rigid Spencer mold. In fact, they didn't fit any mold. From appearance only, they looked like farmers that had been yanked from the Jasper County cotton fields and stuffed in a suit. You definitely wouldn't call either Baker brother polished. The brothers were absolutely clueless about Charleston etiquette, but they also didn't care about upper society rules.

Despite their roughness around the edges, the Baker brothers were reputed as the two best lawyers in the firm. They both finished first in their college class, both received full scholarships to law school, and in law school, both achieved top rank.

Several years ago, word traveled throughout the legal community that the stodgy Spencer & Pettigrew firm was changing its name to Spencer, Pettigrew & Baker. The firm partners supposedly voted unanimously on the addition to reward the Baker brothers for their longstanding tenure, superior work product, client loyalty, and, of course, lots and lots of billable hours. But the Bakers said, "Thanks, but no thanks. We are two rednecks from Hardeeville. You'll hear shots again at Fort Sumter before the firm will be named after a Baker."

Lucy found the Baker brothers' self-deprecation refreshing, particularly amongst all the other stuffy partners at the firm. She had more in common with the Bakers than anyone else in her workplace. After all, they had grown up in Hardeeville, which was almost like Edenville, only Hardeeville had three thousand less rednecks. And like Lucy, Eugene and Randy seemed to detest the mandatory firm social gatherings. They never attended. Based on the stories Lucy had heard about them, she questioned whether their presence was excused due to their power or simply that the partners preferred their absence.

Lily Phillips, a former colleague, had been Lucy's source of knowledge about the Baker brothers. Previously under Eugene's tutelage, Lily worked ridiculous hours. But, Eugene was right beside Lily grueling away late every evening and weekends. He didn't ride on his reputation as the go-to attorney in the entire state for "break the company" issues. Eugene was a hard-nosed, no-nonsense litigator. Lily used to brag that she worked for the most powerful man in the firm, despite his reckless appearance and uncouthness. Eugene sported a coif that was out of style. In fact, there probably wasn't a year that it ever would have been in style. His suits were equally dated, and his jackets were blanketed with dandruff. He chewed on an unlit cigar, dripping tobacco juice on all that was near him.

Once, Lily was down on her knees putting away documents from the rows of floor-to-ceiling, recessed cabinets. Eugene walked by and chewing on his unlit cigar, grunted: "Now that's where I like to see a woman, on her knees." Neither Lily nor anyone else ever complained to firm management about Eugene. It was either due to his power in the firm or that no one took his comments seriously. He was faithful to his wife and treated his secretary, associates, and paralegals like partners in his success.

One of Lily's best stories about Eugene took place after he won a huge case. The numerous documents involved were being scanned so they could be stored electronically. Eugene didn't trust electronic files—he liked his paper copies. Lily filled one of the large mail carts with the documents and pushed it into his office. Eugene, as usual, had his feet propped up on his desk, chomping on his cigar.

"Lilylicious," Eugene said, "what in the hell are you doing?"

"We don't have the space for all these documents, so you need to limit the scope of what you want to keep," Lily said.

Eugene peered over his outdated, thick, horn-rimmed glasses.

"If it has my writing on it," he barked, "it means that I looked at it carefully, and I want to keep it. If it has tobacco juice on it, it means I looked at it carefully, and I want to keep it. Anything else can be pitched."

"Scribble and dribble. Got it, sir," Lily said, wheeling the cart from his office.

Eugene was a family man. When he wasn't in the office, he was a doting husband and father. He wasn't a member of a country club, didn't have a standing Saturday golf game, and had no social aspirations. He just loved to work, loved to litigate, and loved his family.

Eugene's brother, and Lucy's new boss, Randy Baker, though equally smart and unpolished as his older brother, was more of a maverick. Randy was a chain smoker and flagrantly ignored the firm's nonsmoking policy. He had survived at least three mini-strokes that had made his slow, methodical speech even slower. Since his strokes, he had vowed to exercise more and smoke less. He never vowed to kick his smoking habit altogether.

Lucy couldn't believe that she would now be working with the incomparable Randy Baker. She sat anxiously in his office waiting for him to appear. She checked her appointment calendar yet again and confirmed that this was the correct date and time. His tardiness permitted her time to survey the items haphazardly displayed on his bookshelves.

She laughed out loud when she saw the red baseball hat emblazoned with the name of his beach home, "Randy's Roost." During his single bouts, Randy apparently liked to entertain his "lady friends" there. Lily was working with Eugene one Saturday when Randy arrived.

"Looks like somebody got stood up this weekend," Eugene said, laughing.

"Not stood up but damn ditched. Those hats were a shitcan idea. My lady friend wore one to the Piggly Wiggly and wouldn't you damn know it, she saw somebody there with the same hat. They got to talking so guess who never got dinner last night?"

Lucy recalled another Randy story about the time he was deposing his client's wife. As she was describing the lifestyle that "she had become accustomed to," he waved his cigarette in the air as if to say he'd had enough. His long bushy sideburns caught on fire and smoldered as the wife detailed her "help," including the lawn service, maid, and gardener. The opposing counsel stood and lurched across the table, swatting the side of Randy's face with his 11 x 14 legal pad. At first, Randy thought his adversary was reacting to Randy's demonstrative disgust of the wife's spoiled life. Then, he caught a whiff of his burning hair.

Other than various tacky knickknacks, Randy's office contained more plaques and awards than pictures. The sole photos included his children and his current wife—number four. Perhaps the bitterness he felt in paying his monthly alimony bills was the reason he only accepted male clients. Randy startled Lucy when he entered his office as she was perusing his photos.

"Sorry I am late. Had a racquetball match. Trying to stay in shape for the ladies."

Randy had not showered. He wore his breakfast on his perspiration-stained t-shirt. He sported a pair of Reebok tennis shoes that were so old, Lucy couldn't remember the year when they were popular, if ever. A ratty, pair of shorts and compression hose completed his ensemble. He instantly punched the intercom button on his phone and summoned his assistant to fetch him some coffee.

Cynthia, Randy's secretary, was the only woman who appeared to be a consistent presence in his life. She had been working with Randy since his first day on the job. Her attitude was definitely old school in that her role was to make Randy's life easier so his sole focus could be billing hours. In addition to making his morning coffee and retrieving his lunch, Lucy heard that Cynthia even paid all Randy's bills. She was as loyal to her eccentric boss as the Charleston hot summer days were long.

Cynthia dutifully arrived with Randy's coffee as he was peeling off his compression hose. Cynthia handed him his mug. He handed her his compression hose. She wobbled out of his office like this was an everyday occurrence.

"Between those damn support stockings and my sleep apnea mask, I got no chance with the young gals," Randy said, taking a sip of coffee.

"Sort of like life, isn't' it?" Randy said.

"Excuse me?" Lucy asked.

"A gift from a client," he said, holding out his coffee mug for Lucy to read the inscription printed in large, bold letters: *A Giant Cup of WTF.*

Yes, Lucy believed she was going to like working for this man. He definitely was not the typical Spencer partner.

"We have work to do," Randy said. "Here's the Putnam file. Mr. Putnam has made a wad in the insurance business relating to executive compensation packages. You could say he prints Franklins. We need to serve some discovery ASAP. So, get started on some interrogatories."

"With all due respect Randy, I have been in the corporate group," Lucy said. "I understand that this is one of the largest equitable distribution cases in the state's history. To be perfectly honest, I don't even understand what is involved in equitable distribution."

"First of all, equitable distribution is an oxymoron," Randy said, in his slow, drawn-out speech. "There is not one damned thing equitable about distributing assets."

"I've never drafted an interrogatory. The last time I heard of the word was when I was a first year law student in my Civil Procedure class."

Randy attempted to alleviate Lucy's angst over her assignment by insisting that anything goes with his cases.

"An interrogatory is just fancy word for learning shit scoop. I'm sure you've read a trashy novel or two in your day. Interrogatories are like developing the plot."

Lucy didn't want to disclose to her new boss that she had never even owned a "trashy novel." In fact, growing up, she had only made it through one chapter in her friend's Harlequin Romance book before it was confiscated by her mother; she was grounded for two weeks.

"You'll be fine," Randy drawled. "Ask anything you'd want to know. Think about all the goat fuck that makes up her entitled lifestyle—one that she got from getting married to a man who has worked his ass off for the last thirty years. And, you're a woman. I've never understood women. Why do you think I'm on my fourth marriage?"

As Lucy patiently listened to Randy's lilting description of her role, she recalled another Randy Baker trademark. Lily used to mock Randy's unique way of injecting his colorful curse words in sentences. Lucy had never heard the phrases "shit scoop" or "goat fuck" even in Edenville.

Though Lucy could have listened to Randy Baker all day, she politely excused herself to work on questions for Tiffany Putnam. Corporate issues were foreign to Lucy when she joined the firm six years ago. The learning curve had been long and meandering. Conversely, domestic issues were real life and more relatable. Frank Hamilton did not expect that she may actually enjoy her time of penance in this new practice area.

Lucy couldn't wait to tell Sammie about her assignment and her new boss. She thought Sammie would love working with Randy Baker, if Frank Hamilton ever got around to moving her out of corporate like he had originally threatened.

Fool me once, shame on you; fool me twice, shame on me...

Chapter Twenty-Two

Sammie

Sammie read Dougie's letter over and over. It became apparent that she had overreacted. Her overreaction had been grounded in mistrust. The bottom line was that she hadn't erased Cathleen McKinney's notes. Heather was an innocent victim of her unburied suspicions that Dougie's relationship with his boss had crossed professional boundaries. Her insecurities and current weariness had colored her interpretation of the Heather situation.

The temporary break with Dougie had been good for many reasons. It had given her clarity that she needed to get away from a legal practice. The exhaustive analysis required of every infinitesimal detail was spilling over into her personal life and impairing her judgment. After Mack got a little older, she would reconsider a career, but right now, she needed to be at home. She needed to regain control over her life.

Sammie's decision was reinforced by Walker's call announcing that the trip to New York was postponed. These last-minute changes were no big deal to the Walkers of the world, but Sammie had spent all weekend preparing physically and mentally. The trip had expedited her planned weaning of Mack. She had packed extra blouses and pads for fear that the stressful negotiations would trigger any residual milk letdown. For once, the unnecessary preparations, including her premature weaning of Mack, didn't bother her.

Sammie was going to prove to Dougie that she was committed to their family. On Monday morning, while waiting on Walker's marching orders, Sammie began working on a budget. Dougie was doing well at Worth, but Sammie was ashamed that she didn't have a better handle on their financial situation. She made a list of their consistent monthly bills. *The lawn service will have to go*, she thought. In reviewing their miscellaneous expenses, the Starbucks runs would be easy eliminations. Her shoe fetish, however, would be more difficult, but necessary. If things got tight, she was prepared dip into her trust account.

Sammie then realized that she didn't know anything about her account. She knew that she received quarterly statements, but she had never even looked at them. It hit her that she spent so much time analyzing the details of the firm's clients' matters that she had totally neglected her personal affairs.

This was going to change, she vowed. First, she would figure out her brokerage account. She needed to become better educated about the diversity of the investments in her trust fund, the rates of return, and the fluctuations in the balance. Most importantly, she needed to learn if she could access her account to supplement Dougie's income.

The only thing she really knew about her account was that it was managed by Parks Callaway of Callaway Securities. Parks was the founder and her father's longtime broker. Certainly, someone at his company could help her with some basic questions, like how to access her account, rather than her father's long-time advisor.

Sammie's thoughts were interrupted by a call from Manic Janet summoning her to Walker's office. She grabbed a legal pad and headed to the fourth floor. As usual, Walker pointed to the designated associate chair when Sammie arrived. She sat patiently until he finished his call. He barked numerous changes to the documents while Sammie was speedily taking notes.

"We need to circulate revised drafts by 6:00 this evening," he yelled. "Get these back to me as soon as possible so I have time to review them."

Sammie's assignment seemed utterly impossible to timely complete. The bright side was after Walker's review and submission to the seller, she should have several hours before their comments would appear. She should be able to meet Lucy at CCCs for dinner. But, then again Walk-All-Over-You's range of commands changed faster than a chameleon's colors. She alerted Lucy, just in case.

Sammie worked at a feverish pace and had a solid product for Walker's review by 4:45. Interestingly, Walker wasn't even in his office. Sammie left the revisions on his chair. She wasn't going to waste time waiting for him to return. Callaway Securities probably closed at 5:00 p.m. She wanted to eliminate this task from her to-do list.

Sammie ran back to her office and called Callaway Securities. She explained the reason for her call and was put on hold for assistance. She was unprepared and shocked when Parks Callaway picked up the call.

"Sammie, this is Parks Callaway. I know we've never met, but I hold your father in high regard. How can I help you?"

"Well, I didn't mean to bother you and so late in the day," Sammie said. "I just had a few and hopefully simple questions about my brokerage account, if this is a convenient time."

Parks Callaway was extremely friendly and seemed genuinely excited to hear from her. But from Sammie's six years at the law firm, she certainly wasn't naïve. She knew how these relationships worked—even Frank Hamilton would have sucked up to his largest clients' offspring.

They shared niceties and talked about Sammie's parents and their excitement about being grandparents.

"I am embarrassed to say that I have never really paid attention to my quarterly statements," Sammie blurted, after a pause in the introductory chit-chat. "So, I was calling to see if online access is available. I'd like to start monitoring my account more closely."

Mr. Callaway probably handled numerous complicated transactions daily and though significant to Sammie, her account was likely miniscule compared to his other client portfolios. She felt stupid talking to the owner of the company about such a mundane issue and her obvious lack of knowledge of her account.

"I have been meaning to call you to discuss your objectives," Mr. Callaway said. "Your father invested wisely, and there is a good mix of high risk/high reward growth investments, which is appropriate if you are in for the long haul. But we should discuss the portfolio ratios since you are accessing the account for cash."

Sammie was mortified. She had never intended to access the fund for cash at least before now. Did he assume that because of her call? She felt like an ignorant, spoiled, trust fund brat.

"I trust my father's long-term strategy," Sammie stammered. "I just feel like it's time that I become a little more knowledgeable and at least monitor the returns on the investments. So, I wanted to see if there is a way to do that."

"Certainly, we have a link on our webpage to accounts," Parks said. "We can establish a username and confidential password for you. After you log in the first time, you can change either or both. I will send you the link to set it up."

"Yes. Thank you. Could you send to my work email? Our email is very secure."

"You should receive something shortly. Let me know if you don't receive it or if you have any questions. I know you are very busy with your job and a newborn, but when you catch your breath, I am available any time to meet. I'd love to treat you to lunch. I like to meet at least quarterly with clients and am always available to you, Sammie. Take care. Good-bye."

Sammie felt a sense of satisfaction in the productivity of her day. She had efficiently responded to Walker's demanding orders, drafted a budget, and called Callaway Securities. The icing on the cake was dinner with Lucy. She was excited to confide in Lucy her decision to return home and resign from the firm.

While Sammie was waiting on the email with her username and password, she accessed the Callaway website to familiarize herself with the format. She clicked under the heading "Leadership," and Parks Calloway's picture appeared. *He was handsome and had her father's trusting blue eyes—a good trait for a financial analyst*, she thought. Parks' photo made her wonder what potential clients thought of the headshots on the Spencer law firm website, especially Walker Winston, III's. Trusting was not an adjective that came to mind.

Her perusal was interrupted with an email alert. It was from Callaway Securities with her confidential access information. She went back to the website and entered her information. Her account instantly appeared on the screen. She chastised herself for not having taken this step years ago.

As Sammie found the link to her account balance, her heart started racing. Then, like clockwork, she felt it—the letdown. Milk gushed from her breasts. There must be some mistake, but there it was in black and white on the screen—a $400,000 reduction in the balance. Then, there was a knock on her office door.

He'd steal the flowers off his grandma's grave...

Chapter Twenty-Three

Lucy & Sammie

Lucy had made good progress in drafting her first interrogatories and was getting hungry. She was looking forward to her dinner with Sammie at CCCs. She hoped that Walk-All-Over-You hadn't dropped another unforeseen assignment on Sammie. But, her last text was: *So far, so good*.

Lucy and Sammie hadn't talked since Lucy's move to Randy Baker's practice, other than passing chit-chat in the breakroom and sporadic texts. None of these communications was a means to stay in touch with a best friend. Sammie seemed happy so Lucy assumed everything was okay on the home front. But, then, you can't decipher a friend's well-being from brief appearances or text messages.

Lucy headed down the hallway to Sammie's office to check her status. Her door was shut, and Shirley wasn't at her desk. Lucy knocked on Sammie's door, but there was no answer. Lucy wondered if she had already headed to CCCs. Lucy opened the door and was startled to see Sammie in her office. She seem rattled.

"What's wrong?" Lucy asked. "Is Walker being an ass?"

Sammie stood up and pointed to her soaked blouse.

"I can't go like this. I am going to head home."

"Oh, Sammie, that's no big deal. No one will notice, and I have been looking forward to catching up with you. I know this is none of my business, but have you considered quitting that? I mean, I don't know how you are juggling all that milk pumping the week before a closing."

"Actually, I have stopped pumping," Sammie said. "I started weaning Mack over the weekend because of the New York trip that has now been postponed. I guess my milk glands haven't figured it out yet."

"Well, I will take you to change. I'm starving, and if Granny Sammie drives, we won't have time for dinner."

Lucy was talking a mile a minute about her assignment in the Putnam case, but Sammie's mind was on her trust account. She should have paid closer attention to the performance of the investments. Her personal affairs were no longer going to take a backseat to the law firm.

Sammie suddenly realized that Lucy was headed in the direction of her house. Sammie decided to go with it. She wasn't ready to divulge that she had been staying at her parents since catching Dougie and Heather in the hot tub. And, according to Dougie's letter, he was out of town. She could gather her trust account quarterly statements. She would study them later. She felt like an idiot that she never had opened even one of them.

As Lucy turned onto Sammie's street, she got distracted with an email from Walker and worried that he was summoning her back into the office.

"Your sitter sure drives a nice car," Lucy said, interrupting Sammie's review of the message.

A black Range Rover was parked in the driveway.

"I don't know whose car that is."

"It has a Georgia plate," Lucy said, pulling in behind the luxury vehicle.

"This is weird. Dougie is out of town. A burglar wouldn't be driving a Range Rover, right?"

Sammie questioned her recollection of Dougie's letter. The kitchen light was on, but that wasn't strange. They often left a light on.

"This is creepy," Sammie said, as she walked up the driveway.

"Where are you going?" Lucy asked.

"To check out the garage," Sammie said.

Sammie's mind was already considering explanations for the car—Dougie and a co-worker may have ridden together to call on a customer. But, her legs felt like rubber as she attempted to peer through the window inserts in the garage door. They were too high and Lucy's additional two inches in height didn't help.

"We need a chair," Lucy offered.

As they started up the steps leading to the secluded patio for a chair, Sammie heard the bubbling water from the hot tub jets. They both saw the discarded clothes near the hot tub at the same time. The back door to the sunroom was open. Lucy grabbed Sammie's arm.

"Get those clothes and meet me in the car," Lucy whispered, firmly. "I got this."

Sammie didn't answer. There was someone other than a burglar in her house. As Lucy walked from the sunroom into the kitchen, she spotted the mortar and pestle that Sammie had purchased to test her homemade pesto out on Lucy. Before then, Lucy had never even heard of such a kitchen accessory. But, from the white powder and the straw on the counter, she knew that Dougie hadn't been cooking with the kitchen tool.

Lucy quickly retrieved her phone from her pocket. She snapped pictures of the paraphernalia on the kitchen counter. Then, she heard a woman's shrills down the hallway. She quietly proceeded in the direction of Sammie's bedroom. She had her camera ready as she opened the door.

Sammie's head was buried in her hands when Lucy jumped in the car.

"It's not a good situation, Sammie. I went to get Mack, but he isn't there."

"He's at my parents."

"Thank heavens. You can stay with me tonight," Lucy instructed. "I am going into the office and get what I need to finish my assignment. I will tell Manic Janet that you had to leave—a sitter conflict or something, I don't know. I'll get your laptop. Anything else?"

Sammie only shook her head. When Lucy returned to the car from the office, Sammie was sobbing uncontrollably.

"What am I going to do?" Sammie mumbled, between her sobs.

"You are going to leave the son of a bitch."

Sammie's mind was racing. How could she have married Dougie Morgan? The signs were there from the beginning. Isabelle's words came back to her: *He has broken every heart in Charleston County*. She wondered how long he had been cheating. She was crushed by her naiveté and gullibility. She felt like a fool and failure. What would she tell her parents?

They rode in silence all the way to Lucy's apartment.

"Take my room. I've got to finish these interrogatories. I'm going to sleep on the couch."

"I am not going to kick you out of your own bed. I'm not going to be able to sleep anyway."

"Well, you've got to try. I don't know what to say. I know you are dealing with lots of emotions, but you deserve so much better. This may sound crass and insensitive but after tonight, I'm pretty sure Dougie is probably screwing around with Heather too."

"What do you mean?" Sammie asked. "Wasn't he with Heather?"

"Well, I've never met Heather, but you said she was a cute blonde. I will spare the details but the woman in your room was not a blonde."

"Who was it then? This is crazy. I obviously wasn't satisfying him," Sammie sobbed. "Why was I not good enough for him?"

"Seriously, Sammie? Did you just say that? None of this has anything to do with you. You ARE good enough. No, you're better than good enough. You are one of a kind. It's Dougie that has the problem. And, you can't fix it. Damn, I don't know. I'm no psychologist but he's obviously a liar and cheater. You can't blame yourself."

"Why is all this happening to me? I'm just so mixed up right now, Lucy."

"I know you are. But, try and get some rest."

Lucy's place was small, and the walls were thin. For the next several hours, Lucy could tell that Sammie was trying to muffle her sobbing. She felt badly leaving her alone, but it wasn't going to do any good rehashing the evening's events or all the other crap that she had likely kept bottled up.

With all that had transpired, Lucy was amazed at her ability to focus on her work. It was like the night's events opened her eyes wider to deceitfulness and that anything was possible. Who would have ever thought that a spouse of Samantha Spencer could cheat?

After Lucy finished the list of questions for Tiffany Putnam, she checked on Sammie. She was asleep, at least for now. Lucy tried to recreate the earlier scene that already was a blur. She jotted some notes. She had learned more than a thing or two from Randy. If she were ever deposed in *Morgan v. Morgan*, she needed to memorialize all the details.

Lucy scrolled through the pictures on her phone and zoomed in on the drugs on the kitchen counter. She hadn't noticed the colored capsule bottle when they were there. She zoomed in further—Dolorine was legible on the label. She then zoomed in on the pictures from the bedroom. They were not as clear. Unfortunately, the photo only captured the back of a naked woman with long black hair. She started thinking of all the ways this could play out if Dougie played hardball. Their word against his. No smoking gun. But then there were the clothes.

Lucy checked on Sammie again before returning to her car to retrieve the only solid evidence they had. The shorts were inside out. She noticed a monogram across the band—"CM." *Only in Charleston*, she thought. Her closet contained not one stitch of clothing with a monogram or even a designer logo. But, it was becoming quite clear that Dougie Morgan's proverbial closet sported many brands. The only question was who he would play next.

A worm is the only animal that doesn't fall down...

Chapter Twenty-Four

Glenny & Sammie

"Please tell me that you didn't work all night," Glenny said, exasperatingly.

"No, I didn't," Sammie answered, "but, it was a late night. I stayed at Lucy's."

"That's a relief. Mack and I just had the best walk. We went down by the Battery and..."

Sammie couldn't wait for her to finish the play-by-play of the morning's events.

"I need to talk to you," Sammie interrupted.

Sammie couldn't even make it inside. She collapsed on the wrought iron bench in their front yard and sobbed. Sammie's breakdown confirmed Glenny's suspicions that there was more than tension in her daughter's marriage.

Sammie told her mother everything—the notes from Cathleen McKinney, Dougie's explanation, Heather and Dougie in the hot tub, Dougie's explanation, and his lie about his mother's recommendation of their nanny. She revealed Lucy's and her discovery the previous evening and even their discovery of Frank Hamilton and Barbie on the conference room table. Finally, she told her mother the story that Frank Hamilton had relayed about her grandfather.

"Oh baby. My sweet babies," Glenny said, sitting down beside her daughter.

Glenny grabbed both of her hands and looked Sammie in the eyes.

"Sweetie, I have to tell you something too."

What now? Sammie thought.

Sometimes, you just gotta rip off the band-aid...

Chapter Twenty-Five

Glenny Spencer

"Your father and I know about the withdrawals from your trust account," Glenny divulged to her daughter.

"What do you mean know about withdrawals? What withdrawals?" Sammie asked, realizing that the reduction in her account wasn't due to market conditions.

"I assumed you found out," Glenny said, "that's why you showed up here with Mack."

Glenny paused and took a deep breath.

"Recently, Cort met with Parks Callaway, his broker, to discuss some new investments. Parks mentioned that he needed to change the structure of your account since you had been accessing the principal from your highest performing fund. I kept questioning Cort about why you would need so much cash, but he kept reminding me that you are adult now, have your own life, and smart enough to know what you are doing. And, it is your money after all. Then you mentioned the scheduling conflicts and the tension in your marriage. When the letter from Dougie arrived, well, Sammie darling, we started believing there were more serious problems. Cort finally agreed with me that something wasn't right. He asked Parks to freeze the account and look into it."

Glenny's eyes filled with tears, and she bowed her head.

"I knew I should have asked you. I was trying not to meddle," Glenny said. "Oh sweetie," returning her arm around Sammie's shoulder.

"So, what did he find out?" Sammie asked, though suspecting the news wouldn't be good.

"Parks learned that the withdrawals were all processed by one of his assistants," Glenny continued, "Camilla Girard."

"Oh my gosh," Sammie said. "Her brother is Kurt Girard. I remember him from high school. Kurt was at Tradd Prep, and Camilla was at Pinckney Hall."

"So, you know her?"

"Not really. They moved to Charleston my senior year. She was several years behind me. But, why would she take money from my account? Her father made millions from selling a software company in Atlanta before moving to Charleston," Sammie said.

"Yes, the Girard account is now Parks' largest account. They retired to Charleston to be closer to family. Camilla is Parks' niece. So, let's just say that Parks is in a sensitive spot with the whole thing."

"So, did Parks find out why she took it?"

"Oh, Sammie. We thought you must have learned about her. Do you really want to hear this?"

When your world has been rocked off its axis, one's view becomes skewed. Rose-colored glasses are a thing of the past. Whatever her mother was getting ready to disclose, Sammie thought she could handle it.

"Go on," Sammie said.

"Let's go inside. I'll put Mack down for a nap and meet you on the porch swing."

Now, Sammie knew that Camilla wasn't the only one involved. There was much more to this story. It hit Sammie that it may have been Camilla at the house and not Heather. That the Range Rover was hers. But, why the Georgia license plate? They had moved years ago. When her mother joined her on the swing, she was prepared for the news.

"Camilla's side of the story is that she and Dougie used to date. After you returned to Charleston from law school, she broke up with him when she found out that he was seeing you."

"Found out that he was seeing me?" Sammie asked, incredulously. "We dated for seven years!"

"Apparently, he was seeing you both at the same time, if she is telling the truth."

Sammie's gut told her she was. She and Dougie's relationship had been, for the most part, a long distance one. She had tried to be supportive of his juggling two jobs which prohibited him from visiting her.

"So, she took my money to get back at him?"

"No, her story is that she and Dougie reconciled. He convinced her that he had rights to the account. He told her that Cort would use his power to gyp him out of what was legally his, so he was getting his fair share before he left you. When Parks pressed her on when they had reconciled, she reminded Parks that he had recently met Dougie at the Kiawah Beach Club, I guess to corroborate her story."

Sammie was putting two and two together. Dougie's newest doctor customer in Kiawah likely didn't exist and his weekend fishing trip with the doctor didn't occur.

"Why didn't you tell me this?" Sammie asked, feeling more like a fool.

"Because Parks does recall seeing Camilla there this summer with a young man. When he went over to speak, she introduced him, but he is certain that she didn't say his name was Dougie Morgan."

"Why would he remember that? He doesn't know Dougie. I have never even met the man before."

"I was getting to that part."

Sammie didn't know if she could handle any more.

"Parks knows all about Dougie because he is your father's half-brother.

"Oh, dear Lord. Why don't I know this?"

"I guess we thought some things were better to keep private. Your grandmother doesn't know about Parks. Parks' mother is Joyce Callaway. She was your grandfather's secretary. And, she's the reason Cort never joined the firm."

"So Frank was telling the truth about what he and Dad saw."

"The only truth about Frank's story is that your grandfather had a mistress. But, what he told you and Lucy is a lie. His story is not how your father learned about Joyce Callaway."

Everything seemed to be coming full circle. Sammie couldn't help but think that if she and Lucy hadn't caught Frank Hamilton with Barbie, she would have never learned about Parks Callaway, Joyce Callaway, or the reason her father hadn't joined Spencer, Pettigrew & Hamilton.

"Frank Hamilton was threatened by your father. He resented the fact that Cort had a family birthright to a position in the firm. Even back then, Frank used to tell your father that he was going to be the first to beat a Spencer out for the managing partner job."

"All of this must bring back terrible memories for Dad. I'm so ashamed."

"Well, let me finish. This has been such a burden on your father all these years. That is, if you want to hear the rest."

"OK, unless you tell me that I have a half-brother or sister somewhere."

Glenny's reaction to Sammie's comment was like her daughter had driven a stake through her heart.

"You know I worship Dad, but if you told me..."

Glenny interrupted. Sammie could hear the pain in her voice.

"Do you really think that, Sammie?"

"I guess I don't know what to believe anymore. I'm sorry. Go ahead and finish."

"The summer of your father's second year in law school, he and Frank both clerked at the firm. Joyce was assigned to Frank that summer. Apparently, he began suspecting that there was something going on between Joyce and your grandfather. He started following your grandfather when he left the office."

"Are you serious? What a creep."

"Yes, and it gets worse. At the end of the summer when the offers were announced for associate positions, Frank and your dad were going out for drinks to celebrate. Frank insisted on driving, but instead of heading to a bar, Frank drove away from town. Frank kept telling Cort that it would be worth the drive. Frank turned into a motel in North Charleston. Cort saw his father's car. Frank then pointed out Joyce's car. He told Cort that he had discovered their rendezvous spot several weeks ago. It was his security for ensuring he got an offer. But, since he got his offer, he wanted Cort to know that he didn't have to worry about him saying anything. He would keep Cort's secret. Of course, your father didn't know anything about the affair. After that night, your father knew he couldn't return to the firm. That's when he applied for jobs in New York. Your grandfather was incensed that he could even consider such a thing. He told your father that he was abandoning his heritage. He threatened to cut him out of his will if he refused the firm's offer."

"Why would Dad let me work there?" Sammie asked.

"Sammie, that was many years ago. The firm didn't cause the affair. And it is the best firm in South Carolina, and it's all you've ever wanted. After your grandfather retired, Frank was elected as the managing partner. Frank called Cort to report that he fired Joyce—that he could come home now and join the partnership. I guess he assumed that Joyce was the reason that your father took a job in New York."

"So, was that when Dad moved back to Charleston?" Sammie asked.

"No. We returned after your grandfather got sick. Cort was worried about his mother. And, he viewed my miscarriages as punishment for leaving his mother and the firm. He was carrying a great deal of guilt."

"What? I thought you met Dad in Charleston."

"No, sweetie. I met your Dad in New York. I was a designer for a fashion house in New York. When we moved to Charleston, I started working at the boutique shop on King Street."

Sammie couldn't believe that she was just learning about her family's history.

"So, when did Dad learn about Parks?" Sammie asked.

"After your grandfather died. Joyce came to the funeral and asked to meet with your father. She said she had some things from the time that she worked for him that he may want. When he met with her, she told him. Your father wished he had confronted your grandfather that summer. He ignored it. He was too ashamed, scared of his father, and too concerned for his mother. Of course, there is no guarantee that any confrontation would have changed the course of the future, but he feels responsible for Parks. There is a unique bond between them. Anyway, Parks is very loyal to your father, so you don't need to worry about the withdrawals being repeated. Now that you know, I hope we can all move forward."

How could Sammie possibly move forward when she felt like she was suffocating under layers of deception? With all that she had dealt with the last two days, the last person Sammie wanted to see was her father. She didn't think she could face him. She could visualize the disappointment in his eyes. Sammie strongly suspected that his early return from a business trip was precipitated by her mother's disclosure about what had transpired. When he walked in the door, he dropped his bag, darted to her, and squeezed her tightly.

"Life is hard sometimes, Sammie, and often times, it's just not fair. Bad things shouldn't happen to good people, but they do. You are strong and tough," he said, kissing her forehead. "And, always remember life is a marathon, not a 400-meter dash. Along the way, there will be failures, lots of pain, and circumstances for which you can't prepare or control. But, you must keep the faith while chugging along, holding your head high."

Sammie was being baptized into the sometimes troubled waters of adulthood. She was being immersed into a darker world where even your parents weren't immune to weakness, fear, or worry, where you plunged into uncontrollable waters, and where you were presented with tests for which you can't prepare. She didn't appreciate it then, but those enlightenments were the ones where she would learn the most.

A trouble shared is a trouble halved...

Chapter Twenty-Six

Sammie & Lucy

Admittedly, after Sammie's initial disclosure about Dougie and Heather, Lucy suspected something was going on but tried to curb her cynical thoughts. Now, there was no question that he was screwing around—the only uncertainty was with how many women.

The deluge of Glenny's revelations had broken Sammie's spirit. She wasn't in any mental state to practice law. She barely had the energy to get out of bed. Now, that the Seamark deal was on hold, it was a good time to catch her breath. She noted Dougie's travel schedule and nanny departure in her request for a leave of absence, which quickly percolated throughout the firm. It had been a couple of weeks since Lucy had seen her. Lucy's calls and texts to Sammie had gone unanswered.

"Sorry I have been so out of touch," Sammie said when she finally called Lucy. "I've needed time away from everything to think. To be honest, I was disappointed in myself for letting you talk me into going into the boardroom. After that, my life started spiraling out of control."

Where was this going? Lucy thought. *Is Sammie blaming her for this chain of events?*

"Can you meet for lunch some day this week? I need to talk to you."

"Sure. How about tomorrow at CCCs?"

"Is Fleet Landing too inconvenient? I've been craving their shrimp and grits. The weather is going to be nice all week and thought we could snag a table on the water."

"No problem. Can you believe that I've never been there?"

"Yes, actually I can. It's a whopping two miles from the firm," Sammie said, laughing.

"I know, crazy, right? I just looked at the lunch menu. If I bring Randy the whole fried flounder, he probably won't mind how long I take. That is, if I can substitute the red rice for french fries."

"I can't wait to hear more about what it's like working for him."

"It's actually great. You'll love it too. That is if you're coming back. You are coming back, aren't you?"

"I'll see you tomorrow and fill you in. I can't wait to see you."

"Same. I miss you."

When Lucy hung up, she had a strong feeling that Sammie wouldn't be joining her in Randy's practice.

Sammie arrived early to ensure that she secured an outdoor table and one that afforded the most privacy. She even ordered a Bloody Mary hoping it would calm her nerves. Her parents now knew the truth. It was time to confide in her best friend.

Lucy was always prompt, but at 12:15, Sammie worried that she may have been sucked into a work emergency. She perused the menu while she waited to get her mind off of her intended mission.

Sammie thought she knew the history of the concrete, maritime structure that now housed one of her favorite restaurants. The menu provided the rest of the back story.

In 1942, the Navy constructed the Fleet Landing building for off-loading sailors. Prior to the Navy, the spot was the home of the Cooper River ferry. Before the construction of the bridge, the ferry was the means of transport across the Cooper River to Mount Pleasant. The reference to Dougie's hometown unsettled her. She pushed aside her drink and opted for her water.

"Sorry I am late. I couldn't find a parking spot. I probably could have gotten here quicker if I had walked."

"No worries. I was afraid that Bill Blauers had absconded with you."

"Nope. I'm all yours. I think I may have a bloody too. That looks great."

"You can have this one. It wasn't such a good idea after all."

"Are you alright?" Lucy asked, wondering again the purpose of the lunch.

Sammie's stiff posture, the tone of her voice, and her avoidance of any eye contact was signaling this was not a carefree outing. Lucy obliged Sammie's offer for her drink and took a big gulp.

"I've been doing a lot of thinking," Sammie said. "Setting aside the egos we have to deal with at work, I always thought the firm was a safe and solid environment. But all that changed when we caught Frank and Barbie."

"I was wrong to push going to the conference room. It seems so trite now. I'm so sorry," Lucy said, wishing she had listened to her gut and declined Sammie's lunch invitation.

"No, that's just it. I'm glad you did. Had we not caught Frank, I'm confident he never would have mentioned anything about my grandfather."

The waiter suddenly appeared. Since the shrimp and grits were the reason they were at Fleet Landing, Lucy was surprised when Sammie only ordered a cup of gumbo. Lucy decided to splurge and try Sammie's favorite dish on the menu.

"I'd also like the whole fried flounder with french fries to go. I'm earning all kinds of points with Randy in delivering his lunch," Lucy said to Sammie, as the waiter walked away. "You are going to love working with him too. I can't wait for us to work together again.

"That's what I wanted to talk to you about," Sammie said.

"You're not coming back are you?"

"No, I'm not."

"Did you resign?" Lucy asked.

"Not yet," Sammie said. "But I am going to. I'm dreading meeting with Frank to deliver the news."

"Frank Hamilton is the last thing you should worry about. I wish you would tell lover boy where to stick it, but you're too honorable."

"I'm not concerned about telling him. I just don't want to witness his satisfaction that there are no more Spencers around."

"What do you mean?"

"I haven't told you everything."

Sammie told Lucy about how Frank Hamilton stalked her grandfather and discovered his affair with Joyce Callaway, her father's half-brother, Parks Callaway, and the withdrawals from her trust account. While she was bearing her soul, she unveiled the notes from Dougie's boss.

When it rains, it pours, Lucy thought.

"That is some crazy shit, Sammie."

"Well, that's not all of it. Parks Callaway's niece is Camilla Girard, she works for Parks now. Parks noticed that the common denominator with the withdrawals was Camilla. She authorized every transaction. Parks confronted her. According to her, she and Dougie are in a relationship."

"Geez, Sammie," Lucy said. "Do you think that is who we caught him with? Those clothes by the hot tub, they had a monogram with a "C.""

"Guess so," Sammie said. "Dougie was been spending a lot of time in Kiawah, supposedly at some new pain clinics opened by a doctor who had a place in Kiawah. Camilla's parents have a place there. I bet he was seeing her and not the pain doctor."

"All I can say is to hell with Dougie Morgan, Camilla, Heather, and Dougie's boss. And Frank Hamilton too."

"I know but if Frank hadn't told us about my grandfather, I would be struggling more than I already am—letting Dad down that I quit his family's firm."

"All your dad wants is what is right for you. And, even without all the personal shit you are dealing with, I don't think we realize the toll that the hours are taking. It's a slow burn. For once in your life, you've got to think of yourself and Mack. You've given the firm one-hundred and ten percent, if not more. And whether you feel like it now, you have given everything to your marriage too. Dougie's actions have absolutely nothing to do with the kind of person that you are. Don't ever doubt yourself."

"I can't help it," Sammie said. "I can't stop thinking that I am responsible for the failure of my marriage and that Mack is going to suffer. These thoughts are driving me crazy. I can't focus on anything. I'm in no shape mentally to return to the firm. Truthfully, I'm not fit for any job right now."

"You are going to be fine. You will think this sounds crazy, especially coming from me, but catching Frank and Barbie, hearing about your grandfather, and discovering the truth about Dougie are signs. A higher power is talking to you, and you need to listen."

The only thing that should be buried in the sand are the eggs of a loggerhead turtle...

Chapter Twenty-Seven

Sammie & Glenny

Sammie expected that her resignation from Spencer, Pettigrew & Hamilton would be liberating. For once, her time would be hers and hers alone. And, she was going to use it wisely. Her mental stability was counting on it.

She kept hoping that her peaceful mornings with coffee on the porch swing and relaxed outings with Mack would soothe her pain. But, all she could think about was the unraveling of her marriage. She felt like she was stuck in quicksand. She needed to find the strength and resolve to tackle a property settlement and custody agreement. But, the major roadblock was her sense of failure.

Surprisingly, Dougie hadn't pushed either. She assumed that he understood he had no leverage, and there was no need to rock the boat. After all, he was living in a nice neighborhood with no house payment—a satisfied mortgage had been a gift from her parents after the delivery of their first grandchild.

Sammie tried not to think about how Dougie was spending his time, and if he was enjoying his freedom. She was ashamed that she had stooped to driving by their house, and more than once in the middle of the night. She had never snuck out as a teenager, but she was making up for it as an adult. When none of her drive-bys provided any clues, she wondered if he had moved in with Camilla and if he was relieved that their marriage was over.

Once again, Sammie started blaming herself for Dougie's actions. Despite Lucy's consistent encouragement that she wasn't to blame, it was the other things that Lucy had said that were influencing her.

"You can't know how people feel when you haven't walked a mile in their shoes," Lucy always said when Sammie dismissed Lucy's feelings of inadequacies in Charleston society.

Sammie found it particularly poignant that her mother used to preach the same sermon to her when she was growing up. Sammie wondered if she and her parents had unconsciously said or done things to alienate Dougie. Her upbringing had been charmed compared to his.

She found herself reading Dougie's letter again. It seemed like months had passed, instead of weeks, since he had left the letter in her parents' mailbox. She was beginning to see things from his point of view. He had revealed his insecurities. He had convinced her that Heather was an old friend. His words had ignited her passion for him, for their family, and a happily ever after. She had planned to quit her job and make her family her only priority. Sammie's emotions had swung from gratifying contentment to hellish misery. She felt foolish that she had even considered reconciliation.

But, as more days passed, she ached for some sort of explanation. How could he have expressed the things he had in his letter and in less than a week later been with someone else? His lack of contact was making her feel more dejected. When she finally heard from him, Sammie was not prepared for his message.

I hope you had a good trip to New York. I assume that you are still tied up in your deal since I haven't heard from you about a time to talk. I love you, Sammie. I didn't think it was possible I could ever have a deeper love until Mack was born. You both mean the world to me. Please let's have a face-to-face talk soon.

Sammie immediately called Lucy.

"I know this sounds crazy, but it's been killing me that I haven't heard anything from Dougie. But, he sent me a text and wants to meet."

"Don't do it, Sammie," Lucy said, emphatically.

"I knew you would say that, but I have to think of Mack. I want to make sure that I do the right thing. Can you send me the photos that you took?"

Lucy knew that the photos didn't prove anything other than the back of a naked woman on a bed, and the photo was blurry of that image. She knew Dougie would manufacture some explanation. Sammie had always put a positive spin on facts instead of seeing the ugly truth, and she was especially vulnerable now.

"Forget the photos. You need to think about what you saw—the clothes by the hot tub not to mention the notes from Dougie's boss. And then he lied about his mother recommending your nanny. The photos don't prove what is going on here."

"I know, but I'd like to see them."

After hanging up, Sammie regretted confiding in her friend. She appreciated that Lucy had her best interest at heart, but Sammie found it more interesting that Lucy was now abandoning the wisdom she had dispensed in the past. Sammie wanted to be fair to her husband for the sake of her son. Lucy couldn't possibly understand these emotions or the effect of a new mother's volatile hormones. If Sammie's legal training had taught her anything it was to focus on the facts. And these were the facts.

First, Sammie knew her best friend. If the photos clearly identified Dougie with a woman, Lucy wouldn't mince words. She would have described them as indisputable, instead of telling her to think about what she saw.

Second, Dougie's letter said he would be in Charlotte and then Georgetown. She had not seen his car. The person in bed with a woman could have been the owner of Range Rover. It could have been a co-worker who rode with him to Charlotte.

Third, the only fact she knew about Cathleen McKinney was that her notes crossed a professional line. Assuming Dougie was telling the truth about his innocence and her pursuit of him, but for her father, he never would have been put in that situation. She should have refused her father's offer of assistance with Worth Pharmaceutical.

Next was Heather Yardley. Norma had admitted that she knew Heather. Though Norma said she didn't recommend her, Sammie questioned if that was true. During her sleepless nights, Sammie had dissected every conversation with her mother-in-law. She recalled Norma's comment after they announced her pregnancy. She had wasted no time sharing her opinion: "I hope you appreciate how fortunate you are to be able to stay at home. Most mothers aren't afforded that luxury." After Sammie communicated her intent to return to work, Norma told her in no uncertain terms to think about someone other than herself—that Dougie was more than capable of providing for his family.

Sammie never told Dougie about that conversation. She didn't want to drive a deeper wedge between them. She hadn't given Dougie a chance to explain his mother's denial. It was possible that Norma didn't want Sammie to know that she was involved in the nanny search based on her objections to Sammie's returning to work.

Finally, Camilla Girard. The explanations about the withdrawals from her account were from Camilla's side. Parks Callaway couldn't verify that Dougie was with Camilla at the Kiawah Beach Club. The more Sammie thought about Camilla's tale, it couldn't be true. If they had a relationship in the past, it had been over. There is no way Dougie could have been seeing them at the same time. She and Dougie had spent every summer together. Scorned lovers could do crazy things. She owed it to her son to hear Dougie out before believing a stranger.

The alternative scenario kept Sammie awake the entire night—that Dougie had cheated and with numerous women. The next morning, another text from Dougie caught her in a senseless state. She hadn't slept a wink.

Good morning! Just wanted to say that I love you and miss you and Mack terribly. Give him a hug for me.

She should have waited, at a minimum, until she had her senses. But, she couldn't help herself, especially after his mention of Mack. In her foggy state of mind, she forgot her legal training to never show your hand.

My trip to New York was canceled. Guess you had a change of plans too. I came by the house to get some things. I saw everything.

Everything? What is that supposed to mean? I was out of town the same time you were.

Now, Sammie didn't know how to respond. She saw that Dougie was typing some more. She waited.

I let one of the sales guys stay at the house. We went together to Charlotte. He had other calls in the area after I left for Georgetown. Didn't think about checking with you first. Call him.

Send the number, she typed, before erasing it. She knew she wouldn't call. It wouldn't prove anything. But, if he was seeing Camilla, wouldn't he have gone to her house in Kiawah? His Georgetown visit didn't make sense, unless he was telling the truth.

Never mind. Obviously, you're crazy. You're looking for reasons to make up shit about me. If you want a divorce, why don't you just say so? I can't be in a marriage where I can't be trusted!!

Tears instantly flowed down her cheeks. Was she going crazy? She heard Mack crying but she couldn't move. Her whole body was trembling.

Glenny appeared in her doorway cradling Mack.

"Can you feed him, Mom? I don't feel so hot. I didn't sleep at all last night."

"Of course. And you do look terrible. What can I get you?"

"Nothing. I'm going to try and get some sleep."

Sammie noticed that her mother's eyes honed in on the phone in her hand.

"Get some rest," she said, closing Sammie's door.

Sammie put a pillow over her head to muffle her sobs. She felt completely inept as a mother, a wife, and a daughter. She had never felt so alone. She had never been more confused.

When her door opened, she pretended to be asleep. She didn't move when she felt her father's hand on her forehead. Her mother's doting throughout the day did nothing but make her feel worse. She should be taking care of her son instead of curled up in a ball under the covers. She drifted off at some point only to be awakened by a text notification.

I retained an attorney today. He said that you abandoned me and kidnapped our son. Things aren't looking so good for perfect Samantha Spencer. You are going to pay for this so get ready.

Glenny found Sammie with her head laying on the toilet seat.

"I'm taking you to the doctor," Glenny said, wiping Sammie's face with a cold washcloth.

"I actually feel much better."

"Good. I made some soup. I'll go fix you a tray."

"Thanks, but I've been in bed all day. I need a hot shower first, then some soup."

The truth was Sammie didn't feel better. And, the shower made things worse. The steady stream of hot water felt like daggers in her chest. She collapsed on the shower floor and wept.

To keep her mother at bay, Sammie pulled it together, that is, in front of her. But Dougie's late night texts extended her sleepless nights.

Did the law firm kick you out or could you not cut it? I used to think you were like Cort, but you are Glenny to a tee—a pathetic dishrag and doormat.

I forbid you from stepping foot into the house or driving through the neighborhood. My attorney is getting ready to file a No Contact Order against you, so you have been warned.

Your smug father never thought I was good enough for you. Well, guess what, your entire Spencer line is not good enough for me! I will get full custody of Mack, just watch.

The rants often began at midnight and would continue for several hours. While one side of her brain told her to block him, the other wouldn't allow it. She justified her inaction as a need to be prepared. His latest tirades intimated that her family would be served with a lawsuit soon.

My lawsuit is coming, and it's going to be good. It will show your treasured Charleston society the true story of the self-righteous Spencer family.

Dougie's texts had called her and her father every name in the book from spoiled, arrogant, and elitist to master manipulators. Though these were hurtful enough, his latest allegations scared her.

Remember this photo and text? You will be seeing it again…soon.

The photo was of the mortar and pestle Sammie had purchased for a pesto recipe that she had made for Lucy. Before Mack was born and Dougie was out of town, Sammie would sample new dishes and get Lucy's feedback. Lucy never cooked so she enjoyed being Sammie's taste-tester. Sammie had read that the old-school bowl and grinder was the best way to make pesto and faster than a knife to crush basil, pine nuts, and garlic into a creamy paste.

Sammie had taken a photo and texted it to Dougie with a message: *Tried this new kitchen tool tonight with Lucy. Amazing results.*

He had omitted the second photo—the one showing the final product with her new kitchen tool—the pesto sauce.

I will expose your stealing my Worth samples and using your "kitchen tool" to turn the pills into powder for you and your hick friend to snort. I have witnesses who will testify.

Now, she understood the scene from one of the photos Lucy took from their kitchen counter the night they found the clothes by the hot tub. She frantically searched through her phone to find both her original photos, but she had deleted them.

Sammie knew Dougie's allegations were false. But, she also knew he would find some lawyer who would believe the appalling lies spewed in his text messages and enjoy the publicity of a salacious lawsuit. It was more than her reputation at stake—it was her parents and possibly even Lucy's. She hadn't slept in weeks. She had no energy. She could barely endure a one-mile walk with Mack in the stroller before needing to rest. And her resting spot, the Waterfront Park, provided the privacy she needed to shed her tears. She would bypass the famous Pineapple Fountain and head straight to the pier to one of the large, wooden swings. She'd remove Mack from the stroller, hold him tightly in her lap, and have her private meltdowns while watching the cruise and container ships enter the Charleston Harbor. The waters surrounding her homeplace had always brought her such peace. But not now. She felt as if she were drowning. She wanted to drown.

Glenny tried to coax Sammie to go jogging. Glenny's abrupt change in her attitude showed just how worried she was about Sammie. Previously, she had agonized about the toll her daughter's consistent running routine took on her body. Her daughter was a pleaser in all aspects except for her exercise regimen. Sammie ignored her mother's chastisement, advocating that it was the one activity that she did for herself and on her own schedule. Her runs in the rain, the dark, and wee hours of the morning were important to clear her mind and invigorate her spirit. But, Glenny hadn't seen her run since her separation. She assumed that her daughter's previous six-mile runs had been replaced with six-mile walks since she would be gone for a couple of hours. Glenny didn't know about Sammie's detour to the swings at Waterfront Park and that her time away had primarily been occupied by swinging and staring out into the Cooper River while crying her own river.

As Glenny grew more concerned over her daughter's well-being, she noticed that Sammie's return from her walks coincided with the delivery of the mail. Sammie would sit on the wrought iron bench by the mailbox until the US Postal Service arrived. Then, she would put Mack down for a nap before retreating to her room and shutting the door. Her sleep patterns were erratic. Her spark, energy, and zest for life had vanished.

To distract from her own escalating distress, Glenny started organizing the attic—a chore she had put off for years. She had forgotten all about the box containing her old sketches. As she studied the designs, her examination evoked an unexpected nostalgic reaction. She flashed back to Sammie's naptime and mornings at preschool when she secretly penned her ideas. In later years, she worked on them when her husband was away on business trips, or Sammie was in class, soccer practice, or sailing. During those lonely times, Glenny would pull out her sketch pad and escape into her creative world. She wiped a tear from her face wondering why she had hidden her aspiration from her family. *Was it guilt? Was it embarrassment? Was she filling a void of some kind?*

Glenny suddenly realized that her daughter needed another outlet. She had been wrong to make her daughter feel that motherhood was the only job she needed to give her fulfillment. Sammie needed a job. She needed something that provided her an identity other than being Mack's mother. And, she definitely needed a schedule to get her back on track. She scoured job openings and called several of her favorite boutiques. Sammie certainly had an eye for fashion. Her daughter might enjoy the interaction with customers. The question was how to broach the subject.

Glenny decided that the direct approach would be best. Their family had spent more than enough time skirting issues. When Sammie returned from her walk, she was going to sit her daughter down and have a heart-to-heart.

"How far did you go today?" Glenny asked, when Sammie returned.

"The usual," Sammie said, avoiding eye contact with her mother. "We're both worn out and ready for naps."

Sammie's statement reinforced Glenny's resolve. Napping during the day was something Sammie had never done, but it had become a routine these days.

"I was hoping we could have some porch time. We haven't done that in so long. I'll fix us some mint tea while you get Mack down."

Sammie picked up on her mother's efforts to fill her time with activity. In the last several weeks alone, she proposed that they start a 10,000-piece puzzle, paint her bedroom, and take an online cooking class. The most outrageous offer was signing them up for tennis lessons. Her mother had many talents, but athleticism was not one of them.

Sammie relented to porch time. If the past was any indicator of what she could expect, they would rock silently unless Sammie had something on her mind. Her mom usually let Sammie direct the course of any serious discussion or request for advice. But not this day, times had changed.

"I know this is a strange suggestion from me, but I think you need a job," Glenny blurted the minute they sat down.

Sammie started laughing. It felt good to laugh. And, the look on her mother's face was priceless, which made Sammie laugh harder.

"What's so funny?" Glenny asked, painfully.

"I'm sorry, Mom. But that comment is so unlike you. I don't know how I thought of this, but do you remember the book that I made you read to me every night?"

"*Goodnight Moon*?"

"Nope."

"*Go Dog, Go*?"

"Nope, I'll give you a hint—the one about the baby bird hatching while his mother was away looking for food."

"Yes. How could I forget that one? I'm surprised I can't recite it word for word. The bird started searching for his mother. He came upon a dog, a cow, a boat and then that bulldozer...what did the bird call it? Wait...don't tell me. He called it a "snort" because of the sound it made. And then the snort deposited the bird back into the tree right when the mother bird came back with a worm. What on earth made you think of that book?"

"Because of what the baby bird kept yelling. Don't you remember that?"

"Oh, yes, the name of the book was *Are You My Mother?* I get it now. Cute, Sammie. But, I am your mother despite my suggestion that you get a job. Darling, you have to admit that you are not yourself."

Sammie started to tell her mother about Dougie's abusive threats. But, what good would that do? If Dougie was going to drag her and her parents through a meritless lawsuit, she would deal with it then. She had burdened her parents enough with her situation.

"I just need a little more time," Sammie said.

"Time for what? To wallow in your misery? Just hear me out. While you were on one of your walks with Mack, I found a box with some of my sketches. I mean old designs that I had done from the time you were born throughout high school. Your father doesn't even know about them. I don't know why I never showed them to him other than I was embarrassed. I never thought I could make it as a designer. I didn't have a role model encouraging me to pursue my dream. I've told you about my difficult pregnancies and how elated we were to have you. Perhaps, I felt guilty after that for even thinking that I could be a mother and a designer. It was one or the other in my mind. But, you, my headstrong, determined child showed me that you can do both. Granted, things didn't turn out the way you envisioned with a law practice, but that was not because of you."

"Are you suggesting that I go back to the firm?"

"I am not going to tell you what you should do other than you need to do something—anything. But, perhaps right now, you can try something new. Some boutiques on King Street are hiring. You are a natural at fashion so maybe you need some retail therapy. You could work part-time."

"Mom, though I appreciate your motives, that doesn't interest me."

"If that's not challenging enough, perhaps you could teach a course at Pinckney Hall. You could help coach the regatta team as well," Glenny offered.

"It has nothing to do with being challenged. I'm sure retail presents a lot of challenges. I just don't think I could bear a job where I am cooped up inside all day. At least not right now. The walls would start closing in."

"I just don't want you to have the regrets that I do."

Her mother's comment hit home in more ways than one. It was the first time that Glenny had indicated any remorse in not pursuing her dream of fashion design. Sammie's problem was being a lawyer had been her dream, and she had chased it. She couldn't continue to hide under the covers, close off the world, and wait for the axe to fall, but for the first time in her life, she had no motivation to do anything.

You and I are about to have a come to Jesus moment...

Chapter Twenty-Eight

Cort & Sammie

Cort had rarely seen his daughter since she separated from Dougie Morgan. He was always up before the sun, and Sammie would be in bed. When he got home after the sun had gone down, she had already gone back to bed.

Immediately, after he walked through the door after a long day, Glenny would tearfully update him about their daughter's activities, or lack thereof. He tried to soothe Glenny's growing angst.

"She will eventually snap out of it," he reassured Glenny, reminded of his grandmother's words.

And, he believed it because Sammie was, after all, just like him, and he had snapped out of it.

The trysts between Sam Spencer, III, and his secretary, Joyce Callaway, were exposed to Cort at the end of his last summer clerkship at the firm. They had burst more than Cort's bubble of his father's status, respect, and honor. He knew he could never step foot into the law firm that was his supposed legacy. Cort questioned his strength, manliness, and pride when he would break down and silently cry for the Spencer state of affairs. After his father died and Joyce Callaway disclosed the existence of his half-brother, Cort worried about the effect on his fragile mother if she ever learned who fathered Parks Callaway. He vowed to protect his mother from the truth. So, he left New York and returned to Charleston. He buried the secret when he buried his father, Samuel Parker Spencer, III.

Sammie's melancholy was resurrecting more than Cort's recollections of his prior struggles. They were restoring memories. And, for the first time, they were giving him clarity.

Growing up, Cort's mother's mood was erratic. He never knew which mother would rise with the morning sun. There was the lively one whose cheery, sapphire-blue eyes sparkled as she sang "You Are My Sunshine" while flipping pancakes for his breakfast. Then, there was the somber one whose dull, gray eyes were vacant and cavernous. That version of his mother would robotically place a cereal bowl and spoon by him before returning to bed. On those grim days, his grandmother would pick him up from school and fix supper. When the grim days outnumbered the cheery ones, he overheard his grandmother complain about him numerous times. *Cort's wearing me slap out. Cort could wear the horns off a billy goat. The Lord knew what he was doing when he gave children to young'ns.*

His grandmother's chastisement of his mother made him feel bad. He preferred his mother over his substitute one. And, he picked up on his grandmother's resentment. But, he empathized with her. And, for the first time in his life, he understood the cause of his mother's troubles. She had known about Joyce Callaway all along. He vividly recalled his grandmother's reprimands to his mother. *You have the same shoes to get glad in that you got sad in. You're about as useful as a steering wheel on a mule. I didn't ask for an invitation to your pity party.*

But, as each day passed with no snapback from Sammie, Cort grew concerned that Sammie may be more like his mother than himself. And, paradoxically, his wife was stepping into the shoes of his grandmother. Though she would never complain like his grandmother, Glenny's exhaustion at the end of the day was apparent. He knew that Sammie's plight was the culprit. Glenny had discouraged Sammie from hiring a nanny. She was perfectly capable of taking care of her grandson. There would have been nothing to bring her more pleasure. But that joy was turned upside down when worry took precedence—just like his grandmother.

Cort found himself in a place that he had never been during his entire marriage. He absolutely dreaded walking through the door each evening. Sammie's despair was casting a menacing cloud over the entire family.

Cort decided he was taking things into his own hands. The long walks that Glenny reported Sammie was taking with Mack weren't doing the trick. In fact, he surmised they were doing quite the opposite. The time out of the house under Glenny's watchful eye provided Sammie with time to mull over her shattering circumstances. He was going to demand that she get out of bed and join him for his early morning runs. He was convinced her lack of exercise attributed to her doldrums. She needed endorphins, the body's natural pain killers, to diffuse her stress. She needed to feel her heart pumping, not from ache but stimulation.

Cort knew that Sammie faked being asleep when he knocked on her door to extend his invitations. His knowledge wasn't from the fact that her phone was always cradled in her hand but that her lit phone screen evidenced recent activity. He left her notes each morning that he had hoped she could join him on his morning run. "Maybe tomorrow," he concluded every note.

Each morning after Sammie read the notes, she cried. She was ashamed of the worry she was causing both her parents. And, her dad's invitation to join him on his morning run was the first in her lifetime.

For as long as Sammie could remember, the early mornings belonged only to Cort—before he had to answer phone calls and emails, attend meetings, or analyze performance charts and business plans. After bank time, there was family time. Like every minute in every day, he used his time wisely. Sammie appreciated that her disciplined routines and fastidious nature has been passed to her from her father.

But the *Maybe tomorrow* ending in her father's notes had become replaced with *Snap out of it! You have the same shoes to get glad in that you got sad in.* The kicker was Glenny's insistence that Sammie get a job. Sammie awoke every day to a potential opportunity that her mother had located. This morning's was a docent at the Gibbs Museum of Art.

"You love art and history. This would be perfect."

Her parents' words were starting to take hold. She couldn't continue to be confined to her bed and tormented from the texts that Dougie continued to send throughout the night. She couldn't continue to wake up to *Maybe tomorrow*. It was time.

"I appreciate all your ideas, Mom. The one about teaching a course at Pinckney Hall and helping with the regatta team got me thinking."

"Oh, good. What's that?"

"Maybe my old boss at the marina would know of something. Right now, I need to be near the water."

"What a great idea," Glenny said. And she meant it.

PART THREE

This, too, shall pass...

Chapter Twenty-Nine

Sammie

Mr. Barry, the longstanding dockmaster at the Charleston Ashley Dockage, was elated to hear from Sammie. When Sammie requested to meet with him, he didn't ask why. His tone didn't even reveal any curiosity—just excitement. He asked Sammie to come see him as soon as possible.

As Sammie walked down the long ramp to the dock house, the smell of fish and saltwater descended upon her like a heavy fog. The harborage scene immediately soothed her anxiety. She loved everything about a marina.

The names of the yachts and sailboats had always intrigued her. Some identified the occupations of the boat owners—*Pair a Docs*, *Verdict*, and *Banker's Hours*; some, the owners' hobbies—*Game Day*, *Checkered Flag*, and *Reeled In*. Still others reflected a humorous spin on life misfortunes—*Ship Happens*, *Alimony III*, or one of Sammie's favorites, *Free At Mast*. Then, some were simply named after the owners—*Greg's Getaway*, *Cabot's Fever*, and *Peg's Paradise*. Sammie could walk the docks for hours studying the names stenciled on the vessels' sterns.

As she approached the dock house, Mr. Barry was helping a boat washer hook up hoses to the utility pedestal. She had seen Mr. Barry do a lot of things. He wore many hats, but she had never seen him help a boat washer. In the past, he frowned upon the boat washing companies that "cluttered his dock," but as she got closer, she understood his change of heart. The boat washer was cute, young, and was wearing a skimpy bikini. Sammie laughed to herself and instantly felt at ease. When he finally tore his attention away from the boat washer, Mr. Barry saw Sammie.

"Sammie, it is so good to see you," he said, giving her a huge bear hug. "Married life must be treating you well."

"I am not just married, I have a baby," Sammie said.

"Well, something else that isn't fair. You spit out a baby and still have the figure of a teenager."

"Thanks. My son is the reason why I called," Sammie said.

"Well, isn't he a little too young to be a dockhand?"

"Yes, he is," she laughed. "But you know how time flies, so I'm sure before too long, he'll be hanging out at the docks like his mother."

"Yep, lots for a young boy to look at," Mr. Barry said, squinting in the direction of the boat washer.

"No doubt. I remember when boat washers irritated you. Times have changed."

"Sammie, I've gotten smarter in my old age," he said, winking.

He moved away from the boat washer, and Sammie followed him to the dock house.

"I don't know if you remember that I'm a lawyer," Sammie said.

"I did. I don't forget much especially when it comes to a pretty face. I always said that it wasn't quite fair that you got blessed with brains and good looks, not to mention that you're one helluva skipper."

"Oh, Mr. Barry, other than your attitude towards boat washers, you haven't changed a bit. What I wanted to discuss with you is that after I returned to work from my maternity leave, I had a nanny that didn't work out. Mack's father is in sales and travels a lot. Practicing law is too stressful right now. My summers working here are some of my fondest memories. If you have anything I could help with, I'd love to work with you again."

"I always thought you were an angel, but now it's confirmed," Mr. Barry said. 'When I got your message yesterday, I couldn't believe it. It dawned on me that you may be able to steer me in the right direction. But even better if you want to help me with this. I've been scratching my head for about a week 'bout a request from a potential long-term slip rental. It's for a large yacht, and you know the bigger the boat, the bigger the slip fee. But there are, let's say, strings attached."

They walked into the dock house, and Mr. Barry fumbled through papers on his desk.

"Here it is. It's jibberish to me. It's a list of business office requirements sent to us by a public relations firm in Atlanta. I can get the lease for some hotshot's yacht if I can supply a business office complete with certain equipment and someone who knows how to use the stuff."

Mr. Barry handed Sammie a letter with an engraved heading: The Davis Group. "Reliable Results", the firm's trademarked slogan, was elegantly placed along the bottom. The requirements were just standard: 35 ppm, 1200 x 1200 dpi color laser printer, 20 ppm scanner with PDF conversion capability, fax machine, Mac Pro with OSX Server (preferred) with secure internet access, proficiency in the Microsoft Office programs—Word, PowerPoint, Excel, and Outlook.

"This is actually pretty basic stuff," Sammie said.

"We'll nail this sucker with a business office and someone who can speak this language. That should seal the deal. So, what do you think about running my business office?" Mr. Barry asked.

Sammie didn't give a second thought to surrendering her Juris Doctorate degree, at least temporarily, for another kind of JD—Just Dockhand at the marina.

"Where are you going to put the equipment?" Sammie asked.

"We've actually added space for a lounge," Mr. Barry said, pointing to a room off the back of the dock house. "It can be used as a business office too. An amenity my competition doesn't have, not to mention a perty esquire."

"Can I take this list with me?"

"Yeah, take it," Mr. Barry said. "You think I can rent this equipment?"

"Yes. I'll prepare a budget with some options."

"When word gets out that a PR expert is docked here to work on some scandal, I won't need a lounge to get renters. No tellin' the free publicity we'll get from this. This is divine intervention. I tell ya, you are an angel."

"I'll research things and give you an update tomorrow," Sammie said.

Spencer, Pettigrew & Hamilton seemed in the distant past. She found it astounding how the one place that used to monopolize every waking hour of her life and dictate the direction of every day could be so quickly forgotten. A lesson in itself. Sammie was proficient in everything on The Davis Group's list, but at the firm, she had access to full-time technical support if there were ever any glitches. And with technology systems, things seemed go awry at the worst time. Though she had forgotten the name of the firm's head of technology, she remembered that he was responsive and excellent.

Sammie left Lucy a message on her cell.

Hey. I have some exciting news. So, call me back when you're free, and I'll tell you about it. Also, I need the name of the firm's IT expert. My brain has turned to mush. I can't remember anything.

When Lucy returned Sammie's call, she offered to talk to Kevin Miller, the firm's technology guru. Sammie was thrilled when Lucy reported that Kevin moonlighted on the side and would be happy to help her. Lucy said he'd prefer if she called his cell number and use his personal email. Lucy provided both.

Sammie emailed Kevin the letter.

"Call me after you have reviewed the attached letter, and I'll explain. I know you hate hearing this, but it's fairly urgent," Sammie wrote.

Kevin immediately responded.

"How about 1:00 tomorrow at CCCs? I can meet you on my lunch break."

Sammie appreciated his quick response. Since she was no longer a Spencer attorney, Kevin wasn't at her beck and call. Sammie, however, would have preferred meeting Kevin anywhere other than CCCs, the restaurant across the street from her old employer. She no longer enjoyed the priority seating offered to Spencer attorneys. She arrived early hoping to snag a table in a quiet corner. Kevin was characteristically prompt. He arrived at 1:00 on the dot.

"Hey Sammie, it's good to see you. Everyone misses you."

"You are too kind. You know that things go on there without skipping a beat. I was just a fungible unit, easily replaced and soon forgotten. Surprisingly, I don't miss the firm at all."

As soon as she said it, she realized it didn't come out right.

"I meant I don't miss the late hours, the lack of control in my schedule, and honestly, all the games—having to jump because someone had the authority to make me jump."

"I hear ya, girl."

"Of course, you understand. The partners are the only ones who seem to have forgotten what it feels like to be treated like a pawn. And I'd appreciate if you keep this conversation between you and me—I mean I've told Lucy. Anyway, I have a new job."

"At The Davis Group?"

"No. but at the Charleston Ashley Dockage. I used to work summers there helping with the sailing program. And the best thing is "Bill Blauers isn't there.""

For certain, Sammie hadn't missed billable hours. Like most law firms, the value of the attorney to the enterprise was the number of billable hours spent on client matters. Billable hours were measured in six-minute increments. The six-minute increment time requirement was so affixed in your brain that it would spill over into everyday tasks.

After errand runs, Sammie would notice from her Garmin watch that she had spent .8 hours at the grocery store, .5 hours at the drug store, and another .4 hours driving home. This time keeping habit even crept into her attempted retreats from the rat race. She finished the running route in 1.1 hours. Her pedicure took .9 hours. Sammie was looking forward to an off-the-clock lunch with Kevin.

"I always did wonder how Bill Blauers kept up with both you and Lucy," Kevin said. "But what does the Charleston Ashley Dockage have to do with The Davis Group?"

"OK, Kevin. This really has to be confidential. What I'm going to tell you really is on the QT. It's classified information."

"Yes, I still work at the same place you did."

"I know, but since it's not law firm stuff, I just had to make sure. You know I trust you. Anyway, I went to meet with my old boss to inquire about any jobs. He was interested in establishing a business office to secure the slip rental from The Davis Group. The company is some elite PR firm in Atlanta that specializes in crisis management, and in particular, high-profile dignitaries that slip. The rumor is that there is some scandal getting ready to break, thus the reason the PR firm's yacht is coming to town. Given the size of the boat and the scheduled length of dockage, it would be a hefty slip fee. So, you're looking at the Charleston Ashley Dockage's new Business Manager. I was hoping you could help him set everything up or provide me a referral for someone who could."

"I recall that everything is pretty standard. Does he want to purchase or lease the equipment?"

"Lease—so he can see if this concept will work after all of this blows over."

"I can work on a proposal tonight," Kevin said. "By the way, the firm is cool with me helping folks on the side, as long as they aren't adverse to a firm client. I've never heard of The Davis Group but will make sure no one is handling anything against them."

"The company wasn't a client when I was there. But, a lot can change in ten months. If there are no conflicts, how soon could you install everything?"

"You know these vendors are always marketing to the firm, so I have good contacts with several of them. I should be able get it all going within a couple of days."

Sammie noticed Kevin glancing at his watch. She hoped it was law firm habit and not his lunch companion. For once, she didn't have to hurry back to the office and gear up for the afternoon grind. But, he did.

Church potlucks teach you not to put more on your plate than you can eat …

Chapter Thirty

Harold Barry

Harry Barry thought he must be doing something right. The list sent by The Davis Group was foreign to him. Then Sammie showed up and not only could interpret it but also said it was "basic stuff."

Wi-Fi had been the extent of Harry's entry into the fast-paced technology world. His opinion was that a marina should be a place of escape, to spend time outdoors, and reconnect with nature. But, he had relented due to the constant complaints from his retired slip renters. What he really found crazy was that they needed WI-FI to access *Facebook*, *Instagram*, and other silliness on their phones and computers. He hadn't considered that additional technology would attract slip renters that needed to do business. But now with high-speed Wi-Fi, and a business office complete with a computer, a scanner, and a printer, his marina would be the hottest ticket on the Ashley. This business office stuff got him thinking about other ways to distinguish his marina. He couldn't wait to share his new idea with Sammie.

When Sammie arrived and shared the conversation with her geek friend, Harry thought that he was on a roll. This was all working out nicely.

"You got me thinking, Sammie," Harry said. "What do you think about another amenity? Fetchin' stuff our renters need, from groceries, seafood, alcohol, to boat bumpers. We could deliver it all right to their boat. What do ya think?"

"That's a great idea," Sammie said, without hesitation.

Although excited about the upgrades to his marina, Harold Barry worried about the rental costs of the hi-tech stuff and how to pay Sammie. He pushed his uneasiness aside. Now, the most important concern was landing the PR big-wig from Atlanta.

Don't let your eyes be bigger than your stomach...

Chapter Thirty-One

Lucy

Lucy spent the rest of the afternoon reading depositions from Randy's past cases. They were as entertaining as they were masterful. The subject matter was definitely more interesting than wading through corporate bylaws, and probably juicier than any romance fiction novel because these were real facts from real cases. Lucy was beginning to understand the art of deposition questions. Randy kept his questions short, simple, and pointed.

As the day of the deposition approached, Randy reviewed Lucy's questions and complimented her outline. Randy counseled to use her prepared questions only as a checklist to ensure that all topics were covered.

"If Tiffany veers off course, don't interrupt," Randy advised. "Everyone quickly forgets their lawyer's instructions to only 'answer the question that is asked.' She'll get off track, they all do. And, that's when the shitola gets real."

Lucy knew it sounded easier than it would be in reality. Randy had even referred to Carolyn Waters, Tiffany's attorney, as an "aggressive piranha." Unlike Lucy, Ms. Waters was an expert in divorce cases. She likely had been practicing with Ms. Putnam for hours before the deposition.

Lucy changed outfits three times the morning of Tiffany Putnam's deposition. She didn't want to appear too young for fear Carolyn waters would eat her alive. She didn't want to appear too stodgy because she wanted Tiffany to feel comfortable as if talking to an old friend.

Once she met Tiffany Putman, Lucy felt a little more at ease. She had pictured a worldly and sophisticated woman, like Daisy Hamilton. Tiffany, however, belonged to the coarser side of the nouveau riche and was much younger than Lucy had imagined. *A pig with lipstick*, Lucy thought. Lucy's knowledge of fashion designers was limited, but she did recognize the Louis Vuitton logo on her huge handbag. That accessory alone significantly exceeded Lucy's entire annual clothing budget.

The "ED" lawyers, what the equitable distribution lawyers called themselves, consisted of a small circle. They knew each other well. With Carolyn Waters' knowledge that Lucy was new at this, she was circling her fresh bait. Lucy could smell blood in Waters' mouth. Randy sat in the corner as if he was getting ready to watch a matinee. All he needed was a large tub of popcorn. No doubt, Randy preferred his with loads of fake, liquid butter.

Suddenly, Lucy was apprehensive. This was a foreign atmosphere from a corporate boardroom. The court reporter retrieved items from her large bag—a Bible, a tape recorder, and a stenomask. Lucy had recently learned that a stenomask was a large mouthpiece with a built-in microphone. It permitted the court reporter to record all the attorney's questions and the deponent's answers without being heard by the participants.

After Tiffany placed her hand on the Bible and swore "to tell the truth, the whole truth and nothing but the truth," the reporter affixed her stenomask and motioned for Lucy to begin.

"Ms. Putnam, my name is Lucy Tate," she said, mustering all the confidence she could. "I am the attorney that will be taking your deposition today. Have you ever been deposed before, Ms. Putnam?"

"No," Tiffany responded, curtly.

Randy's tutorial about the art of taking a deposition jumped in Lucy's brain. Obviously, Carolyn Waters had instructed her client to only answer the question without any commentary.

"Although your attorney has instructed you on the procedure, let's go over some guidelines," Lucy said, attempting to forget about Carolyn Waters' measuring her up. "The court reporter will be recording your responses, so you need to answer with verbal answers and not a nod of your head."

Tiffany nodded. She glanced at Carolyn Waters embarrassed that she so quickly failed to follow instructions.

"Yes, I understand."

Lucy decided to disarm Tiffany and let her know they were both new at this type of inquisition. After all, Carolyn Waters already knew as much.

"This is my first deposition too," Lucy said. "I'm a little nervous, so we'll just muddle through this together."

Lucy went through the list of questions obtaining the obligatory background information, Tiffany's birthday, educational background, work background, how she met Mr. Putnam, and when they began an intimate relation.

A temporary placement service assigned Tiffany to Mr. Putnam's insurance agency after her separation from her first husband. Her first husband didn't have the assets of Mr. Putnam, so the distribution fight in that case was allocating debt not assets. Poor thing had to find a job and work for a short stint before she landed Mr. Putnam.

"What did your job duties entail at Putnam Insurance?" Lucy asked.

"I was James' scheduler. His previous one had quit. He needed someone immediately. I am good at scheduling and organizing things, so the temp agency thought that I would be a good fit. The agency said that there was a good chance that I would be hired permanently, and I was. James was very busy and keeping up with his appointments was a full-time job. I did a great job and..."

"Tiffany, just answer the question that is asked," Carolyn Waters interrupted Tiffany. "We don't want to waste Ms. Tate's time."

Tiffany had gotten off track as Randy forecasted. Lucy was surprised that the meandering began so early in the process.

"That's alright. I don't mind. When you began your job with Mr. Putnam, was he married?

"Well, he didn't wear a wedding band. He never mentioned his wife, and his office didn't have any pictures of a wife. And, he flirted with me like crazy!" Tiffany said, perkily.

"What did Mr. Putnam do that made you think he was flirting with you?"

"At first, he was just very complimentary of the job I was doing. He said that I was the most organized scheduler that he ever had. I thought he was just being nice, but then I noticed him checking me out from top to bottom. Then, he started turning up the heat. He said things like I made good coffee, I brightened up the office, I had a sexy voice answering the phone..."

Lucy could see Carolyn Waters kicking Tiffany under the table. And it worked. Tiffany abruptly stopped talking.

"Did Mr. Putnam initiate physical contact with you?"

"Uh. Duh. Yes. Lots of times," Tiffany said, grinning from ear-to-ear.

"Do you recall when the physical contact started?" Lucy asked.

"Yes, I remember it very well. It was in Columbia. James had meetings with several executives. He said he needed me to keep him on schedule. He asked me to book us both a room and find a good place for dinner. After dinner and a bottle of wine that night, he propositioned me."

"How did he proposition you?"

"Well, he asked if I wanted to get a nightcap. He said that his room had a mini-bar. I don't know why I went to his room. I guess because he was my boss, and I needed that job. He made me a rum and Coke. I'm pretty sure it was mostly rum. I'm not a big drinker, and the wine at dinner had already gone to my head. My memory of all the details is a little blurry, but I remember that he was aggressive. He started kissing me, and I was scared to stop him. And so, well, that night was our first time."

Tiffany testified that after that trip, she continued to book hotel rooms, at James' request. She was, after all, afraid of losing her job.

"When did you learn that Mr. Putnam was married?"

"I can't remember the exact date but do remember that I was very upset and almost quit. I remember I cried all night. He sent me flowers the next day. He asked me to schedule a night for us to talk. He poured his heart out to me. He said that his marriage had been over for years, and I made him feel alive and loved."

Lucy felt like she was listening to a broken record. This was Frank Hamilton's story being told by Tiffany Putnam instead of Barbie Benfield. By now, Tiffany was on a roll oblivious to her attorney's attempts to hush her up.

"He said that he was going to leave her," Tiffany said, ignoring the kicks from her attorney. "The only thing she loved was his money and her dog, a Bichon named Herend, after her favorite fine china. Herend went everywhere with her. He sat on her lap when she drove her Jag. He slept with her. She even had a baby carriage for that dog. James said that Herend took over his role a long time ago."

Lucy went on to establish that the trysts continued even after Tiffany learned of James' marital status. It all blew up when Tiffany was finally invited into his 11,000 square foot, seven-bedroom house, and Mrs. Putnam returned early from a shopping spree in New York. Tiffany provided a very detailed summary, all while ignoring Carolyn Water's kicks under the table. According to Tiffany, upon their discovery, Yvonne Putnam yelled, "You've never seen the number of zeroes that will be at the end of this check." She stormed out, and James left the next day. He and Tiffany were married a year later.

Carolyn had lost control of her client.

"This is a good place to take a break," Carolyn Waters offered. "Can you direct me to a restroom? Tiffany, come with me."

"You are doing a very good job, Lucy," Randy said after Tiffany and her lawyer left the room. "You're a natural. After today, you won't be able to play that 'I don't know what I'm doin' card,' but I liked it. Tiffany felt like she should help you out. You need to move on to her spending habits. The way you got her talking, we'll never get out of here."

When Carolyn Waters returned with Tiffany, Tiffany looked like a reprimanded child. Up until the break, Tiffany was quite pleased with her performance. Lucy wondered if Carolyn had simply scolded her for the excess information or strongly counseled her client about lying under oath.

According to James' accounts, Tiffany had pursued him from the moment she walked through the Putnam Insurance doors. Also, according to James, Tiffany met his wife her first day on the job when Yvonne dropped Herend off after his grooming at the nearby doggie salon. James' version was that Tiffany offered to dog sit for his wife. Also, Tiffany was known to suddenly appear at the hotels she had booked for James. Whatever really happened, she became Mrs. Putnam #2 and was trying to get her freshly manicured fingers on half of his $400 million net worth—the net worth remaining after paying Mrs. Putnam #1.

After the break, Lucy delved into her expenses—those needed to continue her lifestyle. She had a housekeeper, lawn care service, which didn't include "Justin." Justin changed her arrangements of fresh flowers weekly. Then there was her laundress, cook, grocery shopper, pool cleaning service, and personal wardrobe shopper. Tiffany now had dogs of her own, Coco and Chanel. Coco and Chanel were

Terriers with long hair and loved "having their hair done," requiring the addition of a dog groomer to the staff.

In addition to Tiffany's staff, Lucy established her weekly schedule. She was quite busy. She had tennis at the club on Mondays, Wednesdays, and Fridays (that is if she wasn't leaving for one of their two beach houses). Manicures, pedicures, and facials filled her Tuesdays. Bridge was on Thursdays, garden club, and book club were monthly "commitments." The most stressful part of her schedule, it seemed, was tormenting over which O.P.I. polish to select each week. The right choice between 'Come to Poppy', 'You're a Pisa Work', or 'Cha-Ching Cherry' could make or break her life.

When they finally finished, Lucy wondered where she could sign up for Tiffany's job. Somewhere along the way, Tiffany's "job" became her priority, and she neglected the needs of the one financing her job. Now, he wanted out.

Exasperated, Ms. Waters extended her hand.

"It was nice to meet you, Lucy. I'm sure we'll be getting to know each other well since you are working with Randy now. As soon as the deposition is transcribed, I will need some time to review it to ensure that Ms. Putnam's responses were entered accurately."

"Well that wasn't so bad," Tiffany added.

Lucy agreed that the deposition wasn't so bad. Randy had the more difficult task—going over all the financial information to establish which assets had been accumulated during the marriage. Clearly, Tiffany wasn't in Mr. Putnam's life when he was struggling thirty years ago. She came along after his business was established and successful.

"You were fabulous," Randy said. "You are going to do just fine with de-vorce bullshit. Tiffany Putnam is some bitch, isn't she?"

"Funny thing," Lucy said. "I kind of liked her. True, she's definitely forgotten her previous life. I can't decide if I'm jealous of her or pity her."

"That's not your job, Lucy," Randy said. "Your job is to preserve as much of James' assets as possible."

Lucy was exhausted from the stress of conducting her first deposition. There was no time to celebrate its completion. She had to finish the outline for day two of the Tiffany show. Tomorrow was Randy's turn.

Money can't buy you happiness, but it can buy a big yacht...

Chapter Thirty-Two

Lucy & Sammie

Surprisingly, Lucy was enjoying her mandated move to Randy Baker's domestic practice. Family law matters were much juicier than the sterile corporate world. Lucy couldn't wait to tell Sammie all about it, including her first deposition with Tiffany Putnam. She arrived at CCCs early.

Lucy ordered a beer, pulled out her legal pad, and worked on Randy's outline for Round Two while waiting on Sammie. This line of questioning was going to be more difficult since she didn't understand the business valuations that had been procured by Randy's accounting experts. What she did understand was that Tiffany Putnam was spending James' money about as fast as he was printing it.

Lucy tried to understand how such a smart man could get swept away by such a bimbo. Are intellect or ambition not important to these men? Are they so sex-starved that they lose sight of true compatibility? Lucy had never had a steady boyfriend but knew that the size of a bank account wasn't as important as having common hobbies and interests. But then there was Sammie. She'd found, or so she thought, someone just like her.

As she was deep in thought and struggling to find relevant areas for this next line of questioning, she heard Sammie's patented greeting.

"Hey there, Counselor."

Lucy jumped out of her chair and hugged her.

"I've missed you so much. You look great!"

Sammie reached over and squeezed Lucy's hand.

"Oh Lucy, I have missed you too."

Rudy, the bartender, approached them instantly.

"I see that you two are having a girl's night. What can I get for you, Sammie? Has your wild cohort talked you into a drink?"

"Yes, she has. A gin and tonic, please."

"Whoa, girl," Lucy said. "Going for the hard stuff. Make that two, Rudy."

Lucy twisted around in her stool turning her back to the inquisitive bartender and lowered her voice.

"So, tell me about your new job."

"Well, I told you that a potential slip renter sent my old boss a list of equipment he needed. It's some public relations executive who is on his way here on a big yacht. The rumor is that he's coming to Charleston to work on some type of scandal. Kevin is working on a proposal. You're looking at the Charleston Ashley Dockage's new Business Office Manager."

"This sounds perfect for you," Lucy said. "Not to be Debbie Downer, but what if the dude selects another dockage location?"

"Mr. Barry, the dockmaster, said with or without this slip rental that he's been looking for ways to distinguish his amenities since the competition is so tight. His loyal, retiree slip renters have been more demanding about technology, so he figures he can satisfy them and attract new renters."

Sammie was bubbling over with excitement.

"I am so jealous. Sounds much better than Bill Blauers. Do you have a set schedule? Can you take Mack to work with you?"

"Mom is willing to help me for as long and as much as necessary. It was actually her idea that I find something to do. Mom has been unbelievable. I've been a mess. I have wanted to talk to you about it, but I know how busy you are."

"Sammie, I will always be available for you. You are more important than Bill Blauers. You know that, right?"

"I do. But, I didn't want to burden you with my issues. I guess I needed to wallow in self-pity for a while. I knew that you would tell me to move on—to forget about the past. And I knew that, but, I just couldn't. I'm getting better."

Sammie withheld the details about what she had kept inside the past ten months. Her self-pity had escalated into a full-blown depression precipitated by Dougie's abusive and threatening text messages. She didn't want to relive any part of it. She had turned the page.

"Well, I feel like shit. Some friend I am. I had no idea that you were hurting. I assumed all the times you cancelled on me for lunch or runs was because we had clashing demands on our time. I didn't want to be a pest and pressure you into something you didn't want to do. That has never turned out well."

"Ha. I feel like that was a lifetime ago. So much has happened since then. This new venture will help me get my mind back on track. So enough about me. Tell me about your deposition, you litigator, you."

"Tiffany Putnam is just a shallow skank that believes she is owed $200 million for "organizing" her ex's life with the help of the yard guy, pool guy, maid, etc., etc. Hell, she even has someone to do the cooking and laundry. And, get this, she has a doggie groomer and a personal wardrobe shopper. Her lawyer couldn't control her. Sammie, I had her eating out of my hand. It was so much fun. I can't tell you the adrenaline that was pumping through my veins. Surprisingly, it is much better than the boring deals or corporate bullshit. Randy is amazing. He is so calm, so cool, and unpretentious. He's the real deal. I understand now how he and his brother are such superstars. They are genuine to the core. This move was the best thing that could have happened to me. But speaking of that, we need to order dinner because I have to prepare an outline and get it to Randy tomorrow for review."

"Hey, Rudy, we're ready to order. No dutch tonight. I have Lucy's tab."

Sammie leaned over and whispered in Lucy's ear.

"It's a down payment for my retainer. I'm almost mentally prepared to settle things with Dougie. When I'm ready, I want you to handle my divorce and make firm history in representing the first woman."

What goes around, comes around...

Chapter Thirty-Three

Sammie & Camilla

The minute Cort and Sammie were out the door for their morning run, he uncharacteristically started talking.

"Parks informed me that all of your money has been returned. In fact, his niece paid back every penny, with interest."

"How thoughtful of Camilla to use her dad's money to return what she stole for my husband."

"Young lady, I thought I taught you better than that. It's always best to remain silent than to speak about things that you have no knowledge of. It's my understanding that before her father sold his software company, they had a very modest lifestyle. According to Parks, Ms. Girard has worked since her first lemonade stand. She used her own money. Apparently, she is quite an entrepreneur. She has her own line of women's belts and handbags."

"Then why does she work for her uncle at Callaway Securities?" Sammie asked, snippily.

"Parks volunteered that information too. She doesn't make enough money yet to support herself with her creations. And, she wants to learn as much about the investment industry as possible in the event she has investors one day. Parks is quite proud of her drive and independence."

Sammie had never compared herself to others. Glenny forbade it. Her mantra had been drilled into Sammie for as long as she could remember: *You can't possibly compare yourself to others when you haven't walked a mile in their shoes. Everyone's journey is unique. Pay attention to yours and yours alone.*

On her 10th birthday, her mother's mantra was reinforced by a quote from Marilyn Monroe painted on a piece of canvas. It still hung on her bedroom wall:

Trying to be someone else is a waste of the person you are.

But now, as an adult, Sammie couldn't help but compare herself to Camilla Girard. Sammie had no creative talent. And, the only skill she had acquired was being a lawyer. She couldn't even cut it at that job. Instead, she had returned to her childhood bedroom and childhood workplace. She was going backwards instead of forward. No wonder Dougie was in love with Camilla.

"Well doesn't she sound perfect?" Sammie asked her dad, mockingly. "Then, there is that one teeny flaw of dating a married man."

Cort was seeing a side of his daughter that he had never seen before. And her cattiness was not becoming. He'd probably said too much already, but he wasn't through.

"Camilla views you in the same light. You broke up a nine-year relationship with her soon-to-be fiancé."

"What? She is certifiably crazy."

"Let me finish what Parks told me. Camilla says she and Dougie started seeing each other the spring of her sophomore year in high school, when you and Dougie were seniors. Upon her graduation, Camilla enrolled in the Clemson Arts Program and continued to date Dougie there. She learned about you the summer you were studying for the bar exam. Through her eyes, you only dated her long-term boyfriend for several months before you got married."

"We dated for seven years, Dad."

"I know that, but Camilla didn't. You're the cheater to her."

"I don't believe any of this. Dougie and I were together every summer."

"I told Cort the same thing. But, you were clerking at the firm both summers and working long hours and weekends. Camilla spent at least one summer abroad and others at her parents' home in Kiawah. It's definitely plausible. And, she didn't tell Parks everything. She wants to meet with you. She wants to tell you in person. And, by the way, she broke up with him, again."

They ran in silence. No doubt, Cort knew that all of this had to be upsetting for Sammie to hear. Cort hoped that his daughter wouldn't have a setback. But, she needed to know the truth. All of it. She needed to know her husband's true colors.

Cort sensed those colors long ago. Though he admired Dougie's blue collar background and the number of jobs he had worked over the years, he never trusted Dougie Morgan.

He wasn't too old to remember the Dougie Morgan types—woo you with their charms while lying directly to your face without blinking an eye—fooling everyone, even smart, ambitious girls like Sammie Spencer and Camilla Girard.

But, Dougie Morgan had done more than rock the psyche of his daughter and his half-brother's niece. Dougie's actions kept him up at night. Cort's morning runs along the Battery, previously needed to energize him for the workday ahead, were now required to clear acts of retribution against Dougie Morgan.

Worrying does not take away tomorrow's troubles, it takes away today's peace ...

Chapter Thirty-Four

Sammie & Camilla

Sammie had stopped beating herself up over what she could have done differently in her marriage. She had quit wrestling with whether she should have paid more attention to Dougie's jobs and less about her own. If Camilla's story was true, none of the questions she had grappled with made any difference. It appeared that he had never loved her like she deserved to be loved. She had been his second choice, and she wasn't even sure about that.

Now, she agonized over how stupid she had been. She should have recognized the signs when she was at Yale. Then, she assumed that they were busy juggling competing commitments, and their separation was simply a little hiccup. Everything was always great when they reconnected in the summers. But, according to her father, Dougie had been seeing Camilla during the summers as well. Sammie couldn't figure out how that could be. *How did she not sense that he wasn't totally committed to her? How could he have pulled that off?*

As Lucy had candidly pointed out, Sammie approached life with blinders on, but that's what she wanted in a relationship. She wanted to trust blindly. She didn't want to question the faithfulness of her partner. She wanted unconditional love.

Sammie's current torment, however, was meeting her nemesis face-to face. She counseled herself to stay strong, put on an air of confidence, and keep her emotions intact—to approach the situation as she had done numerous times when dealing with opposing counsel. The problem was it seemed like years since she had been in a conference room surrounded by the pomp and circumstance of adversaries. And, this was worse. It was personal. And Camilla Girard's resumé intimidated her more than any Ivy League educated lawyer.

Camilla was flexible about the date and time of the meeting, but she insisted upon the location—Herons. Cort's communication of the meeting logistics irked her for several reasons. Camilla shouldn't have any standing to insist upon anything. The request for a meeting had been bold enough but to mandate the location was over the top. In addition, Herons was outside the gates of Kiawah Island, where the Girard's had a second home. It was Camilla's home turf. It wasn't convenient for Sammie. Without traffic, Herons was a forty-minute drive from Charleston. Finally, the only time Sammie had been to Herons was the night she and Dougie celebrated their engagement and Dougie's job offer with her parents. That was the last place she wanted to meet Camilla. But, Cort assured her that Camilla had her reasons.

Sammie knew her father had her best interests at heart, but she was irritated with him too. He seemed to be sympathetic to Camilla. Oddly, it seemed his deference was more than the fact that she was Parks' niece. And, in Sammie's mind, her father and Parks Callaway were taking extraordinary measures to ensure Sammie followed through with Camilla's plan.

Cort was taking a day off from work to babysit Mack. Parks was providing childcare reinforcement. Her father and his half-brother were having their first sibling sleep-over. Cort assured both the women in his life that two grown men were certainly capable of handling an eleven-month old. But, to ease any worry, Parks' wife was on standby.

Glenny's motivation was to take care of her daughter's emotional well-being. She booked a suite at The Sanctuary, the oceanfront, luxury, 5-star hotel inside the gates of Kiawah Island, made dinner reservations at its elegant Ocean Room, and booked appointments at its world-class spa.

Sammie thought she could endure any meeting for what awaited her afterward. Had their suite been ready when they arrived, she would have blown off the lunch at Herons and escaped to their balcony with a Bloody Mary and immersed herself with the panoramic views of the Atlantic Ocean. Instead, she canvased the large lobby for the nearest bar. Her mother, however, had retail therapy in mind instead of liquid courage.

"I'm proud of you, sweetie," Glenny said, as they proceeded down the grand hallway past the bar towards the art gallery and retail wing. "And so is Cort. This whole situation has been hard on your dad and Parks. All you've got to do is hear her out. And, if it gets to be too much, you can leave."

As Sammie left the hotel for Herons, she surprisingly found herself looking forward to whatever Camilla had to say. She knew that her mood would have been drastically altered had her father not disclosed that Camilla had broken up with Dougie. But, for that fact, she would have assumed Camilla planned to announce their impending nuptials and discuss shared custody of Mack. Now, that scenario was off the table. So, anything she had to say seemed irrelevant.

Irrelevance and curiosity are two different animals, though. Sammie wondered what precipitated the breakup. And she was also intrigued about Camilla—every detail from her physical appearance to her pretenses.

Sammie had trolled social media for any kind of photo of Camilla Girard. Anything with her name, however, was solely linked to her business—Camilla Girard Designs. She had worse luck with her website. It was temporarily unavailable. The page only displayed the news of the expansion of her line of offerings.

> I am excited to announce that in addition to belts and handbags, Camilla Girard Designs is adding a variety of hair accessories from clips, scarves, to headbands. We are in the process of updating our website for online purchasing. In the interim, follow Camilla Girard Designs on Facebook and Instagram.

Her *Instagram* and *Facebook* pages only showcased her belts and handbags, not the designer. Sammie had even trudged through her parents' attic for her Pinckney Hall high school yearbooks. Parks' rendition of the facts indicated that Camilla started dating Dougie her sophomore year in high school, Sammie and Dougie's senior years. But, there was no Girard in the sophomore class in Sammie's senior yearbook, or any class for that matter. Sammie found that odd because she remembered Kurt telling her that his sister was at Pinckney Hall.

After Sammie parked at Herons, she pulled down the visor to access the mirror. Glenny Spencer never left the house without her light pink lipstick, her only make-up. Sammie had picked up this practice from her mother. She retrieved the new lip gloss from her purse that her mother purchased for her at Signature Oak, one of the hotel's specialty gift shops. The pink gloss, along with the cocktail napkins emblazoned with Coco Chanel's quote: *Don't be sad, just put on some lipstick and attack*, was her mother's light-hearted way to ease Sammie's nerves. But now, this ritual seemed silly when remembering a t-shirt that she saw in the same gift shop quoting Drew Barrymore: *Happiness is the best makeup; a smile is better than any lipstick you'll put on.*

She popped the visor back in place, put the lip gloss back into her purse, took a deep breath, and headed inside to meet Camilla Girard.

If you're always looking in the rearview mirror, you won't see what's right in front of you...

Chapter Thirty-Five

Sammie & Camilla

When Sammie entered Herons, the hostess asked if she had a reservation.

"I don't, but I am meeting Camilla Girard."

"Oh, you must be Sammie," she said, spiritedly. "Camilla is here. She's outside on the patio. Enjoy your lunch."

The perky hostess obviously knew Camilla. She hadn't even glanced at the reservation list for the table location. Instead, she turned her attention to her phone, without offering any escort to the patio.

Sammie meandered past the tabletops in the bar area and through the dining area. The pit in Sammie's stomach returned passing the tables of happy couples enjoying their leisurely lunch. She was certain that she wouldn't be able to eat a bite. The laidback atmosphere spilled onto the crowded patio where she passed more couples and tables of women in their tennis and golf attire. Surveying the patio for a table occupied by her concoction of Dougie's ex—a preppy, young female wearing a Lilly Pulitzer shift and Tory Burch sandals—she unknowingly walked right by Camilla.

Sammie noticed a striking woman headed towards her. The woman wore a denim, sleeveless jumpsuit with a western style belt. Her short, jet black hair was a choppily-layered pixie cut, highlighting her big eyes, high cheekbones, and multiple ear piercings. She couldn't pinpoint her style, but she would characterize it as "elegant bohemian." She noticed a jewelry cuff on her long, slim, toned arms as she extended her hand.

"Hey Sammie. I'm Camilla," she said, confidently.

As Camilla's hand enveloped Sammie's, she noticed that her long fingers accentuated the dark blue polish on her short fingernails. Her full lips shimmered like glass from the effect of her soft pink lip gloss. Sammie regretted the decision to ditch hers.

Camilla was the complete opposite of Sammie's stereotyped image. Her aura was disarming. Sammie's confidence took a nose-dive. She felt like a provincial schoolmarm.

"We're over here," Camilla said, pointing to a table occupied by an older man with a receding hairline. Sammie couldn't believe that Camilla had the gall to bring a date. She tried to squash the additional negative thoughts stirring in her head—Camilla's propensity for older men. As they moved closer to the table, the man's features were more discernible. Sammie thought Camilla's taste included not only older men but also handsome, older men. The man had a distinctive look—a mix of rebellion and adventurer.

Sammie noticed the man's brawny physique when he stood up from his chair and extended his hand. The ruggedness of his hands were registering with her when he spoke.

"Hey, Sammie. It's been a long time."

She had pieced it together by now, but her gaze must have expressed confusion instead of comprehension.

"Kurt. Kurt Girard."

"I know. Gosh, it's been so long," Sammie said, stammering and realizing that these had been the first words she had uttered in Camilla's presence. "Like, I haven't seen you since high school."

Sammie didn't think that the lunch could get any more unbearable. The last words Kurt Girard had spoken to her were as clear as the day he muttered them at the senior dance between Pinckney Hall and Tradd Prepp: "I would have never pegged you as a SOBB." The sting of his words didn't hurt as badly now as then, but they had permanently scarred her. But for those words, she may have never gone to the beach party with Isabelle. His words altered the trajectory of her life.

"I tried to tell Camilla that I shouldn't come—that it would make the situation worse, but she insisted."

Sammie was seeing why Camilla called the shots. She was a force to be reckoned with.

"I told Kurt that he thinks too much, that you probably wouldn't even remember him. I mean it was one party, a long time ago."

Sammie found herself blushing. He remembered it. He had shared it with his sister, at least some of it.

"But, I needed Kurt to be here. He's always been my rock. I was super stressed to meet you," Camilla said, visibly shaken.

Sammie wanted to gloat in Camilla Girard's angst. She wanted to hate her. Instead, she found herself wanting to give her a hug. Looking into Camilla's eyes, she saw a reflection of her own pain.

"Dougie is a narcissist piece of shit," Camilla said, regaining composure. "I am a good person, Sammie. I've always believed in myself. But, Dougie turned me into a person that I never thought I would become."

Their waitress arrived to take their order.

"Would you like to hear the lunch specials?"

"Not until I have a shot of your best tequila," Camilla said.

"Make that two," Kurt added.

"Three," Sammie said.

It was the moment they needed. They all laughed.

"How did you meet him?" Sammie asked.

"At Rutledge."

"I thought you were at Pinckney Hall."

"I was for a semester. I hated it. Everyone was so mean to me there. It's difficult enough moving during high school and worse when you're a newbie."

Sammie flinched. Her classmates had called Kurt the same thing.

"In retrospect, I probably didn't do myself any favors. I missed my friends in Atlanta. They knew me. They understood me. At Pinckney, it was like everyone expected me to be something I wasn't—like them. I was going through this phase—what the Pinckney girls called 'artsy fartsy.' But, they were right. I was an art nerd. When I realized I would never fit it, I ratcheted things up a notch. I dyed my hair purple and went sort of goth. My parents knew that I was just rebelling against the mean girls but let's just say the administration didn't appreciate my creativity. It was either ship up or ship out."

"I'm sorry."

"Well, the way I look at it now, it was perfect for me. I thrived there. Rutledge was an arts magnet school and a very good one. Dougie was taking one of the intro art classes as an elective for an easy A since his mother was the teacher."

Sammie had no idea that Norma taught art. How could she have never known that?

"So, this was the spring of your sophomore year?" Sammie asked, wondering what else she was going to learn about her husband and his family.

"Yes. And, well, you know Dougie. He had this chip on his shoulder like me. Let's just say we connected instantly. I was head over heels. He accepted me for who I was. But for him, I would have never considered Clemson but as it turns out, its Art Program was excellent."

The waitress arrived with the tequila shots.

Camilla slugged hers back.

"I'll take another," she said.

"So, another round?" the waitress asked.

"Sure," Kurt said, "and another while you're at it—put everything on my bill."

Sammie downed her shot and worried about a second. But, she wasn't going to throw water on this dialogue. If necessary, she would walk the four miles back to The Sanctuary.

"Uncle Parks said that you started dating Dougie after that. Is that right?" Camilla asked.

"It depends on what time you are referring to. We got together at a Rutledge beach party in May of my senior year and I thought, obviously incorrectly, that we dated exclusively after that. We were together that summer and every summer after that."

"That ass. I spent that summer backpacking with Kurt in Europe. And then I did a summer abroad my junior year in Italy. Other than that time apart, we were together almost every weekend."

"What did you do the summer of your senior year in college?" Sammie asked.

"My parents have a home in Kiawah. I worked here—at Herons."

Sammie recalled that Dougie took a weekend job that summer at nearby Bohicket Marina.

"How convenient for Dougie," Sammie said.

"What do you mean?" Camilla asked, confused.

"I was busy studying for the bar exam that summer, so Dougie picked up a weekend marina job to 'save for our future,'" Sammie said, now understanding how he could have dated them both. "I was surprised when the job was at the Bohicket Marina instead of Shem Creek, but with you being here, that makes sense now."

"He's a tool. I can't believe this. He didn't have a job at Bohicket. He spent weekends with me on Kiawah, that is, when I wasn't working. As you probably know, he lived at home to 'save for our future,'" Camilla said interjecting quotes in the air. "I loved Norma and Olin—you know, salt of the earth people, but I got it. He couldn't get here fast enough from RePro on Friday nights."

Sammie winced. Camilla was more familiar with all aspects of Dougie's life. Camilla knew his parents far better than she ever had. She'd never even met Dougie's parents until they were engaged. And, now she knew why—Camilla.

"Are you okay? I've probably said enough. I just wanted you to understand that I wasn't a homewrecker. Honestly, I viewed you like that."

"Well, I had no idea about you, until the withdrawals from my account."

"I'm so ashamed about that. What an idiot I was. But, I put back every penny, Sammie. I made a list of the withdrawals and the amounts—so that you can ensure that it's all there."

Camilla reached for her handbag from the arm of her chair Sammie couldn't help but notice it. It matched Camilla's unique style. Camilla presented Sammie with a spreadsheet. Sammie was shocked when she saw the itemized columns of dates, amounts, and calculated interest. She would provide this to her father later, but she was confident that everything had been returned. Oddly, she trusted Camilla.

"There is more. I want to get it all out so that I can move on. But, that is probably selfish of me. I appreciate that this is hard to digest."

"I want to hear all of it. Go ahead."

"Like I said, the summer I worked here, I started picking up on weird vibes from Dougie. Until then, he was always so present when we were together. But, he started checking his phone all the time and making excuses about having to go back into Charleston. I found that odd since he hated living with his parents. When I asked him about it, he turned it back on me. He would say, 'nagging doesn't look good on you, Camilla.' 'Is this a sign of what I will have to put up with when we're married, because if it is, I'm out.' Of course, his comments hit home. I had always been independent and trusting. But, I couldn't help what I was feeling. I knew deep down something wasn't right. So, instead of 'cross-examining' him—his words—about his trips back to Charleston, I had a tracking device installed in his car."

Sammie's stunned reaction registered on Camilla.

"I know, right? I mean if you have to take such extreme measures, it's a pretty strong sign of a toxic relationship. But, I rationalized it because I could quit wondering what he was doing. I could quit 'nagging.' As they say, the proof is in the pudding. One address was a consistent stop. I broke down and told Kurt everything. He knew the address—it was yours. That's when I learned that you were the pudding, so to speak."

The waitress interrupted Camilla's story. For the moment, she didn't seem to mind that they were drinking their lunch. Kurt ordered another round.

"So, by now, we knew all about your family. Our grandmother had come clean to Mom about Uncle Parks. You do know about all that, right?"

"Yes, I know that my grandfather is Parks' father."

Camilla and Kurt instantly looked at each other. Sammie couldn't discern if their expression was surprise or relief. But, then she caught Kurt shaking his head at his sister as if to say, "Don't go there."

"Right," Camilla said, pausing. "Well, that's not my story to tell. All I can say is that I couldn't believe the Spencer family was rearing its ugly head back into our lives. I know that sounds crass but I'm just being honest with you, Sammie. To put it bluntly, we hated what your grandfather did."

Sammie found her dig a little remarkable given that Joyce Callaway certainly wasn't an innocent party in the situation. But, then again, she was picking up that there was more to that story than she knew and possibly even her parents.

"I confronted Dougie. I didn't tell him how I knew he had been spending time at your house, and he didn't ask. He matter-of-factly said that he had applied for a job at Worth Pharmaceutical. You were dating one of his friends from the marina, and your father had connections with the company. He said that your dad was giving him interview tips. Given my family's contempt for Sam Spencer, he didn't want to upset me. The job was a great opportunity and fit his skill set. Everything he was doing was for us, blah, blah, blah. He made me feel awful that I had even brought it up. I almost called the mechanic who installed the tracking device to have it removed. But, for some reason, I couldn't. Something felt off. After another sketchy reason to return to Charleston, he was tracked going from your house to the Kapp's. He never mentioned that he still did the Kapp's yard work, so I got suspicious. I called Kurt. He agreed to check it out. Kurt lives in Wando, so he made it over there in about twenty minutes. When he arrived, there was no sign of Dougie outside doing any yard work. He parked across the street and waited. After a couple hours passed, he saw Dougie and you leaving together. I knew what had transpired. I mean we used to laugh about if that deck could talk. We had sex there more than the bed of his pickup. So, I broke up with him. I didn't see him again until the night you and your parents came into Herons to celebrate your engagement. Unbeknownst to me, he had requested my table—this table."

Sammie had been so giddy about the double celebration dinner for Dougie's job offer at Worth Pharmaceutical and their engagement, she didn't pay attention to the exact table location. But, there was no reason not to believe Camilla about this one minor detail. She vividly recalled the important one. Dougie selected the restaurant, date, and time.

"When I approached the table and saw Dougie and your family, I about fainted. When he announced it was an engagement celebration, and I saw the ring on your finger, I felt sick. I was trying to stay composed and remember saying that it sounded like champagne was in order. I went to my boss and told him that I didn't feel well, and I needed to leave. I ran out of restaurant as fast as I could. I quit the next day. I didn't think I would ever be able to step foot in here again."

Sammie couldn't believe that Dougie could be so heartless but obviously there were lots of things she hadn't known about him.

"After I quit Heron's, I started working with Uncle Parks. I realized quickly that I wasn't cut out for an 8-5 office job. And, the drive every day into Charleston was a bitch. I was so exhausted that I never had time to work on my business. And, I desperately needed my creative outlet during this period. So, I reduced my hours to two days a week and picked up a job with the resort cleaning service. I get paid by the house—so to speak. It gave me the flexibility to work on my designs and try to get my business off the ground. One of the townhome complexes I clean is beside of the Beach Club. Dougie and I used to go there a lot. I knew that I was finally putting Dougie Morgan behind me when I went there for dinner one night. I was sitting at the bar when someone came up behind me and asked me if the chair beside me was taken. Of course, I instantly recognized his voice, turned around, and it was him. He told me that it was fate that we were there at the same time, though I suspected that one of his buddies told him I was there. He said that he missed me, that he married you on the rebound, and that he was miserable. He said your family controlled your lives and that you were obsessed with your job and making partner. He said he would do anything to get me back. When you love someone like I did Dougie, I wanted to believe everything he said. I'm embarrassed to say that he stayed with me that night, and we started planning our future together. He said the only thing that was stopping him from leaving that very night was the account with Callaway Securities. He wanted to get his fair share. He understood the power your father wields. I'm sure now that he never intended to leave you for me. I was merely the vehicle to your account, and I hate to say that I was a willing participant. Based on my grandmother's shoddy treatment by Sam Spencer and his law firm, I wasn't too worried about any repercussion to him or to me."

"So, when was this exactly?" Sammie asked.

"It was last June, the first day of June to be exact."

By now, Sammie's head was swimming from the shots. But this last bit of information made her nauseated. She and Dougie had left for the hospital at 11:00 p.m. on May 31, Mack's due date. For first mothers, she learned that her labor had been quick. Mack was born at 7:10 a.m. on June 1. Terpertha, her nurse, woke Sammie up early that evening to feed Mack.

"Is everything okay?" Terpetha had asked.

Sammie assumed she was referring to her pain management.

"Your husband got a call and high-tailed it out of here faster than a hot knife through butter."

Worried, Sammie checked her phone. She hadn't missed any calls but there was a text from Dougie. *I didn't want to wake you. I headed home to go to bed. I'm exhausted. I'll be back first thing in the morning. I love you so much.*

Instead of sleep, he "high-tailed" it to Kiawah to find his old girlfriend, spend the night with her, and make plans for their future.

"I don't feel so hot," Sammie said, chugging some water.

"You don't look so good either. You're really pale," Kurt said, jumping from the table.

"Oh, Sammie. I didn't mean to upset you," Camilla said, dumping water onto her napkin. She reached over and placed the napkin on Sammie's forehead.

Kurt returned with a basket of bread and crackers. Sammie helped herself to a corn muffin and more water.

"We should probably order," Camilla said, waving at the waitress.

"Y'all go ahead. I have what I need right here," nibling on the muffin. "But I will take a Coke."

Camilla and Kurt ordered a round of Bloody Marys for themselves and the fresh catch of the day. Sammie was thankful that her earlier plan to hit the bar had been altered by retail therapy. Right now, she worried that her stomach couldn't even handle the sight of a Bloody Mary or the smell of fresh fish. She excused herself. She barely made it to the bathroom. As her head laid on the toilet seat, she was reminded that Dougie Morgan was the only person that had caused such retching. But, no more. She did more than flush her vomit. She purged herself of his lies, his infidelity, and his manipulation. Right there, in the bathroom stall, she prayed for her son. She vowed that she was going to fight for full custody. And, she would fight to the bitter end.

A child's first steps are only achieved after stumbles and falls. Subsequent steps through life are no different...

Chapter Thirty-Six

Sammie

The plague of sleepless nights, tossing and turning, cold sweats, and a racing mind seemed to have dissipated. During the last ten months, Sammie had learned a lot about Dougie Morgan. Although there was probably more that she didn't know, she knew enough. Her mother was right. It was time for her to put the past behind her, resurrect her identity, and find joy.

Sammie finally had got a good night's sleep. The next morning, she excused herself from joining her mother for a long stroll with Mack. Instead, she headed to the marina with Kevin's proposal. She was hopeful that Mr. Barry was still interested in his business office but if not, she decided she would be happy as a clam running errands for the slip renters. Sammie found herself smiling as she approached. Yet again, Mr. Barry was assisting another cute boat washer.

"Hey, Mr. Barry, is boat washing another amenity that you are considering?"

He laughed.

"Hard times call for thinking outside the box. A man's gotta do what's he gotta do. You got some numbers for me?"

"Yes, I have the proposal right here."

"Great. Let's go sit in the dock house so I can concentrate on these numbers. This boat washing is sort of distractin', if you know what I mean."

"The Davis Group is offering to pay an extra fee for exclusive dibs to the office while the boss man is here. This one gig will bankroll my business office overhead," he said, excitedly, while reviewing the equipment rental costs for a six-month term. "This hotshot is scheduled to arrive in five days," Mr. Barry said. "Think Kevin can get everything here by then?"

"I'll find out. He has these vendors eating out of his hand due to the business he sends them with all the law firm stuff."

Sammie immediately contacted Kevin to relay that Mr. Barry was interested in the six-month rental plan.

"How soon can you get everything installed? The head of the Davis Group is scheduled to arrive soon."

"I don't think that will be a problem. Everything is available and on hold for me. I'll call my guys now, but unless you hear from me, I'll plan to have everything installed in the next couple of days."

"That would be great. Thanks so much, Kevin. I really appreciate it."

Mr. Barry sealed the deal on the slip rental when he promised that "his business office would be sufficiently upgraded to meet the demands of The Davis Group, and Mr. Davis would be given top priority." He also said Mr. Davis was very intrigued with the fact that a former corporate lawyer was the office manager.

"I guess you are now on the clock," Mr. Barry added. "I have your first project. Grant Davis himself sent this document for me to sign. Interpret this for me."

Sammie read the document.

"Well, one thing is for certain. There is definitely something brewing. This is a confidentiality agreement. Basically, it says that you agree not to disclose any information you obtain from The Davis Group to any third party, including information relating to, arising from or associated with the business being conducted by The Davis Group. The time period covers not only the term of its lease of the slip but also forever."

"This is some shit, huh?" he said. "I don't mind signing it. I don't discuss the business of any of my renters. Hell, I could probably write a book on the stuff I've witnessed from these rich fuckers. And, I do mean 'fuckers,' if you catch my drift."

"Whatever, but you can't disclose that *Sea Relations* is being docked here or that the vessel is owned by Mr. Davis. This document prohibits you from saying one word about anything related to the reason that boat will be here. If you do, you can be sued for damages including actual and consequential damages."

"What in the hell is a 'consequential' damage?" Mr. Barry asked.

"Consequential damages can include anything that a creative plaintiff's lawyer will argue that you should have been foreseen for not holding up your end of the bargain. For example, if Mr. Davis had to hire additional security due to word getting out that he is here, he could try and make you pay for it. I could strike the word 'consequential' and tighten up some of these points, but any changes could backfire. He may think you are trying to wiggle around keeping quiet. He likely won't accept any proposed change anyway. So bottom line is if you don't sign it, he won't sign your lease."

"Well, like I said, I don't blab the business of my tenants to anyone," Mr. Barry was chomping at the bit for the dockage fee and free publicity—not promoted by any gossip from him, of course.

"I do know that, but the stakes are higher here," Sammie said, trying to make sure he understood that he was playing with fire. He could not afford to ignore the document's provisions. "You just need to be aware that there could be serious consequences for any violation. He could ruin your business and your reputation."

"Loose lips sink ships!" he said. "This is an opportunity of a lifetime. Where do I sign?"

The former lounge converted nicely into a relaxed, professional business office. The three walls of windows let in beams of low country sunshine and incredible views of sailboats, yachts, and the activities on a marina. Even the boat washers were a welcome view compared to Sammie's previous confined office space. Sammie thought that this setting would suit her just fine.

"Oh Sammie, I almost forgot," Mr. Barry said. "Mr. Davis says he needs one of those confidentiality agreements from you too. Said you would understand since you are an attorney."

"I don't like that. He is questioning my integrity."

"Well, I guess he is questioning mine too. And you said if I didn't sign it, he would head to another marina."

"I'm aware of that, Mr. Barry, but as an attorney, a strict code of ethics governs my behavior, not this document," Sammie said, trying to dance around why his request for her to sign was more egregious. "This ethical code mandates that I keep matters confidential, or I could lose my law license."

Sammie's attempted explanation overlooked that the information learned from customers of a marina business office didn't carry the same protections as an attorney-client relationship. She had yet to appreciate that severing her ties to the firm gave her the same status as a marina dockhand.

"You said I could lose my business and my reputation. Don't see how that's really any different," Mr. Barry said, huffily.

"This man likely has a team of attorneys working for him, so he knows the rules about professional responsibilities. If I just sign this without a fight or at least without any proposed comments, he'll likely not respect my judgment. When giving Kevin the business office requirements, I've already discussed the fact that he is here. I can't sign something that I have already violated."

"Geez, Sammie. I really want this lease dockage," Mr. Barry said.

"Call him back and tell him that I refused to sign it but explain why. That I said it wasn't necessary since there were legal rules governing my behavior, and they are stricter than his document."

Mr. Barry took off his hat and started scratching his head. Sammie could tell that he was worried about communicating with a man who probably never hears "no."

"Mr. Barry, if he threatens to go to a competitor, I'll sign it. But, I want you to present my rationale and with no waver in your tone. It will only demonstrate that I am an independent thinker."

After Mr. Barry relayed Sammie's refusal and the reason, Grant Davis demanded to meet with "the obstinate attorney" after he docked.

"He said that if you couldn't work things out, he'd head on up to the Lockwood Marina."

As the meeting time approached, Sammie couldn't figure out why she was nervous. It wasn't like she hadn't met and worked with powerful businessmen before. She concluded that it was due to the importance of this dockage agreement to Mr. Barry. She didn't want to mess things up for him. She knew that the powerful executive was playing the "if I can't get my way, I'll just take my toys and go elsewhere" card, but she also knew that he would likely follow through on it. She was worried that she may have already blown it for Charleston Ashley Dockage. She anxiously walked down the dock to *Sea Relations*.

She arrived at the stately Westport yacht but didn't know where to go. As she stood on the dock admiring the vessel, the sliding glass doors off the back deck opened, and a good-looking man came to the back platform.

"Are you Ms. Morgan?"

"Yes, I am."

"I'm Billy. I'm the captain of *Sea Relations*. Come this way. I'll help you aboard."

After Billy helped her onto the platform, she followed him up some stairs that led to an expansive back deck with teak flooring.

"Mr. Davis is waiting for you in his office."

Sliding glass doors on the deck opened into a cozy salon. A navy, striped sofa was filled with oversized pillows with various nautical designs. A mounted sailfish hung on the wall. The room was masculine yet elegant. The den led into a sleek contemporary kitchen with stainless steel appliances. From the kitchen, Sammie followed Billy up to the next level, which resembled the lobby of an eclectic New York ad agency. The room offered several distinct settings for creative thinking. A chrome and glass table faced a long row of windows with a view of the water. A wall was covered with fishing trophies, not from a trophy shop but from the sea. Sammie recognized a tuna, marlin, and a wahoo. Sammie knew that a wahoo was the fastest fish in the ocean and wondered if the man behind the office doors had reeled it in.

Billy knocked gently before opening the office door.

"Mr. Davis, Ms. Morgan is here."

Billy was certainly easy on the eyes, as Mr. Barry would say. But, Grant Davis took your breath away on impact. Sammie felt heat rise from her face. Grant Davis was at least 6'3 and lean. He was prematurely gray, which made it difficult to gauge his age. Sammie decided to take charge immediately and display some confidence since she probably looked like a smitten schoolgirl ogling over a professor. She extended her hand and gave him a firm handshake.

"I'm Sammie Morgan. It's nice to meet you."

"I must say that I didn't know what to expect—a former corporate lawyer who is now running the business office of a harborage and refuses to sign my confidentiality agreement."

"With all due respect, your agreement is vague, at best, and a good lawyer could rip it apart," Sammie argued, confidently but feeling weak at the knees.

"Certainly, you have seen, and probably drafted, these agreements numerous times and understand their importance and necessity."

"Yes, sir. You are correct. I have drafted them numerous times. The reason I refused to sign it was because I am a licensed attorney, sir. If I am retained to work with you in some sort of capacity, I am required by ethical rules to maintain confidences."

"Well, well, well... Ms. Morgan is a feisty attorney. I like that. But I don't think I've ever met an ethical lawyer."

He reached into his back pocket and pulled out an alligator leather wallet. He opened it to display a wad of green bills and handed Sammie a $100 bill.

"You have now been retained by The Davis Group to assist us in our business here in Charleston. Your first assignment is to make my confidentiality agreement bullet-proof. I need it tomorrow. While you're at it, have your marina boss sign the new agreement."

"I can have you a revised agreement by tomorrow. I should advise you that if Mr. Barry signs a revised agreement, it wouldn't be enforceable. There is no legal consideration," Sammie said. "Mr. Barry signed the original document in return for the slip fee."

"Touché. I'm willing to take my chances on the consideration point with your boss. I need your new version by noon. We are being retained in another matter, and I want to send to them your new iron-clad agreement."

"Noon, it is," Sammie said, thinking he sounded more like the Spencer partners than a PR expert.

"Aside from the work that you are doing for Mr. Barry, I will pay you separately when you provide me advice and counsel. Keep up with those hours. I'm confident that you are familiar with that practice."

"I certainly am," Sammie said, thinking that Bill Blauers was one of the reasons why she left the firm.

"And I would like to discuss with you some of the background regarding why I am here," Grant Davis said. "I need some immediate help with typing and circulating an outline. I don't want to work on that remotely with my office. It's too risky."

"Would you like to meet me at the business office?" Sammie asked.

"No, I would like for you to come here," Mr. Davis said, emphatically. "I know that, despite any signed agreements, it will eventually get out that I am here. I know dock chatter all too well. I want to keep as low a profile as I can."

"Sounds good. I'll be back at noon tomorrow with your new agreement."

Sammie started to return the $100 bill but then realized their communications wouldn't be protected by the attorney/client privilege if she wasn't retained. *This man knew what he was doing, and this was going to get interesting*, she thought.

She arrived promptly at noon the next day with a new document comparing her revisions to his original agreement. Her proposed deletions were highlighted in red, with her proposed additions noted in green. The printed document looked like a lit-up Christmas tree. Upon seeing the colors and understanding the comparison process, Grant Davis laughed.

"I won't tell you how much we paid an Atlanta attorney for my draft," Grant said. "It appears you retained one 'and' and one 'but' and looks like the rest is trash so that means I blew about $5,000 a word."

"That's good work if you can get it," Sammie said. "I didn't realize how significantly I had edited your document until I compared the two documents with the comparison program. The comparison version may be too difficult to read due to the number of proposed changes, so I brought a clean version of the revised agreement."

"I appreciate that, and I appreciate your concern for my eyes. I'll let you know if I have any questions. Please, sit down. I need to discuss some additional assignments."

"I am available to help you, but I need to discuss time commitments with Mr. Barry," Sammie said, feeling like Grant Davis was going to dominate her time. "We didn't foresee that I would be retained to do legal work and be paid independently."

"What do you mean?" he asked.

Sammie then wondered what sort of promises Mr. Barry had made to get this dockage.

"We discussed two employment arrangements for me," she said. "In addition to the business office work, I will be running errands for our renters. The website has not been updated yet, but one of the amenities is a gopher service per se. If you need groceries or boating supplies, we will bring them to you, for a fee. So, I have another obligation to Mr. Barry."

"Spencer lawyer turned marina gopher," he said, chuckling rather condescendingly. "Is there something you need to tell me about your departure from your reputable law firm that my due diligence missed somehow? Which would be a first, by the way."

Due diligence? What sort of investigation had he conducted on her? And why? She figured he was a master at reading people and situations so best to get the Sammie Morgan story on the table. Grant Davis was used to hearing about life's twist and turns, that's why he was a successful PR guy. He took the twist and turns and helped straighten them out, or at least in the world of public opinion. Like her dad always said, "it is what it is. Deal with it and move on."

"I loved being a lawyer, and I didn't mind my 18-hour days before my son was born," she said. "But, I realized that I couldn't sustain that pace. So, I am taking a break from practicing law, at least temporarily. I used to work summers for Mr. Barry teaching at the sailing school here, and it just so happened that he was starting his business office and needed someone familiar with the technology and software systems. The timing couldn't have been any more perfect. My son is almost a year old. I have been going a bit stir crazy. I wanted to work but something with flexible hours. I guess you could say I was a sea creature in a former life. I love to be near the water. I decided to try this out for the time being. So, that is it in a nutshell."

"I was curious how a Spencer, Pettigrew & Hamilton corporate lawyer ended up here. Ironically, I had been researching Charleston firms in the event I needed local help. Don't take this the wrong way, but I don't trust lawyers but was going to have a stand-by firm on retainer, just in case. My job requires that I think ten steps ahead. When Harold pitched his business office and the lawyer who was going to be running things, I did a little checking up on you. Since the Spencer firm was on my short list, let's say you sealed the deal with my dockage here. So, the way I see things, your new boss won't have any issue with the arrangement I am going to propose. Would you like some coffee or tea before I begin?"

"Water would be great."

He buzzed Billy, who within seconds arrived with a tray of fresh fruit, cheese and crackers, bottled waters, and a pitcher of tea. His large hands gripped a water bottle and tossed it to Sammie.

"So, a little about me, Ms. Morgan, I'm a sweet tea junkie, one of my vices," he said, pouring himself a glass of tea.

He stepped from his desk.

"Let's sit over here," pointing to the large red leather sofa in his office. "I'll give you a brief summary of the issues where you can be of assistance."

She searched for a piece of paper in her backpack.

"Don't take notes. Just listen," Grant Davis said.

Pigs get fat, hogs get slaughtered...

Chapter Thirty-Seven

Lucy

Round Two of Tiffany Putnam's deposition was as entertaining as the first. Lucy watched and listened to Randy in complete awe. He was so smooth and relaxed. The deponent could easily forget that he was not on their side. His slow manner of speaking, though not done intentionally, was a big advantage in a deposition. Tiffany Putnam grew impatient and answered questions before Randy finished posing them. More than half the time, she incorrectly guessed his intended direction, so they were getting all kinds of sideline information. Carolyn Waters was beside herself and becoming increasingly irritable with her client as the day went on. By mid-afternoon, Randy had a better rapport with Tiffany than Tiffany did with her own lawyer.

Randy questioned Tiffany extensively about James Putnam's business, his clients, how he came to obtain the clients, timelines, and his product offerings. He was clearly establishing that she had no clue about any of it.

Randy also confirmed that the $5,000,000 oceanfront home on Kiawah Island hadn't increased in value since their marriage despite Tiffany's $600,000 complete makeover for the home's interior. Since becoming Mrs. Putnam, Tiffany's expenses for upgrades to the $3,000,000 million penthouse in West Palm Beach, Florida, more than exceeded its increased value.

During a break from the deposition, Lucy ran into Kevin in the breakroom.

"Hey, I had lunch with your former sidekick the other day," Kevin said. "Sammie looked good."

"I heard," Lucy said. "I had dinner with her that night, and she told me about how you were helping her out. I think it all sounds great. But most of all, I'm so happy for her. I don't know what all she has told you, but she needs a break right now. I'm glad she has something to keep her mind occupied. Speaking of occupied, did you know I moved into Randy Baker's group?"

"Yes, I heard that and thought it was a, well, how should I say this, an interesting move for you," Kevin said.

"I am in the middle of Round Two of a wife's deposition in a huge ED case—that's equitable distribution, how the marital assets get divvied up," Lucy said.

"I know that I don't have a law degree, but I do know what ED cases are, Lucy," Kevin said, flatly.

Lucy worried that she sounded condescending. Kevin was going to think she was such a jerk.

"Well, you are smarter than me then, because I had no idea what Randy was talking about when he said ED, and I'm still learning," she said, trying to salvage any damage. "It's like I'm starting all over as a first-year associate, but I am really enjoying it."

"I bet you are a natural," he said. "What are you doing after work? I need to go to the marina and take some measurements. I've installed all the equipment, but there is a great bargain on a desk that I think Sammie would like but don't know if it will cramp the space. If you want to ride over with me, you can see Sammie's new job site, and if she's around, maybe we could all get a drink afterward."

"That sounds great," Lucy said. "I'm going to need a drink, or three, after this day is over listening to this poor, pitiful woman detailing the 'life that she has become accustomed to.' And I've never been to a marina."

"I'll call Sammie to see if she will be there," Kevin said. "When do you think you'll be done for the day? I'm flexible, so no worries about the time."

"We're moving slowly," Lucy said. "You know with Randy's slow speech, things take a little longer. But, I don't think we'll go past 6:00 since we have another day of it tomorrow. If it looks like it will run longer, I'll call you."

"Ok, see you later, Lucy," Kevin said.

Lucy was trying not to get too excited. This was the closest thing to a date for her in quite some time. He was probably just being nice to include her since Sammie would be there. Regardless of Kevin's intentions, she couldn't concentrate on Tiffany's drivel, this woman needed a reality check. There were millions at risk to their client, and Lucy just wanted to leave and go to the Charleston Ashley Dockage with Kevin.

At 5:15, Randy was obviously growing tired and said they would continue in the morning. After Lucy escorted their guests to the elevators, she stopped by her office to check messages. Surprisingly, Roberta or Gladys Kravitz, was still at her upholstered cubical. She was usually running out of her cube at 4:55 like there had been a fire drill. She peered over her workstation at Lucy.

"Kevin Miller came by to see you," Roberta said.

She cross-examined Lucy with her eyes, waiting for a hint or tidbit of information. Roberta was another scorned woman, on a different scale than Tiffany Putnam but equally as resentful.

"I told him that I wasn't aware that you were having any computer problems. He said that you didn't have a computer issue," Roberta said, "but he left a note in your chair."

"Thanks," Lucy said, summarily. "What has you here working late?"

"I just needed to tidy up," Roberta said.

Tidy up, hell, Lucy thought.

Lucy shut her door and read Kevin's note.

It's 4:45, and you must still be with Bill Blauers. Call my office extension (3571) when you are done. The system will automatically page me. Sammie is at the marina and will meet us at the dock house. She is excited you're coming, and I am too.

Kevin obviously left the note right before time for Gladys to dart out. She was thankful that the note was in a sealed envelope. Lucy knew that her secretary had been attempting to examine its contents. Lucy dialed extension 3571.

"Hey there," Kevin answered. "Are you done? If so, I can leave right now."

"Yes, I just came by my office after dropping off the parties. I need to go back into the conference room and see if Randy needs anything, but I think I'm good."

"Ok, I'll go get my car. The marina parking is limited and strict about guests so I thought we could ride together, unless you want to drive separately."

"I'd love to ride with you," Lucy said.

"Great, I'll be out front."

Lucy hurriedly ran down the hall to the conference room. Any other time, she would have loved to have talked to Randy to see what he thought about the deposition. He was a hoot, but tonight she actually had something other than work to occupy her time. Randy was still there and reading over his notes.

"She's like a damn vulture but as nastified as rancid fucked roadkill. Bring your outline for Round Three to the Waffle House up on Meeting Street. We can go over it at breakfast. I'll be there at 6:00 a.m."

"Yes, sir. I'll get started on it," Lucy said, making a quick exit before he had time to form another sentence.

Any other night, Lucy would gladly stay to work. She could draft questions about Tiffany's staff and personal schedule until the cows came home, but these accountant spreadsheets and assets were a whole new ballgame for her. But, work would have to wait until later. She packed her laptop and all the data and headed out to meet Kevin.

Lucy didn't know what kind of car Kevin drove but wasn't too surprised that it was an old, navy Grand Jeep Wagoneer with tan, leather interior. She wasn't a car enthusiast. In fact, she couldn't recognize years, or models, much less the makes of many cars, but the classic Wagoneer instantly brought back great memories with her bestie from high school, Tracy Luck. Tracy's dad was a car mechanic and had restored an old Wagoneer.

"Hey, I love your car," Lucy said, hopping in. "My best friend from high school's Dad had a Wagoneer. We used to go joyriding in it. Some fun times."

Unlike her friend's, Kevin's Wagoneer was upfitted with a sunroof and sound system. Dave Matthews was crooning through the speakers. Kevin's rumored tattoo was peeking out of his rolled up long-sleeve shirt.

"I love Dave Matthews," Lucy said. "What other music do you like?"

"I have a diverse range," Kevin said, "but it all has to stand the test of time, like my woody," he said, winking.

"What do you mean woody?" she asked.

"Oh, sorry, I thought since you were familiar with Wagoneers, you knew that they were called 'woodies.' I didn't mean to scare you."

Lucy laughed. They headed down East Bay to Lockwood Drive, the road that paralleled the Ashley River and was home to three of Charleston's marinas.

"I hope Sammie knows what she is getting into," Kevin said. "I understand that she is excited about working for her old boss. He's pretty crusty but seems like a good dude. This PR guy, though, sounds mysterious."

"Well, you know more about it than I do," Lucy said. "I spoke to her just briefly during our last break to tell her how excited I was to see a marina up close and personal and couldn't wait to see the hotshot's yacht. She abruptly said that we couldn't go near it. I did think that was strange."

"Yep. But, Sammie is smart," Kevin said. "Hell, you and Sammie are the two of the sharpest women I've ever encountered. I'm not just saying that."

"Sammie is very smart," Lucy agreed. "And she's tough, tougher than I would have ever imagined. Has she mentioned anything about her husband?"

"No, she hasn't mentioned him at all. She just talks about her son and needing more flexibility and less stress. I totally get that. I didn't pry about why her husband couldn't help her. I just figured he was a selfish egomaniac who thinks his job is more important or can't accept the fact that it isn't. I've seen it all."

"I am not going to breach any confidence with Sammie because she is my best friend but let's just say that he is a royal piece of shit and there are a lot of other names for him too."

"Jobs like the ones at Spencer aren't a dime a dozen," Kevin said. "And the fact that she is a Spencer is an added benefit. That guy has it made."

"Let's just say that he 'had' it made," Lucy said.

They turned into the gravel parking lot amongst the Porsches, Range Rovers, and what looked like a Ferrari. The only Ferrari Lucy had ever seen was in the movie "Ferris Bueller's Day Off."

"Is that a Ferrari?" she asked.

"Yes, and there was an Aston Martin in here the other day," Kevin said.

"Well, I've never even heard of that one."

Lucy had impressed herself in recognizing the Ferrari and Wagoneer, but an Aston Martin was truly a foreign car to her.

They pulled into a spot that had a sign: *Reserved for Boat Owners and Registered Guests. Guests must receive a pass at the dock house or will be towed at the owner's expense.*

"I guess we need to secure a pass first, so you don't get towed," Lucy said, pointing to the sign. "This seems like the kind of place that will tow you in a skinny minute—even if you have a woody."

"It's okay," he laughed. "Mr. Barry knows my woody, no pun intended there for sure."

When walking down the ramp to the docks that housed all the big boats, Lucy quickly understood why this atmosphere appealed so much to Sammie. While the boats were ostentatious, and the place oozed money, there was a competing, more powerful sense of calm and peace. Mr. Barry was walking up the docks and waved at Kevin.

"How did a techno geek end up with such a looker?" Mr. Barry said, winking. He extended his hand and said, "I'm Harold Barry."

"It's nice to meet you. I'm Lucy Tate. Sammie and I used to work together before you stole her from me."

"I need to meet the person at your firm who does your hirin'," Harold Barry said. "I thought Sammie was one of the few broads that had brains to match her looks, but someone's done found themselves another one. Darlin', if you want to break out too, just give me a call."

Sammie had mentioned that Mr. Barry was a flirt but as harmless as a big teddy bear. With that inside information, Lucy replied, "Give me your number then, and I'll call you when my bullshit radar needs testing."

"Man, this is too much for an old seaman to handle," Mr. Barry said. "A gal with brains, good looks, and a sense of humor. You got yourself a keeper there, Kevin."

Other than his last awkward comment, Lucy thought Mr. Barry was a card. She was feeling better about Sammie working here. Though Harold Barry obviously could dole out the shit, she was confident that he wouldn't take any. He would have Sammie's back.

"Sammie has already been working with all the fancy equipment," Mr. Barry said. "There's not a problem already, is there?"

"No, I just want to measure the space that's still available," Kevin said. "One of my vendors has a cool desk that he is trying to get rid of. It's not for rent, you'd actually have to buy it, but it's a good price. I thought you may want to get Sammie a little gift for securing your new renter."

"I don't know anything about that," Harold said, shaking his head. "Or I should say, not since I've had to sign my life away with some legal document about the top-secret bullshit."

They went into the dock house. The natural light highlighted pictures of fishermen posing with their various catches from the sea. Lucy found the marina a welcoming, happy place. It was the polar opposite of the stuffy, sterile environment of the Spencer law firm. Sammie was busy on the computer. She didn't even hear their entry.

"Hey, girlie. This place is amazing, but I need to keep a close eye on this guy," Lucy said, looking towards Mr. Barry.

"I see that you've met my boss," Sammie said. "Nothing like my former bosses at the firm, huh?" Sammie asked, beaming.

She's going to be just fine, Lucy thought.

"So, Kevin, what do you need to measure?" Sammie asked. "I think everything is great. The setup is most efficient."

"I just wanted to confirm how much space was left in case the business office may need some additional equipment."

"Speaking of equipment, I got you a cell phone for orders. Sammie is also my Gal Friday," Harold said to Lucy and Kevin. "We're going to crush the competition by making deliveries. The phone has unlimited texting but limited minutes for calls. I figured you don't want calls but written orders so there is no confusion."

"What's the number?" Kevin asked. "Lucy and I need a beer," Kevin said, finishing his measurements.

"Ha, ha," Sammie said. "Mr. Barry, see what you've started. Zach's Crab Shack is next door. It has really cold beer and, best of all, river views. I'll go with you."

Kevin, Lucy, and Sammie walked back up the docks. The ramp was steeper due to the low tide, making it difficult for Lucy to climb in her work pumps. Kevin lifted her up and propped her on his hip.

"Geez, lawyers aren't used to making client visits on docks," Kevin said.

Sammie thought she was imagining things. If she didn't know better, she would have thought Kevin and Lucy had something going on.

Zach's Crab Shack was not what you'd expect of a restaurant next door to the marina parking lot with all its $100,000 foreign cars. Shack was an accurate description, but it had character—large, wooden-framed windows propped opened by nautical cleats. Though it was just a concrete block, it had the feel of an outdoor bar. There were dollar bills stapled all over the walls and ceiling with various messages written on them. Square box fans were secured to the ceiling. An oversized Blackbeard pirate flanked one end of the bar. In the back corner was a juke box. Lucy hadn't seen one of those since her college days at the fraternity houses.

"Go pick some music for us," Kevin said, handing Lucy a five-dollar bill.

Lucy couldn't help but think that this gesture was a test—to find out if she was a complete nerd with no musical IQ. She scanned the list. At a place like Zach's, she should have known that she couldn't go wrong with any pick. She decided to go with ones that had stood the test of time: "I Was Made for Lovin You" by Kiss; Steely Dan's "Peg"; and ABBA's "SOS."

Lucy joined Sammie and Kevin at a bar table with three tall wooden stools. They had already ordered a round. Lucy took the remaining stool close to Kevin's. When they were finishing their beers, the band, Kiss, boomed from the juke box.

"Is that one of your songs, Ms. Tate?" Kevin asked.

"It sure is."

"You are probably the only Spencer attorney who knows the band, Kiss."

"Well, you have your woody, and I have my Kiss," Lucy quipped.

"What did you say, Lucy?" Sammie asked, her eyes widening.

"Never mind, it's a joke," Lucy said. "Kevin made fun of me on the ride over. He has a Jeep Wagoneer—apparently, also referred to as a 'woody.' I had never heard that before."

"That makes two of us," Sammie said.

Again, Sammie wondered about her two former colleagues. They had this chemistry, and this comfortable banter. She didn't recall that they had been friends at the firm. She and Lucy had only interacted with Kevin when they had a computer issue. Lucy squelched Sammie's increasing curiosity.

"I hate to be a party pooper," Lucy said, "but I have to meet Randy at the Waffle House at 6:00 tomorrow morning with a deposition outline in hand. And, I haven't even started on it. It's looking like an all-nighter for me. I won't be able to stomach listening to Tiffany Putnam's charmed life with a hangover."

"I need to go as well," Sammie said. "I have a deadline too. I have to get a document to Mr. Davis tomorrow by noon. But I am on Cloud Nine to spend time with y'all. And, Lucy, I'm so glad you got to meet Mr. Barry and see my new office. You know you can come by anytime. Come to think of it, we should do this weekly."

"I wish you didn't have to work tonight," Kevin said, driving away from the marina. "I'd like to take you to dinner."

"I'd like nothing better," Lucy said. "I had so much fun. I just have to start cranking on this outline. It will be Waffle House time before I know it. Tomorrow is the last day of these depositions, so I'd love a raincheck."

"How about tomorrow night?" Kevin asked. "Or doesn't Randy take weekends off?"

"No, he doesn't. But hopefully he won't give me an assignment that has to be completed by 6:00 a.m. on Saturday. Dinner sounds great."

"I'll come up with a good place," Kevin said, pulling into the parking lot.

Lucy leaned forward to retrieve her computer case off the floorboard.

"Sorry, you should know better than to lean forward with a short skirt in a woody," he said.

"Is that so?" Lucy responded, sassily and leaning towards his face.

Instantly, they were kissing...hard. No first peck for them.

"I really have to go," she said, pulling away. "It's going to take me at least an hour before I can concentrate. I'll see you tomorrow."

"Night, Lucy. I'm already hating this guy, Bill Blauers. You promise you're going to ditch him tomorrow?"

"Oh yeah. He'll be kicked to the curb tomorrow night," she said.

Her insides were like butterflies. *How did all this just happen? Did she see this coming? Had she been unprofessional at work, flirting with him without realizing it? Screw it*, she thought. The rebellious side of Lucy Tate—the one that played the yard game on Ms. Hathaway's lawn and the one that entered the Hamilton Boardroom was yelling, "pick me, pick me." It was time that she picked the side of Lucy Tate that lived a little. She couldn't wait for tomorrow night.

If it's too good to be true, it's too good...

Chapter Thirty-Eight

Sammie & Grant Davis

"I appreciate your rationale for refusing to sign my confidentiality agreement, but we need to document our legal engagement," Grant said. "Here's a draft letter that sets forth the terms of your employment. I attempted to keep it simple after seeing how you butchered my other agreement. I am paying Harold a rather generous fee for use of the business office. My work needs to take priority over everything else."

Sammie was betting that the "generous fee" would likely cover the annual rental costs for the equipment. Mr. Barry was going to love that his innovative idea for a business office paid off so quickly.

"In summary, it provides that The Davis Group retains you as special counsel for a period of three months. I thought you may appreciate not having to record your time, so I am providing a flat fee of $5,000 per week. I appreciate that you have your gopher duties—which I have described a little more eloquently in our agreement as 'runner services.' I have also provided that such runner services can be utilized by The Davis Group."

Five thousand a week? Was he serious? Sammie needed to carefully review this contract.

"I'm quite confident that you will want to review this, so I'll step out," Grant Davis said. "I thought we'd have a working lunch. I'll serve as your gopher while you are marking up my contract. Would you prefer a sandwich or shrimp salad? Billy's shrimp salad is the best you'll ever have, by the way."

"I'd love to try Billy's shrimp salad. Being a local Charleston seafood connoisseur, I'll let you know how it ranks. And another water, please."

So, with that, the suave Grant Davis left Sammie Morgan with his handwritten engagement letter.

Sammie instructed herself to ignore the exorbitant fee. *Focus*, she counseled herself. *Pretend this is a document for a client.* She read it over three times. He had kept it simple. Her first revision was to clarify the time period since it was vague. She left the law firm due to her unpredictable schedule and certainly wasn't going to be on-call at any time of the day for three months. She inserted "The Davis Group retains you as special counsel between the hours of 9:00 a.m.-4:00 p.m., Monday-Friday, for a period of three months from the date of this letter (referred to as "Work Schedule"). The Work Schedule can only be exceeded by mutual agreement of the parties. She read the engagement over several times. It was concise and other than clarifying her hours, she found it more than fair.

Grant Davis returned about thirty minutes later with a tray of food.

"Wow, this is impressive. Maybe Mr. Barry should add you to the amenity selection as the resident chef."

"I have many talents, Sammie, but I've served my time in the trenches—I've been there and done that."

"Too bad," she said. "It appears you could be pocketing some big tips. Anyway, here's some slight revisions to your engagement letter."

"Now, why am I not surprised?" he smirked.

He put on his reading glasses. He read it over several times.

"You continue to impress me. This is acceptable."

He pulled out a pen and signed the bottom and handed the pen to Sammie.

"I'm not a suspicious person, Mr. Davis, but you need to initial the changes that I made in the body of the document."

"Yes, ma'am. Anything else?"

"No, that's it," she said, signing her name.

"If you feel better about typing this up, we can both sign the typed version as well," he said.

Sammie felt that she had already gotten off on the wrong foot commenting upon his agreement and the engagement letter.

"No, this works," she said.

"About your gopher services, I understand from Mr. Barry that he has provided you with a cell phone for calls and texts about errand requests," Grant said. "I'm sure you appreciate that I don't want my information to be public. I'd like to have more control over my communications. So, I am providing you with a cell phone to be used exclusively for my requests," he said, extending a new phone. "You don't need the number since I will be the only one communicating with you."

"That is fine," she said, placing the phone in her backpack but thinking he was skittish about possible leaks.

"Please start eating if you can focus on what I'm saying while being a food critic," he said. "I'm sure you have heard of your Senator Scott Hill and are probably aware that he is a rising star in his party. He was strongly considered as the Vice-Presidential running mate in the last election. Senator Hill has a pristine record. And you likely also know that many women find him 'easy on the eyes.' I don't know how much you know about his personal life. His wife, Caroline, is the only child of a very accomplished businessman who has invested wisely in the pharmaceutical industry. Have you ever heard of Drug Innovators?"

"No, I haven't," she said.

"Senator Hill's father-in-law was the primary investor when it was a fledgling start-up biopharmaceutical company. Last year, it received FDA approval for a break-through drug, and the company is now valued at $300 million dollars. So, let just say that Mrs. Hill's father has done very well for himself. Unfortunately, Mrs. Hill has been battling ovarian cancer and her prognosis, at this point, is uncertain. It has been a difficult year for her in radiation and chemotherapy."

"That's so sad," she said unconsciously, before realizing this was not the time to interject any opinion.

"Yes, it is," he said before continuing. "One of my best clients is a pharmaceutical company. I work with it on a range of issues but primarily before the roll-out of any new product. I also get involved with its legal counsel in formulating a public relations strategy if any claims arise due to a drug's adverse side effects."

"That's interesting. I hear about all the warnings on television commercials for various drugs, obviously written by lawyers. But I had no idea public relations experts were involved as well," she said, finding his area of expertise fascinating.

"I don't get involved in the advertising so much, only if someone has a serious side-effect attributed to the products' use. You know the press eats that kind of thing up, and it can spin out of control quickly."

"Sorry to interrupt. I haven't worked with pharmaceutical companies, so I may have a question or two as you go," Sammie said.

"Don't hesitate, though I get the impression that you are not shy in that regard. So, where was I? The company that I work with specializes in a very effective pain medication. It is highly successful but if not used properly, can be highly addictive. The drug is getting lots of attention because of its profitability and monopoly in the market."

Her head was about to explode. This was sounding too close to Worth Pharmaceutical's drug, Dolorine.

"I don't mean to interrupt again but would this company be Worth Pharmaceutical?" she asked.

"Yes, it is. So, you're familiar with Worth?"

"Yes. My husband works for Worth. He hasn't worked there long but is in sales. I may have a conflict of interest."

"If you let me finish, I think you will see that we are working for Worth. But I appreciate your raising that connection. And, I will emphasize again the confidentiality of this information. Based upon your earlier recitations about your ethical code, I assume that you appreciate that you cannot share any of this with your husband."

"Of course. I just needed to make you aware of this connection before you went any further."

"Point noted. If you husband is in sales, he must be aware that the Senate Finance Committee is investigating the company due to some allegations that a formulation of the drug was rejected that would, arguably, make it less addictive. Has your husband mentioned this investigation to you?"

"No. He never talks about his job other than customer locations. He travels a lot. We communicate about his schedule, stuff like that."

"It is well known that Senator Hill's lifestyle has been financed by his father-in-law who has pharmaceutical companies to thank for his accumulated wealth. Many of these companies are large contributors to Senator Hill's campaign finance fund. These facts, coupled with Ms. Hill's use of the pain products under investigation, made Senator Hill the logical choice for us reaching out to him. The company simply wants a fair shake. The company recently created an External Affairs/Communication Division and promoted a very smart woman as its director. She was previously a rising star in the sales division. Her name is Cathleen McKinney. Do you know her by chance?"

"No, we've never met," Sammie said, feeling uneasy. "But, she is my husband's boss," Sammie said, withholding her opinion of Cathleen McKinney.

Though there may be no conflict of interest, Sammie didn't want to work on anything associated with her.

"It's a small world, isn't it? Senator Hill has been meeting with Ms. McKinney extensively during this process to become educated on the facts so that he can objectively evaluate the FDA claims. It appears that the working relationship has become, well, more than just professional. They were recently spotted together in Key West. We are investigating the "together" aspect of it. But, this could get very sticky. Worth retained me to work with Senator Hill due to the detrimental effect any perceived relationship may have on the hearings."

The notes from Cathleen McKinney to Dougie came flooding back to Sammie's mind. But this time, she felt no sympathy for Dougie. It sounded like Dougie had met his match in Cathleen. She suddenly wondered if Grant's "due diligence" on her had somehow uncovered Dougie's employment by Worth, or if he knew about Dougie and Cathleen. There were too many coincidences.

"With all due respect, Mr. Davis" …

"Sammie, please call me Grant," he interrupted.

"Okay, Grant, all of this is outside of my area of expertise. I am not a PR specialist and don't know anything about the pharmaceutical industry."

"No," Grant said, "but you do appreciate that the English language is very powerful. I am the PR specialist. I don't need any help in that regard. You are obviously well-trained in drafting documents and the legal ramifications if the precise words aren't used. You are proficient in word processing as well, correct?"

"Yes, I know all the programs that were identified on your list to Mr. Barry. I just want us to be on the same page with our expectations because your fee is very generous."

"Sammie, you pay for the best when you're in my business. I assure you that any lawyer we involve will be charging $1,000 bucks an hour. You know the drill. Some lawyers use a case to make a name for themselves and overvalue their role. You don't have any career motives from this engagement. In fact, this situation couldn't be any more perfect. My instincts are typically right on target. But, if it makes you feel better, I have a team of lawyers that can review everything in more detail, if necessary. It's nearly 3:00. I don't want to exceed your "Work Schedule" on the first day, so here's an outline of talking points that I need for a conference call tomorrow. Type these up and have the document to me by 10:00 tomorrow morning. And don't forget your phone. I may need some things."

"It's already in my briefcase," Sammie said, holding up her backpack. "I'll see you tomorrow."

Sammie wasn't going to be a stickler on the defined Work Schedule just yet. He was paying her too much. There was no way she was telling Lucy about the terms of her engagement. Lucy would again chalk it up to how things fell into place for Sammie. But after all the discoveries of the last year, Sammie thought she deserved a nice break.

On the way back to the dock house, Sammie called her mother.

"I actually have a legal assignment for one of the slip renters," she relayed. "I may be a little late."

"Take your time, sweetie. We are going to the club for dinner. Mack always draws a crowd of lookers. If you're done in time, you can join us."

"I think I'll just stay here," Sammie said. "I can focus on this assignment without feeling rushed."

Truthfully, Sammie wanted to avoid questions from her parents' country club friends. The news had likely percolated through town about her resignation from the family firm.

As she was proofreading the document, her new cell phone buzzed. She reached in her backpack.

I need 2 pounds of shrimp, ketchup, horseradish, arugula, mozzarella, tomatoes, and if gopher is available, I'll prepare dinner for her.

Now, this was interesting. Sammie thought that she shouldn't read anything more into it, but she was suddenly curious if Grant Davis was married. He wasn't wearing a wedding band. She had noticed that when he tossed her the bottled water. She reasoned that he was probably just lonely. The boat was awesome, but it couldn't be fun being cooped up and hiding from the public all the time.

She texted back.

Just finished so gopher can drop off outline with order. I'd love dinner. Be there in hr, that ok?

As she printed the document, turned off her computer, the phone buzzed, *perfect*.

Sammie was excited about dinner. Grant Davis was smart, confident, powerful, and filled a room with his presence. And he seemed grounded. Not many men in his position would put aside their ego and listen to a female. But he listened, processed her points, and agreed to her proposed changes to his confidentiality agreement and engagement letter.

She drove fast to Lowcountry Seafood, the closest market on this side of the peninsula. Naturally, the market had fresh seafood but often a great selection of vegetables. But she wasn't certain it would have arugula. It would take fifteen minutes longer at this time of the day to make it to the Piggly Wiggly. She quickly assembled everything from the list except arugula. Spring mix would have to suffice.

When she got back to the marina, she checked her watch. She had a couple of hours to enjoy dinner before her parents returned with Mack.

As she approached *Sea Relations*, Billy was out on the back deck cleaning the sliding glass doors. He saw the bag of groceries and ran to help.

"What do you have?" he asked, puzzled.

"Can't you tell I am a workaholic?" Sammie said, jokingly. "I have two jobs here. One is at the business office and the other is running errands. So, let me know if you ever need anything from shrimp to bumpers. These are ingredients that Mr. Davis requested. He is cooking dinner tonight. I guess it's a working dinner."

She didn't know why she felt like she owed Billy an explanation for her being there.

"Quite impressive. I can assure you that none of our stops, and we've had a lot, have this type of service. Grant's not back from his run."

"Run as in jogging?" she asked.

"He prefers early mornings but often will go again at night," Billy said. "Need any help?"

"No, other than I need to get the shrimp on ice," Sammie said. "I'd hate for Mr. Davis to get sick from food poisoning with my first delivery. It could spell disaster for Mr. Barry's newest guest amenity."

"Sure, this way. He should be back soon. He was only going to run six."

"Only? What is his usual distance?"

"It really depends on his stress level. If he's had a bad day, he'll go ten or more."

Sammie hoped that he had a good day. She couldn't stay long.

"I'm on sort of a tight schedule. Do you know what he had in mind so I could start preparing stuff? I'm assuming the ketchup and horseradish is for cocktail sauce," Sammie said, as she mixed the two ingredients.

"And shrimp," Billy said, laughing while retrieving a large pot.

He started simmering the water.

"Care for a drink while you wait?" Billy asked. "Grant has everything so whatever your pleasure."

They settled on the back deck with a beer.

"I love this time of day on the water," she said.

"Me too," Billy said. "I run with Grant some mornings, but this time of day is my winding down time."

"I don't have a running preference really," Sammie said. "After a morning run, I feel like I'm more alert throughout the day, but there is nothing like an evening run to dull the edge."

"Running is how I met Grant," Billy volunteered. "We both ran a marathon down in the Keys. It was some fifteen years ago. We met at the docks after the race. We both had our medals and race t-shirts in hand, started talking about the course, our finishing time—you know, race stuff. Then, Grant had a much smaller boat that he ran himself. I was captaining a 90-footer then. Grant shared that he was looking for a larger boat but was reluctant to hire a captain—you know due to the sensitive nature of his work—but knew he couldn't handle a bigger boat by himself. Grant took my number and called about six months later. I was ready for a change and new challenge, and this vessel is pretty rockin'."

About that time, Grant emerged. He was soaked. Lucy would love running with him. He sweated like her.

"Well, it's nice to see that my two employees are having drinks and relaxing while the old guy is trying to stay alive. I apologize, Sammie. I didn't know I would be this long."

He grabbed a water from the outdoor wet bar refrigerator.

"I'll be right back."

Grant was back in no time with two glasses of wine, his hair still wet from his shower.

"I'm replacing your beer with one of my favorites—an Oregon Pinot," he said, swirling the wine, breathing the aroma, and taking a sip. "Delicious?"

"Agree," Sammie said. "But before I forget, here's the outline for your call tomorrow."

"Right now, I'm famished," Grant Davis said. "Let me cook, and we'll discuss a plan over dinner. Speaking of dinner, I see that the water is simmering, and the cocktail sauce is made."

"I need to leave before too long so thought I'd get things started. Do you need any help?"

"No, you've done enough," he said. "You are my guest, remember? Billy will keep you good company while I cook. Shrimp doesn't take long. It's nice out tonight. Let's eat outside. Be back shortly."

Billy and Sammie continued to talk about Billy's background, his family, and when he became passionate about boating. He was easy to talk to, like an old friend. Grant came out intermittently to set the table and pour more wine. Interesting that he was the king of this castle but was acting like the hired help. Conversely, the hired help was enjoying drinks, chatting it up, and listening to music.

The meal was light and fresh but filling. The fresh shrimp and homemade balsamic dressing drizzled over the tomato and mozzarella salad was delicious.

After dinner, Grant asked Sammie if she had time to go over the outline.

"The reason I quit the firm was to spend more time with Mack," she said. "But, if you want to call me with the changes tonight, I can work on them later. Or I can meet with you first thing in the morning."

"Tomorrow is fine," Grant Davis said. "That will give me sufficient time to think about any additions. But don't go yet, I need to pay the gopher for our dinner."

"Don't worry about it," she said. "You are paying me more than enough. This one is on me."

"Ms. Morgan, you cannot breach our contract on the first day," he said. "That is grounds for termination. I'll be right back."

Grant returned with a wad of cash.

"For your services," he said.

There were several $100 bills.

"Mr. Davis, I cannot accept this," she said handing him back the cash.

He raised his eyebrows with a look of disdain. He took one of the $100 bills back.

"That's for calling me Mr. Davis," he said. "Now, scoot, see you in the morning."

Sammie felt like she was walking on water. She didn't need the money, but it assured her that he was not taking advantage of the situation.

As she pulled into her parent's house, her hotline buzzed. *Grande Starbucks coffee & oatmeal for me + whatever gophers eat for breakfast.* Sammie smiled. She looked forward to seeing him the next morning.

Chapter Thirty-Nine

Lucy

Round Three of Tiffany Putnam's deposition was more of the same. Lucy had enough of this woman. After the first day, Lucy didn't have the level of scorn for her that Randy did. But, she was beginning to see why Randy took cases only from men. Lucy thought that she, too, would have a hard time representing the Tiffany Putnams of the world.

Clearly, Tiffany had pursued James for his money and never loved him. He was an idiot for cheating on his first wife, Yvonne, with Tiffany. But then again, based on Tiffany's deposition, Yvonne didn't love him either. Regardless, Yvonne had been there from the beginning. Tiffany waltzed into the union after James Putnam had struck gold, so her belief that she was entitled to half of his assets was beyond comprehension.

At the close of the deposition, Randy offered Tiffany $20 million in cash, her choice of either the West Palm Beach penthouse or the Kiawah oceanfront house, and $30,000 a month in alimony for ten years. Though Ms. Waters attempted to hide her smile thinking about the payday this would bring her, she simply said that she and her client would discuss the offer. But, Tiffany ignored her lawyer and rejected it outright.

"That bastard is crazy if he believes that he can leave me destitute," she said. "I'm entitled to half. That's the law."

With that, she picked up her $5,000 Chanel purse and stormed out. Randy calmly shrugged his shoulders at Ms. Waters.

"The offer expires at 5 p.m. Monday," Randy said. "I hope you enjoy your weekend, Carolyn."

"So, what do you think she will do?" Lucy asked Randy. "It sure seems like a generous offer."

"You never know with these women, Lucy," Randy said. "For some reason, they develop a sense of en..tit..le..ment." (Only Randy could turn four syllables into at least eight). A judge could award her more, but it will be a long battle. The greedy BIT-ches get antsy, so we'll see."

Lucy was beginning to think these ED laws were for the birds, at least in these circumstances. She had a lot to learn. She felt that Tiffany wasn't entitled to anything. She should have to work to earn her money the old-fashioned way, from the sweat of her salon-perfected brows.

"You did a fine job on these outlines and your exa...min...a..tion," Randy said. "You can take the weekend off, unless you want to join me at the Waffle House in the morning."

"I'm going to have to pass on breakfast," Lucy said. "I have a long run planned tomorrow. The Waffle House and jogging aren't a good combination."

Lucy was beginning to wonder what Randy's wife did. Randy had invited her no fewer than ten times to the Waffle House since she started working for him.

"Doesn't your wife cook for you, Randy?" Lucy asked.

"Hell fucking no," he said. "You'd think I'd get it right by the fourth time, but I'm apparently as big of a dumbass as James Putnam."

"I'm sorry. I hope you have a great weekend. I'll see you on Monday."

Lucy really enjoyed working with Randy, but she had a date. She needed to shower and change before her likely firm-prohibited date picked her up. Given the number of firm policies, she was confident that one outlawed dating employees. But, she certainly wasn't going to research it. It was always better to ask forgiveness rather than permission.

Lucy headed to her condo on James Island. Crossing the bridge over the Ashley River. She realized that she didn't know where Kevin lived. She doubted that he lived on the peninsula, so their date location was probably more casual. She tried to call Sammie during a break but got her voicemail. Sammie had not returned her call despite Lucy's message that she had an urgent fashion question. Sammie knew about Lucy's date. Surely, the legal affairs of a marina couldn't be that demanding. Lucy tried her again. Her call went straight into voicemail.

Sammie, it's me again. I hate to bother you, but Kevin is picking me up at 7:30. I need your advice on an outfit. Pllllleeeaasse call me back. Headed home now to stare at my closet and stress.

As Lucy pulled into her garage, her phone rang. It was an unknown number. She wasn't about to answer that call. It hadn't taken her long to discover that an unknown caller was often a partner on the line with an emergency project. Lucy let the caller go into voicemail.

It's Sammie. I hate I missed you. This is one of my gopher phones. I don't even know the number. I'll call you again when I finish this pickup. You will look beautiful in anything even it is a paper bag. Answer next time!

Lucy placed her cell on the bathroom counter and jumped into the shower. Just as she began rinsing the shampoo out of her hair, her cell phone rang. She bolted out of the shower leaving a puddle of water as she reached for her phone.

"Sammie?" Lucy asked, hoping it was her.

"Yeah, it's me," Sammie said. "I was afraid you wouldn't answer. I know how you avoid unknown callers. I'm on one of these gopher phones. Where are you going?"

"I don't know. That's my dilemma. I'm guessing that Kevin is not the stuffy restaurant type."

"Well, if you don't know where you're going, I'd go with your shift dress. The one with the colorful, paisley print with the openings in the sleeves. That dress is versatile and would work with casual or fine dining. It would look adorable with your new ballet flats."

"I knew you would know the right thing. I miss you. How are things with the PR stud?"

"Fine, I'm staying busy," Sammie said. "What's strange is that I don't miss the firm at all. Other than you, of course. I want to hear all about your date on our run tomorrow."

"Ha. Hopefully, I will have something to talk about other than Tiffany Putnam. Call me and let me know what time works."

"Have a great time. I am excited for you. I really like Kevin."

"Yeah, he's yummy. Bye, sweetie, and thanks."

Lucy put on the dress that Sammie suggested but ditched her flats. They looked too esquire-ish. She felt like a 16-year old getting ready for her first date. It had been a long time. Her heart skipped a beat when she heard the doorbell. She thought that she gasped when she opened the door. Non-legal attire definitely accentuated Kevin's assets. His muscular arms were more visible beneath his short-sleeved shirt fully exposing his modest tattoo of small waves encircling his bicep. There was no designer logo on his shirt or blue jeans. His look was simple but sexy.

"Wow!" Kevin said. "Lucy Tate, you look fabulous. I like your place. Do you like it over here?"

"It's fine. I'd rather be closer to the water. I didn't even ask you where you lived when you offered to get me. I hope I wasn't too far out of the way."

"Not at all. I'm on Folly Beach, and one of my favorite restaurants there is Taco Boy. Do you like Mexican?"

"I love Mexican. But don't let me overindulge on chips, salsa, and queso."

"Well, I'm not making any promises because this place has the best homemade salsa, queso, and margaritas. All pretty addictive."

"How long have you been with the firm, Kevin?" Lucy asked. "I know it's been at least six years because you were here when I started."

"I remember. I recall thinking now here's evidence that you can be a female lawyer and hot at the same time."

Lucy blushed.

"I have been at Spencer for eight years. Prior to that, I was with a tech company. A Columbia law firm was one of our clients," Kevin said. "Eugene Baker was working with one of the attorneys there and had all kinds of technical issues. I helped him daily for about a week. He asked me for my card. He said that his firm was looking for a new technology director. He scheduled an interview for me on the spot."

"That is so great. Spencer would have never considered me unless it had to."

"What do you mean 'had to?'"

"I won a diversity scholarship that the firm endowed. It was exclusively based on my class rank. White men were eligible, if that tells you anything."

"Ha. After I researched the firm, I knew I didn't have a shot at the job. I didn't doubt my qualifications but, as you know, Spencer is not very diverse. Every partner is more than lily white—all Charleston born and bred, private school educated, and Ivey League degrees," Kevin said.

"To be honest with you, I can't believe I have survived and am one year away from being one of those lily white partners."

"I didn't mean to insult you. I just couldn't help but think when the others discovered that I was black, my interview would be cancelled. When it wasn't, I thought that I was the one who needed to be more open-minded. But, there is no denying that the place is about as stodgy as butterscotch pudding. I have enjoyed it, but, no offense, I've had my fill of attorneys. PICNIC problems are not challenging."

"Did you say 'picnic' problems?" Lucy asked.

"Yes—Problem In Chair Not In Computer."

They had a wonderful Mexican meal. Kevin was right. The salsa and queso were addictive. Lucy didn't drink much. Billable hours and alcohol were not a good combination. She had a slight buzz from the margaritas. All the tequila forewarnings scrolled through her brain: *Tequila makes your clothes fall off,* and *tequila is a sneaky bitch.* Her thoughts were interrupted by Kevin.

"What ya thinking about? It's like you went somewhere."

"Oh, I was thinking that tequila has the potential to make me crazy."

"How crazy?" he asked. "I'll order you another one, or we can go to my place at Folly Beach. I have some tequila at my house, or if you're scared of crazy, I have some beer."

"I'd love to see your place and switching to beer would be a wise move on my part."

Unlike the gated, manicured resorts with their 5000-plus square foot multi-million dollar homes, Folly Beach was an accessible, unpretentious town. A game of volleyball, frisbee, or cornhole was always in full action in the sand among the visiting college students from the Citadel or College of Charleston.

Kevin described his Folly Beach residence as a "fixer upper hut." He fell in love with it because of the view of the marsh, the Folly River, and the proximity to the ocean.

Arriving after dark, Lucy couldn't see the views, but she could smell the salty, ocean air. His "hut" was about the size of her condo—800 square feet but with twice the charm. He grabbed two Coronas from his fridge, cut some limes, and they retreated to the screened-in porch. He lit candles and put on music.

They talked awhile before Lionel Richie's album of duets with popular country artists filled the room. The crashing of the whitecaps and the chirping of the crickets provided perfect accompaniment to Jimmy Buffet and Lionel's rendition of the old classic, "All Night Long." As Lionel started singing "Stuck on You," Kevin took the beer out of Lucy's hand and started dancing with her.

"Who is this singing with Lionel?"

"You don't recognize that South Carolina boy?" Kevin asked. "That is Darius Rucker. No better combo than Lionel and Darius."

Kevin pulled her closer as their feet shuffled across the porch. He leaned down and started kissing Lucy's neck. She didn't know if it was the effects of the earlier tequila or the awesomeness of the evening, but she was light-headed. His lips then moved to hers. They kissed through the entire next song, "Endless Love" with Shania Twain. She could feel Kevin's hip bones pressed firmly against hers while they danced. As the song ended, Kevin blew out the candles, took her hand, and led her back into the house.

"You ready for me to take you home or could I talk you into another beer?"

Lucy wondered what more alcohol could lead to.

"I don't need anything else to drink, but I'm not ready to leave," she blurted.

Lucy couldn't believe she had said that. She grew anxious and could feel sweat emanating through every pore. Kevin's kiss stopped her overactive brain.

"I'm not ready for you to leave either."

Her legs felt weak. Her insides felt mushy. For once in her life, Lucy Tate couldn't form a sentence. He kissed her again. Time seemed to stand still. Her mind and body relaxed. They ended up on his sofa, though Lucy couldn't recall how.

"I better take you home now before I don't," Kevin said, when they came up for air.

"I could borrow some PJs," Lucy said.

"PJs?" Kevin asked, laughing. "I haven't heard that in a long time. But I can find some PJ's for you," he said, walking into his room.

"This is the best that I can do," he said, reappearing with a t-shirt.

The t-shirt was stiff and looked like it had never been worn. On the front pocket was printed: Charleston Ashley Dockage.

"Mr. Barry gave this to me for helping him out with the equipment," he said. "Kind of cool, huh? You can break it in for me."

"Well, that Mr. Barry is always thinking of ways to market his marina, huh?" Lucy said, laughing.

She retreated to the bathroom, put on the t-shirt, and brushed her teeth with her finger. She climbed into bed and pulled up the covers. The room was cooling off from the breeze blowing through the large screened windows. She heard Kevin locking the doors and turning off the lights.

"Is it too cold in here for you?" he asked, noting that she was buried under the covers. "The salt air helps me sleep, but I can shut the windows or find you some warmer pajamas."

"No, leave them open," she said. "This is much better than my white noise, sleeping machine."

He unbuckled his belt and dropped his jeans on the floor. His body was divine. She smiled at the sight of his white cotton boxer briefs. As she hugged the covers to her neck, she thought about the last time that she had ended up in bed with a guy. It had been years, after her judgment was impaired from celebrating her final law school exam.

Lucy thought he knew that she was checking him out as he walked into the bathroom. Work clothes did not do him justice. She started feeling silly asking for some "PJs." She must have sounded like a schoolgirl at her first sleepover. After he climbed into bed, Lucy curled up next to him. He put his arm around her and kissed her softly on the forehead.

"How do the PJs fit?" he asked.

She rubbed his chest. Then, her hand moved to his six-pack abs. Before she comprehended what she was doing, her hand was touching the elastic band of his boxers.

"Too big, do you have something else?"

"I'll see what I can find," he said, lifting the t-shirt over her head.

By now, she had pushed his boxers down to his knees. He rolled to the side of the bed, kicked them off, and quickly retrieved something from his bedside chest. Before she had time to think about what was happening, they were melded together. They were ravenous for each other. For once, Lucy didn't mind the sheen of sweat covering her body. Kevin was slick with sweat too. The cool breeze from the windows couldn't cool the heat bursting from their connection.

"For a minute, I thought we may slide right off the bed," Kevin said, rolling off of her. "Let me get us a towel and water.""

He got up and went into the kitchen. He came back with a bottled water, a towel, and an ice-cold Corona.

They sat up in bed and shared the beer. Then he took a big swig of water, leaned over, and kissed her while slowly releasing the water from his mouth into hers.

"Now, that's how I like to hydrate," Lucy said.

So, he did it again and again. Somewhere between three or four swallows, they were back at it. He opened the drawer of his nightstand again.

Afterward, he snuggled up behind her and draped a leg over hers with his arm across her waist. She could feel his breath on her neck and the rhythm was as steady as the ocean breeze. She was so relaxed. She wished that she could bottle this evening, this feeling of companionship. But, not surprisingly, the uninhibited Lucy Tate had left the building and the interrogating lawyer had returned. *How many girls had slept in his bed? How many times have his legs and arms been draped around someone else? How many condoms did he keep in his nightstand? When was the last time someone was over? Would everything be okay in the morning? Would it be awkward at work?* Somewhere amongst all the questions, Lucy Tate fell fast asleep and didn't move until the sunrise peeked through the windows.

Beware of a wolf in sheep's clothing...

Chapter Forty

Sammie

Sammie couldn't wait to take Grant Davis breakfast and engage her brain. Her mother had been right about getting a job. The marina gig was the medicine she needed. It made her get out of bed. It made her wear something other than her pajamas or exercise clothes—her only wardrobe since officially moving into her parents. The problem was everything else remained in the boxes that Dougie had a delivery service dump on her parents' front porch. She hadn't had the energy to open the first one until now.

"Mack, what do you think Mommy should wear today? I'm thinking about jeans and a sweater. What do you think?"

Mack cooed, beat his hands on the bumper bar, and lurched forward in the stroller urging her faster.

"Faster it is," Sammie said.

As Sammie was dressing, she reconsidered the navy sweater she selected. When Glenny had purchased it for her, she thought it was perfectly professional but hadn't realized that the back neckline was much lower than the front. It revealed too much skin for the Spencer law firm, in Sammie's opinion, but it seemed perfect for a marina setting. Her patented ponytail provided cover for most of her back. *Conservative with a twist*, she thought.

As she was walking down the docks to *Sea Relations*, she ran into Mr. Barry.

"What have we got here?" he asked, looking Sammie up and down.

"I have on my delivery girl hat this morning," Sammie responded, straightforwardly. "I had an order for Starbucks from *Sea Relations*."

"Besides Mr. Hot Shot, has anyone else placed an order?" he asked.

How was she going to explain that Grant Davis had provided her with a phone for just his texts?

"Actually, no. When we were working yesterday, Mr. Davis asked me to bring coffee. We are meeting again this morning. But, we need to advertise that service," she said, trying to divert the conversation from Grant Davis.

"You're right. Could you come up with some type of flyer on your fancy equipment?" he asked.

"Yes, that's a great idea. I'll start on that soon."

Billy met her at the back deck and grabbed the coffee.

"I brought you something too."

"I really appreciate that," Billy said. "The boat captain is usually overlooked. Follow me. Grant is waiting for you upstairs."

Instead of his office, Grant was in the large room outside of his office with great views of the Ashley River. Papers were spread across the large chrome and glass table.

"Good morning, Sammie," Grant said, peering over his reading glasses. "I don't know what I'm more impressed with. Your legal abilities or delivery service."

He took his glasses off, placed them on his desk, and took a sip of his coffee.

"I have a surprise for you," he said. "Senator Hill has been offshore fishing with one of his buddies and will be returning today. I thought it would be more productive and private if we interviewed him in person."

Sammie couldn't believe that she was going to be in the same room her senator discussing a potential scandal.

"His buddy is dropping him off here around noon—in *Silver Lining*, a Grady-White Canyon 366—not a wise move if you want to arrive under the radar."

"I'm partial to sailing," Sammie said. "I don't know much about fishing boats. I'm assuming by your comment that *Silver Lining* is impressive?"

"You might say that. Other than his choice of arrival, my initial research indicates that the man is very smooth, so I want you to pay close attention to every word he says. Take notes this time. We need every fact nailed down. Your legal training will prove useful in our interrogation. Feel free to jump in and ask for clarification if something doesn't measure up."

Grant went over the facts, as he understood them and questions for the senator. Sammie was furiously taking notes.

"I'll get this typed up. Is there anything else?"

"Yes, there is. You are very smart and meticulous. It's good to have you on the team."

Sammie returned to the business office and typed the list of questions. Her hotline buzzed. She had begun noticing the connection between an errand request from Grant Davis and the tingling of her skin. She quickly looked at the text: *a fine cigar for after.*

Grant Davis didn't want just any cigar but a "fine" one. For some reason, she wanted to exceed his expectations but didn't know anything about cigars. She couldn't take too much time with the request or she would miss the delivery of her senator aboard *Silver Lining.*

Mr. Barry startled her when he suddenly appeared in the makeshift office.

"Have you gotten to that flyer yet?" Mr. Barry asked.

She wanted to ask him to identify a "fine cigar" brand but vetoed her idea.

"Not yet. This is a big day. Our own Senator Hill is arriving soon on some Grady White fishing boat—but remember what you signed. Do not breathe a word about that. I'll get a flyer to you soon."

She printed the questions and sprinted out of the business office. She didn't turn back to wait for any response. She ran at full speed to her car. *Not a day for skinny jeans,* she thought. She knew of one cigar store on King Street due to the distinct tobacco smells that seeped out to the sidewalk. She hoped her hunch was right. She rushed to the counter.

"I work at the Charleston Ashley Dockage, and one of our best slip tenants has requested a 'fine cigar.' My boss wants to impress him. Price is not an issue."

"Ahhh, I can help you. It will certainly impress," the worker said. "I have an Arturo Fuente Opus X BBMF—stands for Big Bad Mother F. I won't offend the lady, but you know the rest. They are very difficult to find. $65."

"Sold," she said, handing him the cash and running out.

Sammie thought the cigar would be perfect. A BBMF for a BBMF. Too bad she couldn't tell Mr. Barry about this. He would love the name. She raced back to the marina and ran down the ramp to the docks. As she was walking at a fast clip to *Sea Relations*, she heard loud music coming from the Ashley River from an approaching center console fishing boat. So much for keeping his arrival under the radar. *Egos and testosterone have a way of asphyxiating the brain*, Sammie thought.

Grant was on his aft deck shaking his head. As Senator Hill exited the fishing boat and walked towards *Sea Relations*, Grant retreated trying to avoid the onlookers and motioned Sammie inside.

The senator was better looking in this setting than the various media portrayed him in the Senate Chamber. His sunburned face accentuated his head full of blonde hair. Coupled with his fit and tall physique, he had movie star quality. He wore Sperry boat shoes, khaki shorts, and a fishing shirt. Billy escorted him in.

"Senator," Grant Davis said, coldly, "I see that my work is cut out for me. I thought you'd be smarter than to call attention to your arrival. If someone recognized you, I'm confident that the dock chatter is already abuzz. So, let's get down to work as quickly as possible and get you out of here."

Senator Hill's carefree swagger seemed perplexed by Grant's scolding. He extended his tanned hand and switched gears. He advanced a serious tone introducing himself to Sammie.

"I'm Samantha Spencer, senator. I work with Mr. Davis. It's nice to meet you."

Sammie didn't know what possessed her to use her maiden name. The connection with Worth and Cathleen McKinney were too close for comfort. Grant raised his eyebrows at her introduction.

"Have you had lunch, senator?" Grant asked.

"I have not, but my buddy, Tripp, is cutting up a tuna that we caught for some filets. He is planning to serve us lunch if that's okay with you."

"That sounds wonderful. My captain will help him. In the interim, let's begin."

Grant looked at Sammie.

"Samantha is an attorney, so our communications are protected and privileged. We've prepared questions that may be hurled at you with cameras rolling. Of course, we don't know the facts," Grant said. "That's why you are here. But, our questions are only a preview of what may come. I am here to help you, but I cannot do my job unless you are one-hundred percent truthful."

"I am a straight shooter. Trust me, I'm not here to play games. I wouldn't be here if I didn't appreciate the fact that I need help," he said, his voice cracking, "and some water."

"While you look these over, I'll get you some water and check on lunch," Grant said, handing Senator Scotty Hill the list of questions probing into the details of his infidelity.

Sammie watched him intently, noting his reaction to each question. When one hit a sensitive area, no response was necessary. Senator Hill's body language clearly revealed the answer. He was not the same man who nonchalantly walked off *Silver Lining*. He was more like the tuna that was being sliced opened and grilled.

Grant returned and watched the distinguished United States senator. He studied the squint of his eyes, the furrow of his eyebrows, the twitch of his shoulders, and the way he squirmed in his chair.

The potential disaster that awaited him was finally sinking in, Sammie thought.

When Senator Scotty Hill finished the questions, he massaged his temples.

"I love my job. I am honored to serve my constituents. I experienced a severe lapse in judgment, but I am not here to make excuses. I'm ready to begin."

Sammie prepared to take notes but was becoming nauseated. It was like watching Dougie after she found the notes from his boss—same body language, same facial expressions, and the same woman.

*Politicians are like cream in buttermilk;
and there is no cream in buttermilk...*

Chapter Forty-One

Senator Scotty Hill

"Grant, as you know I am a member of the Senate Finance Committee, and our committee has launched an investigation into painkiller prescription drugs, particularly, opioid drugs. The misuse is epidemic. Some members of the committee want to curtail access to these medications. I, however, have witnessed firsthand the benefit of these drugs. My wife, Caroline, couldn't have survived the past two years without them. She is battling ovarian cancer and has been taking Worth Pharmaceutical's pain drug, Dolorine."

Just the mention of Worth made Sammie ill at ease.

"Caroline is a fighter, but without Dolorine, I don't think she would have been able to accomplish the things that she has over the last year. I am a big fan of this drug. My critics think it's because Worth is a generous contributor to my campaign fund. But, that's not true. It's simply that it is the best pain management drug on the market."

The senator had certainly regained his composure. He sounded rehearsed.

"Plus, I understand that your father-in-law has done quite well in investments in startup biopharmaceutical companies," Grant said.

"That is true, but my support of Dolorine has nothing to do with big pharma's campaign contributions or my father-in-law. My support is due to watching someone you love deeply suffer and the relief this drug has provided."

He closed his eyes, took a gulp of water, and took a couple of deep breaths.

"During the course of this investigation, I was eager to learn everything I could— information that I would only learn through our investigation, especially less addictive alternatives or undisclosed side effects. I was contacted by Cathleen McKinney, who works for Worth."

Sammie attempted to smother the emotions that flamed inside her at the mention of Cathleen McKinney. Sammie knew where this was headed.

"Prior to this time, I had never met nor heard of Ms. McKinney. She offered to educate me about Dolorine and help me understand the clinical trial data. We met on several occasions."

After a long pause, Senator Hill continued.

"Do either of you know Senator Tony DeVore?" he asked.

"I know that he serves with you on the Senate Finance Committee investigating Dolorine," Grant answered. "From Florida, correct?"

"Yes," Senator Hill said. "His constituency is very interested in reducing drug prices. In his opinion, we are on the opposite ends of the spectrum with the pharmaceutical industry. I know that he questions whether I am capable of being fair—that I am too connected financially to the drug companies."

"Do you know him?" Senator Hill asked, looking directly at Sammie.

"No, I don't," Sammie answered, but wondering why in the world he would think that she knew any politician from Florida.

"Senator DeVore will stop at nothing to increase his notoriety in the senate. He views me as an impediment to his rise in power. He cannot be trusted and will manipulate any situation in his favor. The Senate Finance Committee's investigation provides him the perfect opportunity to highlight that 'pharma is my back pocket.' After I learned that he was keeping tabs on my visits with Ms. McKinney, I said that we meet somewhere other than in my office to avoid further detection by Tony DeVore. She made some joke that we should meet on a deserted island. I laughed and agreed that when she had secured such a spot to let me know, but in the interim, I didn't think it was wise to meet in Washington."

Sammie was getting an inside look at this heinous woman's maneuvers. She was finding it difficult to stay objective.

"Within the hour, she called back to say that one of the Worth executives had a yacht docked in Key West at the Sun Key Marina, and the boat was available on Sunday for such a meeting. The location couldn't have been better because Tripp, my buddy who brought me here, had invited me to go fishing in Key Largo that week. I decided to fly into Miami on Thursday morning, drive to Key Largo, fish with Tripp, and then drive on down to Key West on Sunday morning."

Sammie was trying to forget Cathleen McKinney and stay focused on her memorialization of his story.

"Later in the week, Ms. McKinney called my office and left a voicemail. She had details about the meeting. I called her back, and it was during this conversation that she said she was trying to find a way around my having to pick up a visitor's pass at the dock house. I was impressed with her sensitivity to the confidential nature of our meeting. She seemed to have thought through every detail."

"Excuse me for interrupting—you called her back from your phone in your D.C. office?" Grant asked.

Sammie was disappointed in herself for not catching that lack of detail. She wasn't listening as a lawyer but as a bitter wife.

"Yes, but on her cell phone. She had left her cell number on my voicemail. That was the last conversation I had with her in D.C. I called her back sometime Friday evening when I was in Key Largo. During that conversation she said that you could bypass check-in at the dock house with a gate code."

He paused and turned to Sammie.

"I apologize but the code she gave me was 6969 pound. She said that it was probably the idea of a horny dockmaster but that she liked the idea...I can't recall exactly, but I viewed it as another flirtation."

The woman was despicable through and through, Sammie thought.

"It was during this conversation that she told me the yacht would be available all weekend, so we could have a more leisurely schedule. I told her that Saturday would work better because I could get back to Miami on Sunday for a flight back to D.C. She also told me on that call that *Prescribed* was at the end of Dock #3."

"Who else knew that you were going to be in the Keys?" Grant asked.

"My wife, my assistant, and my chief of staff knew that I went to Key Largo, just not Key West. I wasn't dishonest. I just didn't fully disclose my itinerary. No one knew I was in Key West, except Cathleen McKinney. I didn't stop at the dock house since I had the code to the gate and the yacht's location. I went straight to the boat. I don't recall even seeing anyone that Saturday morning other than some deckhands, who didn't pay any attention to me."

In checking her notes, Sammie confirmed with the senator that the gate code, the change in the meeting from Sunday to Saturday, the name of the boat, and its locations were communicated in Key Largo on the senator's cell.

"Exactly," he said. "I arrived around 9:30 or so that Saturday morning. She had coffee waiting in the dining salon with documents stacked in piles on the table. The first thing that hit me was that she was not dressed for a business meeting, but, then again, we were in Key West on a yacht. She had on some type of bathing suit coverup, which failed to cover up that she was wearing a skimpy bikini."

She was sure aggressive and blatant about her objective, Sammie thought.

"Samantha, please excuse me for saying this, but I have had many attractive women hit on me, and Cathleen McKinney was no exception. Trust me, the fact that I was on a private boat, in a private location with a sexy and smart, half-naked woman was not lost on me. But I knew that I had a lot of documents to review in a limited period of time. Before hunkering down, I walked around a bit to stretch my back—it was tight from the drive. She led me to the sundeck. As I walked around, she took off her cover up and began sunning in a lounge chair. She commented that the environment wasn't conducive to work and that she was becoming sidetracked...or something like that."

Senator Hill paused for water.

"I told her to take her time and enjoy the sun. I went back inside and started reading hundreds of pages of documents about formulations and clinical trials to understand the scientific and biological bases for the medications. She eventually came in and asked me if I had any questions. She was still wearing her bikini.

Sammie was impressed with the senator's ability to concentrate and digest so much information while Cathleen likely hovered over him half-naked.

"She was obviously knowledgeable about Worth's products inside and out. She explained the various formulations and why certain ones were rejected based on Worth's research and development data or clinical trial results. I was impressed with the resources invested and all the various factors considered before seeking FDA approval. After several hours, it became clear—or at least from the data and internal analysis that she provided from the Worth chemists and product development group—that the formulation of Dolorine submitted to the FDA provided the maximum pain relief with least risk of side effects."

Sammie was wondering when he became side-tracked. Her stomach was turning cartwheels.

"It was late by the time I got through everything. I should have left that evening but was exhausted. By then, she had given up on her romantic overtures. We slept in separate bedrooms."

Sammie wasn't buying this rendition of her senator's story, especially given what she knew about Cathleen McKinney's antics.

"That morning, when I was leaving, I noticed a man walking the docks. He followed me to the gate. We were the only two people on the docks that morning. I saw him when I got into my rental car. I called Cathleen. I told her that we had company and to be on the lookout for a man with a white baseball cap, gray shirt, and navy shorts. I was hoping I was just being paranoid, but something didn't feel right."

Grant listened silently throughout this whole rendition and watched Sammie intently. Sammie thought he was making sure that she was taking copious notes.

"As I was driving back to Key Largo, she called and said that the man had been loitering outside the boat for the last hour. He had not seen her, but she waited a couple of hours before leaving. She called back later and said that when she left, he was not on the docks near the boat. As she exited the gate, she saw him on a bench reading the paper. Now, all of this is what she told me, so I don't know if it is true or not. She said he watched her get into her car, and then he quickly jumped up and made his way to the parking lot. She pulled into a nearby boat storage lot and parked behind a boat trailer. She got out of her car, hid behind the boat, and watched for cars leaving the marina. She saw a red, Mercedes sedan go by and circle back several times. The driver had on a white baseball cap like the guy that I saw when leaving. She couldn't get the license plate. She stayed in the lot an hour before leaving. She didn't see the car again."

"So, from your story,'" Grant said, tersely, "even if nothing intimately happened between you and Ms. McKinney, you know that a meeting on a boat at a remote location could be spun a million ways."

"I do know that. It is why I am here. I have replayed these events in my head a thousand times. I am one-hundred percent confident that no one knew I was in Key West. Tripp didn't even know where I went. I only told him that I had a meeting on Saturday. The man could have been there on Saturday, but I am thinking he didn't start his stakeout until Sunday. Our original plan was to meet on Sunday. My hunch is that Tony DeVore has tapped my office phone, and this dude was hired by him. It's just a gut feel."

"Are you absolutely sure that you learned of the code for the gate to the marina while in Key Largo?" Grant asked.

"I remember that I started to write down the code on a pad but stopped when I heard the number. There was no way I was putting that number in writing. I know for a fact that I learned of that code in Key Largo while on Tripp's boat."

"Well then, the white-capped gentleman either had the code or had to check in at the dock house. We'll find out."

"And according to my notes," Sammie added, "she told you the name of the marina during the call you took in your office. If your phone was tapped, that information would have been available."

"That's correct," Senator Hill said.

"Have you seen or talked to Ms. McKinney since that weekend?" Grant asked.

"No, I have not. The only time that we spoke is that Sunday when she told me about the suspicious Mercedes and seeing the same guy that I did. That is when she said she would get you involved—that you helped the company with PR issues and that you could get to the bottom of this. I have not heard from her."

"Ms. McKinney is very sharp," Grant said. "She cherishes her job and her power in the company. She will not jeopardize that. She is a master at cover-ups."

Sammie found that comment odd coming from Grant. She was getting paranoid. She wondered what he meant. *Is that why he hired her and was paying her so much? Did Grant know about Dougie and Cathleen? Had Cathleen involved Grant's company after Dougie threatened to expose her?*

"Senator Hill," Grant interrupted Sammie's racing suspicions, "I trust that you have been honest. How this situation turns out for you depends on one thing. Were you seen with Ms. McKinney on a yacht in the Keys? If you were, no one would believe you were there solely to learn about Dolorine. If you were not seen, we can prove that Senator DeVore is illegally tapping phones and hiring private investigators in a power struggle. Trust me, it won't turn out well for him. Let me caution you, though, if he is involved, he is watching you. Don't do anything stupid. And stupid numero uno would be meeting Cathleen McKinney again in any location."

Senator Hill looked like he had been through the ringer. He was clearly distraught.

"Oh, trust me, Grant. I appreciate all too well what this could to do me, and, more importantly, what it could do to my wife."

"I will get started immediately on having your office checked for bugs. After that, I'll obtain the list of visitors from the Sun Key dockmaster. I've docked this boat there many times, so I won't have any problem on that front. Docks not only have big boats but also big ears. For once, chatter among the docks may work to our advantage. But, we don't need any dock chatter before I learn about the phone. Senator Tony DeVore obviously has strong connections all over the state. If it gets out that I am inquiring about the visitor list, and the senator gets wind of it, he may have a change of heart about stalking you."

Billy arrived with the fresh tuna filets. Sammie was feeling nauseated and couldn't eat. She didn't know how Senator Hill could either. If this got out, he would be fried by the public. No one would believe him. Even vulnerable Sammie Morgan wasn't buying it. But then again, she knew Cathleen McKinney. No one was safe.

Don't buy a pig in a poke...

Chapter Forty-Two

Sammie

Sammie was still trying to digest the information from Senator Scotty Hill. Since she had no appetite, she excused herself from the lunch to type up the interview. Grant said he would let her know when the senator left so they could go over her transcription. As Sammie walked back to the business office, she noticed a voicemail from Lucy.

Hey Sammie. Guess what? I have a date with Kevin tonight. Can you believe it? There is a break in this deposition, so I was trying to reach you for some fashion help. Leave a voicemail if you don't get me, and tell me what to wear, please! I don't know how long this deposition will last.

As Sammie began to return Lucy's call, her mother called.

"Hey darling? Are you having a good day?" Glenny asked.

Sammie wanted to disgorge the events so far, but she couldn't breach her confidentiality agreement. And, she knew her mother wouldn't approve of her working on anything remotely connected to a sex scandal.

"I have a favor," Glenny said. "I want to take Mack to one of your father's banking conferences in Florida. I get so bored during these five-day conferences. Your father is tied up in meetings and then dinners the entire time. I would love Mack's company. We could have so much fun. I could take him swimming, biking, and strolling. It would really mean a lot to me, and you know how I love to show him off. Will you at least think about it?"

With all that was happening with Senator Hill, Sammie thought that her mom's invitation was a godsend.

"Are you sure, Mom? Let me call you right back. My phone is getting ready to die. I forgot my charger."

"Where are you?" Glenny asked, when Sammie returned her call. "My phone says it's an unknown number."

"This is a marina phone. But about the trip, I know Mack is easy but traveling with him on a plane to Florida and for five days?"

"Yes, I'm sure," she said. "I would have said something earlier, but I was worried it might be too much. But we have gotten into a wonderful routine, and I really want to take him."

"Well, it would actually help me out," Sammie said. "There is a lot going on here. Funny how I thought this job would be so flexible. I can't get into all of it, but I am working on a legal matter for one of the slip renters."

"What is your schedule for the rest of the day?" Glenny asked.

"I am headed back to the business office to type up a document. It should only take a couple of hours. What time are you leaving tomorrow?"

Sammie's "hotline" buzzed while she was talking to her mother. She hadn't even started typing the interview yet.

"We leave at eight in the morning for the airport," Glenny said.

"I will be there as soon as I can and will get everything packed."

"Okay, but I'm thinking a shopping trip is in order. Mack is growing like a weed," Glenny said.

"An order just came in. I'll see you when I get home."

Sammie looked at the text that she got from Grant. *What now*? She got the cigar. She was skipping fresh tuna filets. But, she shouldn't complain. After all, he was paying her rather extravagantly for her legal work.

The text read: *Need deck of cards. Don't eat. Saved you a filet. Hurry back.*

As Sammie entered the dock house, Mr. Barry was there.

"So, do tell," he said.

"Well, you may be getting that national attention that you want," she said. "If not, at least you'll recoup the costs of all this equipment. He is also paying me directly for legal work so that what I learn will be protected by the attorney-client privilege. So, you don't need to pay me anything for the business office work. It looks like this is a win-win for you all the way around."

"I reckon' all that is true, but we'll see. There is something about him that I don't trust," Mr. Barry said, huffily.

"I'm working on a flyer announcing your new gopher service. After you approve, I will distribute them."

Sammie started typing up the interview with Senator Hill. Afterward, she drafted a proposed flyer for the new gopher service.

The **Charleston Ashley Dockage** appreciates you docking with us. We are here to make your visit to Charleston stress-free and enjoyable. In addition to all the other fine amenities, we are offering an **errand** service. We will deliver groceries, marina supplies, the freshest fish from our local markets, and many other items. Text your requests and place the desired delivery time and slip #. There is no charge for the service, but gratuities are appreciated.

Sammie put the draft flyer on the counter, printed the typed interview, and headed out to find a deck of cards. Sammie knew that Lucy would be beside herself agonizing over what to wear and reeling that she hadn't called her back.

Sammie used her hotline phone as she headed to her car. Lucy didn't answer. Sammie left a message that her phone was dead and that she would call her back.

Sammie rushed to her parents' house to help her mother get ready for the trip and tried Lucy again on the way. Lucy still didn't answer. Sammie laughed and thought that Lucy was determined to go on this date. They both had learned the lesson of answering a call from an unknown number—it usually meant getting sucked into an assignment from a law partner. After the third attempt, Lucy finally answered.

"I'm glad you finally got my messages. I knew you wouldn't answer a call from an unknown number. I know you all too well. This is one of my gopher phones, so I need to be quick," Sammie said.

Sammie coached Lucy on her outfit and told Lucy that she liked Kevin. He had impressed her getting the business office set up so quickly. He was no nonsense.

Sammie packed Mack's things for the trip. Her mother was so excited about their trip and rambled on and on about what she and Mack would do. After Sammie got Mack bathed, fed, and put to bed, she started to head back to the marina.

"Do you have a deck of cards here?" Sammie asked her mother. "One of my jobs at the marina is running errands, and one of the renters wants a deck of cards. If you have some, it would save me a trip to the store."

Glenny went into the den and opened a drawer.

"Take your pick. These are from my bridge days. I was never any good at it. But, it did provide some social interaction. Maybe you should find a card group."

"I don't have time to do the things I want to do now," Sammie said.

"Well, you need to make time for yourself. Why don't you see if Lucy can go to dinner with you tonight? You know you are welcome to go to the club any time."

"Lucy has a date tonight," Sammie said. "I'm so excited for her. She has been calling me today stressing about what to wear. She has no confidence in her wardrobe."

"Well I understand why she calls you. You have a knack for style," Glenny said.

"I've never thought about it, but if I do, I know where I got it from. After all, my mom was a designer for a fashion house in New York and still has the best outfits at any party."

"All I need now to get noticed is to have my beautiful grandbaby with me," Glenny said. "He turns more heads than an expensive designer outfit ever could."

Sammie returned to the docks. The senator and Tripp had left. They apparently hadn't made as big of a production of leaving as arriving.

"We have a filet waiting for you," Billy said. "I must admit Senator Hill and Tripp know how to do things right. You are gonna love this tuna. And, we have salad, beets, and my famous pimento cheese."

"Great. It has been a long and interesting day. What did you think of Tripp? I understand that his fishing boat is extraordinary."

"Yep, Tripp is a pretty cool dude," Billy said. "He apparently doesn't have to work for a living. His father is some powerful CEO. Tripp can fish every day or do anything else he wants for that matter. Most of the guys I run into like him are pretty obnoxious.

But, he's a good guy. And he obviously thinks a lot of the senator. They have been friends since college. I don't know what's up but do know from being around Grant that you don't meet with him unless there is some type of crisis."

Sammie refrained from commenting on the pickle involving Senator Hill.

"By the way, the boss man is letting me earn some extra cash since he'll be docked a while. I'm leaving tomorrow to co-captain a trip from the Keys to the Cayman Islands."

"That sounds great," Sammie said.

"Sammie," Bill smirked, "when you are running a boat that distance, it's a lot of work for the captains. But, I can't complain. I do love my job. Since I haven't seen the town yet, I'm gonna hit the bars tonight. You can give me some recommendations. I'll let Grant know that you are here. Oh, and one more thing. It's none of my business but be careful."

Sammie wondered what Billy meant by that comment. *Was he talking about Grant? Or the senator? Or the whole mess? Had he picked up on the vibes between her and Grant?* As her mind was racing, Billy returned with the tuna filet, beets, salad, pimento cheese, and crackers. Grant was behind him with wine.

"I hope you like this wine. It's a French Burgundy. I don't follow the general rule of white wine with seafood. Besides, I like breaking rules sometimes. It's my wild side," he said, winking at Sammie. "Try this and see what you think."

"This is great," Sammie said, taking a sip.

He held up his glass.

"Here's to the South Carolina senator and Worth Pharmaceutical. Without them, I wouldn't have had the pleasure of meeting you."

Sammie touched her glass to his, but the toast made her feel uncomfortable. She wished she had never heard of Worth Pharmaceutical and certainly didn't want to be toasting anything to do with that company.

"Look at this feast," Sammie said, deflecting any further conversation about Worth. "I am starving. Billy overdid it. He must be trying to make up for leaving you for the Caymans. How are you going to get along without him?"

"Oh, I don't know," he said. "I hear that this marina has a new service and will fetch me whatever I need. I'm going to take full advantage of it while Billy's away."

Sammie tried to suppress a big smile by taking a bite of the tuna filet. She was enjoying the calming effect of the wine.

"That would make Mr. Barry very happy. He is quite proud of his new idea, but I don't think he can pull off catching fresh tuna. It's incredible."

"While you eat, I'll review this transcription. We'll see if your note-taking skills match your lawyering skills," he said, filling his wine glass again before going inside.

Billy returned, ready for a night on the town. He looked even better all cleaned up.

"So, Sammie, where should I go?"

"Well, you can't beat the bars on East Bay. Start at Jimbo's Oyster House. You may end up parked there all night. It has a great bar and great seafood," Sammie said. "And oysters," they said, simultaneously.

"Do you want me to take you?" Sammie asked, obligatorily but hoping he declined.

"No, I'll catch an Uber. I don't want to get on Grant's bad side," he said.

His comment along with his earlier comment to be careful left Sammie feeling anxious.

After Billy left, Grant reappeared with his cigar.

"I decided to enjoy my BBMF cigar while I finished reading this interview."

Grant read, noted questions, and corrections. He was attractive with his reading glasses, his intense concentration, and even smoking the cigar. She couldn't remember a time in recent history where she felt so relaxed. She was alternating her gaze between him and the sailboats anchored in the river. There was a soothing presence to Grant Davis.

"It appears that you are more than an excellent scrivener," Grant said, removing his glasses and setting aside his pen. "These cigars are hard to find. Will Samantha Spencer share her source?"

"So, you picked up on my name change when I introduced myself to Senator Hill."

"Indeed, I did. I don't miss important details."

"It's not an important detail and actually just popped out," Sammie said. "My maiden name is sort of known in the area. If he was familiar with the Spencer name, I assume I was thinking I would gain some credibility points. Or, subconsciously, it might have been an attempt to distance myself from Cathleen McKinney, since my husband, or I should say, my former husband, worked for her. Truthfully, I don't know."

"You mentioned your husband's association with Ms. McKinney before. I get the feeling that the relationship was more than just professional. Did Cathleen entice your husband like she did Scotty Hill?"

Sammie could feel herself blushing and hated this uncontrollable reaction that conspicuously revealed the answer to his question.

"I suppose there are some similarities. Like Senator Hill, he denied anything happened. I never caught them or anything. But, then when I learned about others, it didn't really matter if he was telling the truth or not."

"I'm sorry. Were the others also at Worth?"

"No. But, I don't want to talk about any of that."

Sammie decided to go on the offensive to avoid other embarrassing questions.

"I want you to tell me about Grant Davis," she said, as her color subsided. "Are you married? Do you have children?"

"I was, and I do. I have a daughter and a son who are both in college. They are great."

He paused and took a long draw on the cigar and blew out a big pillar of smoke.

"Other than my children, whom I adore, I can't say that I have anything in common with their mother. It's strange how you can live with someone and not realize that fact until your children are out of the house."

Grant picked up his glass, swirled the wine around and around, and then took a sip. He stared out over the water, sipping his wine, and puffing on the cigar. They sat in complete stillness.

"Hey, where did you go? You look like you are miles away. Penny for your thoughts."

"I haven't heard that expression in years," he said, laughing. "I was just thinking it is too bad that marriage doesn't age as well as wine."

Sammie's marriage didn't even have time to ferment, she thought.

"I have been struggling with how my son will be affected," Sammie said. "At this point, I don't even want his dad involved. Do you think that is selfish?"

"I certainly can't opine on that without any facts. But even then, only you can answer that."

"I think it's great that your children were raised in a loving home with both parents for so many years," Sammie said.

"I presume so," he said, pausing. "We never fought, but I wouldn't characterize our home as loving."

"How would you characterize it?" Sammie asked, hesitantly.

"Good question," he answered, taking a sip of wine.

Sammie was fearful that she had overstepped her boundaries. She started to change the subject to break the silence.

"Co-existence," Grant finally answered. "I would say my wife and I co-existed."

"What do you mean?" Sammie asked, deciding to push a little further.

Grant swirled the wine and stared off into the water again. It may have been the water's reflection, but his eyes seemed to moisten as he answered.

"Our marriage died many years ago. We went through the motions of pretending to be a family for our children. The best way to describe it, I suppose, is like having a roommate. We shared nothing in common, but she was easy to live with."

"Interesting analogy," Sammie said, "though, it's really sad to me. You had to have some attraction or commonality at the beginning. Did you try counseling?"

"We did. I think the counseling sessions highlighted and confirmed our incompatibility. My ex-wife is content to sit at home, watch reality shows, read trashy books, and spend money. Online shopping is a favorite pastime, since it can be done without ever leaving the comforts of the sofa. We were too young when we got married. You don't know then that a marriage has to have a foundation of something other than physical attraction and good romps in the sack," as a playful chuckle replaced his serious, austere mood.

Mr. Fix-It Man of everyone else's problems was loosening up, and his hard exterior was beginning to show some soft cracks.

"So, what do think, Counselor?" he questioned, jovially.

"You're asking me?" Sammie asked. "Your marriage lasted much longer than mine. I am certainly not qualified to dispense advice. I thought my marriage was perfect. We had the same interests and really loved spending time together. We had tons of fun, and as you so eloquently put it, 'good romps in the sack' too. But apparently, it wasn't enough. I am still trying to make sense of it all," fighting the tears welling up in her eyes.

"Don't beat yourself up, Samantha Spencer," he said, smiling. "I am sure you did the right thing. You don't seem like the type that would make such a drastic move if it wasn't warranted. I, on the other hand, continue to harbor a lot of guilt. So, I guess you think I'm a cad, huh?"

"No, I don't. I think everyone should have a life partner—someone that you love with all your heart and are committed to unequivocally."

She had loved Dougie like that, with all her heart. She couldn't understand Dougie's actions especially after he had a newborn son. He didn't care about anyone but himself. Thinking about Mack, tears formed quickly and this time, she couldn't hold them back. Grant put down the cigar, got up from his chair, sat down beside her, put his arm around her, and hugged her.

"You asked about my life. I didn't mean to upset you. Your son will be fine. There is a good basis for the saying that children are resilient."

Sammie felt safe in Grant's arms. He was the calm in the storm. When a disaster hit, he remained unruffled and confident while executing a meticulous plan to remedy the problem. She felt sorry for him. Who fixes him?

"I'm sorry," Sammie said. "I need to seek counseling myself. But for now, I'm going to relax, enjoy this view, this wine, and this unbelievable meal. And you need to enjoy that rare cigar. Oh, and by the way, I also brought the deck of cards you requested."

"What time do you need to leave?"

"I don't have a curfew. But, I can't be too late."

"How about a quick game of blackjack?" he asked, cutting the cards.

"You don't want to lose your shirt. I am working overtime right now," Sammie quipped.

"That's exactly what I had in mind," he responded slyly, continuing to shuffle the cards, making them loudly crackle as they were expertly folding together.

Sammie wondered what he meant. She wondered if she was misinterpreting his evocative grin.

"I don't understand," she said.

"By now, I know you're competitive. The question is can you handle losing and being exposed at the same time?"

"I still don't understand," Sammie responded, questioning if he was really thinking what she was thinking.

"You will, but I don't want to be accused of cheating. You shuffle the cards while I get more wine."

"I don't need any more wine but help yourself. I'll shuffle."

"Sounds good, but wine is all I am getting. I'm not going to cheat and put on more clothes."

The rules were now clear. He was suggesting that the loser had to remove a piece of clothing. Sammie had never heard of or played strip blackjack. She was intrigued where this would go as she dealt the first hand.

Grant returned and smirked, pointing to his top card—a king.

"You may need extra clothes," he said, laughing at the nine displayed in Sammie's pile.

"I'll stay put," Grant swiftly and confidently said.

Sammie peaked at her second card. From his king and quick decision, he must have nineteen or twenty. She had no choice but to take another card since her second card was a four. She busted with the newly dealt ten of diamonds. Grant laughed as he turned over his second card. It was only a three.

"I see that Samantha Spencer is a little competitive and not very conservative. I'll remember that."

Sammie took off one of her shoes. She dealt again. She had an ace. He had a two of hearts.

"Hit me," Grant said, after peering at his uncovered card.

Sammie gave him another.

"Hit me again," he said.

He looked at his cards, looked at Sammie.

"One more."

If Sammie didn't have blackjack, she would have taken another card. Grant was sporting a similar hand. Instead, he busted. She knew right then that she was in trouble. He was too good at disguising his hand. Interestingly, he left his shoes on and took off his shirt.

His chest and stomach could rival a twenty-year old. He was either trying to really distract her or tease her. Whatever it was, it was working. She wanted to throw her cards in the air.

Grant won the next hand. Sammie removed her other shoe. He won the next two hands. Sammie was thankful that she had worn her running shoes with socks, but she was getting into trouble. No shoes or socks left for her. Except for his shirt, Grant was fully dressed with both of his shoes intact. She did notice, however, he wasn't wearing any socks.

Sammie was relieved when she won the next two hands. Grant's loafers were off and since he was sockless, this hand was important. Her heart pounded. Dougie was the only guy who had ever seen her in underwear. She tried to calm herself down, counseling that she was exposing no more than if she was wearing a bathing suit. But, it wasn't working.

Grant had an ace showing. This presented lots of options. He requested a card, then another, and then another. He paused. He looked at her. He looked at his hand. He looked back at her again.

"I'm good," he finally said.

Sammie thought his pause was to throw her off. She was confident with her eighteen, and she was confident he busted.

Without saying a word, he revealed his hand. The multiple cards equaled twenty-one.

Sammie stood.

"You are so lucky," she said, unbuttoning her pants.

"You're right, I am very lucky," Grant said, standing up and moving towards her. "Let me help you," he said, with his large hands touching her waistband on her button-fly jeans and grazing her navel.

At that moment, Sammie would have sworn that she had two beating hearts, the one fluttering in her chest and the one throbbing inside her stomach. The slow, seductive way that Grant kissed her neck as he slid the metal buttons through the course slits was undeniably erotic. Sammie's body was burning with a desire that she had forgotten. She wanted Grant Davis' hands and lips all over her. When his finger moved across the lace band of her underwear, fear trumped desire. She removed his hand.

"I really need to go," she said.

Life isn't perfect, but your outfit can be...

Chapter Forty-Three

Sammie & Grant

When Sammie returned home from dropping her parents and Mack at the airport, she was excited for her day at the marina. That is, until she returned to the arduous task of unpacking all her boxes of clothes. Her stomach ached from wardrobe gluttony. She sorted her clothes into three piles: clothes with the price tags still attached, ones that she didn't even remember, and ones she could vividly recall the exact place where she had sported the garment with Dougie. This latter pile, she promptly repacked into a box for donating.

She withheld a top and pants from the donation box. She had loved the short-sleeved red and white striped V-neck bodysuit and sailor jeans. She had worn the outfit only once. Then, she thought Dougie's comment that they were going to the Shem Creek Bar & Grille, not the Charleston Yacht Club, had been tongue-in-cheek. Now, she wasn't so sure.

Today, she approved of the chic, nautical ensemble, especially the six buttons on both sides of her pants. She had fallen asleep thinking about the way Grant had handled her button-fly jeans—unhurried, methodical, and luring. A sensual magnetism sizzled between them. Next time, she wouldn't stop him.

Sammie checked her hotline phone continuously while getting ready. After the previous evening, she anticipated a request for coffee or breakfast from Grant. After two hours, she worried that there may not be a next time. She may have sent mixed messages playing along with his strip blackjack game before her abrupt exit. Men like Grant Davis probably didn't tolerate drama or worse, humiliation. She feared she had ruined any chance of a do-over.

A call on her cell phone startled her. It was Mr. Barry.

"I haven't seen much of you," Mr. Barry said. "I was getting worried that Golden Boy had kidnapped you."

"No, but he is keeping me busy. That should make you happy. He has paid for your equipment rental."

"You're right about that, but I'm still waiting for that scandal to surface so we can get some free publicity."

"Don't count on that, Mr. Barry. Grant Davis is very good at his job."

"Harrumph," he growled. "Well, on the bright side, word about our gopher service is getting out. There are some orders here at the dock house. Two of them need stuff today. And, I added your number to the flyer so make sure to check your phone."

Sammie checked her real gopher phone.

The request from *Aqua Therapy* for two six-foot deck brushes, deck cleaner, a squeegee, and hoses evidenced how they were going to spend their Saturday. She could retrieve the cleaning supplies at the same marine supply store as the 75-inch water ski rope order from *Water You Lookin' At?*

"I have two orders on the phone, so I am headed to take care of those now. I'll pick up the others after I make these deliveries."

Sammie remembered that she had planned a run with Lucy this morning. She called her to cancel.

"I can't go running this morning," Sammie said, on Lucy's voicemail. "I am stuck running boat errands. Can you go to dinner Monday or Tuesday? Mom took Mack with her to one of Dad's banking conferences. They return on Wednesday. I want to hear all about your date and catch up. Let me know."

While she was concentrating on gathering the cleaning supplies for *Aqua Therapy*, her hotline phone buzzed. Her knees buckled. *Need OJ or whatever you like with champagne.* Sammie's heart fluttered from relief and excitement.

As Sammie was walking briskly back down the docks, the seagulls' squawking, cawing and squealing, the high-pitched "hee haw" calls from the royal terns, and the willet's rapid piercing "bo-dee-dee-dy, bo-dee-dee-dy, bo-dee-dee-dy" provided the background accompaniment for the pelicans diving head-first into the water for their breakfast. The smell of the saltwater was more discernable with the end of the summer's stifling temperatures and the arrival of lower humidity.

Mr. Barry handed her the orders that were left in the dock house.

Pier Pressure—five pounds of shrimp, Titos Vodka, Charleston Bloody Mary mix, and two lemons; *Joe's Jollies*—six bratwurst, mustard, ketchup, onion, six ears of corn; *Rising Tide*—4 quarts of mud minnows & a slip float-rig.

When she got back to Grant's boat, he was relaxing on a chaise lounge chair on the aft deck.

"I started making a pitcher of mimosas but ran out of OJ," Grant said. "I was hoping you would join me for brunch."

"It seems that the word is getting around about the errand service. I've already handled two, or three counting the OJ, and have three more. Mr. Barry just handed me these orders," Sammie said, showing Grant the list. "But, it should only take me about an hour or two."

"How about I come with you? I need to get off this boat. It's about time that I see some of downtown Charleston."

"That would be great. One of my favorite restaurants has a great brunch."

"How about I pick up some things while we're out? I don't watch much TV but am a college football junkie. I'm getting peer pressure from this order from *Pier Pressure*— I am thirsty for a bloody," Grant said.

"Seems there is another football junkie docked here," Sammie said, glancing at an incoming text on her marina phone: *case of Budweiser, four pounds of hamburger, hamburger buns, 24 wings, Ranch, Ruffles, French onion dip. Pls deliver to Game Day by 2:00 on Saturday.*

"Well, let's get after it," Grant said.

Sammie was relieved that they made it past the dock house without a sighting by Mr. Barry.

"My car is the white BMW. We should go to Haddrell's Point Tackle Supply first for the float-rig and mud minnows," Sammie said.

"Mud minnows?" Grant asked. "They don't sound appetizing."

"They are to flounder and redfish—it's like fishing with candy."

"I like shopping with this candy," Grant said, opening Sammie's door.

He leaned in and kissed her.

"That's to inspire you to step on it."

Sammie did just that. She sped down Lockwood Drive to Broad to East Bay. She was on a mission to knock out the orders.

When they returned, Sammie seized one of the large carts that the marina provided for owners. Grant helped her unload the bags from the trunk into the cart. When she bent over to retrieve the last bag, Grant wrapped his hands around her waist and pulled her against him.

"I'll let you make the deliveries while I make us some lunch and our bloodies. Any special instructions on how you want your drink?" Grant asked, whispering into her ear. "I like mine hot."

"So do I."

Sammie couldn't wait enjoy a Bloody Mary with a very sexy man. She hurriedly headed first to *Game Day*, the only order with a specific deadline. Their pregame party was already underway.

"You're just in time," one of the occupants said, boisterously. "I'm Steven Wayne. What's your name darlin'?"

"I'm Sammie."

"You're sure cute, Sammie. Who are you pulling for in the game? You know your answer determines the amount of your tip."

Sammie didn't even know who was playing but from the attire of the rowdy group and Steven Wayne's "A True Cock Fan" shirt, it was obvious that South Carolina was playing someone.

"I'm pulling for the Gamecocks, of course."

"Thata girl! Cock's rule. Hey, Robbie, come give this perty gal a big tip."

Sammie assumed Robbie was the boat owner whose obnoxious guest had a big mouth for talking and alligator arms when it came to paying. Robbie looked too distinguished to surround himself with the likes of Steven Wayne.

"I'm Robbie Blake. This should cover the costs for our order and make up for my rude guest," he said, handing Sammie three $100 bills. "Tell Harry that his delivery service idea is pure genius," Robbie said.

"I sure will. You guys have fun. Let me know if you need anything else," she said, exiting *Game Day*.

The boat owner had more than covered the costs of their football tailgate on his 87-foot Lazzara but not the crude shirt or comment from his guest. So, she put the cash in her pocket.

As she headed down the dock, her hotline phone buzzed: *On the bow lounge with our drinks. Hurry on up!"* She made the other deliveries to *Pier Pressure, Joe's Jollies, and Rising Tide.*

She climbed the stairs towards the bow lounge on the expansive upper deck of *Sea Relations*. Grant was in the hot tub sipping his drink.

"Come join me," he said.

"I would love to, but I don't have a bathing suit."

Sammie had picked up Grant's ability to turn on a poker face when needed, but she had noticed that he had less control of his emotional face. He looked confused or surprised. She realized that she was sending mixed messages again. The woman who had played strip blackjack, had invitingly kissed him back in broad daylight, and played along with his innuendo about how spicy she wanted her Bloody Mary was now declining an invitation in his hot tub.

"How about a t-shirt and shorts," he asked, standing and reaching for a towel. "I'm sure I can find you something."

"If I'm going to get your clothes wet, I may as well get in with my own," Sammie said, realizing that her bodysuit could technically work as a bathing suit.

"You have enough buttons on these pants?" he asked, laughing.

At that moment, she regretted her selection of her sailor jeans. She had fantasized about him taking them off of her.

"I thought you didn't have a bathing suit," Grant said, checking out Sammie's bodysuit as she entered the hot tub.

"It's a bodysuit," she answered, laughing. "But it works."

The backdrop was as seductive as Grant Davis. It was a beautiful fall day. The air was crisp, and the Ashley River was sparkling from the sun's reflections. The evocative surroundings didn't seem to influence the attentive football fan. The screeching seabirds and the gurgling water from the hot tub jets were competing with the commentators' prognostications from the large flat-screen TV. He seemed to be interested in the game and content to sit on one side of the hot tub while she was on the other.

Sammie had never taken time to watch football. The only attention she had paid the sport was in high school when she devoured the Saturday morning paper to learn about Dougie's performance the preceding Friday night. But, she was learning more than the player's positions and game strategy. She was seeing another layer of Grant Davis. This one wasn't serious or steady—it was childlike and rowdy. She was enjoying watching his animated expressions.

During a commercial break, he hopped out to make two more drinks. By now, knew that Grant Davis didn't miss a single detail and wondered if he could sense her checking him out. She laid her head back and closed her eyes, hoping that the water pounding on her back would beat down the desire building inside her. But, it wasn't working. Instead, she was back on the sofa playing strip blackjack remembering the feel of Grant's hand across her stomach and sliding along the lacy band of her panties. She jumped when he stepped back into the hot tub with their drinks.

"I've been a terrible host. I was so enthralled in the game, I didn't ask you if your Bloody Mary was hot enough."

She felt heat rise from her face, and it wasn't due to the water temperature.

"I didn't mean for my comment to make you uncomfortable. I apologize. But, your essence bulldozes my otherwise disciplined restraint," he said, sitting down beside her.

He removed her hair tie and ran his fingers through her hair. She turned towards him. The sparks that had been smoldering exploded. Their mouths devoured one another while their hands were covering a lot of territory—his unsnapping her bodysuit and hers down his shorts.

"Do you like the halftime shows, or do you want to do something else?" Grant whispered in her ear.

He didn't wait for a response. He scooped her up and carried her to the oversized settee a foot from the hot tub. The open air only added gasoline to the fire.

Grant's halftime performance extended well into the fourth quarter before they returned to the hot tub. No clothes were necessary this time. Sammie leaned back into his chest. He had an intoxicatingly calm effect on her. His cool composure enveloped her and paused her brain. She absorbed the river scenes—the motors of the boats traveling on the Ashley River, the spray of water hoses from the boat washers, the traffic humming over the grates on the bridge—the list of sounds around a marina was endless.

"I never fixed you lunch. How about I make you dinner and convince you to stay with me tonight?"

"I would love to, but I don't have any clothes. The only shirt I have is wet."

"Minor complications," he said. "I'm sure I can find something. We're not going anywhere."

Sammie felt like she was dining in a gourmet restaurant with the jazz music humming through the speakers, the wine, and the aroma of spaghetti sauce, despite she was only sporting one of Grant's t-shirts. His clam linguine rivalled the best Italian restaurant on King Street. She thought that Grant Davis was perfect in every way— handsome, sexy, calm, confident, sensitive, successful, and a good cook to boot.

Grant took his t-shirt off of her for the second time that evening in his stateroom. She felt so safe in his arms. She didn't want the night to end. Sammie questioned how she could have these feelings so soon and so fast? She thought that she should have dated more and had more sexual relationships. She felt stupid that she thought Dougie was the only one for her. Grant Davis was a prince that made Dougie look like the toad he was. In no time, Grant's breathing was steady, and his body was relaxed. Her head was rising and sinking with every cadenced breath. Their connection was so strong, she felt as if they were sharing the same breath.

They dozed off for several hours before Grant's cell phone woke them. It was after 10 p.m.

"I have to take this," he said. "Hey. Hold on just a second," he said to the caller. "I'll only be a minute. Don't you go anywhere," he whispered in her ear. "Have you received my messages?" he asked, leaving the room. "You haven't responded."

His voice then trailed off. She wondered if there were new updates on the senator's situation. Otherwise, who would be calling after 10 p.m. on a Saturday night? But, his call didn't take long.

"Sorry. I have a staff of workaholics, and they know I fall in the same category. But, I have more important things to do tonight than work."

When she woke up the next morning, he wasn't there. She grabbed the t-shirt that was crumbled on the floor and walked up the stairs into the salon.

"Why am I not surprised that you are just as beautiful in the morning," Grant said.

"That sounds like something a PR expert would say."

"Only if it were true. I woke up early with a new matter on the brain. You were sleeping so soundly, I didn't want to wake you. But, now that you're up, how about I serve you breakfast in bed?"

"That sounds wonderful," she said, "except, as you said, I'm up now."

"You missed my point," he said, running his fingers through her hair.

Grant's t-shirt ended up on his stateroom floor again. After, he put his arm around her and pulled her into his chest.

"This is how I want to spend the entire day. Unfortunately, I'm going to have to work on this new matter today," he said. "And, while I am the bearer of bad news, I am going to have to head out early in the morning."

"Tomorrow?"

"Yes. I have Senator Hill's situation under control, but unfortunately there is potentially a bigger crisis. I've got to catch a flight to my Palm Beach office. I was hoping you could give me a ride to the airport."

Sammie knew that Grant's stay was short term but wasn't prepared for it to end tomorrow. She felt empty. She laid her head on his shoulder, closed her eyes, and tried to soak up the feeling of his body next to hers. She wanted to ask him details of his new crisis, find out how long he would be gone, and how long he could stay when he came back.

"Ever heard of Parcepto? It's a pharmaceutical company."

"No," Sammie said, picking up that Grant was deep in work mode.

"How about a drug called Palpo? Given that your ex worked for Worth, I thought you may have heard of it. It's touted as a breakthrough drug, and in my experience, the pharmaceutical sales force is typically on top of information like that. I was hoping you would have some intel so that I wouldn't have to spend all day researching all of this. I'd rather be spending the time with you," he said.

"I'm sorry I can't help you. Dougie and I never discussed anything about work details. It was enough to keep up with his travel schedule."

They took a long shower together. He shampooed her hair, massaged her head with his strong hands then did the same to her entire body. She was already feeling the pain of his departure. Grant had unexpectedly appeared in her life and restored her spirit. *You will survive*, she counseled herself. But deep down, she didn't believe it. He had reignited her desire. She had missed being touched by a man.

"Let's get out of here before I have you back in the sack," Grant said, toweling her dry.

Grant wrapped his silk robe around Sammie and tied the sash around her waist. The luxurious fabric was like butter on her skin. It radiated his scent—masculine, decadent, leather. She wanted to bottle his aroma. He wrapped his arms around her waist, pulling her close. He kissed her neck, moving to her chest. His phone's ringing killed the moment.

"I have another important matter I have to address first," Grant said, before hitting the mute button on his phone. "You are my important matter," pulling her in for a long kiss. "By the way, you look so damn sexy," before unmuting his phone. "Assemble the team for 2:00. I should have a plan by then."

The buzz on Sammie's marina phone alerted her of a message. The text was from *Game Day* with a list of what appeared to be hangover aids—sausage, bacon, eggs, bread, coffee, coffee filters, and Advil. The text ended with an ASAP and a smiley emoji.

"Well, it appears duty calls. I have to tend to an immediate breakfast request from *Game Day*. Apparently, they need some grease and first-aid."

"I'm not sharing you with anyone on our last night so you may have to throw Harry's gopher phone in the Ashley River," Grant said, laughing. "I'm going to fix you a dinner that will beat anything in those Charleston restaurants you think are so wonderful."

"Sounds good. But, at the moment, I need to find my top. It should be dry by now."

"The temperature has dropped. If Harry notices you walking the docks in your 'bodysuit,' you will have some explaining to do."

Grant opened a drawer.

"Wear this," he said, tossing Sammie a sweatshirt. I also need to pay you."

He handed her three stacks of wrapped bills.

"Grant, this looks like too much. You are overpaying me as it is. I can't accept this."

"You can and you will. A deal is a deal. We have a contract, remember? Trust me, you have earned it. A bill from my lawyers would have been twice as much, less efficient, and less helpful. I should be done by early afternoon. Come back as soon as you can and make yourself at home."

Yesterday's bluebird day had been replaced with gray skies and a gusty wind. Sammie wanted to ditch the list, return to Grant's boat, and relax in the hot tub. But, the errand service was part of her bargain with Mr. Barry.

When she returned to *Game Day* with the hangover supplies, the owner was on his aft deck on his cell phone. He cradled the phone on his neck to help her with the bags of groceries.

"That's a load of crap, and you know it. I'll mark this up with our final position. You can take it or leave it. There will be no further negotiations," ending the call and throwing his phone onto the large cushioned sofa. He was obviously irritated with the caller.

"Sorry about that," he said, sighing. "I understand that the marina has a business office for faxes, emails, and that kind of thing. Do you know who I need to contact to use the office?"

"Yes, that would be me. What do you need?"

"I need a document emailed, but it needs some changes first. Looks like I'm going to have to make them myself. My lawyer is on the golf course."

"I can definitely email it. But, I'm proficient in Word if you need me to make your changes."

"Great. How about I meet you at the dock house in about an hour? I really appreciate it. The Charleston Ashley Dockage is definitely number one on my list."

Sammie had time to make it to her parents and change into warmer clothes. She didn't want Mr. Barry eyeing the sweatshirt. En route, her mother called. It seemed like weeks since they had been gone—so much had happened.

"Hey darling!" Glenny said. "Cort and I are having a ball with Mack. I took him shopping yesterday and got him some things. Shopping for a boy is hard. I tried to stay away from the cutesy outfits but couldn't help myself. He's just so darn adorable. What have you been doing? And, do not tell me that you have been working the entire time."

"I have been working if you can call it work. I've been shopping for supplies for the marina guests. Today, I had to get some things for a boat named *Game Day*. The yacht owner has a document that needs revisions, so I'm headed over there now to do that. Anyway, the other matter that I was working on is done. Some front has moved in here. It's cold and dreary."

"Not to rub it in, but the weather here is beautiful. We're getting ready to go for a bike ride. Sam rented this buggy that attaches to the bike. It's perfect for Mack. There are lots of great biking trails. I'm going to get a bike with a child's seat when we get home."

"That sounds so fun. I'm glad you're able to get outside with Mack. I'll call you tomorrow. I love you, Mom."

"Love you too, sweetie. Mack, say bye-bye to your mother."

Sammie heard him giggling again as she hung up. It was exactly what she needed. Her melancholy mood vanished. Grant was leaving, but Mack would be home soon. He was the most important man in her life, not Grant Davis. She was happy. She had a great family and for the time-being, was spending the night with a great man. She wasn't going to worry about what happened next. If anything, Grant had cured her hot tub angst. After all of Dougie's extracurricular activities in their hot tub, she didn't think that she would ever get back into one. Funny how she hadn't given it a second thought with Grant.

Sammie decided to check-in with Lucy. She had yet to hear from her since she cancelled their run and invited her to dinner. She was surprised that she answered on the first ring.

"I assumed since I never heard back from you that your date must have been pretty darn good," Sammie said.

"Oh, girl, yes," Lucy said, dreamily. "Dinner sounds great. Want to shoot for Tuesday night at CCCs around 7:00? If something comes up, I will even go with you to run your errands. And Kevin says hello."

"So, you're still with him?

"Uh huh."

"Well, tell him hello from me and that he better be taking good care of my girl. See ya Tuesday. Can't wait."

Sammie knew she would have to come clean with Lucy about Grant. Lucy would tell her that she was on the rebound and to be careful. But, she wasn't on the rebound. She hadn't intended for any of this to happen. It was like it was meant to be.

Sammie headed back to the marina to meet Robbie Blake. She realized that using her legal training gave her great satisfaction. The Grant Davis and Robbie Blake matters weren't likely to be an everyday occurrence, or even monthly. But for now, her situation couldn't be more perfect.

"I have a new customer for the business office," Sammie said to Mr. Barry, entering the dock house. "Robbie Blake from *Game Day*. He has some changes to a contract."

"So, Robbie has discovered your skills? You know, he's part owner of a professional football team. And single too. He could give the PR stud a run for his money."

"I'm not going to comment on that remark. But, Robbie said that the Charleston Ashley Dockage is his number one marina now that it has a business office," Sammie said.

"Umph. I guess that *Sea Relations* privatephobe was worth something."

Sammie's hotline phone buzzed. Fortuitously, Robbie Blake entered the dock house distracting Mr. Barry. Sammie quickly checked her Grant Davis phone. *Shrimp, two filets and vegetable of yr choice. Can't wait to spend the evening with you & fill you in on new matter.*

Sammie tried to regain her focus as Robbie handed her the document. Even without her new knowledge of his ownership in a professional football team, it was evident that she was working on a player's contract. She typed Robbie's changes.

"I'm actually a lawyer. Until recently, I worked for a large firm here in Charleston. Could I offer a change to your third paragraph?" Sammie asked. "Your current draft is ambiguous."

"Sure, fire away," Robbie said.

Sammie saw Mr. Barry wink at Robbie.

"Wow, that's quite impressive," Robbie said, after reviewing her changes. "Let's go with it. Here's a list of email addresses that need the document."

"Send me a bill for this work, Harold. My lawyer has yet to call me back. And I can assure you that he wouldn't have made these changes so quickly. They would have staffed it up and taken all day to send me another draft. This issue could have ruined my day. I really can't tell you how much this helped me out. How about you two join me and my guests for happy hour?"

"I'd love to, Robbie," Mr. Barry said, grinning from ear-to-ear.

Sammie remained silent wondering how she could get out of it.

"Nice work there, Sammie," Mr. Barry said, after Robbie Blake left the dock house. "Why don't you meet me here at 5:00, and I'll be your escort to *Game Day* for our free drink."

"I've got a dinner delivery for Grant Davis, and he wants to discuss a new matter," which was partly true.

"Too bad. You would have more fun with us than Mr. Confidentiality."

Nothing could be further from the truth, Sammie thought to herself.

"You'll have more fun without me. There's a lot of smack talk on that boat. You'll fit right in."

"I like it when Sammie gets a little feisty. Makes me forgetful. *Reeled In* needs to send a fax. Can you do that on this fancy equipment?"

"Sure can."

Sammie offered to return the document with the fax confirmation to *Reeled In*. Given its slip location beside *Sea Relations*, she could check in with Grant and see if there was anything else she could pick up while she was purchasing the items for their dinner.

When Sammie entered the salon on *Sea Relations*, it was eerily quiet. The only noise was ice puttering in the ice machine. She climbed the stairs to the upper deck, but Grant wasn't in his office. She proceeded down to his stateroom. His clothes were on the bed. Apparently, he had gone for a run. She laid down and took in the room where she had spent the last two nights. The t-shirt that she had worn was beside the bed. She smiled thinking about how many times Grant had taken it off of her. She then remembered the sweatshirt in her backpack.

As she pulled it out, she noticed a label with a monogram sewn into the back—CM. Her legs were shaking as she walked over to the drawer where she thought Grant had retrieved the sweatshirt. The drawer contained a woman's clothes. She picked up a shirt—same label, another "CM" monogram. In fact, every item of clothing in the drawer bore the monogram CM, except a black, lacy bustier with garter straps. The drawer beneath it was filled with papers with the Worth logo. Both of these drawers had locks, unlike the others. She felt sick.

As vomit gurgled up her throat, she ran into the master stateroom and hurled into the toilet. She felt dizzy. She rested her head on the toilet seat. She grabbed the edges of the marbled bathroom countertop and pulled herself up to the sink. She splashed water on her face and instructed herself to get a grip. Cathleen and Grant both worked for Worth. There had to be a logical explanation. But, she saw a distrusting version of herself staring back at her through the mirror. She saw a woman who had been educated by Camilla Girard.

Though she hated bothering Lucy while she was with Kevin, she couldn't wait.

"I hate to bother you and know this is out of left field, but do you still have the clothes that we took from my house? The ones by the hot tub?"

"Of course, I do. I work with Randy, remember? You don't get rid of evidence. I have them in a safe place at home. Why?"

"I can explain later, but when you get home, will you look at the monogram again?"

"I know there was a 'C.' Remember, we thought the clothes were Camilla's. But, I checked them later and the initials were 'CN,' or maybe 'CM.' Did you find out something else?"

"Maybe," she said, but knowing that she had.

Sammie ran out of *Sea Relations*. She tossed her phone dedicated to Grant's texts into the Ashley River and ran to her car. She sped away from the marina and couldn't get to her parents' fast enough. She jumped in the shower, turned on the water as hot as she could tolerate, and tried to wash the stench of Grant Davis from her body. But, the hot water couldn't cleanse her soul. It may never be the same.

PART FOUR

Any job worth doing, is worth doing well...

Chapter Forty-Four

Lucy & Kevin

Lucy was awake and listening to Kevin quietly snoring. Breathing deeply better described the steady and soft cadence. Lucy usually woke up early, and once she was awake, she couldn't stay in bed. She took off like a rocket and didn't stop until her head hit the pillow before starting the drill all over. She was surprisingly relaxed and had no desire to jump out of the bed. She put her arm across Kevin's chest and snuggled up close. He stirred.

"I could get used to waking up with a beautiful woman beside me," he said, rubbing his eyes. "You look like you've been awake for hours. You're not one of those early morning people, are you?" he mumbled between yawns.

"I am an early riser, if that's what you mean by 'those,'" she said.

"Since you are one of those, I hope you don't mind morning breath," he said, kissing her.

She had been awake for what seemed like hours watching him sleep, thinking about their night together, and hoping things wouldn't be awkward between them with the clarity that sunlight brings. He sat upright in bed, his back against the headboard.

"Sit on me."

As she rolled on top of him, he kissed her chest. She grabbed the headboard. Her cell started ringing, interrupting their heated ecstasy. She ignored the reminder of reality.

"I'm going to make you breakfast," Kevin said. "And if you don't have plans today, how about a long walk on the beach? Do either of those sound good to you?"

Lucy involuntarily sighed. She was trying to catch her breath.

"Well, I definitely need some breakfast, but I don't even know if I can walk right now. My legs feel like rubber. I need to check my voicemail. Hopefully, that was not Randy."

"If it is, tell him that you are dumping Bill Blauers for the day. I have a great day planned for us."

When Lucy noticed that the call was from a private number, she knew that she was doomed. She reluctantly listened to the message. It was Sammie cancelling the run they had planned. Lucy was relieved the message didn't relay a work emergency. And, for once, she didn't mind Sammie's conflict. She was now free to hang out with Kevin all day. Her thoughts were interrupted by her growling stomach coupled with the aroma of coffee, bacon, and eggs.

"Boy, it smells great," she said. "Thank the Good Lord that was Sammie calling and not Randy. So, it looks like you are stuck with me."

"Fantastic. Here's some coffee for you to take to the porch. Go sit and relax, if you know how to do that," he said, laughing.

She understood why Kevin loved his location. The views of the marsh and the Folly River were so peaceful. As Kevin was cooking a breakfast feast, she actually relaxed. Head to toe, she was experiencing a calm, restful stillness.

The breakfast was delicious and hit the spot. Though Lucy's mother had consistently drilled into her head that breakfast was the most important meal, she never took time for it. She was always in too big of a hurry to get to the office and start billing hours. But admittedly, she felt much better.

"Ready for our power walk on the beach?" she asked Kevin.

"Power walk? I'm going to get you to chill if it kills me. We can walk as long as you want, but power will not be involved. After our leisurely walk, we are going sit down and watch football. What do you think about that?"

"I think it sounds like a perfect day," she said.

They spent all morning exploring Folly Beach. Kevin reported that the pier was the second longest on the east coast. He was pushing Lucy's ability to "chill" to the limit when he bought bait and rented two fishing rods. Baiting the hook was no problem, but there was definitely an art to casting. She was determined to learn. She was enjoying herself but thought she could probably enjoy anything with Kevin.

Throughout the day, Lucy realized that, other than Sammie, she knew very little about the co-workers that she spent the majority of her time with every day. She learned a lot about Kevin. He graduated from Clemson where he was enrolled in the College of Engineering and Science. When his mother died in his junior year, he needed a second job to pay his expenses and some of his mother's medical bills. The engineering curriculum was difficult, but the computer science classes were easy for him. With all going on with his mom, he switched his major. Kevin had no regrets.

"Sometimes real life creates detours," he explained, matter-of-factly.

They lost track of time and were going to miss the kickoff for the Clemson game unless they started some serious power walking, which Kevin nixed again. When they passed a scooter, Kevin downloaded the app and instructed Lucy to hop on.

Lucy hugged Kevin's waist tightly as he maneuvered through the traffic and tourists. She knew he had a football game on his mind, but she wanted to spend the afternoon like this. She laid her head against his back, closed her eyes, and began reliving their morning in his bed. Her lustful thoughts halted when the scooter came to a screeching stop.

"Be right back," Kevin said.

Kevin ran a fast clip into the local market. He returned in no time with several bags that he placed in the front basket.

"Game day supplies," Kevin said. "More Coronas, chips, and stuff for my famous chili. Hang on."

The man was on a football mission, whizzing in and out of the Folly Beach roads.

"That was fun," Kevin said, parking the scooter. "We'll have to do that again when we have more time. Like tomorrow. We can pack a picnic and get one for the entire day."

Lucy tried to remember the last time that she had been on a picnic. Surely, she had some time in her life, but the only picnics that came to mind were from the Sunday church covered dishes.

"But now, there's a game," Kevin said. "I hope you like college football."

Since joining Spencer, Pettigrew & Hamilton, simple pastimes like fishing, riding a scooter, and watching football had been purged from her life for Bill Blauers.

"Being a College of Charleston girl, I watch some games, but I am not a diehard SEC fan," she said, attempting to display some knowledge of the sport.

"Clemson is in the ACC conference," Kevin laughed. "Not the SEC. If you had said you were a South Carolina Gamecock fan, I may have had to send you packing."

Lucy wasn't surprised by the huge TV. She shouldn't have been surprised at her IT guy's surround sound and other gadgets. His setup made you feel like you were literally sitting in the football stadium.

With the football game blasting, Kevin started chopping the ingredients for his "Tiger Chili." While the chili was simmering, he opened the double doors that led to the porch. The air circulating through the house had that crisp, fall smell that accompanied the arrival of lower humidity. He popped two Coronas and sat down on the couch. He handed Lucy a beer and clanked his beer against hers.

"Cheers," he said. "Here's to several scoring drives."

He winked and took a swig. From the look in his eyes, Lucy totally picked up on his innuendo. He was so darn cute. She became lost in a trance just gazing at him. He stopped mid-swig.

"What's wrong?" he asked. "I hope I didn't offend you. Don't get too serious on me now. My comment was tongue-in-cheek," he said, squeezing her thigh.

"No offense taken," she said. "As long as you give me your tongue and cheek later when you're scoring."

"That's a deal," Kevin said.

The next day, they scootered around Folly Beach to find the perfect picnic spot. Kevin said that driving a scooter was hard work, so it was necessary to stop at random bars to have a beer to refuel.

The bars in Folly Beach were as quaint and carefree as the houses. Lucy's favorite stop was a bar with a dirt floor, long wooden benches, and lots of fun, neon signs. Not surprisingly, most had a drinking theme. She pointed out her favorites: *I don't jog. It makes my lunch jump out of my glass; Sure, I like a cocktail every now and then, last time I checked, it was now;* and *Never drink alone, unless you are by yourself.*

Monday morning came too quickly. Lucy couldn't remember a time when she had enjoyed an entire weekend without Bill Blauers. Her relaxed weekend state was jolted back to reality when summoned to Randy's office.

I was born at night but not last night ...

Chapter Forty-Five

Lucy

"I didn't see you in the office all weekend," Randy said. "In your absence, I got two new matters. Have you heard of The Chandler Cuisine Collection?"

"No sir, I don't think so," she said.

She was trying to decipher Randy's comment about her absence over the weekend. She didn't need to get off on the wrong foot with him.

"It's the group that owns Charleston's finest restaurants," Randy said. "Tanner Chandler is the president, and our new client. It appears that his wife, SuSu, has been banging more than tennis balls with her instructor. Get Linda to give you the number for Nathan Nifong. He's our best private investigator."

Lucy had never met a private investigator. Randy's practice was introducing her to real world stuff.

"Here's the Chandlers' address and her car info," Randy said. "We need to prove that SuSu is doing more than improving her tennis game. We need Nathan on her ASAP. Tanner is leaving for France tomorrow for some fancy restaurant convention and will be gone a week. SuSu was supposed to go with him, but her tennis league has a tournament. She 'couldn't let her team down.' Tanner isn't buying her conflict. He says she sucks, though she should be on the pro tour based on his club bills for her lessons."

Randy was interrupted by a phone call. Lucy's short stint in Randy's practice area had made her cynical towards and confused about marriage. *How do people who love each other enough to get married fall so far off course?*

"Where was I?" Randy asked, finishing his call.

"A restaurant convention in France, and tennis lessons," Lucy said, reviewing her notes.

"The last club bill for those lessons lit a fire under Tanner. He said it's one thing if his wife is screwing around, but another thing if he's paying someone to do it. Tanner is out for blood and wants to sue the club too. He doesn't believe all the lesson time has been on the court. Since I don't care too much for country clubs, I couldn't give a shitcan, but it may create some issues with our pot..nars."

In addition to Randy's unique and random use of profanity, his accent was equally entertaining.

"I need all the information you can find on The Chandler Cuisine Collection," he said. "I want some verification of the profitability numbers provided by Mr. Chandler. We've got to know what's at stake here. Many of our pot..nars are members of this club, so it's got be worth it before I piss them all off."

Lucy wondered how the Baker brothers ended up at the Spencer firm. They were scrappy, smart lawyers who didn't give a "shitcan" about the do's and don'ts of Charleston high society.

"Now, for the second matter," Randy continued. "This one violates my longstanding policy of not representing women, but this one sounds interesting. It is a woman from Atlanta. I told her that I couldn't take any new clients, but that you could talk to her. I'll let you decide if you want to represent her."

"Seriously?" Lucy asked. "I don't think I'm ready to take a matter on my own."

"Oh, you'll do fine," Randy laughed. "I'm always available to answer any questions if you feel like you need some help. You can interview her and see what you think. She is coming in this afternoon at 3:00. Her name is Anna Chatham. Just listen to her story, see if you believe she is credible, and then we can discuss it. But get me the information on the Chandler Cuisine Collection pronto. I don't want to run up a big bill with Nathan if I'm going to refer this one out. But, it will be worth an initial investment of time to find out what's going on. My bet is that SuSu is lobbing some balls, and they ain't tennis balls."

Lucy hurried out of Randy's office to call Nathan. She didn't have a clue what services to request but hoped he knew the drill from working with Randy. He answered on the first ring.

"Nifong here."

"Mr. Nifong, my name is Lucy Tate. I'm an attorney at the Spencer firm and work with Randy Baker. He has a new case and needs your assistance. He asked that I call you."

"Lucy, did you say?"

"Yes, sir, Lucy Tate. I've just started working with Randy."

"Who is it this time?" he asked, cutting to the chase.

"Her name is SuSu Chandler. The wife of Tanner Chandler, for the time being."

"From Randy's clientele, I assume that Chandler is the big-time restaurant guy?" Nathan Nifong asked.

"That's my understanding. Mr. Chandler is of the opinion that SuSu is getting more than tennis lessons from their country club pro. Randy wants you to find out. Given that I'm new at this, I'm not sure what Randy has in mind."

"I do. Randy and I have worked together for many years."

"Great. Their address is 202 Country Club Road. SuSu drives a white Mercedes, and get ready for this—her license plate is LOVE10-S."

"Tell Randy I'm on it."

Lucy was becoming intrigued and fascinated with the lifestyles and extracurricular activities of the Charleston rich and famous. She investigated the net worth of Tanner Chandler and the profitability of the Chandler Cuisine Collection. After doing a couple of searches, she uncovered lots of information about the restaurants, the chefs, the menus, and the extensive wine selection—everything but the financial information that Randy requested. She called Kevin for help.

"What's up, beautiful?" Kevin asked.

"Hey. I need some help. I need access to sites where I can locate financial information about a company and an individual. Can you help me?"

"Shoot, I was hoping you were calling about something else. I can't concentrate on my work from thinking about our weekend. By the way, have I told you that you are awesome and that I had a great time?"

"Yes, you did," Lucy said, grinning. "Several times, and I had a great time too, but don't remind me. I've got to pull this stuff together for Randy before 3:00. I have an appointment with a potential new client—a woman. Randy won't take cases from women, but he thinks it has potential. He wants me to conduct the interview. I'm a little nervous but excited too."

"You're silly," Kevin said. "I'm confident you can pull that off."

"Thanks," Lucy said appreciating the positive reinforcement. "Anyway, before that, I have to collect financial information on the Chandler Cuisine Collection."

"That's the company that owns all the restaurants, right?" Kevin asked.

"Yes, that's my understanding," she said, thinking that she must be the only person in Charleston who hadn't heard of this company.

"The firm has subscriptions to some sites with information. But, I have to come to your office to give you access. I can be there in about ten minutes. How 'bout we try one of the Chandler restaurants after work? You would technically be working on your new matter."

"That sounds perfect," Lucy said, "but for now get down here and give me some access."

When Kevin arrived at Lucy's office door, Roberta/Gladys moved about as quickly as she did at 4:55 p.m. She barreled out of her cube.

"So, Lucy, are you having some more computer problems?" Roberta asked. "I could try and help you before you bother Kevin."

Kevin was onto every secretary and lawyer in the firm, and he didn't tolerate the BS.

"Roberta, how do you think you will help Lucy?" Kevin asked. "If I got paid by the number of times that I help you, I 'd be retired."

She huffed and slinked back into her cubicle. Kevin shut Lucy's door, hugged her, and kissed her neck.

"Now for that access," he said, lifting her skirt.

"Kevin, stop teasing me, seriously," Lucy said, pulling his hands away. "You can access that later after you get me on these sites."

Kevin quickly pecked away on Lucy's computer and printed out some information on the earnings of the Chandler Cuisine Collection for the last five years, their Dun & Bradstreet rating, and the net worth and investments of Tanner Chandler.

"I had no idea these restaurants made so much coin," Kevin said. "Call me when you are done with your new client. If I have time, I'll review all the Chandler restaurants menus, and you can see what suits you."

Lucy gathered the information that Kevin efficiently obtained and headed to Randy's office. She hoped that Randy could figure out a way to handle Tanner Chandler's case without a conflict with the country club. She thought that this case was going to be fun. She couldn't wait to learn about the devices Nathan Nifong utilized in obtaining scoop.

At 3:00, when the receptionist alerted Lucy that Ms. Chatham had arrived, she became anxious. It had taken years to gain confidence conducting interviews in the corporate group. But, family law issues were nothing like corporate matters. She was back to square one as an inexperienced lawyer. She took a deep breath and went to meet her first prospective client in her new practice.

Lucy had inaccurately painted an image of Ms. Chatham similar to Tiffany Putnam, but Ms. Chatham was the opposite. Like Tiffany, she wasn't wasting time on the sale racks at the discount stores. But, she exuded a glamorous, polished air. She had short brown hair, piercing blue eyes, and flawless smooth skin. She wore a cream pencil skirt with a light blue, crisp, cotton blouse. The flared ruffles at her wrists seem to accentuate her large diamond wedding ring. The heels on her killer pumps had a checkered pattern perfectly matching the colors of her outfit. Her ensemble appeared plucked from a fashion magazine.

As Lucy approached her, she extended her hand.

"Are you Ms. Tate?"

Her handshake was firm, but her hands were like silk. The only time Lucy's hands had ever felt this like was after indulging in free samples of expensive skin products at the various Charleston boutiques.

"Yes, but please call me Lucy. We are meeting in one of our conference rooms. Can I get you anything to drink first? Coffee, water, or a soda?"

"Water would be great, thanks."

Lucy escorted Ms. Chatham into the conference room and retrieved the water for Ms. Chatham and a Coke for herself. *Note to self,* Lucy thought, *drink more water and invest in expensive skin products.*

"It has taken me some time to muster the courage to call someone," Ms. Chatham said, beginning her story.

She paused and looked through her purse.

"I thought I had some tissue in my purse. Could I impose upon you for one?"

Lucy opened the cabinet doors spanning the back of the conference room dedicated to Randy's clients. Certainly, most divorce attorneys have Kleenex, but since Randy's clients were men, he may not stock such an item. Lucy worried that this one little mishap evidenced her rookie status. Lucy felt a sigh of relief when she spotted a box.

Lucy plopped the whole box beside Anna Chatham. She gracefully removed a couple of tissues and took a deep breath. She looked down at the table and sighed.

"This is more difficult than I thought."

"Take your time, Ms. Chatham. I'm in no hurry," Lucy said, but she certainly didn't want to be there too long. She had a date.

Again, Anna Chatham took a deep breath.

"I have been married twenty-six years, happily married, I thought. But lately, I have been having some doubts. My husband works long hours and travels extensively."

Long hours and extensive travel seemed to be a familiar theme among Randy's clients. She'd made it longer than the others Lucy had been introduced to so far. But, from Lucy's limited time in Randy's practice, Anna Chatham's suspicions were probably justified.

"I am a writer. In the early years of our marriage, I worked for the *Atlanta Journal-Constitution.* My job was hectic with long hours and deadlines, so I completely understand the demands of my husband's job. I guess what I am trying to say is that I never put pressure on him or complained about his work schedule. About the time our children were in preschool, my husband started his own business. We decided that I would stay at home and start freelancing. I had earned a good reputation while at the paper, so I had enough freelance jobs to provide a perfect balance of challenging work and flexibility. The flexibility was necessary then because his schedule was unpredictable. My husband is a very competitive man. I wasn't surprised by the number of hours he invested in his new venture. But even then, he made time for the children and me."

Lucy worried how long this background information was going to take. She didn't need to hear about the so-called perfect parts of her marriage. She didn't want to appear crass but wanted to bypass all the history and get to the point.

"So have the travel and hours increased to a degree that you suspect the time away is something other than work related?" Lucy interjected.

"Frankly, I never thought that. I began feeling neglected and unappreciated. When I worked, it seemed like he respected me more, was interested in what I was doing, and valued our time together. You know, we were juggling children and demanding jobs. When I started freelancing, I felt like my job wasn't as important."

Ms. Chatham wiped her eyes and sipped her water. Lucy was trying to be patient.

"I tried to talk to him about my feelings and even suggested counseling, but he would brush me off. He told me that I was spoiled, I didn't understand the pressures of his job and to suck it up. But, I did understand the pressures of his job. I had been there once myself. I have tried to schedule time for just us, like date nights, but that agitated him. He missed them due to working late. After the children went to college, he bought a boat. He loved boating. We both did. I was excited and viewed this as a time we could reconnect. Since the children were gone, I could travel with him on his business trips or his boating excursions. I can write from anywhere. But he always has a reason for why it's a bad time."

Lucy wanted to cut to the chase and ask if she caught him shacking up with a boat washer or cute deckhand.

"I finally confided my feelings with one of my best friends. She candidly said, 'Anna, he has a girlfriend, plain and simple.' Until hearing that from one of my closest friends, it had never occurred to me that he could be unfaithful. He is a fastidious rule follower. We have never fought or anything close to it, but after that frank assessment from my friend, I began snooping around the house. I am embarrassed to say that I would go through his briefcase, his car, his pants pockets, his receipts, looking for any sign of infidelity. I have never found anything."

Surprisingly, Lucy found herself thinking that perhaps Anna's husband was just really busy. She started empathizing with him. She knew from first-hand experience that work gives you tunnel vision. You don't realize that you are shutting out everything and everyone.

"Don't take this the wrong way, but our clients typically have found some evidence of impropriety or that things don't add up. I would rely more on your instincts than your girlfriend's comment."

"Trust me. I've gone back and forth in my head about this. But my husband's job is to cover for corporations and individuals that get in trouble. He is a master at spinning things. My friend could be very wrong, but she is right that all the signs are there. He is here in Charleston working on a matter. He knows Charleston is one of my favorite places but flatly rejected my offer to accompany him here. I understand his clients' needs for privacy and confidentiality, but I am his wife. I came here with the intent of doing my own investigating. I'm so ashamed that I didn't want to involve anyone else.. After I got here, it became evident that I am in over my head. But, I need to know the truth because it is driving me crazy. I need to know if he has a mistress."

With that, tears began streaming down the soft, beautiful skin of this classy woman.

"First of all, I am so sorry. You are obviously a very smart woman. We have private investigators that can help you do some investigating—if that's what you want. I can provide you a range of options, and you can see what fits your budget."

"Lucy, my husband has done very well, and I haven't done so badly myself. I will spend whatever it takes for me to be able to bring this to some closure. Currently, he is docked here, but I don't know how long."

"Do you know where he is docked?" Lucy asked.

"Yes. The marina is the Charleston Ashley Dockage, his boat is a 112-foot Westport yacht, *Sea Relations*. It should be easy to find."

"I am familiar with that marina," Lucy said, thinking about the fortuitous location of *Sea Relations*, and that it was time for Sammie to give her a full tour of the docks. "I'll need his phone numbers and a description for our private investigator."

"He's 6'4, 45 years old but looks older due to his salt and pepper hair. He is very fit— he runs a lot. I'll email you some photos, but I have one of his business cards with all his phone numbers," she said, reaching for her purse.

"How long will you be in Charleston?"

"I don't know yet. Here's his business card. I kept my maiden name because, as a writer, I had gained some notoriety before we were married. In retrospect, maybe that was silly. Maybe, he didn't like the fact that I didn't take his name."

Poor thing. She was trying to find reasons to blame herself for his actions, just like Sammie. *Must be a female trait*, Lucy thought. She picked up the card. It was engraved with "Grant Davis, CEO of The Davis Group. Reliable Results." *Holy shit. Grant Davis was the PR guy Sammie was working with.*

"Feel free to call me anytime—day or night," Lucy said, handing Anna her business card.

"Thank you, Lucy. I really appreciate your help."

After escorting her new client to the elevator, Lucy immediately called Nathan Nifong.

"I have another matter for you. I hope you can work it in with the Chandler matter. It has some urgency as well."

She gave him a quick summary.

"If that guy is hunkered down on his boat, we'll start with cell phone records. On the Chandler matter, this one isn't going to be too difficult. Mrs. Chandler is not focused exclusively on her tennis game. When I went by the house to place a tracking device on her Mercedes, she was leaving, so I followed her. She went to a house on the Isle of Palms. The house is owned by Cris Waters. In checking the country club website, the tennis pro is one Cris Waters. Though SuSu had on a tennis outfit, there is no tennis court at this house, and she was there more than sufficient time for me to install the tracking device. I haven't updated Randy yet. If you can do that, I'd appreciate it. I'll get you cell phone records for Grant Davis shortly."

"Thanks. I'll update Randy now."

Lucy went to Randy's office to update him on her interview with Anna Chatham and SuSu Chandler's tennis "lesson."

"I want to take Anna's matter, Randy. She isn't like the spouses of your clients. She actually has her own career. She's a writer. Her husband is Grant Davis, a big time PR executive, who has a yacht that is currently docked here in Charleston. I called Nathan. He is going to start retrieving cell phone calls."

"Ummm, ports of call to the yachtsmen typically include more than their docking location," Randy said. "I'll let you run with that one. When you talk to Nathan again, we need pics to document SuSu's instructor's drop shot. Have him wait until tomorrow when Tanner Chandler leaves on his trip. I don't want to raise any suspicion before then."

Lucy went back to her office and decided to call Sammie. She wanted to confirm that they were still on for dinner tomorrow night, and to learn more about this Grant Davis. Lucy got her voicemail.

"Hey, girl," Lucy began. "Sorry I couldn't talk longer yesterday. But I can't wait to catch up tomorrow night. I ended up spending all weekend with Kevin. He has the coolest house at Folly Beach. We had a blast. Call me if you can and if not, I'll see you tomorrow night at CCCs."

Lucy then called Kevin and got his voicemail.

"I'm finished with my new client interview. Yes, I have a new client. Randy is letting me take this case. I can leave any time, so call me back when you are free."

Lucy started researching The Davis Group, its office locations, number of employees, annual revenues, and other matters when Barbie appeared at her door.

"Lucy, you received a fax," Barbie said, handing her numerous pages.

"Thanks, Barbie. I assumed faxes were obsolete. This is my first."

"Randy is the only attorney who still receives faxes," she said, laughing. "I guess I'll be seeing you more often now that you are working with him."

The fax was from Nathan with Grant Davis' cell phone records for the past sixty days. He was a prolific communicator. While Lucy waited on Kevin, she noted repetitive calls. She called Nathan.

"Did you get my fax?" he answered.

She realized that Nathan was not one for introductory chit-chat.

"If you don't know by now," Nathan continued, "Randy prefers faxes. He either doesn't trust email or hasn't figured out how to use it."

"Probably both," Lucy said. "Can you find out who the numbers belong to?"

"Duh, yes," he responded.

Lucy was embarrassed that her inexperience was so obvious.

"Circle the numbers that you want me to trace," he said.

"On their way. Oh, and Randy wants pictures of SuSu and her pro—or as only Randy could put it—photos of the 'instructor's drop shot'. But wait until tomorrow after Tanner Chandler leaves for his trip. He doesn't want to raise any suspicions before then."

"Got it. Drop shot. Sounds like Randy. Talk to you later. Call my cell if you need to reach me."

As Lucy was studying the list of calls and dates from Grant Davis' cell phone records, Kevin called.

"We are going to the Gullah Kitchen. It looks like our type of place. Can you leave now?"

"Give me about ten minutes. I now have to send a fax to our PI. I have never sent a fax, so hopefully it won't take too long. Can we go by that new martini bar for a drink before dinner? I want to celebrate my first matter."

"Meet me out front. I have my woody—actually both of them."

Kevin and Lucy were enjoying their second martini when Lucy's cell rang. It was Nathan.

"I'm sorry, but this is our investigator. I better take this."

"What's up, Nathan?"

"I started looking up the numbers you circled. One is from a tracfone so there is no way for me to identify the caller. I pulled outgoing calls made from it. There are several calls made to your cell. Based on the length of the call, it appears you had a conversation."

"Tracfones? I hadn't heard of anyone ever using those, so I have no idea."

"Other than you, there is only one other outgoing call from that tracfone. That call was placed to a Cort Spencer."

"He is my friend's father. She works at a marina and has a phone to receive orders for supplies. I guess that is a tracfone."

"Interesting, because Grant Davis must be the only one needing supplies," he said. "Lots of texts from his phone to that tracfone."

"That is strange. She is always busy with orders," Lucy said.

"Well, this Grant Davis is smooth because most of his repetitive calls are to tracfones, other than calls made to a Cathleen McKinney. So far, she appears to be winning the prize for most calls made and received."

Lucy relayed her conversation with Nathan to Kevin and told him about her new client, the wife of Grant Davis.

"Maybe that's how PR guys operate, but it sounds a little strange to me," Kevin said.

"The weird thing is that every time I talk to Sammie, she says she is running errands for slip renters. But Nathan said that the only person who has contacted that tracfone is Grant Davis. Do you think Mr. Barry would give her a tracfone to use?"

"Maybe, Harry seems a bit tight. Remember, when we were there, he mentioned he had a phone for her with unlimited texting but limited calls."

"Now, that you say that, I do. Nathan said that Grant Davis has lots of calls to Cathleen McKinney. That is the name of Dougie's boss. I suppose there is more than one Cathleen McKinney."

Tuesday morning, Lucy was tasked with drafting a Separation Agreement for Tanner Chandler. Before he left for France, Randy had updated Tanner on SuSu's visit to Cris Waters' house on the Isle of Palms. Upon hearing the news, Tanner authorized an all-out blitz on SuSu's whereabouts while he was away. He wanted to know what she was doing every minute of every day. Randy told him that the tracking device would identify her whereabouts, but Tanner said he didn't care how much it cost. He wanted 24-hour surveillance by a human being, not a device. Tanner wanted the Separation Agreement ready by the time he got back. He was planning a homecoming surprise for SuSu that she wouldn't forget.

Nathan was a solo shop. He couldn't provide round-the-clock surveillance. As Lucy explained Tanner Chandler's demand, Kevin offered his assistance.

"I don't require much sleep. A break from fixing computers would do me good. Why don't you check with Randy and see if I can help? It would be fun. You could come with me. We'll get good food and pack a cooler and let SuSu entertain us."

Lucy wasn't ready to disclose her relationship with Kevin to Randy. She had to think about how to delicately offer this proposal. After some thought, she decided to test the waters.

"Randy, there is no way Nathan can single-handedly cover SuSu nonstop for a week. I know Nathan is your go-to guy, so I have an idea. You know Kevin Miller, the firm's

IT guy? I have to admit that he pulled the financial information on Chandler and his restaurants for me. He could moonlight as Nathan's assistant. It would be more profitable for the firm. Instead of paying a third party, the firm would be earning whatever hourly rate we would charge for Kevin. We get to keep Nathan on the job and make money on Kevin."

Randy loved it. Nathan was his best private investigator, and Randy didn't trust PI service companies. Randy recounted a story of a botched job of a PI service that had been retained by the wife of one of his clients. Though these stories were long and cut into billable time, Lucy loved hearing about his past representations.

Randy didn't want his reputation to be tainted by some jackleg PI firm. He loved the idea of a Spencer employee working with Nathan.

"This is a no brainer. The problem is when the potnars hear what Kevin will be doing, I'll be getting other volunteers."

Nathan assigned Kevin a 3:00 p.m.-midnight shift. Kevin updated Lucy that he had followed SuSu to the country club. Apparently, SuSu was attending an event without her tennis companion due to the parade of women entering the club in their designer dresses with gifts in hand.

Lucy delivered Chinese take-out at 7:00 p.m. She found it all exciting. She didn't even care that she couldn't bill any hours while spying with Kevin.

"Sounds like you won't get any evidence tonight," Lucy said.

"I don't know about that. SuSu is wearing a one-piece black jumpsuit that zips down the front. I'm thinking her outfit is strategic. The tennis jock won't have to waste any time with warm-ups later," he said.

"You're having some fun with this, aren't you?"

"For now, yes," Kevin laughed.

While Kevin and Lucy were dining on the Chinese take-out in the country club parking lot, Lucy's phone rang. It was Nathan.

"Hey Nathan, what's up?"

"Your friend who runs errands at the marina—is her name Samantha Morgan?"

"Yeah, why?"

"Well, I've been watching video from the camera in the marina parking lot. My buddy is the dockmaster and helps me out from time to time. Let's just say that I've investigated activities out there before. There is video of a woman walking hand-in-hand with a dude and they left in a BMW. I traced the plate. It's registered to Samantha Morgan. You wouldn't happen to know what Grant Davis looks like, would you?"

"No, I don't, but are you absolutely sure it is Sammie?"

"Well, Lucy, I don't know your friend, but a cute blonde was getting into a car registered to Samantha Morgan, and unless someone has stolen your friend's car, she has someone she's sweet on."

"I'm sorry Nathan, but I need to see the video. First of all, she tells me everything. We're best friends. She would have told me if she was seeing anyone."

"Well, you need to look at it then. I'll download the video to a flash drive, and you can see for yourself. There are two clips a couple of hours apart."

After Lucy hung up, her gut was telling her that Nathan had seen Sammie and that she was probably with Grant Davis. Thinking back on their conversations, Sammie had quickly dismissed all questions about Grant Davis. The fact that Grant Davis was the only one that had used Sammie's phone for orders was equally suspicious. Lucy had to see that video.

As Lucy relayed the information to Kevin, he spotted SuSu.

"Interesting, she just left from the employee's entrance. It's closer to the tennis courts."

"How do you know about that? Are you a member here?"

"Hell, no, Lucy. I thought you knew me better than that. After she went inside, I assumed I had a little time to check out the possible exits. I wanted to make sure that bimbo didn't lose me on my first night investigating. Here, write down on this pad that she exited the employee's entrance at 9:10 p.m. I am supposed to keep a log so it will match up with the tracking device on her car. Her husband wants this all locked down."

"I'm impressed, I think. I would have been here hours watching the front door. You are a natural at this."

"I don't think so. Given that it's an employees' entrance, I didn't give it a second thought. I guess SuSu is sneakier than I thought."

"Or, just on a mission," Lucy added.

"I guess I'm headed down to the courts," Kevin said. "I'll meet you at your place after Nathan gets here."

"Be careful, Kevin. I bet the club has some type of security."

"Nathan already tipped me off about that. He said that the security folks are quite cooperative if you hand them a business card with some cash."

Lucy was bummed that she had her car. She wanted to hang out with Kevin, and she was curious about SuSu's itinerary.

When Nathan relieved Kevin, he handed Kevin a flash drive.

"This is for Lucy. Can you give it to her tomorrow at work? It's important."

Kevin didn't disclose that he was headed straight to Lucy's apartment for the rest of the evening. And Nathan didn't disclose the evidence on the flash drive—that Lucy's best friend was the other woman of her new client.

Don't hang your wash on someone else's line...

Chapter Forty-Six

Lucy

"I have to see what's on that flash drive," Lucy said the minute Kevin walked in. "I won't be able to sleep otherwise."

"I figured as much."

Kevin uploaded the video from the flash drive onto his computer. The images were blurry, but Sammie was identifiable. She was walking hand-in-hand with a man in the direction of her white BMW. The man opened Sammie's door. After she got in, he leaned into her car. Lucy couldn't tell what he was doing but she was thinking that he wasn't helping with Sammie's seat belt. They left the marina.

The video then cut to her BMW pulling back into a marina parking space. Sammie got out and walked in the direction of the camera. It was a clear shot of her. She headed back to her car with a cart. The man helped her load the bags from her trunk into the cart.

As Sammie leaned into her trunk to retrieve more bags, the man moved directly behind her, wrapped his arms around her waist, and pressed his body into hers. He said something in her ear. She turned towards him. He moved closer to her face like they were getting ready to kiss in broad daylight. Instead, she said something then turned to get the cart. They walked together towards the docks with big smiles on their faces.

"Wow. I don't know what to say. I feel like I've invaded her privacy. But, it's also upsetting. Sammie hasn't mentioned that she is in a relationship."

She accessed the photos that Anna Chatham had sent to her and showed them to Kevin.

"I'm thinking this is Grant Davis. What do you think?"

"Hard to tell from these head shots. It could be someone else."

"The man in the video is definitely tall and thin like Anna described. But, whoever it is, why wouldn't she have told me? She's my best friend. We tell each other everything."

"Everything?" Kevin asked, kissing Lucy's neck.

"Well, most everything."

"Just ask her," Kevin said. "Tell her what you saw. You have to find out if it's your client's husband. If so, you're gonna have to disclose it. But, you won't resolve it tonight. Watching that video makes me want to take you to bed right now."

Sex with Kevin paused Lucy's analytically, active brain. After, her blissful state would put her in a deep sleep even without her white noise machine. But, tonight, she couldn't sleep. She finally got out of bed at 5:00 a.m., made coffee, and jumped in the shower. Kevin startled her when he joined her.

"But for my 6:00 a.m. SuSu watch, I'd take you right back to bed," Kevin said.

"I'm coming with you. I'm not going to be able to concentrate on anything in the office. I didn't get any sleep worrying about whether Sammie is messed up with that sleaze bag Grant Davis."

"Absolutely, if you think Randy's okay with it."

"Well, it is work," Lucy said. "I can spend time with my two favorite men, you and Bill Blauers."

"I'll fix us a breakfast sandwich," Kevin said. "Bill Blauers can't do that."

Nathan raised his eyebrows when he spotted Lucy in Kevin's car. She rolled her window down.

"That was Sammie on the video," she communicated to Nathan.

"Thought so. Talk to you later."

Lucy called the office to let Randy know that she had to retrieve some evidence Nathan had on her new case. She also relayed what had transpired since yesterday with SuSu and her tennis instructor.

Then, Lucy called Anna to see if she was available for an afternoon meeting. She decided to show her the video from the marina parking lot. Lucy had to find out if the man with Sammie was, in fact, Grant Davis. She had a sinking feeling that her best friend was indeed the other woman. When Anna Chatham arrived, Lucy escorted her into a conference room.

"Thanks for coming in. As I mentioned, I wanted to update you on what we've learned so far. First, we've obtained your husband's cell phone records for the past sixty days. We attempted to identify recipients of repetitive calls. It appears a lot of the calls are made to tracfones. We can't identify those. Do you know why your husband would be calling tracfones?"

"No, I don't even know what those are," Anna said.

"They are cell phones with prepaid minutes. You can purchase them from a lot of retailers. You don't have to disclose personal information or have any type of cell plan."

"Grant does handle a lot of high-profile cases," she said. "Maybe the reason he has those phones is for the very reason you mentioned—you can't find out who he is calling."

"Other than calls to tracfones, the other repetitive calls are to a Cathleen McKinney," Lucy said. "Do you know who that is?

"No, I do not."

She clutched her hands tightly together. She pressed her fingers into her knuckles. Lucy started thinking that she wasn't cut out for this practice area after all. Her stomach was feeling the anxiety that was all over her client's face.

"Ms. McKinney works for Worth Pharmaceutical," Lucy said.

"Well, Worth is a big client of Grant's firm, so that would make sense," Anna said.

Another logical business explanation, Lucy thought. The man is smooth but not smooth enough to avoid cameras in parking lots.

"In addition to the cell records, our investigator has reviewed video from a security camera in the parking lot at the Charleston Ashley Dockage. He sent me two clips that I am going to show you. I will warn you that you may find it disturbing if the man is your husband."

Anna took a deep breath and squeezed her knuckles harder.

"Well, that is what I am here to find out. Go ahead."

Lucy pulled up the video on her laptop and played the clips showing Sammie and a man walking hand-in-hand towards her car. Anna closed the laptop.

"That is Grant," she said. "I don't need to see anymore."

"I'm sorry Anna," and Lucy was sorry, in more ways than one.

At that moment, Lucy was so mad at Sammie for keeping this secret from her.

"We can get more evidence. It's up to you how much you want to spend. Again, I'm sorry. Is there anything I can do for you? Would you like some water, coffee, anything?"

"No, I just need some time to myself," she said. "I'll be in touch."

Lucy called Kevin.

"How did your meeting go?" he asked.

"Not good. The man with Sammie in the video is Grant Davis. I feel betrayed. I couldn't tell my client that her husband was with my best friend. I don't even know what my ethical obligations are. This is such a mess."

"Yes, it is. I can't help you with your ethical rules, but you need to have a heart-to-heart with Sammie. You wouldn't be disclosing confidential information to tell her you saw her on a video. That video is the property of the marina and was provided to Nathan. It doesn't belong to your client."

"I hadn't thought of that," Lucy said. "Boy, you have picked up a lot of legal knowledge at the firm, huh?"

"Yep. We'll save my education on that front for another day. Aren't you meeting Sammie tomorrow night? Talk to her then. Let's discuss over dinner. I'm going to be stir-crazy sitting in my car most of the night again. I'd rather be fixing attorney's computers."

"Hang in there. Tanner Chandler will be back soon. Let me know where you are, and I'll bring you dinner."

Lucy watched the video again of Sammie and yes, Grant Davis. She couldn't possibly know that he was married. Lucy tried to zoom in and see if he was wearing a wedding band, but the picture became too grainy and distorted. She called Nathan Nifong.

"What's up Lucy?"

"I just met with Anna Chatham. She confirmed that the man in the video is her husband. I am getting ready to go through the cell records you sent me again. Anna seems to think the tracfones make sense given the sensitive nature of her husband's business. Can you retrieve calls for the past six months? He probably has a woman at every port," using Randy's line.

"Yes, I can. But it may be tomorrow. I am relieving Kevin at 5:00 p.m."

Tomorrow was certainly acceptable. Anna said she needed time to herself. By their next meeting, she hoped to uncover someone else other than Sammie. Now, she had to figure out what to say to Sammie. The walls felt like they were closing in. In retrospect, corporate law never tugged at her emotions like this. She called Kevin.

"I can't concentrate. This Grant Davis issue really bothers me."

"Why don't you go for a run to clear your head?" Kevin suggested. "I'll see you later, and, babe, quit thinking about it. Sammie has her reasons for not telling you."

Kevin was right, but Lucy couldn't stop thinking about Sammie and her involvement with this cad. Then, it hit Lucy that Sammie may have already figured it out. She had been so wrapped up in Kevin over the weekend, that she hadn't thought about Sammie's call asking her about the monogram in the clothes they found by the hot tub. Sammie mentioned that she may have learned something new. Lucy surmised that the something new was the relationship between Grant Davis and Cathleen McKinney. Lucy wished that she was seeing Sammie tonight. She knew that she wouldn't think of anything else for the next 24 hours.

He's on a first name basis with the bottom of the deck...

Chapter Forty-Seven

Sammie

Sammie didn't sleep at all. She kept replaying recent events. Half the night, she tried to comprehend her rapid infatuation with Grant Davis. The other half, she spent analyzing her relationship with Dougie from their first meeting to their marriage and everything in between. She found it conflicting that her father, whom she admired so much, was the farthest thing from either of them. *What was it about her that was drawn to bad men? What were the warning signs of narcissistic behavior?*

Her mind quickly turned to Mack. She felt that she was inadequate to raise a child, much less a boy. She wanted her son to be kind to and respectful of women. Mack would be back tomorrow, and his mother needed to find the strength to carry on. She had one day to pull herself together.

The cold front that had moved in also brought rain. All Sammie wanted to do was lay in bed under the covers over her head. She felt as gloomy as the weather. She didn't want to go to the marina. She called Mr. Barry and told him that she had some things to take care of before Mack got home but to let her know if any orders came into the marina office. She would be checking her phone.

She forced herself out of bed. She needed to get out of the house. She bundled up to go for a run.

She opened the gate on the white picket fence of her childhood home—her home with two wraparound porches. Instead of running, she wanted to flee to the upstairs porch swing where she and her mother spent many hours. Lucy had been right. She had been protected by the luxury of a charmed upbringing. Maybe that was her problem. She had no perspective on human frailty.

She had been raised in a loving, supportive environment, which instilled a genuine trust in people. She believed that if you were a kind and honest person and worked hard, you could control your destiny. Perhaps that was the reason she had never agonized over any decision. Her choices thus far in life seemed, well, just natural and had all worked out. That is, until now. She was becoming skeptical of everyone's motives and her judgment.

Sammie was glad that she was meeting Lucy for dinner. However, she continued to debate if she should fill her in on the weekend, the discovery of the monogram clothing in Grant's room, and the Worth papers. Though Lucy wouldn't judge, Sammie was ashamed of her behavior. She knew that Lucy always thought that she was on some higher, moral ground. Well, Sammie had news for her. Sammie's streak had ended—and ended badly. But she knew that her faith, her family, and her best friend would get her through this recent mistake. Yes, Dougie Morgan and Grant Davis were both big mistakes and errors in judgment. Mack was the wonderful product of the first mistake. Nothing good had come from the second.

She's educated beyond her means to comprehend...

Chapter Forty-Eight

Lucy And Sammie

Sammie got to CCCs early. She needed a drink to help her loosen up and come clean with Lucy. Rudy, their favorite CCC bartender, was working and made a beeline for her.

"Hey Sammie, it's great to see you!" Rudy said, excitedly. "It's been too long. How are you?"

"I'm good, but I've missed this place."

"Drinking anything else tonight?" Rudy asked, setting down a glass of iced water.

"I'm meeting Lucy for dinner, but I'm a little early. What is your latest specialty cocktail concoction?"

"I've got this killer new margarita," Rudy said. "Infused with jalapeño. But fair warning, it's pretty spicy."

"Sounds interesting. I'll try it but with extra tequila to muffle the jalapeño," Sammie said, hoping it would rapidly dull her senses.

"Lucy tells me that you are working at the Charleston Ashley Dockage," Rudy said, delivering her margarita. "Quite a change from the firm, huh?"

"Just a little bit," she said, sipping her courage elixir.

"Probably gives you more time to spend with your son. How old is he now?"

"Almost a year old. It's hard to believe."

"Time gets away from us, for sure," he said, "but you sure bounced back into shape. You look great, as usual. And, it will be no time at all before your son will be carrying on your family tradition at the firm."

There were some nice perks that had come with working at the firm. CCCs certainly catered to the lawyers across the street. Yet, while working at the firm, Sammie had never given the CCC's staff much thought. Being removed from the hectic schedule, she was surprised at the simple things around her that she was first noticing. For instance, she saw Rudy's strengths. He had the ability to make you feel important from the moment you sat down.

After Rudy caught up with the increasing CCC dinner crowd bar orders, he returned and leaned over closer to Sammie.

"I guess you've heard about the latest firm gossip," he said in a lower tone. "That's some shit, ain't it?"

"I've sort of been out of touch," Sammie said, withholding that she didn't care about any firm gossip.

"Lucy hasn't told you?" he asked. "I thought the whole firm would be buzzing with that scoop."

Sammie feigned any emotion or interest, though admittedly she was a little curious if it involved Barbie and Frank Hamilton. Thankfully, a waitress distracted Rudy's further sharing his scoop. She was growing more anxious about delivering her own revelations to Lucy. The potent jalapeño in the margarita was not helping her squeamish stomach. She gulped some water to calm her increasing jitters, and then, someone grabbed her from behind.

"Hey girlie!" Lucy squealed, squeezing her tightly.

Sammie turned and gave Lucy a hug. Lucy leaned over the bar and yelled down to Rudy.

"Hey Rudy, champagne, please, when you get a chance," squeezing Sammie's hand, "to celebrate being with my friend. It seems like forever since I've seen you."

"It does seem like forever, doesn't it? You probably have a gazillion things to catch me up on," Sammie said.

"Ha. You know what life at the sweatshop is like," Lucy said. "I will fill you in on Kevin, who I absolutely adore. But, first let me live vicariously through you. Tell me about life on the docks."

Ironically, Lucy's vibrant spirit had a soothing effect, and Sammie didn't want her news to kill the effusive state.

"You go first," Sammie said. "Update me on Kevin."

Lucy didn't even have to say anything about Kevin. Her ear-to-ear smile evidenced that she was smitten. Sammie listened to Lucy go on and on about their weekend, how compatible they were, how it seemed like they had been together forever, all the kind things he had done, and the great sex. Sammie was feeling sad and jealous that Lucy's new romance seemed so perfect. The perfect one that she had found turned out to be a fraud.

"So, enough about me," Lucy said. "It's your turn. I hate to say this, but you look like you did after pulling an all-nighter at the firm billing hours. I thought the marina job would be less stressful."

"Gee, thanks," Sammie said, tensing up from what she was about to divulge. "To be honest, I didn't sleep much last night. Oh Lucy, I don't know where to begin, but I'm a mess once again."

Once Sammie started, she couldn't stop. She told Lucy everything—from what she thought was the best relationship ever, to her discovery of the monogram on the clothes, to the Worth Pharmaceutical papers in what looked like Cathleen McKinney's designated dresser drawers.

"Do you think it's too coincidental?" Sammie asked.

"Honestly, it is very strange that Cathleen McKinney keeps appearing and Worth too. I did think that whole setup was very strange with Grant Davis involving you in his highly secretive business matters," Lucy said. "But he had nothing to do with you quitting the firm and then getting the marina job. Don't get carried away."

"I feel like I am going crazy. And admit it, I am completely inept when it comes to men."

Lucy squeezed her hand.

"You are a beautiful, trusting soul who sees the best in everyone," Lucy said.

"Well, that trust has burned me now twice," Sammie said. "I thought my judgment was one of my strengths. Now, I am questioning everything."

"It is a strength," Lucy said. "You don't have a suspicious bone in your body. That is what makes you who you are and why I love you so much. I've always hated the saying 'Whatever doesn't kill you makes you stronger,' but it's true. More importantly, it makes you wiser. You are going to be just fine. Let's order dinner at the bar. I have something else to talk to you about."

Lucy didn't want to move to a dinner table where it was quieter yet afforded more opportunity for eavesdropping. Lucy needed to talk to her about the video. The bar area was the best spot—a lot more noise to cover their conversation.

"I want to tell you about my first case," Lucy said, after they placed their dinner order. "I couldn't believe Randy didn't reject the case outright because the client is a woman. You know that he has a rule that he only represents men. He let me meet with her and decide if I wanted to take the case."

"You haven't skipped a beat in this new area," Sammie said.

"I don't know about that, but I want to help her. She has suspicions of infidelity and finally got the courage to call a lawyer. She is a writer who gave up her job after children but has continued to freelance. She is beautiful, classy, and polished. Her husband has a successful business in Atlanta and treats her like crap."

"Is Randy Baker's reputation that well-known?" Sammie asked. "I know he has a stellar reputation in South Carolina, but isn't domestic law one of those areas where you need a lawyer in your state of residence?"

"Her husband is here on business. She is very private and ashamed for thinking he could be cheating. But, all the signs are there. So, she came to town to check up on him. Her husband is docked at a marina. When she couldn't get through the locked gate, she called Randy. I don't know how else to say this. Sammie, she is married to Grant Davis."

Sammie turned white. Lucy thought Sammie may faint.

"Oh God, no." she said.

She put her head in her hands.

"Lucy, he told me he was divorced. Obviously, he is a liar, but geez, what are the chances that my best friend is representing his wife? You're not going to tell her what I told you—are you, Lucy?"

"Well, Sammie, before tonight, you haven't told me that anything was going on between you and that dirtbag, so of course, I haven't said anything. There is video of the two of you in the marina parking lot, which she has seen. And, to be perfectly honest, I was very upset when I saw it. I can't believe you haven't told me anything about him. I mean Sammie, we're best friends."

"I wanted to, Lucy, but I was scared. Things were going way too fast, and I was concerned that you would lecture me about being on the rebound and that I needed to be careful—all of things I kept telling myself. But, he seemed so perfect. I should have known better. If Dougie finds out about this, he will crucify me with it. Are you going to tell his wife?"

"I don't know. Part of me wants to discuss all of this with Randy. I am worried that I have some ethical dilemma here that impairs my representation. Shit, I don't know. I've never had to deal with this type of mess before. You sure don't have these issues in the world of corporate law. What do you think I should do?"

"Did you tell her that you knew me?" Sammie asked.

"No, I didn't. I told her to think about what she wanted to do next—that we could get more information."

"I bet there is a long list of people just like me."

Sammie wiped away the tears that were beginning to spill from her eyes.

"Really, I don't care what you tell her," Sammie said. "She needs to know he is a monster."

"I hate to sound like a lawyer, but I will probably have to subpoena you for your deposition," Lucy said. "Your license plate is clearly visible in the video, and our PI knows the car belongs to you. I could let her know that we've located the woman in the video and that the woman confirms a relationship. Then, I'll let her decide if she wants the details and how she wants to proceed. She doesn't strike me as the type that wants to destroy the man."

"I'll leave that to you, Lucy. I will do whatever you think is best. You don't have a choice. She is your client. You can't withhold information, and you certainly won't catch him with me again. His business is finished here anyway. I understand that he has left, and I don't think he is coming back. I should have listened to Mr. Barry. He never trusted him."

"I shouldn't tell you this," Lucy said, grabbing Sammie's arm, "but while we're coming clean, our PI investigated Grant's cell phone calls. There is one number he calls a lot and also receives lots of calls from too."

"Cathleen McKinney?" Sammie asked.

"Yes. She routinely calls him every night around 11:00 and every morning around 6:00."

"I noticed some of those calls over the weekend," Sammie said, "as well as her clothes. That's why I called you about the monogram."

Lucy put her arm around Sammie as the tears started again. She seemed incredibly sad. They sat in complete silence for what seemed like an eternity. Lucy couldn't find any words of comfort. Sammie wiped her eyes. Her demeanor took a 360-degree turn.

"Let's hit some bars," Sammie said, finally. "Are you game?"

"Sure. I just need to call Kevin and let him know my plans have changed. We were going to meet after dinner."

"Tell him to meet us here. We're going bar-hopping. On Grant Davis."

After Kevin arrived, Sammie paid the bill and gave Rudy a $500 tip—all on Grant Davis. She had a stack of cash in her purse "for her services." She didn't want his money.

"How about we head down East Bay then hit King?" Sammie asked. "I'm feeling charitable."

East Bay and King were two of Lucy's favorite streets because she thought they reflected the city's lure—history, views, shopping, and restaurants. East Bay provided extensive views of the Cooper River and was home to her favorite seafood restaurants, while King Street was a shopper's paradise with its antique stores, art galleries, shoe and clothing boutiques.

In addition to its idyllic water views, fabulous food, and rich culture, another extraordinary feature of Charleston was that it was walkable. There were no cabs zipping up and down the historic streets—only horse-drawn carriages filled with tourists or the occasional bicycle rickshaws. Due to the popularity of East Bay and King streets, many musicians planted themselves there hoping for cash tips from the city's visitors. The diverse talent of the street scene added to the vibrant charm emanating throughout the city.

The threesome bar hopped along East Bay distributing $100 bills into guitar cases, jars, famous Charleston sweetgrass baskets, or other collection plates of choice beside the gifted and soulful musicians. They deposited extra Ben Franklins to their favorites: John-O, Clyde, K-train, Je'vaughn, and Margrit.

John-O, always clad in a cowboy hat and overalls, had squatter's rights outside of Magnolia's, Lucy's favorite restaurant. John-O sang old country tunes. Glen Campbell's "Southern Nights" was as much a staple in John-O's repertoire as the shrimp and grits were inside Magnolia's.

Clyde was stationed a couple of blocks down from John-O. Clyde was known for his blues tunes. He was belting out Stevie Ray Vaughan's "Pride and Joy" on his electric guitar when Kevin stuffed a wad of cash in Clyde's shirt pocket in front of his pack of Camel cigarettes.

"K-train was on the corner of King Street singing Van Morrison's "Moondance." Je'vaughn, the Jamaican reggae singer, was a couple of blocks down, playing his steel drum and belting out Bob Marley's "Could You Be Loved." After throwing down more drinks and more of Grant's money, they stopped at Margrit, a petite black woman whose strong voice weighed more than she did. Margrit made sweetgrass baskets at the Charleston City Market during the day and played Southern Baptist hymns on her violin at night. When they passed Margrit, she was swaying as she finished "My Faith Looks Up to Thee." As she began her next song, "Amazing Grace," Lucy walked up and stood beside Margrit and sang along with Margrit's violin accompaniment.

Margrit's eyes widened and her somber mood transformed into joy as a huge smile came across her face. Sammie had never heard Lucy sing but was in awe as the sweetest, strongest voice bellowed down King Street.

"Amazing Grace, How sweet the sound. That saved a wretch like me..."

Lucy and Margrit continued with every verse. When they finished singing, the tourists and locals who had gathered started whooping and clapping. If it hadn't been so dark, Sammie would have sworn Lucy's face turned five shades of red. Lucy hung her head and bashfully walked back to stand with Kevin and Sammie. "Amen sister, Amen," one woman yelled. Another touched Lucy's shoulder and said, "Bless you, child."

"That performance deserves ten bills," Kevin said, dropping $1,000 in Margrit's large sweetgrass basket. Sammie was moved as well.

"Lucy Tate!" Sammie exclaimed. "I didn't know you could sing like that."

"Well, that's what happens when you spend your childhood attending choir practice every Sunday and Wednesday night."

Sammie inserted her arm under Lucy's free arm. The three proceeded down King Street arm-in-arm. Indeed, Sammie was filled with a transformed spirit. In that moment, she knew that grace would lead her home.

If you sup with the devil, you better have a long spoon...

Chapter Forty-Nine

Lucy

Lucy arrived later than usual to the office. She stayed out too late for a work night. In addition to the late-night bar hopping, she attributed her pounding head to the built-up anxiety prior to confronting Sammie. The overindulgence in cocktails had prevented her preparation for what she would say to Anna Chatham. At this moment, she would have preferred lack of sleep to the beating of drums in her head.

Lucy called Anna first thing. She wouldn't be able to concentrate on anything else. She retrieved a large cup of coffee from the breakroom and tried, without success, to get past her secretary unnoticed. Gladys Kravitz peered over her cube.

"I was wondering if you were going to make it in today. I heard that you had a big night out on King Street last night and that you sang with one of the street people."

"This is some small town, isn't it?" Lucy responded, nonchalantly. "I met Sammie for dinner to catch up," she responded, quickly shutting her door.

Lucy twirled around in her office chair, trying to focus on points to discuss with Anna Chatham. She made an outline so she wouldn't omit a single fact. Before calling Anna, she needed a Coke to stop the cartwheels in her stomach. She made it back from the break room without any further inquisition from Roberta. Then, she called Anna's cell. The call went directly into voicemail.

"Anna, this is Lucy Tate. We located the woman in the video. She works at the Charleston Ashley Dockage. She confirmed a relationship with your husband. He misrepresented his marital status to her. She is quite upset and is willing to do anything to help you out. I can give you as much detail as you want, and we can discuss next steps. Sorry to leave this on voicemail. I am in the office all day, so you can call me at any time."

As Lucy hung up, she questioned whether it was appropriate to leave such details on voicemail. She should have discussed the protocol with Randy. She worried that she screwed up. Her first case was getting worse and worse.

Lucy hated her sensitive sweat glands. They weren't only activated during exercise but also by stress hormones. As beads of perspiration popped up on her forehead like popcorn on the stove, she headed to the restroom to try to calm down. She had made it six years at the firm with a perfect record—lots of billable hours, lots of collections, excellent work product, not one client complaint, and no missed deadlines. But now, the year that she was being considered for partner, she had violated the revered rule of no access to the Hamilton Boardroom, caught its namesake screwing the mail room manager, accepted representation of the first-ever female client in the history of the firm's Family Law Practice, learned that her best friend was the other woman in her case, and become romantically involved with one of the firm's employees. Her current resumé wasn't looking so great. As she was splashing water on her face, "Gladys" sashayed in the bathroom.

"Rough night, huh? You need any Advil? I have some at my desk."

"I am fine but maybe we should coordinate our bathroom breaks. I am waiting on a call back from Ms. Chatham and can't miss it."

Lucy made a mental note to ask for a secretarial reassignment from Roberta to Shirley. Since Sammie was no longer at the firm, Shirley, Sammie's former secretary, could easily take her on.

For the next two hours, Lucy worked on the Chandler separation agreement. Randy had been updating Tanner Chandler on his wife's tennis lessons. Upon his return to town, Tanner was planning to present SuSu with her walking papers.

Lucy, engrossed in her current assignment, had forgotten about Anna Chatham until her phone rang.

"Lucy, Hello. It's Anna Chatham. I received your message."

Lucy rummaged around her desk for the thoughtfully prepared outline.

"I've been doing a lot of thinking," Anna continued. "I appreciate all that you have done for me. But, I no longer need your services. Please send me a final bill for your time and the expenses."

"I apologize if my message upset you. I should have waited to communicate with you directly. I wanted to convey the information as soon as possible so that you could think about your next steps."

"Oh, no, Lucy. Your message was fine. I'm not dissatisfied with your work in any way. You are a good lawyer. I've decided that I can't go through with this. I have a pretty good life."

Lucy couldn't believe what she was hearing. While relieved that she was getting fired by her client, Anna's statement bothered her.

"Anna, I am no psychologist, and I will honor your decision. However, I must point out that the reason you even started down this road was because you were unhappy. And, you deserve happiness and to be with someone who treats you like a queen. Do you want to live like this for the rest of your life?"

"Thank you, Lucy. You are young and have a lot to learn," she said. "When you have children, you will see things differently. Our children believe that their parents are happy. Through this process, I've learned that there are varying levels of happiness, and that I have a lot to be thankful for. Grant provides for me very generously. Thank you again for your time. Bye-Bye now and take care."

Lucy sat there feeling empty, tormented for her client, and angry at her at the same time. But, she made one fair point—Lucy couldn't understand the child factor. Nevertheless, Sammie had a child and was strong enough to get rid of the poison in her life. Ironically, Sammie was providing evidence for Anna to do the same. But Anna chose to stay and wither away emotionally while pretending to be happy. Sammie was stronger. And one day, Sammie would find the happiness she deserved.

Don't dig up more snakes than you can kill ...

Chapter Fifty

Sammie

Sammie couldn't get Lucy's rendition of "Amazing Grace" off her mind. Her family's homecoming was more than amazing grace, it was a spiritual reunion—a spiritual awakening. Sammie felt truly blessed.

Mr. Barry had given her the day off. He would cover for her errand-wise, but that she would "have to make it up in a meaningful way." He made her laugh. His inappropriate comments were part of his charm. It made him the unique Harold Barry, Dockmaster Extraordinaire. He was another blessing. She was lucky to have him back in her life.

She hated leaving Mack the next day but was ready to get back into a routine, one without Grant Davis. She was comforted knowing that Mack was in the best of hands with his GG. Soon after she left the house, Mr. Barry called.

"Are you going to grace us with your presence today?"

Was it her imagination or did she detect a serious edge in his otherwise easygoing tone?

"Yes sir. I'm currently on my way."

"Excellent," he said.

His mood seemed to have changed.

"I have an order from *Why Knot*. They need a water hose. They didn't specify the brand or length, but you may need to write this down. They are apparently very particular when it comes to dock lines. They want five 12-foot, 3-strand, and 5-inch diameter nylon lines. They must be navy."

From all of Sammie's sailing days and time on the docks, one thing that she had learned early on was that boat owners could be very peculiar, bordering on superstitious, especially when it came to their boat supplies.

"Though I'm having Sammie withdrawals, I will sacrifice myself for thirty more minutes if you want to bring your best fella a Starbucks Iced Caffè Americano?"

"You are my best fella, and I'm delighted to do that. Call me if you need anything else, and I'll see ya in a little bit."

Sammie completed the run to the marina store for the hose and lines. Approaching the marina, her stomach ached. She worried that Grant Davis had ruined her greatest refuge. As she walked down the ramp, her apprehension subsided. For all the remorse, pain, humiliation, and shame that she felt, he wasn't powerful enough to capsize the life raft provided by the docks.

Though she had only taken one day off, it seemed like weeks since she had been to the marina. Her regurgitation of the events from the past week to Lucy seemed like months ago. She headed towards *Why Knot* to deliver their hose and lines. Based on its size, *Why Knot*, held the third best slip location on the dock. *Sea Relations*, the largest yacht currently at the marina, held the coveted last slip providing the easiest exit to the Ashley River. *Reel Deep* was between *Sea Relations* and *Why Knot*.

After her delivery, Sammie's curiosity got the best of her. She continued walking towards Grant Davis' slip to see if *Sea Relations* was still there. She didn't have to go far to spot the sleek, 112-foot yacht. The other very nice multi-million dollar yachts paled in comparison.

Sammie began thinking about how Lucy was drawn to the Hamilton Boardroom. She felt a similar pull towards the boat. She had an insatiable urge to go inside—like she was caught in an undertow. She had learned long ago that when caught in an undertow, you don't fight it. She relented to the force. She reasoned that she needed to approach the scene with a clairvoyant legal mind.

Her heart was beating out of her chest. Its accelerated rhythm was as steady and loud as Je'vaughn's steel drum. She took a deep breath. She was one-hundred percent confident that Grant wouldn't be there. If she ran into Billy, it was certainly plausible that she left something there. He wouldn't think anything about it.

She stepped onto the swim platform and climbed the steps to the aft deck off of the salon. She noticed a pair of pumps in the basket by the sliding door. The basket collected the forbidden shoe on a yacht without a white sole. She opened the sliding glass door.

"Hello? Hello? Billy?" she called. Her quaking voice didn't even sound familiar to her. It sounded like a breathless intruder. She walked through the salon, and through the kitchen. There were two wine glasses still wet with red wine residue. *Good for him*, she thought. Billy is entertaining on Grant's boat while he is away.

"Hello? Hello? Billy?" she asked again.

She ran quickly to Grant's stateroom where she had found the drawer full of Cathleen's clothes. Her hands were trembling as she opened the drawer. She checked the label. The monogram that was etched in her brain was real. She opened the drawer underneath the clothes, where she had seen the stack of papers. Her recollection was correct, except the volume of papers seemed to have tripled.

She felt a force stronger than her otherwise rule-following nature as she reached in, lifted the items from the drawer, and stuffed them in her backpack. She could return them later. She exited the boat and walked quickly back to the dock house.

As she entered, she was thankful that Mr. Barry had requested an iced coffee. Her delivery of his favorite beverage would temporarily distract him. He was watching the radar behind the counter.

"Iced coffee up, sir," she said, though her voice sounding foreign even to herself as her heart was still beating out of her chest. He looked up and smiled his big, toothy grin.

"I was beginning to wonder if you had forgotten about the old man. This will hit the spot. Thanks, Darlin'."

"Sorry, I delivered the supplies to *Why Knot*, and Mr. Hooker was a little chatty."

"Hooker—what a name. He started to name his boat *Hooker's Paradise*. But, he thought that he may be blacklisted from certain marinas," he said, sipping his coffee. "I told him he should have combined both names—*Hooker's Paradise, Why Knot*? Now, that would have created some dock chatter. By the way, how's your boy?"

"He is wonderful. My mother is spoiling him rotten. They had a great trip. I will bring him by for a visit soon. Though you don't like children on the docks, you'll have to make an exception for him."

"If anyone gets a rug rat's pass, it is you. Speaking of passes, you know all things must pass, and it's time to say adios to *Sea Relations*. Billy called this morning. Good riddance," he grumbled.

Sammie began to panic. She had to find out when Billy was heading out. She had to get the documents back on the boat.

"I really like Billy. He is a solid guy, don't you think?" she asked.

Harry peered over his reading glasses suspiciously.

"Yeah, I guess he was alright."

"I'd like to at least say good-bye to him," trying to suppress her anxiety. "Is Billy here now?"

"Nope," Mr. Barry said. "He did mention that some of the asshole's business partners were coming to stay a couple of nights, and since he didn't work for them, he was going to party with one of his buddies. He didn't say which marina, so I can't help you with your good-byes."

Sammie regretted going back onto the boat. Given the shoes in the basket, Grant's partners must have already arrived. Now, her dilemma was how to return the documents.

"All this time, I thought you were hot on the PR bigwig. I should have known he wasn't your type. I'm disappointed in myself for not seeing that you really had it for Billy. I'll be damned," Harry said, shaking his head.

"You are losing your touch, Mr. Barry. Billy just seemed like a genuinely nice guy who loves what he does. If you can't afford a boat, what better job to have than to run one. I found him interesting, that's all."

Sammie retreated to the business office. She opened the backpack and pulled out the stack of Worth papers. Amongst the documents was a hard drive. She was interrupted with an order from *Second Time Around*. When returning to the marina with the order, an attractive woman passed her. She looked like she had just come off a New York runway and was totally out of place in her business suit and stylish pumps on the docks.

After making the deliveries, she walked down the dock towards *Sea Relations*. It was lit up like a Christmas tree. Someone was definitely on that boat, and it wasn't Billy.

That night, she rocked Mack for a long time. She wanted to bottle his innocence. She had enjoyed a solid family foundation. She worried how to incorporate Dougie into Mack's life. She couldn't keep him from seeing their son completely. He would use that against her when Mack was older. She would have to address it sooner or later but not now, and probably not tomorrow. After Mack started drifting off to sleep, she carefully placed him in his crib. "Sweet dreams, my beautiful baby, sweet, sweet dreams."

Her thoughts drifted to the documents in her backpack. If they were Grant's papers, why would he keep them in his stateroom and not his study?

Sammie opened her backpack and began flipping through the papers. She noticed Dougie's handwriting on a copy of a letter addressed to a Dr. Stanley Drake in Pittsburgh.

Dear Dr. Drake,

This letter follows up on our prior negotiations and agreement relating to a 10% interest in Sailfish II, LLC for $500,000. This investment is based on the Florida business plan. Enclosed is the $25,000 deposit. The schedule for the remainder of the payments is attached.

Sincerely yours,
Douglas Morgan

There was a number of copied checks from Dougie made out to Sailfish II, LLC. It suddenly hit her that the schedule was the timeframe of Dougie's withdrawals from her trust account. Though she never wanted to revisit that issue again, she opened the drawer where she had placed her personal papers. She pulled out the manilla folder labeled: Callaway Account.

She sorted the copies of the checks to Sailfish II, LLC. The amounts and dates matched up perfectly to the spreadsheet Camilla had given her, except for the last two checks. The dates on those were after her father had instructed Parks to freeze her account. Her money, or her father's money, had been used to pay for an investment in Sailfish II, LLC.

Amongst all the individual pages, there was a bound booklet. She began reading the booklet identified as "Florida Business Plan." The Executive Summary discussed the formation of a Real Estate Investment Trust to develop and bundle income-producing properties in South Florida. The first phase would include upscale apartment buildings and medical parks in Martin and Palm Beach counties. The strategy was based on the growing population of retired residents.

So Dougie used her money to invest in some business venture. She was not qualified to evaluate an investment like this, but it seemed to make sense. *Why wouldn't Dougie discuss the opportunity with her instead of secretly investing her money?*

She didn't have the energy to piece it together, but it was clear that she had to get everything back on the boat. Everything except the checks and Dougie's letter. For some reason, she felt a need to protect Dougie. Or, maybe, she was protecting herself. It was her money after all. She couldn't recall any time that she had ever lied to her mother, but she made an excuse about needing to go back to the business office and promised it would be quick.

Sammie's stomach was turning flips as she drove to the marina. From Lucy's disclosure of the video evidence of her and Grant, she was now aware that there were cameras in the parking lot and who knows where else. She parked in the vacant lot beside the marina, used the access code to enter the laundry facility, and exited out the backdoor. She ran down the ramp and went into the business office for cover in case her presence had been captured. She then headed down towards *Sea Relations.*

The entire stretch of dock was so quiet. The only sound was the water lapping up against the pilings. Ahead, there were lights reflecting on the dock, but not a soul was stirring in *Why Knot* or *Reeled In.* That's exactly where she was—reeled in into something that was not good.

It was clear that someone was still on *Sea Relations.* She would have to think of a way to get onto that boat.

The next morning, Mr. Barry was walking towards her as she walked down the ramp with his Starbucks coffee order. He didn't look happy.

"Good morning. Maybe this coffee will cheer you up."

"Umph," he grunted. "It's going to take more than coffee. Damn toilet in women's locker room stopped up again. This is the third time this week."

While Mr. Barry was busy in the women's locker room, Sammie had time to investigate activity on *Sea Relations.* She didn't want Mr. Barry asking questions about why she was loitering in the vicinity of that boat. As she approached *Why Knot,* she recalled the Hooker's plans to explore the creeks and channels between Charleston and Kiawah Island in their yacht tender. She stepped onto their swim platform and accessed their deck. Due to the height of the Hatteras sport fishing boat's flybridge, she hoped it provided a view of *Sea Relations.* As she climbed the outside steps to the flybridge, she was amazed at the expansive view of the Ashley River.

As she gazed down the river, she thought about the Hooker's route. She and Dougie had made that trek numerous times. They would head down Wappo Creek through Elliott's Cut to the Stono River and then the North Edisto River ending at Bohicket Creek. Dougie loved fishing in Elliot's Cut where only local fisherman knew that it was filled with spotted sea trout, red drum, and flounder. Those had been the fun times.

Her reminiscing was interrupted when she spotted a paddle boarder headed out into the river. She recognized that it was Billy. She recalled that he went for a long paddle board jaunt on mornings prior to disembarking for a long trip. Billy was a natural. He made boarding look so easy, so effortless. He stood erect with the paddles methodically moving from side to side, cutting through the wakes left by passing boats like a knife slicing a piece of fresh fruit. Watching his steady rhythmic moves, his paddle moving back and forth, back and forth, back and forth, her mind drifted from the task at hand. The water was calm, and the sun provided natural heat to an otherwise chilly morning.

Suddenly, she was knocked to the floor by the reverberation of a loud boom. Smoke engulfed the sky. Her body ached, and she was woozy. With the assistance of the boat's railing, she pulled herself up. She immediately noticed a dark red mass on the water. Her lifeguard instincts propelled her in. Billy was clutching his board as blood continued to ooze onto the water's surface. Shrapnel was protruding from his chest.

"Billy, it's Sammie. I'm here. Hold on, hold on."

His eyes were closing. She grabbed him and swam towards the docks. He squeezed her hand before he went limp.

"Billy, I've got you. Hang on, buddy."

She could hear sirens in the distance. She hoped an ambulance was on the way. There was already a flurry of activity on the docks. She tried to focus on Billy who was beginning to feel like a heavy anchor. She made it to the dock house where a number of onlookers had gathered. Everyone looked blurry. Mr. Barry pulled her out and wrapped a blanket around her while others tended to Billy. The sirens were deafening. As she watched a stretcher cart Billy away, her body began convulsing.

"What just happened?" she asked, her teeth chattering.

"*Sea Relations* exploded," Mr. Barry said. "I pray that no one is on that boat."

Helicopters buzzed overhead. Mr. Barry picked her up, carried her into the dock house, and placed her on the sofa. He sat down beside her and wrapped his arm around her.

"Are you okay, honey?" Mr. Barry asked.

"I'm fine. I think. Can you find out about Billy? He was bleeding so badly."

Her body was completely numb, and she didn't have the strength to wipe the tears that were now pouring down her face. The dock house phones rang off the hook. The ringing started echoing in her head.

"Right now, I need to make sure that you are okay. Billy wouldn't have stood a chance if you hadn't been there," he said, squeezing her tighter.

Sammie could feel his chest heaving. His breathing was deep, intense, and rapid. He mentioned that her parents were on their way, but she couldn't comprehend anything else he was saying. Her head was spinning, and the scene outside of the dock windows seemed chaotic.

After what seemed like an eternity, she recalled that two policemen arrived with her parents and escorted them to the car while dodging television cameras and reporters. One reporter was keeping pace with them, pelting her with questions.

"Where were you when the boat exploded?" "Do you know what happened?" "What did you see?"

Sammie walked in a daze amidst the questions fired at her. The last thing she remembered was being in her bed with their family doctor and her parents by her side.

His playbox is filled with sinking sand...

Chapter Fifty-One

Lucy

Kevin, who received electronic feeds from every major news source, ran to Lucy's office immediately upon receiving an alert about the explosion at the Charleston Ashley Dockage.

"Listen babe, there's been an explosion at the marina. Apparently, Sammie saved some captain's life. Pull up News 2. They are reporting live. This is making national news."

"What the hell!"

Lucy hands trembled as she tried to pull up the News 2 website.

"Before you freak out, one of the pictures shows Sammie leaving the marina with her parents. She is wrapped in a blanket and looks soaking wet and bloody," Kevin warned, his voice cracking.

As Lucy pulled up the website, there was a large picture of the burning yacht. She clicked on the first video. There were several already posted.

"Kendra Kent reporting live from the Charleston Ashley Dockage where a 112-foot yacht penned *Sea Relations* is still smoldering from an explosion near the yacht's bow. What caused the explosion is under investigation. Firefighters are here along with the Coast Guard and the ATF. At this time, it is unknown whether anyone was on the boat, but at least two people have been injured by the explosion. Billy Andrews, who reportedly is the boat's captain, was paddle boarding and seriously injured by shrapnel from the explosion. His life was saved by his wetsuit and a yacht dockhand, Samantha Morgan, who rescued Mr. Andrews from the water. There are many unknowns here, but we will remain live on the scene. We will report updated information as we learn more about this incident. Back to you in the station."

Lucy clicked on the slides of pictures from the scene and found the one Kevin saw. Sammie was clutched by her parents, blood splattered on her face. There was a picture of the stretcher that must have contained Billy. Another showed the ATF representatives. Their quick arrival time was a benefit of having an ATF field office located in Charleston. They look like martians in their bomb suits, gloves, and helmets.

She had to talk to Sammie. Lucy called her cell. She didn't answer. She then called the Spencers. Their answering machine clicked on.

"Mr. and Mrs. Spencer, this is Lucy Tate. I just heard about the explosion. Of course, I am worried sick about Sammie. I know you are probably getting inundated with calls, but if you have time, please call me and let me know about Sammie. Thanks."

By now, the firm was abuzz with the news. Roberta burst into Lucy's office.

"Lucy, did you hear about Sammie? She is all over the news. A boat blew up at a Charleston marina."

"Sammie's okay, Roberta," Kevin said. "Lucy is upset, so if you can, hold her calls and shut the door, please."

She huffed and left abruptly.

"This is all too weird. Do you think it was an accident?"

"It doesn't look like it with the ATF slithering all over the marina," Kevin said.

"Let's call Mr. Barry," Lucy said, impulsively.

"Lucy, he is probably dealing with a lot right now. Let's just sit tight and see if you hear back from Sammie's parents. She's okay. We both saw her. Don't get worked up. I'm going to get back to work. Let me know if you hear from the Spencers," he said, kissing her forehead.

Lucy had piles of work to do, but none of it seemed important. She attempted to read a document but wasn't processing any of the words on the page. She tried reading them aloud, thinking that may aid in her concentration. She lurched when the sound of her edgy voice was interrupted by the phone's chime.

"Lucy Tate," she answered, masking her severe angst.

"Lucy, it's Glenny Spencer."

"Oh, my gosh," Lucy blurted. "Thanks for calling me back. I am just sick with these news reports. How's Sammie doing?"

"She is resting and is going to be fine," Glenny Spencer said, reassuringly. "I'm so glad you called," she said, her tone changing from calm to concern. "She is likely delirious, but she keeps asking for you and repeating over and over that she really needs her backpack."

"Can I come and see her?" Lucy asked.

"Our doctor gave her a sedative so she could rest. I'm sure she'll call you when she wakes up."

"Did she say what happened?" Lucy asked.

"All that she has communicated is that she was on some boat—something like 'YNot'—I guess she was making a delivery. She heard the explosion and then saw a man in the water."

With this information, Lucy knew that Sammie had likely been on a boat docked near *Sea Relations*.

"And Lucy," Glenny Spencer said, interrupting Lucy's rambling thoughts, "Sammie doesn't know this yet, but we learned that Dougie was on the boat that exploded. That's all we know. I'm sure it will be all over the news soon. I wonder if Sammie knew he was there. I really hate to bother you with this, but can you see if you can find her backpack?"

Lucy suddenly had this feeling that the contents of the backpack may disclose either why the boat exploded or who did it.

His carnival ride just sold out of tickets...

Chapter Fifty-Two

Lucy & Kevin

Lucy immediately called Kevin.

"Sammie's mother just called. Dougie Morgan was on that boat."

"Boy, that's terrible. The news just reported that in addition to Billy, there were two others critically injured but didn't disclose names. Geez. How is Sammie taking it?"

"She doesn't know yet. Her mother said the doctor gave her a sedative. Mrs. Spencer said Sammie kept talking about needing her backpack. She must have had it with her when the explosion occurred. It's on some boat. I'll call Mr. Barry and find out if that makes any sense."

"Then what are you going to do?" Kevin asked.

"I'm going to go get her backpack," Lucy answered, boldly.

"Lucy, have you been watching the news coverage? The place is crawling with suits."

"I have to try. I'm calling Mr. Barry."

"Well, I'm coming with you then," Kevin said. "Bailing you out of jail for interfering with a crime scene is not what I had planned today."

Mr. Barry told Lucy that there was a boat named *Why Knot* docked at the marina and close to the burning yacht. He said that the owners weren't there, so they wouldn't have placed any orders.

"I don't know why she would have been on that boat other than the good Lord put her there so she could save Billy. I always knew she was an angel," Mr. Barry said.

Mr. Barry agreed to meet Lucy and Kevin in the vacant lot adjacent to the marina and escort them in.

When they arrived, Mr. Barry was visibly shaken.

"I'm so sorry about all of this," Lucy said. "What a mess. How is Billy?"

"Last time I checked, he was no longer in critical condition, unlike the others. Did you hear?" he asked, pausing and taking a deep breath. "One was Douglas Morgan. What the hell was he doing on that boat?"

He looked down at the ground and shook his head.

"I don't know the shit that went down between Sammie and her ex, but she sure doesn't need some embarrassing exposé. What a dumbass."

"Who was the other person on the boat, Mr. Barry?"

Lucy's gut told her it was Cathleen McKinney.

"Didn't recognize the name. Some swanky businesswoman—probably a crony of Grant Davis. Now, look at my marina. It's going to take months to fix all of this. And who the hell is going to want to dock here after this mess? All the things I did to get that scumbag's business. It's a damn train wreck!"

Clearly, Mr. Barry was dealing with a lot. A hunk of his dock was gone, and police tape draped the entire length of the remaining part of the dock. The resident 112-foot sleek luxury yacht that previously was jealously ogled was now smoldering and kept afloat by cables and unattractive reinforcements. The dock was secured and swarming with TV crews and ATF officials.

"The ATF is restricting movement in and out of the marina until the investigation is complete," Mr. Barry said. "Let's just hope I can get you past security without any questions. Just keep walking. Let me do the talking," he instructed, as he escorted them down to the docks.

They approached the security guard posted at the dock entrance.,

"These two work for me," Mr. Barry said, authoritatively. "You got any update about those injured?" he asked, distracting the armed officer with his questions.

With its prime location in the last slip on the dock, the bow of *Sea Relations* faced the water. Had it faced the other way, the explosion would have damaged a number of the other yachts. *Why Knot*, cushioned from the blow by another boat, didn't appear to be damaged at all.

"I'm sure the boat is locked, but I will cover for you," Mr. Barry said. "All that time that she spent on *Sea Relations*, I just thank the Lord she wasn't there. Just hurry and find her stuff."

After inspecting the first-floor deck, they climbed the stairs to the deck above. Sammie's backpack was in plain view. The sweeping views of the Ashley River were remarkable from this spot, so maybe it was innocent as that—she had just taken a break to enjoy the setting. But then again, it wasn't like Sammie to board a boat if she knew the owners weren't there, view or no view.

"Let's get you two out of here," Mr. Barry said. "Tell Sammie that I'm thinking about her and to take all the time she needs. It's messed up. The one hired to keep that senator's troubles under wraps is the one that blew it all to pieces, literally. Isn't that some shit? This marina is getting more publicity than I ever imagined. But, it's not good," he said, shaking his head.

He reached in his pocket and pulled out a flash drive.

"Put this in Sammie's backpack. It's video from the parking lot cameras. The ATF folks have copies. See if Nifong can learn anything. I know that Nifong works for you, Lucy. Harold Barry wasn't born yesterday. But, let's keep this between us."

Kevin and Lucy walked nonchalantly but quickly to avoid any attention. Lucy was beginning to think that Sammie's backpack had some critical information. She was getting ready to find out.

"Your place or mine?" Kevin asked, putting his arm around Lucy's waist and pulling her close. "I've logged enough hours on the Chandler matter, I can take an afternoon off."

"Let's go to yours. I'm feeling sort of squeamish. I need salty air."

On the way to Kevin's house, Lucy called Nathan.

"Been watching the news about your client's husband's boat gettin' blown to smithereens—pretty spooky stuff," Nathan answered, in his cut-to-the-chase manner.

"I know. That's why I'm calling," Lucy said. "Kevin and I just left the marina. Mr. Barry gave us a flash drive with footage from the parking lot cameras. He wants you see if anything appears suspicious."

"Will do. I'm at the office. Want to drop it off now?"

"Sure, we'll be there in about ten minutes. Thanks, Nathan. You're the best."

After they dropped off the flash drive, Lucy left a message with Linda, Randy's secretary, that she would be working remotely the rest of the day. They hunkered down with the backpack on Kevin's porch. They decided to divide and conquer. Lucy tackled the papers. Kevin seized upon a hard drive.

Lucy examined a business plan relating to an investment in South Florida for the development of medical parks. The prospectus detailed demographics and market analysis—boring and benign, but seemingly legitimate.

After an hour or so, Kevin interrupted Lucy's reading.

"Lucy, have you heard of a Senator DeVore?"

"No. Why?"

"There's something fishy going on. This hard drive definitely belongs to a Cathleen McKinney."

"She was Dougie's boss at Worth. Sammie found some of her clothes on *Sea Relations*. She thinks there is something going on between her and Grant Davis. But, why would her hard drive be on Grant Davis' boat?"

"No idea, but there are several emails to a weird email address that mention a senate investigation initiated by Senator Tony DeVore into Worth Pharmaceutical."

Lucy googled Senator Tony DeVore. The search instantly revealed numerous hits. She clicked on the DeVore.senate.gov website. One thing was evident. He wouldn't turn heads. He looked like a dweeby accountant. She clicked on the heading: *About Senator DeVore*. Lucy read Kevin the senator's profile.

> Currently serving his second term in the U.S. Senate, Senator DeVore previously served three terms in Congress. Prior to his service in public office, he was the lead investigator with Florida's Central Division of the Alcohol, Tobacco, Firearms and Explosives, where he was a leader in recouping money from the tobacco industry into Florida's Medicare/Medicaid funds. Senator DeVore is an

advocate for our senior citizens and the growing population of retirees in Florida. He seeks to improve the quality and costs of health care for our seniors. As such, he serves on the Senate Finance Committee and its Subcommittee on Health Care. Senator DeVore works tirelessly in his efforts for affordable prescription medications. He is also dedicated to eradicating the epidemic of prescription drug abuse.

"Of course, these profiles are promotional strategies, but he sounds and looks like a homegrown goober who cares for senior citizens," Lucy said.

"Interesting, indeed. There are a plethora of emails between Cathleen and this weird address. This could take a while," Kevin said, while scrolling through the email account.

"Plethora? Oh geez, you sound like the lawyers you work for. That is a turnoff, by the way," she said, teasingly.

"Don't you worry about that, babe. One thing you can count on, I am no Spencer lawyer wannabe. I do want one Spencer lawyer though. How 'bout we take a bootie break?"

"Don't tempt me. It's going to take all my energy to focus on this clinical trial data but after that, I'm all yours."

Their concentration was interrupted by the ringing of Lucy's cell.

"Hey Nathan. You got anything?"

"I'm not sure. There is video of a red Mercedes sedan with Florida tags. The car was at the marina several times over the last week. The vehicle is registered in the name of Trevor Wilson, who owns a company called CrocoGator Surveillance. Check out his website—lots of reptiles. Anyway, Harry's never heard of him or his company."

"We are finding references to Tony DeVore, a Florida senator, in an email account," Lucy said. "Did you say the car had Florida tags?"

"Yes. The owner is a private investigator. Harry says what his slip renters do is their own business. But, as you know, it wouldn't be the first time that a hired investigator has paid his marina a visit."

"Got it. Thanks. Call back if you find anything else."

Lucy continued reading about clinical trials. One related to a Parkinson's drug called Palpo. After reading pages and pages of data, she could only glean that the proposed medication was effective but had an unexpected and unintended side effect. Participants reported rapid hair growth. The side effect was not isolated to men. The bottom line was that Palpo was sent back to the research and development department to isolate that component for the consideration of a new drug line to compete with the booming hair replacement market. The new drug wouldn't be limited to men but marketed to women as well.

"So far, it's not making sense," Lucy said. "I must be missing something. These clinical trials relate to a drug for Parkinson's disease called Palpo. The participants experienced an unintended side effect of significant hair growth. Why would this be controversial?"

"I thought Worth was into pain medications. Google 'Palpo,'" Kevin said, continuing to read through the email account.

"Why didn't I think of that?" she said, feeling rather inept in this field of investigation. Catching people screwing around was cut and dried compared to this.

Her search on Palpo quickly revealed that it was being developed by Parcepto Pharma. The Parcepto website announced:

> A recently completed clinical trial establishes that Palpo significantly effects dopamine, the brain chemical that controls body movement. Clinical trial participants reported less tremors and muscle stiffness with even small doses of Palpo. Trial participants have no undesirable side effects. The company is excited to move forward with its application for FDA approval.

"Sorry to interrupt you but Palpo is a drug developed by a company called Parcepto Pharma, not Worth. How would Worth have copies of their confidential clinical trial data? Sammie must have been onto something. You think this is the purported scandal that Senator Hill was involved in? The mess that brought Grant Davis here?"

"Maybe," Kevin said. "But this Cathleen McKinney has something going on with a colleague. Listen to this email: *I have learned that you are sweet on one of your young employees. You need to stay focused on the deal. We don't need any distractions.* Cathleen responds: *Trust me. This is worth it. He can help us. You know the deal, baby. Hell, you invented the deal.* The reply: *Exactly. Some sales punk can't help us at all. Thus, the reason for my inquiry. I'd turn a blind eye if it helps us. The key word is us. I enjoy that I am a beneficiary of your array of talents. You're good but not that good. Don't be fucking around for sport.* She replies: *I love it when you get jealous. As you say, it's only for business with anyone else.*

"Oh my gosh. I think that email is talking about Cathleen and Dougie. Can't you find out who is emailing her? I think it's Grant Davis."

"I could if the account was on the law firm's server. You'd be surprised by your colleague's extracurricular activities."

"So, is that how the porn viewing by Charles Ross was discovered?" Lucy asked.

"Ha," Kevin said. "No comment other than nothing must be a secret even within the walls of a law firm. Listen to this one," Kevin said. *And before you get any ideas about the Florida senator, that's a no-go. I draw the line on pencil dicks.* The response: *Invest in a blindfold. We have to squelch his investigation. Work your magic on him. Need some insurance.*

"If she is communicating with Grant Davis, they are both despicable. He and that bitch slut make a perfect pair."

"Bitch slut?" Kevin asked, laughing. "You are starting to sound like Randy."

"Sorry, not very ladylike, huh? I do enjoy Randy's creative combinations of profanity. But, shoot me if I become a regular at the Waffle House. Speaking of food, can we take a break? I'm starving."

Kevin boiled some fresh shrimp and opened two Coronas.

"If that email address belongs to Grant Davis, that woman's got some balls to screw around on his boat. What did the email call Dougie? A 'sales punk'? Do you think Grant Davis would blow up his own boat? Do you think he meant to kill them? I'm thinking that all this data about Parcepto is irrelevant. The explosion could simply be about a love triangle. And, I wonder if Sammie knew Dougie was there, and that's why she went up on *Why Knot* to see if she could see anything."

"Whoa, Nellie," Kevin said. "Hold your horses . Don't get carried away. I'll start reviewing Cathleen's other emails. There's a lot more to get through. But, I need a break.

He got up, rubbed Lucy's shoulders, and then sucked her neck. Her whole body tingled.

"A hickey would be hard to explain to Randy," she said, getting up and leading him into the bedroom.

The break was what Lucy needed to settle her. Time stood still in Kevin's arms. Afterward, he hit the shower while she read a report from the chief of Worth's Research and Development Department.

> This research was undertaken due to the increasing number of complaints about the addictive nature of Dolorine. As the pre-market studies verified, the effects of Dolorine are substantially enhanced when crushed and ingested by nasal insufflation.

> The R&D department is pleased to report that a modified version of the Dolorine product has been developed that is more difficult to crush. Even when crushed, it does not become a powder form that can be easily ingested through nasal insufflation. Further, the new product's effects are greatly diminished when crushed. We believe that this new formula will greatly reduce, if not eliminate, the allegations that Worth is contributing to the epidemic abuse of this important drug. We are very proud to present this report to you."

The shower water stopped.

"Oh my gosh, Kevin. I found something," Lucy called.

He stepped out of the bedroom with a towel wrapped around his hips. Beads of water glistened on his chest and hair. He ran his hands rapidly through his hair spraying water on Lucy.

"You're amazing, did you know that?" Kevin asked. "But for that shower, I would have needed a long nap, and you're back at it in full force."

"Well, now I forgot what I was going to tell you. Get some clothes on and fast, please. You're distracting me—and you have a lot of emails to read."

He reappeared dressed in some lounge pants.

"What did you learn?"

"This is an R&D study that evidences that Worth knew that Dolorine was being abused. And that it could be crushed and snorted. I told you about what we found at Sammie's, right? I took a picture. I thought it was cocaine but there was a mortar and pestle on the counter. Dougie must have been enjoying his sales product. Wonder if Senator DeVore knew about this report and was why he initiated the investigation?

Because Worth knows of less addictive alternatives but has done nothing to change the formulation."

"Sounds like you're making progress. How does the South Carolina senator play into this? Isn't he the reason Grant Davis was in Charleston?"

"Yeah, I can't figure that one out. Hopefully, you'll learn something from that hard drive. And, I'm not talking about yours."

"Don't remind me. I'm just getting my energy back."

Kevin regained his focus and worked diligently for a while. With the background Lucy now had, she went back through the papers to see if she had missed any connection to the South Carolina senator.

"I don't want to jump the gun, but I have some information on the Senator Hill connection," Kevin said. "You want me to keep reading or update you now?"

"No. I am done. I'm not seeing anything."

"Well, for starters, Senator Hill's wife is loaded. Her father has made a lot of money in the pharmaceutical industry, the industry which throws a lot of money into Senator Hill's campaign funds. Both Hill and the Florida Senator are on the Senate Finance Committee investigating Worth Pharmaceutical's pain product. These emails are cryptic at best. I couldn't testify in a court of law, but I would bet everything I own in Vegas that this weird email address is, indeed, Grant Davis. But whoever it is, the person, Cathleen McKinney, and Senator Hill were setting a trap for the Florida senator.

"But how could they set him up? That doesn't make sense."

"Think about it, Lucy. You work with Randy now. What's the best way to get a politician in trouble?"

"Good grief. You think the plan was for Cathleen to seduce him? Didn't she refer to him as a 'pencil dick'? But maybe she had a change of heart if it helps her company. God, that woman is disgusting. You think she did? You think that DeVore had something to do with the explosion?"

"That's what I am thinking," Kevin said. "Didn't his bio refer to a stint with ATF?"

"I think we've only stumbled on the tip of something bad," Lucy said. "I'm going to be sick. I think we return the backpack to the marina, and whoever finds it will deal with it."

"Think about that," Kevin said. "You don't want Sammie being dragged into this. And there is no way to return the documents on the boat surrounded by police tape."

"Certainly, Sammie doesn't know about any of this. She thought the scandal involved Senator Scotty Hill," Lucy said.

"Don't freak out," Kevin said, "but I've read some other stuff. About Sammie."

"Now, I'm really going to sick," Lucy said. "Do I want to know?"

"I'm pretty sure Sammie was set up," Kevin said.

"What do you mean set up?" Lucy asked, incredulously.

"I told you about the emails where the sender chastises Cathleen for banging the sales punk, right? Let's just call the sender Grant Davis. Anyway, Grant Davis is saying he'll have to fix that and is on his way to Charleston. Then this one. It's the last exchange on this drive. *This is easier than I thought. Fell into my lap. You must be doing something right because your boy toy's wife works at one of the marinas.*"

"So, he chooses the Charleston Ashley Dockage because Sammie is there. I did think it was very strange that some PR executive would involve Sammie in such a high-profile matter. She didn't discuss with me what all she knew or what she did. She apparently spent a lot of time running errands for Grant Davis and was smitten. He must have seduced her like Cathleen did Dougie. You think Anna Chatham set me up as well? I mean she dropped her case after I disclosed her dirtbag husband's affair. You think that's their way of keeping Sammie quiet?"

"I have to admit, those all sound plausible now," Kevin said. "But we've learned all we are going to from this backpack."

"First, I've got to call Mrs. Spencer and tell her that we have the backpack and warn her that that it contains highly confidential documents," Lucy said. "They shouldn't mention anything to anyone about her backpack or that Sammie had been on *Why Knot.*"

"Good idea," Kevin said. "I'll touch base with Mr. Barry and get an update."

After Lucy's conversation with Glenny Spencer, she could tell from Kevin's body language that Mr. Barry had bad news. When he hung up, his face was ashen.

"What? What is it?"

"Dougie died," Kevin said. "And so did Cathleen McKinney—both were on *Sea Relations*. Mr. Barry said that reporters were everywhere. He said not to come back and to tell Sammie to stay away. He also mentioned that the FBI had arrived and were up his ass with questions."

"Guess we're stuck with the backpack."

You'll catch more flies with honey, than vinegar...

Chapter Fifty-Three

Tate & Horton, Counselors at Law

Frank Hamilton smugly delivered the news to Lucy that her consideration for partnership had been extended for a year due to her switch to the Family Law practice. He reported that the title of partner at Spencer, Pettigrew & Hamilton was only bestowed on those that were recognized experts in their respective field. He was confident that Lucy would attain that status, she simply needed more time.

Surprisingly, Lucy remained calm throughout the entire impromptu late meeting requested by the managing partner. Her sweat glands had even been held at bay. Sitting in the tufted, cream, leather chair facing his expansive pedestal desk, the lights from the ships within view from Frank Hamilton's floor-to-ceiling windows enlightened her. Instead of casting a reflection across the Cooper River, they were spotlighting the fact that she had been chasing a bogus goal at Spencer, Pettigrew & Hamilton. She had been seeking acceptance into a culture that she perceived was more intellectual and sophisticated. But, her simple and unpretentious roots had provided her with a strong dose of perspective.

When leaving Frank Hamilton's office, Lucy ignored his shallow words of encouragement. Instead, she felt empowered by them. They were a sign that it was time for her to take control her destiny. And that, she did.

Sammie was still recovering from the aftermath of the explosion but seemed eager for a visitor. With flowers in hand, Lucy took a deep breath as she rang the Spencer's doorbell.

"I resigned from the firm," Lucy said, explaining that her consideration for partnership had been extended another year.

"What?" Sammie asked. "Are you crazy? It's only one year. After that, you will be the firm's first female partner. Think about all the hours you have logged. This has been your dream. Don't tell me that you are questioning whether you're good enough or any kind of crap like that."

"Sammie, just listen. I've decided to start my own firm. Kevin is my new Chief Information and Technology Officer. Our new firm name is Tate & Horton. The Horton is Ben Horton, you know the litigator with Calhoun & Roberts?"

"Are you serious? How did this happen? How did you get hooked up with Ben Horton?"

"We were in law school together. I ran into him at a law school reunion event several months ago. Apparently, he had been number one in our class since our first year until I knocked him down to second. He told me he was actually relieved because he knew Spencer, Pettigrew & Hamilton wasn't the place for him. But, like me, he was saddled with debt and couldn't have snubbed the Pettigrew Scholarship since it paid for the third year tuition."

"Ben is the star in that firm," Sammie said. "His trial wins are profiled a lot in the legal journals."

"I know, right? I couldn't believe it when he told me about his class rank. I had no idea. He fell into the category of someone who worked hard but played hard, or harder. He rocked a Woodstock look—long hair, always wore some type of poncho, and what I called Jesus sandals. His mode of transportation was a skateboard. He was one of the few cool people in law school."

"He still rocks the long hair," Sammie said.

"Long hair for Spencer lawyers, yes, but in law school, he had a ponytail. Anyway, at the reunion, he told me he was considering making a move. Apparently, his firm's compensation system is archaic and political. I told him Spencer wasn't much better. We started commiserating about our long hours, lack of control over our lives, and unfair compensation for our hard work. Kevin and I have been talking about how great it would be to do our own thing and be our own boss. Our plans accelerated when I got a call recently. From Lily."

"Lily Phillips?" Sammie asked.

"Yes. It made me realize I need to get off of the billable hour hamster wheel and pay closer attention to my contacts—you know, 'networking.' Anyway, since she left

Spencer, she has been with several pharma companies. She is now in-house counsel at Parcepto Pharma. Parcepto is interviewing potential law firms to represent it in some litigation. She wanted Spencer, Pettigrew & Hamilton to submit a proposal."

"Good grief, not another pharma company," Sammie said.

"Yep. And it involves Worth. You know how we couldn't piece together those documents you found? It's all making sense now," Lucy said.

Sammie's recovery from the explosion was instantly thrown to the wind.

"What do you mean?" Sammie asked not wanting to hear even the mention of a pharmaceutical company ever again.

"Parcepto is suspicious that Worth has a mole in its R&D Department that leaked confidential clinical trial results and formulations to Worth. Lily said that they had gotten word that Worth was getting ready to submit an application to the FDA for a groundbreaking hair replacement drug. Parcepto has a similar drug in its pipeline. With the press that Worth has been getting about the explosion and the senate investigation into Dolorine, Parcepto believes the time is right to bring suit. Hit 'em while they are down."

Sammie realized then that she had never told Lucy about the papers that she had kept—the ones involving Dougie and the withdrawals from her trust account. Listening to Lucy's conversation with Lily, she grew panicky. The investment by Dougie with her money may have been a bribe for that data. The real estate prospectus, a cover.

"Lily thought it would help me with partnership consideration if I brought a significant piece of litigation to the firm."

"So, did you submit a proposal?" Sammie asked.

"No. Frank Hamilton nixed it. Said the firm had a conflict."

"A conflict? What kind of conflict?

"Who knows. Kevin checked the client database and couldn't find anything. Weird, right? But, as my Sunday school teacher, Juanita Hathaway, used to say, 'When the Lord closes a door, he opens a window.' I met with Ben and told him about the Parcepto request and asked if he would be interested in pursuing it with me in our own firm," Lucy said.

"This is so exciting, Lucy. I can't believe it," Sammie said.

"After I resigned, I told Lily that Tate & Horton would be honored to submit a proposal. Not surprisingly, Lily said that the company had only requested proposals from established large firms but that the interviews hadn't gone well. The firms were foaming at the mouth about the potential fee and boasted about all the lawyers available to comprise the Parcepto team. Lily relayed that the hourly rates for the senior litigators ranged from $1,000 to $2,000 an hour—thinking that the company would be impressed that the attorneys could command such a rate. When questioned about recent cases that the so-called high-priced lawyers had actually tried before a jury, the responses were similar. 'We are victims of our success. Our opponents are fearful to go to trial against us, so beneficial settlements are customarily obtained.' She directed us to highlight Ben's trial record and present an alternative fee structure to hourly billing."

In compiling the proposal, Ben Horton's resumé of litigation victories spoke for itself. Lucy added Kevin's technology background, expertise in electronic discovery, and offered a modest flat fee to cover their costs until trial. Her fee structure, she thought, showed that Tate & Horton wasn't interested in milking the case for billable hours. The upside for the firm would be a percentage of any recovery. The fee structure demonstrated that they had skin in the game and were willing to take risks for the client's benefit.

Parcepto was impressed with Ben's jury trial results and liked the creative fee structure. They were equally impressed that the proposal included a technology expert, Lily reported. Tate & Horton was invited for in-person interviews. The meeting went well, but they knew it was still a long shot due to their size.

"I really hate to bring this up, but isn't there some ethical obligation to disclose the information you have?" Sammie asked.

"What ethical rule is that, Sammie?" Lucy asked. "Nothing was obtained through a client representation. We have no duty to disclose the information."

Sammie was thrilled about Lucy's new venture. Her excitement, however, was dampened by the opportunity presented by Lily. Worse, Sammie had in her possession relevant documents that she hadn't shared with Lucy. Her only comfort was thinking that a pharma company like Parcepto wouldn't hire the small start-up firm for such a significant matter.

"As it turns out, there are benefits to keeping your mouth closed—like the information about Barbie and Frank."

"What do you mean?" Sammie asked.

"Remember that Barbie was taking massage therapy classes, right?" Lucy asked. "Well, she bought that building on upper King that you and I have talked about—you know the one with potential but needing a lot of work—the one beside the shoe store that you love. Sammie, Barbie has transformed it. It is unbelievable. It has heart of pine floors, 15-foot ceilings, and majestic windows. She opened a spa on half of the first floor, and get this, the Chandler Cuisine Collection is opening a restaurant on the other half."

"No way," Sammie said. "I know the building."

"She calls it *The Benfield*. She has additional space upstairs. It needs some work, but she offered to lease it to me below market. She said it was her way of thanking me for treating her as an equal and not some low life mail room employee. She was also grateful that we didn't report her after what we saw."

"I guess it pays to be nice," Sammie said.

"Everything is coming together at the same time. Parcepto's interview team was impressed with Ben's long list of trial victories and read every article written about him. So, Tate & Horton landed its first representation. Isn't that great?"

"Yes," Sammie said, with as much excitement as she could muster. But, she felt sick. Once again, she was finding herself in the middle of one her best friend's cases.

Church isn't over until the choir stops singing...

Chapter Fifty-Four

Ben & Lucy

Sammie was growing weary about the case against Worth Pharmaceutical. Ben and Lucy had met with Sammie continuously to try and piece the parts together. She had continued to withhold from Ben and Lucy the letter from Dougie to Dr. Stanley Drake and his checks evidencing an investment in Sailfish II, LLC. Dougie's letter clearly established Dr. Drake's affiliation with Sailfish II, LLC. And, it was more than suspicious that an R&D chemist in Parcepto's research and development facility in Pittsburgh could be the brains behind medical park facilities in Florida. But, from Lucy's summary of the evidence collected to date, no discovery produced by Worth nor any of their interviews with their Parcepto contacts mentioned Sailfish II.

"Have you learned anything about business affiliations in Florida?" Sammie asked one day trying to understand their lack of interest in the prospectus that had been in her backpack.

"What do you mean?" Lucy asked, suspiciously.

"I recalled that you mentioned something about Florida in the email exchanges on Cathleen's hard drive. Just curious what the connection was."

"Oh," Lucy said. "Those related to Senator Tony DeVore's initiation of the investigation into Dolorine."

Sammie was feeling deflated.

"According to the Parcepto CEO, Senator DeVore's campaign was always begging for money from their Political Action Committee. He'd heard Tony DeVore's campaign pitch a thousand times—Parcepto's interest were aligned with his. Both looked out for senior citizens. So, the Parcepto PAC made a sizeable contribution to DeVore's campaign fund. In return, Parcepto encouraged an investigation into pharma companies that were perpetuating the opioid epidemic and shelving less addictive formulations, specifically Worth. It was a quid pro quo. For Parcepto's campaign contributions, DeVore would use his position as chair of the Senate Finance Committee to launch the investigation into Worth. Senator DeVore was in Parcepto's back pocket. Parcepto told DeVore that the investigation wouldn't be meaningful unless he subpoenaed all clinical trial data. Parcepto secretly hoped that the opioid investigation would uncover information on the suspected mole in its R&D Department. It didn't. But, when we were in Pittsburgh interviewing folks, we learned that two chemists saw Charles Webster meeting with Dr. Stanley Drake in a hotel one day at lunch. We thought this was a major break-through because Webster was a former board member of Parcepto and a current board member at Worth. He is also Scotty Hill's father-in-law. And, Dr. Drake had been tasked with creating Parcepto's new formulation for the hair growth product. So, in our assessment, a meeting with a Worth board member and a Parcepto chemist was significant. But, our sources wanted to remain anonymous because they would be implicating themselves."

"What do you mean, implicating themselves?" Sammie asked.

"Lucy has this amazing ability to get people to talk," Ben added.

"It's called confession," Lucy said. "My Preacher Daddy must have rubbed off on me more than I knew. Why would two employees be taking their lunch hour in a hotel?"

"Oh," Sammie said. "Got it."

"I promised them that we wouldn't disclose that fact," Lucy said. "No one needed to know about two witnesses, one would be sufficient. But, neither wanted to testify without further corroboration."

Lucy told Sammie that they were running into dead-end after dead-end. They had interviewed every member of Parcepto's R&D team, but for a Sarah Peyton Daniels. Sarah Peyton was on paternal leave helping her father recover from a stroke. She was "not important," according to Parcepto's General Counsel's office and the other R&D chemists. She was new to the company and the lowest ranking chemist. She wouldn't have any information relevant to the case. Lucy was inclined to accept the client's assessment of Sarah Peyton. But not Ben, he wanted personal confirmation.

Ben Horton was known for his charisma in front of a jury. But, Lucy was becoming more impressed with his dogged determination not to leave one stone unturned, even if in the eyes of anyone else, it wasn't even a pebble.

"Sarah Peyton's father lives in Greenville, South Carolina so on our way back to Charleston from Pittsburgh, Ben insisted upon a detour," Lucy said, refraining from adding that she was anxious to get home to see Kevin but had no choice but to accompany Ben.

"Sarah Peyton corroborated what we learned in Pittsburgh about the results of the clinical trials. Sarah Peyton was initially reluctant to discuss anything other than clinical trial data, research methodologies, and other scientific verifications, but she was warming up to Lucy," Ben said.

"I told her that some of the other scientists slipped and referred to Stanley Drake as 'Dr. Snake'. I asked her if she had any idea how he got that nickname. She said that no one trusted him. He didn't collaborate with others in the Parcepto R&D Department—that is was aloof and standoffish, especially to her. She attributed his attitude towards her because she was a female from the south."

"Lucy began commiserating with Sarah Peyton about Southern stereotypes and female prejudices," Ben said. "Lucy told her that the biases are what inspired her to start her own law firm."

"I told her that she landed in a good place," Lucy said. "That the Parcepto case was our first big case, and the company took a chance on us. And, there weren't too many companies who would offer paternal leave. Even so, many people would be fearful "Sarah Peyton then relayed that she was having lunch one day while her father was in physical therapy. She spotted Stanley Drake with South Carolina's U.S. Senator, Scott Hill. She thought it was strange and contemplated approaching the table and introducing herself to the popular senator, but she decided against it because of Dr. Drake's treatment of her in the office."

Ben and Lucy knew this sighting was significant since it established a link between Senator Hill and the Parcepto R&D chemist, which corroborated their theory behind the meeting with Hill's father-in-law, Charles Webster, and Dr. Drake in Pittsburgh. But they also knew that a good defense attorney would rip timid Sarah Peyton Daniels apart on her recollection. And, there was a humongous missing link. Worth didn't have any pending FDA application for anything similar to a hair replacement product. If Worth had bribed a chemist, and paid for a supposedly revolutionary drug formulation, wouldn't it be jumping at the opportunity to take it to market?

of the backlash if they took it. I told her that I admired her."

"Lucy reeled her in," Ben said. "As we were leaving, she said, 'There is one other thing. I don't know if it is important or even relevant.'"

It was becoming clear to Sammie, that she may be the only one that could connect the dots between Worth and the stolen formulation.

Ben and Lucy assumed that Worth would offer some type of settlement to avoid any negative press associated with a trial that could affect its stock price and avoid the legal fees that skyrocketed during trial preparation and the costs of a trial. But Worth was holding firm to its position. The suit had no merit whatsoever, it repeated. Worth had not offered even a penny towards a settlement.

"We believe that the Parcepto lawsuit was a preemptive measure," Ben said. "No wonder the company went with us. We were cheap. Our payday only came if the company obtained a settlement or a jury verdict. We were competent enough to show that Parcepto meant business. The lawsuit would, at a minimum, put on hold an application with the FDA by Worth for a hair loss replacement product. I think we've been duped by our own client," Ben said.

The trial date was set. Tate & Horton had no choice but to proceed.

A dead bee can still sting...

Chapter Fifty-Five

Sammie

Glenny and Sammie were enjoying a gin and tonic on the swing while watching Mack play with his boats in the new addition to the Spencer's house—a large, plastic kiddie pool on the upstairs porch. Mack was obsessed with boats. Thanks to Glenny, Mack had an entire fleet.

After Dougie's death, Sammie sold their house and furnishings and officially moved in with her parents. Over the past eighteen months, her childhood home had blanketed her with the comfort and stability she desperately needed. When she had broached looking for her own place, Glenny had been armed with a hundred reasons against it. Two reasons resonated: "Mack needs a father figure." "He is forming a special bond with his grandfather." Sammie felt immobilized. But, now, her mother's words, "you need more time," were truer that Sammie wanted to admit.

She yearned so desperately to return to that place and time where her life had been "perfect" as Lucy had characterized it. She wanted to go for a mindless run, read a book, or get lost in the sputtering noises Mack made when driving his boats.

Now, the heavy weight on her soul was Lucy's exposé that Sammie had been setup. Grant Davis needed to know what Sammie knew. He needed to learn if Sammie knew about her husband's affair with Cathleen McKinney, if she knew that her husband was a participant in a scheme to buy a promising new drug formulation from a competitor's chemist. The supposed scandal involving Cathleen and Senator Hill was a ruse. She had to give it to Grant Davis, he had thought about every angle. Since she had been retained as counsel to The Davis Group, anything she learned from her representation couldn't be disclosed. Further, Worth would argue that any documents in her possession resulted from her representation. She felt foolish for playing into their hands.

Sammie anguished over the upcoming *Parcepto Pharma v. Worth Pharmaceutical* trial. Ben assured her that any documents in her possession would have to be disclosed by the parties during the discovery process.

Sammie couldn't help thinking that Ben underestimated the crafty and unscrupulous Worth attorneys and Grant Davis. Those documents and computer hard drive were on that boat for a reason—for Grant to destroy them. But, the documents hadn't been destroyed because Sammie took them, or as Worth would argue, stole them. And, on top of that, she had even withheld Dougie's letter to Dr. Stanley Drake, Parcepto's chemist, and evidence of payments for a competitor's drug formulation.

Without Dougie or Cathleen available for questioning, the evidence produced through rounds of interviews, document productions, and depositions had only loosely linked Senator Hill to the Parcepto R&D chemist, Stanley Drake. No direct evidence of any bribe for the highly confidential and promising "Hair Revitalization" drug formulation had been discovered.

Ben's gut was that there was a scheme, and it had been perpetuated by Senator Scotty Hill's father-in-law, Charles Webster. As a former member of Parcepto's board of directors, and a new, major Worth shareholder, he was the common denominator between Parcepto and Worth. Both Webster and Senator Hill had been observed meeting on separate occasions with Parcepto's chief chemist. But, that's where the trail stopped.

It appeared Worth would be getting away with everything. This dilemma added to Sammie's suffering. Ben and Lucy had poured their heart and soul into the case and spent an entire month interviewing Parcepto chemists at their client's R&D facility in Pittsburgh. Given their fee proposal, they were fronting the expenses and losing their shirt on their reduced hourly billing rate. Their new firm was already severely in the red. And worse, their case had lots of holes. A damage award of zero would not be a good kick-off for their new enterprise. But, that's what Lucy predicted—a "big Goose egg."

You'd rather have it and not need it than need it and not have it...

Chapter Fifty-Six

Sammie

Sammie accepted Robbie Blake's invitation to join him on a three-week Caribbean cruise. It was the medicine she needed. This excursion would get her out of town for the upcoming *Parcepto Pharma v. Worth Pharmaceutical* trial. But, after Lucy's last dire update on the weaknesses in their case, she felt guilty for leaving. She felt like she was abandoning her best friend. Every attempt she had made to steer them to investigating the Florida connections hit a dead end. When Sammie asked about the connection to the Sailfish II, LLC prospectus in her backpack, Ben and Lucy viewed it as a legitimate investment possibly being considered by Cathleen McKinney or Grant Davis. None of the information they had obtained in the discovery produced by Worth or in their interviews of Parcepto employees disclosed anything about the limited liability company in Florida.

Behind the scenes, Sammie had attempted to uncover the individuals behind Sailfish II, LLC—the entity identified in Dougie's letter that received payments from her trust account. But, her access to the Florida Division of Corporations files was limited and had only uncovered more limited liability companies. It was like a corporate game of nesting dolls. The managing member of the Sailfish II, LLC was East Coast Ventures, LLC. The managing member of East Coast Ventures, LLC was yet another limited liability company, Medical Park Properties, LLC. Behind Medical Park Properties, LLC was yet another layer.

Sammie wasn't surprised by these findings because as a Spencer corporate lawyer, she had formed numerous limited liability companies in the same fashion. It was a shell game. The more layers of corporate insulation, the less exposure to the individual investors. With the trial starting and no settlement on the table, she was determined to get to the bottom of Sailfish II, LLC—to keep digging under the corporate layers until she found a human being.

To do this, Sammie needed to visit the corporate division office in Tallahassee. She called Robbie Blake.

You can't call an alligator a lizard...

Chapter Fifty-Seven

Tate & Horton

Lucy was learning a lot from Ben Horton. Before now, she didn't realize there was an art and strategy in selecting a jury. Ben had meticulously reviewed the profiles of the jury pool. Most of the opening day was spent in questioning the potential panel. Ben was extremely satisfied with the mix of twelve men and women that had been selected.

"Our case may be weak, but our jury is strong," Ben said. "Corporations may be impressed with New York lawyers, but not South Carolinians. Our jury won't be fooled by the arrogance of the non-resident lawyers."

 Lucy was crossing every finger and toe that Ben's instincts were right, at least about their jury.

Ben's opening statement to the jury laid the groundwork that Charles Webster had made a lot of money in the pharmaceutical industry. His connections were helpful to his son-in-law, Senator Scotty Hill, whose campaign fund received generous contributions from Worth Pharmaceutical. Worth had used Senator Hill's influence in nixing an investigation into the company's epidemic pain medicine, Dolorine. It awarded Charles Webster with a seat on its board of directors. Webster's previous stint on Parcepto's board provided him with inside knowledge of a promising new Parcepto drug formulation for hair replacement. Ben forecasted the evidence that would be presented: a meeting in Pittsburgh between Charles Webster with the Parcepto chemist in charge of the hair revitalization formulation and a meeting between the same chemist with Senator Hill in South Carolina.

"The evidence will demonstrate that Worth was desperate to salvage its reputation in the marketplace from the bad publicity involving the known addictive nature of its pain medication, Dolorine. It needed a noncontroversial drug in its portfolio. Charles

Webster advocated a revolutionary hair replacement formulation being developed by Parcepto. And, he knew how to make that happen."

In his opening, Joseph Forsythe, the New York lawyer representing Worth Pharmaceutical, admonished the jury to pay close attention to the testimony.

"This is a complicated matter. You must focus on the salient points."

Ben passed Lucy a note. *He has already offended every juror—he is not only talking down to them but over them. Salient? Really??*

"As you have already witnessed, the plaintiffs' attorneys will try to confuse you with testimony about sightings between a chemist employed by Parcepto and your senator, Scott Hill, and even with your senator's father-in-law, Charles Webster. The connection with these sitings is a head scratcher and frankly, hogwash."

Ben passed another note. *Hogwash? Head scratcher?*

"Senator Scott Hill meets with lots of people, as does his father-in-law. And, though, Charles Webster is a shareholder of Worth, the company has lots of shareholders. Worth isn't required to, and cannot possibly, police the activities of all of its shareholders or their other investment opportunities. This case falls under the category grasping at straws."

Aside from his blustery condescension, Lucy tended to agree with the haughty Worth lawyer.

"We have good facts, but the problem is there is no crescendo," Lucy told Ben. "The connection between Worth and Dr. Stanley Drake is tenuous. The jury will want more proof," Lucy said. "And hot shot Joe Forsythe will hammer home that there is absolutely no evidence of confidential information leaked from Dr. Drake to Worth."

Joseph Forsythe would begin his cross-examination of Worth's witnesses the next day. Ben and Lucy began a long night of strategizing how best to salvage their case. Lucy called Kevin.

"Hey, we are on our way back to the office. Ben is picking up some dinner, it's gonna be a long night. Any special requests?"

"No," Kevin said. "I was just getting ready to text you. You just received a FedEx package," Kevin paused, "from Florida."

Buzzards and chickens come home to roost...

Chapter Fifty-Eight

Lucy

Curiously, the Federal Express box originated in Tallahassee, Florida. The contents appeared to be formation documents for several limited liability companies. She thumbed through the lengthy legal filings. Then, her heart jumped when she saw hand-written notes from Cathleen McKinney. She set aside the laborious corporate filings and started reviewing them.

I enjoyed meeting you at the regional sales meeting. You have gotten off to a great start! You have star potential. Congratulations!
Best,
Cathleen McKinney

It was great spending time with you at the retreat. You are building quite a network. Keep up the good work! Worth values relationships. Relationships are the key to success.
Best,
Cathleen McKinney

Well, I must say that I am not surprised that your sales exceeded all expectations. How do you keep busting the projections, Dougie? What is your secret? If you share your secrets at the Christmas party, I'll share mine.
XOXO,
Cathleen

I can't wait to see you at the Christmas party. I hope you're still going solo so I can give you an advance tutorial of some new products. I'll be wearing your favorite red dress—at least at the party. Can't wait for our private after-party!

XOXO,
CM

After reading them, she knew Sammie sent this package. But how? She wasn't in Florida but the Caribbean. Also, in the package was a letter from Dougie to Dr. Stanley Drake, the Parcepto chemist who was in charge of formulating the revolutionary hair growth product.

Dr. Stanley Drake
15 Ridge Road
Pittsburgh, PA
Dear Dr. Drake,

This letter follows up on our prior negotiations and agreement relating to a 10% interest in Sailfish II, LLC for $500,000.00. This investment is based on the Florida business plan. Enclosed is the $25,000.00 deposit. The schedule for the remainder of the payments is attached.

Sincerely yours,
Douglas Morgan

A number of checks from Dougie to Sailfish II, LLC were enclosed that matched the payment schedule attached to the letter but for the last two payments. Worth could argue that the document simply showed a Worth employee's independent investment in some company.

Lucy turned to the Articles of Organization from the Florida Division of Corporations for the limited liability companies. The first Article of Organization related to Sailfish II, LLC. The managing member was identified as East Coast Ventures, LLC. Whoever had sent these documents understood the LLC shell game and also provided the Articles of Organization for East Coast Ventures, LLC. The managing member of East Coast Ventures, LLC was yet another LLC, Medical Park Properties, LLC. Having prepared these multiple layers of protection numerous times, Lucy flipped through all the articles to the last entity in the stack, Drug Innovators, Inc., and its president, one Charles Webster.

She called Ben's cell.

"Where are you?" she asked.

"Ten minutes, away," Ben said.

"Hurry. I received a FedEx package—from Florida."

Lucy had been so focused on the getting to the bottom of the LLC string to uncover the human at the end that she failed to see another link. But Ben did.

"Look at who is to receive all legal notices," he said, pointing to the notice section in the Articles of Organization.

"Holy shit," Lucy said gaping at the identical provision for every single filing.

All written communication should be sent to the registered agent:

Joseph Forsythe
Cavagnaro & Forsythe
PO Drawer 84
New York, New York

"Time to inform the Judge of an addition to our witness list, Joe Forsythe."

Stretching the truth is like stretching a rubber band, it will eventually snap...

Chapter Fifty-Nine

Lucy & Sammie

Lucy was giddy to see Sammie. She couldn't wait to hear about her Caribbean Island excursion on Robbie Blake's yacht. Sammie had met the professional sports team owner when delivering orders. She had been about as tight-lipped about her trip as she had been about her falling for Grant Davis. She worried that Sammie was getting sucked in by another man. She used to trust Sammie's judgment but between Dougie and Grant Davis, she wasn't so sure about Sammie's assessment in the male category. Despite Lucy's reservations about another faulty romance, the timing of Sammie's Caribbean vacation was opportune. She knew that Sammie hadn't wanted to be around during the *Parcepto Pharma v. Worth Pharmaceutical* trial.

Now, Lucy understood that the timing of Sammie's Caribbean jaunt had been intentional. Sammie could avoid a subpoena to testify if she was beyond the jurisdiction of the U.S. court system. After all, she had provided the documents that blew the case wide open. Lucy couldn't wait to tell her about the huge settlement.

Sammie's flight had painted her a golden brown and lightened her blonde hair But, there was more to Sammie's glow than being on island time the last three weeks.

Lucy jumped up from the bar stool and ran to give her a big hug.

"This is Kevin Miller and the one and only Lucy Tate," Sammie said to the three others accompanying her.

"Oh, girl, we have heard so much about you. I'm Camilla Girard, my brother, Kurt, and our fab captain, Robbie Blake."

After introductions were made, Kurt and Kevin proceeded to buy a round of drinks.

Camilla grabbed Robbie's hand and headed to the juke box.

"Girl, what is going on? Camilla and Kurt Girard? My head is spinning. I want the deets. But first, how did you pull off sending me the information from Florida?"

"Well, based on the update you gave me before I was supposed to leave, I knew it wasn't looking good. I felt so bad that I had in my possession crucial documents. I told you that I was attempting to return the documents when the boat exploded. That is true. But, what I didn't tell you was that I had removed the checks Dougie had written to Sailfish II, LLC and the letter sent to Dr. Stanley Drake. Of course, then, I didn't know who he was or anything about the investment. But, the payments matched up perfectly to the spreadsheet that Camilla had given me about the withdrawals from my trust account, except for the final two payments. Those were scheduled to be paid after my dad had Parks freeze the account. So, I knew my money was being used for something. And, whatever it was, I didn't want to be involved. Given the players, my gut told me it was something fishy. Then, from what you told me about the Parcepto case, I assumed the payments were for the stolen formulation. When none of the documents disclosed by Worth in discovery disclosed anything on the Sailfish II, LLC, I started thinking that Worth may not have been involved in the pay-off to the Parcepto chemist. It could have been a scheme only involving Dougie, Cathleen, Senator Hill, his father-in-law and Grant. But, then, it hit me that another consistent player was Tripp, Senator Hill's fishing buddy. I didn't know his last name or even if Tripp was his first name and not a nickname. But, I did remember the boat name, *Silver Lining*, a Grady-White Canyon. Mr. Barry helped me look it up. The boat is owned by Henry Wilson Bridges, III. Tripp is a nickname for a third generation. There are lots of those in Charleston."

"And, the president of Worth Pharmaceutical is Henry Wilson Bridges, II. Girl, you are so smart," Lucy said.

"So, I knew then that there was a connection with Worth. Kurt, Camilla, and I were supposed to fly into Naples to meet Robbie—that is where his boat was docked at the time. Kurt and I went to Tallahassee first before we went to Naples. We combed through all the records at the state's Division of Corporations and found the trail. In case we found something, I took everything with me to send to you."

"You are the best. I feel badly now for thinking you had fallen for another yachtsman."

"No, that would be Camilla. So, in a nutshell, Kurt is a seventh grade teacher in a pretty rough area in Wando. He started an after-school program to keep the kids out of trouble and expose them to new activities. One is sailing. He asked me to help. Anyway, Robbie became interested and donated money for several sailboats and even purchased a Jon boat. That's how he met Camilla. She teaches art design for the program. So, Camilla is dating Robbie, and well, I've been seeing Kurt."

Camilla and Robbie returned from the juke box.

"Sammie was just filling me in on how you two met," Lucy said. "Robbie, I think it's so wonderful what you are doing for the after-school program."

"Well, I don't do anything but help support it. These two have the talent and volunteer their time."

Kurt and Kevin arrived with a round of beer for the table.

"Okay, everybody has to go pick a song," Camilla said, as The Zach Brown Band song "Where the Boat Leaves From" blasted. This one is mine.

"Cheers to great friends, old and new," Camilla said.

They clinked their bottles. Then, they each headed to the juke box to pick a selection.

When the next song began, George Strait's "How 'Bout Them Cowgirls," Lucy stood up and broke into a big grin. "This is my song. Here's to Barbie Cowgirl Benfield. Drink it," she yelled holding up her beer bottle.

"Speaking of Barbie, Camilla has some exciting news," Sammie said, beaming.

"I have my own design business that I have been operating from home. I decided it was time to look for space. Sammie told me about The Benfield. When my partner and I saw it, we fell in love with it. Barbie said the upfits will be finished soon."

"I asked Barbie who was moving in, but she told me it wasn't her story to tell," Lucy said. "So, you are going to be Tate & Horton's new neighbors?"

"Yes," Camilla said. "Sammie, you tell her who my partner is."

"Your new neighbor is Camilla Girard and Eleanor Spencer Designs. Mom is Camilla's partner. And, in addition to the sailing instruction for the after-school program, I am going to help Camilla and Mom. Part of the upfit is a playroom for Mack."

"That is excellent! Oh, this makes me so happy."

"This song is mine," Kevin said, grabbing Lucy's hand and pulling her onto the dance floor.

Lucy wrapped her arms around his neck. She knew the song. "I Was Made for Lovin' You." The disco rock song by the band, Kiss, was the first song she had played on the juke box the night she and Kevin first visited Zach's Crab Shack. The other couples migrated to the dance floor.

The group stayed on the floor when "Only Wanna Be With You," by Hootie and the Blowfish clicked on. Robbie was really proud of his song from the band founded from at his favorite school—the University of South Carolina. Neither Camilla nor Kevin, both Clemson graduates, objected to his selection. Camilla was smitten with Robbie Blake, and Kevin loved Darius Rucker, the lead singer.

Kevin motioned the bartender for another round as Eric Church's, "Drink In My Hand," his selection, played. Sammie began worrying that her song had been skipped. When Camilla had instructed everyone to choose a song, she knew immediately the perfect song. She seriously doubted, however, that her selection would be among the juke box offerings. But, it was. And it seemed apropos when her selection was the last song that played. Though the others stayed on the dance floor with their dates, the song was just a classic 1970's song to them. But to her, it was much more. She wondered if it would even register with Kurt. It did. He wrapped his hands around her waist, pulled her close.

"I remember," he said.

She forgot about all the others. She was transported back to their first dance in high school. In her mind, the boxed fans attached to the ceiling at Zach's Crab Shack transformed into the disco balls in the high school gym. Kurt sang every word to Bob Seger and the Silver Bullet Band's "We've Got Tonight" in Sammie's ear.

"What a large time," Robbie said, after the juke box played the last song. "Does anyone need something to eat besides me? I'll take care of dinner. I know someone who can run a mean errand."

"Ha ha! My gopher duties are now only dictated by Camilla and my mom," Sammie said.

The group left Zach's Crab Shack for Robbie Blake's yacht, *Game Day*. It was a clear night. It was as if every star in the galaxy wanted to celebrate with them. Robbie popped the cork on some champagne and filled glasses. Sammie noticed that he grabbed two extra glasses as he led the way to the flybridge.

"I have some exciting news too," Robbie said, turning back to the group following him up the stairs.

"Sammie, I want you to meet my new boat captain."

On the top open deck stood Billy along with Mr. Barry.

"Billy," Sammie yelped, running into his arms.

Then Mr. Barry cleared his throat.

"Do you have to be a boat captain to get noticed around here?"

"No, you don't," Sammie said, hugging her old boss.

Robbie poured glasses of champagne for Billy and Mr. Barry.

Lucy raised her glass.

"Here's to kindred spirits and new adventures. Blessed be the tie that binds."

PART FIVE

Don't let the truth get in the way of a good story...

Chapter Sixty

Anna Chatham

The sun was intense. Anna Chatham had always been careful with sun exposure. But today, she didn't care if she got a little pink. The sun's strong rays made her feel alive again.

Over the last several years, she had become an empty and lifeless shell, motivated only by the question of whether her husband was cheating. Now that she knew the truth, she felt liberated.

Perhaps Grant's recent interest in her was due to her renewed, independent spirit, or maybe, he was putting on a good marital face for the investigation. Whatever it was, she was now with him at the exclusive Ocean Shores Club in Islamorada basking in the sun while he was shopping for a new boat.

Before this weekend, she couldn't remember the last time they had even kissed, but the sex that morning was like old times. No, it was better than old times. Then, she had wanted to please him. Now, she desired to please herself.

Although Grant had dallied with many other women, he was married to only one—her. She gladly accepted her husband's invitation to get away for the weekend. His business was doing better than ever. In fact, Worth was getting ready to drop Grant a huge fee for additional public relations expertise. Worth had been accused of stealing a drug formulation. That, coupled with suspicions as to why one of its high-powered executives ended up with a lowly sales associate on a burning yacht, would garner a significant fee.

Despite all, Grant's reputation was intact. The Bureau of Alcohol, Tobacco, Firearms and Explosives concluded that the explosion was an accident. She didn't know who was more relieved, Grant or her. She wasn't even concerned that an investigation was being initiated to determine whether the ATF had been paid off. She knew that neither she nor Grant was involved in that. Now that the explosion was ruled an accident, Anna Chatham was feeling confident that none of her friends or their children would hear of Grant's indiscretions with Cathleen McKinney, the marina dock trash, or who knows else. After all, Grant's job was keeping a lid on things. He certainly would do his best job for the person that mattered most to him—Grant Davis.

Anna Chatham decided to celebrate all these events. She confidently approached the pool bar to place a drink order. As she scanned the cocktail menu, she decided on the Diva Boomer Martini, a mix of Chambord, berry vodka, rum, and rimmed with pink sugar. Though she was feeling like a diva, especially after her performance that morning, the real appeal of the drink was because it was a boomer. As she sipped her martini, she closed her eyes and replayed the footage of Grant's yacht burning. *Yes, some things were just meant to be*, she thought. Her fortuitous meeting with the knowledgeable boat mechanic was definitely one of those things.

She vividly recalled everything about that day, except how she ended up at Art's Oyster House. She had been reeling from the voicemail that she had received from Lucy Tate. She could still hear it in her head: *The woman in the video has confirmed a relationship with your husband. He told her that he wasn't married.*

It had been painful enough to view the video. She could only remember walking into some bar and choosing a stool far away from all the other bar visitors. She tried hard to fight back tears. She must have looked pitiful and out of place. Then the large boat mechanic said, "Hey babe, looks like you made a wrong turn, but I'm glad you did." He exploded with this squealing high pitched laugh. "Let Barnyard buy you a drink, darlin'."

Anna Chatham's professional training temporarily distracted her from her self-pity. She was always intrigued with human interest stories and delving into people's backgrounds. She was instantly curious about how a Charleston resident came to be called Barnyard. She couldn't help but think that the name properly stuck because it aptly fit this character. His laugh sounded like a pig. His red bandana tied tightly around his oversized head was the perfect accessory for his 6'6 and 300-pound frame.

Anna Chatham, the writer, learned a lot about Barnyard that day and he, about her. One glass of Chardonnay turned into too many. But who was counting? She poured her soul to this stranger.

Barnyard knew the Charleston Ashley Dockage well. He moonlighted there. In fact, he had a job there early the next morning. His title at his real job at the Charleston Port was Master Mechanic. According to the bartender, Barnyard was the best of the best when it came to making a boat run. He even joked that he was referred to as Dr. Barnyard because he could diagnose and fix anything ailing on any type of boat.

As Anna Chatham was checking out of her hotel the next morning, a growing number of guests gathered around the TV in the lobby bar mesmerized by an explosion that had just occurred at the Charleston Ashley Dockage. As she watched the footage, a sinking feeling engulfed her like the black smoke engulfing the sky. She recalled Barnyard's advice, "You got to get him where it hurts." But, an explosion had not been the plan as far as she could remember.

Her initial remorse over the unintended casualties had been replaced with a weird satisfaction. Thinking about that day, she smiled and ordered another Diva Boomer Martini. Who would have thought that she played a role in the events that had transpired? That had been the best bang for her buck—worth every penny.

She secretly toasted Bart Yardley, who because of his inability to pronounce his "t's" as a child, became known as Barnyard. Life was good for Anna Chatham.

There's more than one way to skin a cat...

Chapter Sixty-One

Bart Yardley

Bart sat at his favorite spot at the bar hoping to catch replays of the basketball game he had missed the night before—the L.A. Lakers and his man crush, LeBron James. His favorite bartender served his usual first-aid breakfast after a grueling all-night shift—a dozen oysters and an 18 oz. cold, draft Budweiser. One night after having too many beers, he had told the bartender, "Art, if you'll serve me just one more beer, I'll love you as much as King James." So, on that drunken night, Bart began calling his favorite bartender "How Great Thou Art." The nickname stuck.

Bart slurped down his last oyster coated in Texas Pete hot sauce and his second beer. The beer was working its usual magic. The aches reverberating from every muscle and joint in his body began to numb. Then, the game highlights were interrupted by a special news report. He hated breaking news. Nobody at the bar cared about the real world. *Everyone in the bar was there to forget, for this little moment in time, the crazy shit happening around them*, Bart thought. But as the camera panned in on a smoldering boat, Bart became interested.

"We are reporting live from the Charleston Ashley Dockage where we have an update on those injured from an explosion that occurred earlier. The boat captain has been released from the hospital, but the two that were aboard the luxury yacht perished."

Beer spewed. Bart quickly wiped his mouth with his hand.

"What the hell?"

"Yeah," said Art, "you haven't heard about the yacht that blew up in the marina? Two people were on it."

"Quiet," Bart instructed chatty Art. "Let me listen to this."

"We have learned that the two deaths were employees of Worth Pharmaceutical Corporation—Cathleen McKinney, the Director of Worth's Communication Division, and Douglas Morgan, a Worth sales representative. As previously reported, the owner of the 112-foot Westport yacht docked at the Charleston Ashley Dockage is Grant Davis, who runs a public relations firm in Atlanta. According to a Worth representative, the company periodically utilizes the PR firm. Mr. Davis was at his Palm Beach office at the time of the explosion."

Bart was about to choke. Someone had beat him to the punch. His new friend, Anna C., and he had only planned a small incident—something that would force evacuation of the boat's occupants and some substantial cash for repairs. There had been no talk of an explosion with deaths. Bart thought that the classy broad's husband must have been up to more than she knew.

"Who did they say the dude was that died?" Bart asked Art.

"Grew up over the bridge," Art responded. "One of my customers earlier said he went to Rutledge, was a superstar athlete there, and married some Charleston hoity toity."

"What was the name?"

"Douglas Morgan," Art said. "I've been hearing this shit all morning. Did you know him?"

"Yeah, I knew him," Bart said. "He used to be a friend of mine. Shit. Pour me another one."

Bart couldn't come to grips with this information or his emotions. Was he happy or sad? He was finding it difficult to mourn the death of Dougie Morgan. He recalled that sweltering day when he was headed to his fifth boat repair at Shem Creek. He was wet from head to toe with sweat. It was his last service call of the day. Wouldn't you know it, *Sea Catcher* was docked about as far away as it possibly could have been. Bart didn't know if his wobbly legs could make it down the docks to the boat.

As he approached with beads of sweat dripping from his face, he thought he must be seeing things—hallucinating from heat exhaustion. If he hadn't been so exhausted, he would have killed him then. On that boat was his buddy Dougie Morgan banging his younger sister, Heather.

Everybody knew he was a player in high school. Who wasn't, really? But, Dougie was out of college with a real job when Bart caught him with Heather.

"I know what I'm doing! You don't own me!" Heather screamed at her brother.

After Bart caught them, he wrote Dougie Morgan off. He had been dead to him since that day. But when he heard Dougie had hired Heather to babysit his kid, Bart exploded. Heather assured him it was all good and that their relationship was in the past.

Bart knew that Dougie was up to no good on that boat with the hot shot businesswoman. *Dougie Morgan got what was coming to him*, Bart thought. He returned to his cold beer and the basketball replays. He didn't give Dougie Morgan another thought. Instead, he raised his glass to Anna C.

He's the cream of the crap, and the crap of the cream...

Chapter Sixty-Two

Grant Davis

Grant was with his wife, but all he could think about was Cathleen. He couldn't get her off his mind. They had made a great team inside and outside the bedroom. They were both masters of their craft—meticulously outlining strategies and executing them with precision. That is, until Dougie Morgan arrived on the scene.

When Cathleen fell for the low-life sales punk, things had gone south, Grant thought. She had fallen to the most pedestrian temptation—physical attraction. During all the years he had known Cathleen, they had remained intently focused on the strict implementation of a plan and completely devoid of emotional attachment.

Though Grant didn't buy it, Cathleen had attempted to defend her transgression. Dougie Morgan was smart and cagey. She didn't know how but he had pieced together Project Eden. He threatened Cathleen. He would expose the entire scheme unless he could reap some of the benefit. He wanted in. So, a deal was struck for his ten percent ownership interest in Sailfish II. Grant recalled her patented laugh when she said she needed something on Dougie Morgan "to keep him honest."

Though the original execution of the scheme had faltered, Grant was secretly gloating about the ultimate outcome of Project Eden. Worth had settled the Parcepto litigation for a rather significant sum. Its terms were under seal and would never be disclosed. The evidence that had been presented at the trial up to the time of settlement was weak and easily countered and defended in the public opinion arena. The Davis Group would receive a large fee to make certain.

Similarly, Drug Innovators was sitting on a gold mine for a new hair growth drug. The application was now pending with the FDA. After approval, Worth would be purchasing the company owned by Charles Webster. The less controversial drug would propel Worth into a new dimension. Drug Innovators and Worth would reap huge profits in the $4 billion hair loss industry, making peanuts out of the amount paid to Parcepto as settlement.

Despite Cathleen's dalliances with Dougie Morgan, she had masterfully followed the plan in addressing the accusations that Worth was capitalizing on the addictive nature of its Dolorine pain medication. As planned, Cathleen's seduction of Senator Tony DeVore led to his termination of the Senate Finance Committee's investigation. Grant smiled recounting her abridged version of that plot.

"'Easy peasy, lemon squeezy after I got tanked and closed my eyes," she had said when they viewed the video, clearly identifying the senator with another woman.

During Cathleen's pillow talk sessions with Senator DeVore, she disclosed that Senator Hill had requested a secret meeting with her to discuss the senate investigation. According to Cathleen, her recital of the scripted bait was Oscar worthy. She spun a story that included the number of calls Senator Hill had made to her, the requests for visits, the flirtatious gestures, and then the invitation to a yacht in Key West. "He is seducing me, plain and simple," she told Senator DeVore.

The groundwork had been laid, no pun intended, Grant thought. They knew that Tony DeVore would jump on any opportunity to obtain incriminating evidence on popular Senator Scotty Hill from South Carolina. They anticipated a private eye at the Sun Key Marina. What they didn't anticipate was Senator DeVore's boldness in tapping Senator Hill's office phone. An added bonus. The desire for power, Grant had learned, led to impulsive, foolish behavior.

In terminating the Senate Finance Committee's investigation into Worth's pain killer line, Senator DeVore announced that there was no evidence of Worth's manipulation of the addictive nature of its pain meds nor of its suppression of less-addictive formulations. Grant Davis wrote Senator DeVore's script in exchange for the sex video with Cathleen McKinney and the agreement to keep his wiretapping under wraps.

The only person that could have ultimately spoiled Project Eden was Samantha Spencer Morgan. Grant smirked, thinking about the way he planned to uncover anything she knew. Unlike Cathleen, he pulled the long straw in that plan. Samantha Morgan was much better looking than Senator Tony DeVore. *A tolerable romp in the sack*, he thought. He certainly hadn't had to close his eyes.

The more difficult job had been maintaining his cool during the investigation into the cause of the explosion.

"I can't prove anything," Grant told the joint team of ATF and FBI investigators, "but Cathleen McKinney told me that she had in her possession some documents that were very damaging to Senator Tony DeVore. I was to meet her at *Sea Relations* the day after the horrific explosion," Grant Davis divulged during his interviews. "That evidence had been taken to *Sea Relations* and now unfortunately is literally up in flames. I do find it curious that Senator DeVore previously worked for the ATF. Of course, we will never know what the documents disclosed or what she learned. So tragic," Grant said, as solemnly as he could muster.

Grant Davis had been cleared of any involvement in the explosion of his boat. So, he only had to put on a happy marital face for a little while longer. But, Anna seemed to have a newfound, fancy-free liberation. Grant couldn't remember the last time she had an alcoholic drink before 7:00 p.m. She was on her second martini, no less.

As Grant and his wife were relaxing by the pool, Grant was relishing in his influence. He had set off another chain of events—an investigation into a possible cover-up of the cause of the explosion by the ATF and Senator DeVore. After recounting all the events, he decided to join his wife with a martini. He secretly toasted his beloved Cathleen and his own Oscar worthy performances, knowing that he could always buy another boat. Cheers!

Acknowledgements

In July 2012, I traveled with my youngest son to a junior golf championship in Torrey Pines, California. While on a run alongside the Pacific Ocean, this book was born. I began putting it to paper on the plane trip back to North Carolina. Since that time, there have been many rewrites of this novel and changes in my life. I'm grateful for my constants.

My three sons, Andy, Walt, and Peter, will always be my greatest accomplishments. Pam Dickson and Sylvia Jurgensen were my first two readers a decade ago but have been friends for more than four decades. Laura Cavagnaro has been my loyal, wise, and fun compadre from our freshman year at Wake Forest University, through law school, and now, my primary editor (we should write a book!).

Also, a shout out to Liz Newell, who continues to espouse the wisdoms passed down from her mother and grandmothers. Her "Liz-isms" are peppered throughout.

Needless to say, after ten years in the making, there are many people to acknowledge:

Peggy Payne, an accomplished published author of several books, for her input, insights, and guidance; Kim Hasty, a writer and journalist, for her review and recommendations; Stephen Norton, published author, for his constant positivity, creative energy, and my book title; Rachel Cox, my formatter; Susan Lower, for her critique and meticulous detail; Christos Angelidakis, my talented cover designer; Grace Casey, founder and creative director of Marrow Design; and Erica Levy Photography.

And to the constants in my non-fiction world—my legal profession. The title bestowed upon these invaluable souls is "support staff," but a more accurate description is "life support." Thank you Lisa, Debbie, Mary, Kathy, Kim, Rochelle, Donna, Debra, Tammy, and all the others.

Made in the USA
Columbia, SC
22 June 2023

18732142R00192